The Beachcomber

By
Michael Gering

Uncovering The Hoax, The Mystery, The Myth, And The Whole Truth
INSIDE THE JFK COLD CASE FILES

The Beachcomber
By
Michael Gering
Published by Spirit Helper Productions

© 2013 Michael Gering, First Edition
© 2015 Michael Gering, Second Edition

THE LIBRARY OF CONGRESS
COPYRIGHT OFFICE
TXU 1-170-649
ISBN 978-0615927954

Printed in the United States of America
Cover photo: Erica Varela / Ralph Drew
LA Times invoice# 030113-rd-2   3/5/2013
Maryrose Grossman avarchives@nara.gov

Author photo:
Photographer, Damion Thompson, www.youtube.com/itsallarts
Hairstylist, Johnny Hsiung, 310-245-5266
Azalia Salon, 310-471-8894

EMAIL THE AUTHOR at: beachcomber005@yahoo.com
website: http://michaelgering.weebly.com

The Meek Shall Inherit The Earth

(A favorite quote from the soul)
John Obrien
An Irishman—Forever,
A Legendary Human Rights Activist

This is a world of chance, free will, and necessity,
and chance by far rules—either; it has the last
and the featuring blow... at all of these events.

Herman Melville

The Legendary Pillars Inside The JFK Parthenon Of Legends

We The Jury--I Stand With You All--Today And Always

JIM MARRS

OLIVER STONE

FLETCHER PROUTY

JIM GARRISON

CLAUDIA FURIATI

ANTHONY BRUGIONI

ROBERT GRODEN

HAROLD WEISBERG

DAVID LIFTON

JAMES FETZER

LEN OSANIC

JESSE VENTURA

THOMAS HARTMANN

LAMAR WALDRON

HOWARD JONES

DOUGLAS WELDON

PENN JONES

JFK Assassination experts all across America and the World--
Your Dedication And Passion For The Truth
Inspires Every American Countryman
I salute all of my fellow jurors.

For Alex Alexandrovich Gering
Vietnam and Korea changed both of our lives forever--

We miss her presence with us everyday
Karin Esther Lennartson Gering
10/20/2004
This book was delayed a decade to honor her passing

To the ten million five hundred thousand men
air lifted to Vietnam from 1965 through 1975;
the over two million Vietnamese who died there;
and the 58,000 U.S. Service men who never came home.
Had JFK not been assassinated 11/ 22 / 1963:
All of your lives could have been saved
as Tip O'Neill lamented—there would
not have been that terrible loss
of life had JFK—lived.

Memorial Day—May 26th, 2015

To Our Military Families And Our Many
Military Veterans Returning From
Service Tours In Iraq—And Afghanistan—And
Wherever Duty, And Our Country Has Called You

Thank you for all of your sacrifice to our country.
John F. Kennedy had your back –
Richard M. Nixon and Lyndon B. Johnson,
they both told some vicious lies and they did not have your back.

Special Thanks

My friends at The Kennedy Library Maryrose

To all my great friends and family and legendary figures I love

ALL THOSE WHO INSPIRED ME

George Carlin / Tony Bondi / David Milch / William Goldman / Peter Nelson

Claudia Furiati
The Extraordinary Author Journalist And Writer
You told this story to the world first.

Special thanks Janet at Ixtlan

My Pharmaca Pharmacy family, the Sclar family, the Gering family,
the Shafers, the Allen family, the Mattas family.

Linda Mellor, Kathy Shafer, Cheryl Mattas, Melanie Allen
(No brother on the planet has more in life than I have
in these four awesome sisters.)

Tim, I will pick up the wrecked T-bird in the backyard and reanimate it soon…
Sara Shafer, Timmy Shafer, Jeremy Mattas, Travis Mattas
I am so proud of all of you and your accomplishments, Uncle Michael

The Fantastic Four Musketeers Of Michael's Machine:
Carlos Nunez, Wade A. Morman, Damion Thompson, Joseph E. Steinberg
A.J. sometimes we bite the bullet in life and we preserve the good name by
doing the best we can behind the eight ball or through all of our
difficult times of adversity.

To the good chin wag we missed all these years and a cup of coffee 50 years later.

Special thanks for financial assistance in rights acquisitions
to Mr. John Richards and his kind, lovely dear sister; Lou Ann Richards

"God bless the child that got his own."

"We walk the road we grew up on and we let go of all the rough stuff
to see the good stuff."

Dignified with dignity chin up – In the undignified era of our time.

THE VAGABOND WRITER

THE VAGABOND BOOK

Author's Note

For some like my father called me a real circle talker, and also in his viewpoint, I was once thought of as like… The Beachcomber–just a bum. But you can call me Michael, an omniscient third person, and a bucolic voice of meek reason, within this fruit-filled world that in a worthy trade cobbler's sense, how truly strange it is that man's imagination, would be kibitzing in these unique and vivid visions of so far away and beyond a thousand bitters.

I am but a tethered soul on median post that's been heavily pounded dizzy into a quiet voice of reason, in an otherwise imbalanced, out of kilter planet, and as this voice, or sometimes weary commentator, who at this particular time in his life is feeling the spirits needing of such a voice, to calm the unruly waves of discord. I seek forth tendered by spar in indefinable intractable duty. I sprung from the giant fish-beast like a gross regurgitated old sea tortoise rejected by a mighty hurl deep from the belly of Jonah. I am duly shackled to a huge heavy scar-filled and fractious shielding shell, who is forever damned, wishing to blow my spout like my cousins the sea whales, plowing the swells abroad, and I like them am feeling rather—impaled, but yet undaunted as I'm rolling along to the changing tide of the sea's restless currents, appearing, doing my deeds, and then disappearing again… in lengthy spasms.

As I tend to keep going forward to try to put a stop to and also quell the many axes swung in evil, as the axes fell in Cuba, and, the axes fell here in America, in the new era of the United States, the millennium of the axis of evil which was hammered into full operational splicing horrors in its effects to our constitution, as well as our spirits. The intention to spell and fully lay bare these myriad labyrinthine channels, through the darkest depths of man's or the cabal notions of all dubious eccentricities, in those lost-souls in these uncommonly disturbing, and very dangerous times. In seeing it laid bare we will try to rekindle or build a more trustworthy and palatable, solvent soluble alternative. It shall be declaration with freedom built within truth. The new truth that existed in all of our free declarations, both civil, and in civility, and properly with the liberty and justice for all, including J.F.K.; believing the country will withstand the trial as we get the truth from deep within our government. It will not break us. We will emerge stronger. As we still all enjoy the pursuit of happiness. We all toil with our existence, in overseeing the brinks of the world's habits, of these sad or dreary planetary dramas of ever changing vistas, for want and need of divining some long-overdue hope in our vivid and drought-laden horizons.

The Beachcomber

CUBA

It is difficult not to be emotionally pulled when you visit the tropical paradise Cuba. The exotic island, with its world-class beaches, landscapes steeped in both traditions of Spanish-African cultures, and its mulatto rhythms of conga drums pounding late into the night... its abundance of warm-hearted smiling and giving people, sharing with you a cup of sweet dark rum and spiced roast pork at every corner. Its culture of celebrations from Night Carnival and May Day to Mardi Gras, and vast assortments of nightclubs, music halls, jazz bars, and eateries with specialist servers in the finest of drink, the finest of music, the liveliest most spirited of dances, and top it all off with the finest of handmade tobaccos in Cuba's *specialist art* of the world's best cigars.

The theatre and Cuban National Ballet are in high esteem and internationally acclaimed for their repertoire, which include both classical and modern ballets. Cuban painters and artists have managed to retain freedom of expression in spite of difficulties involved. Everything from Afro-Cuban mythology and folklore, to the intense movement of street art. The streets are turned into studios of outdoor living canvases, however, *some were confiscated*, some artists left for Miami. But the Cuban artists' networks are active in Miami: Jose Bedia, Luis Marin, Jose Iraola, Thomas Esson, Nereida Garcia, Frank Leon, Juan-Si, and, of course, Thomas Sanchez, all began their careers in Cuba before immigrating to U.S. soil and residences. But Cuba remains a painter's paradise and still harbors a burgeoning community of talent. The late Wilfredo Lams' distinguished works are displayed inside Havana's Artes Museum.

Cuba has produced outstanding writers. Guillermo Cabrera Infante, Alejo Carpentier, Servero Sarduy, Lezuma Lima, and also Miguel Barnet, and Jose Marti are leading lights of the Latin American Literature Era. In cinema, Cuba has the New Latin American Film Festival which attracts the film community from all over the world, and its Coral prizes are the Latin equivalent of the Oscars.

The people love to have a good time and indulge in everything from baseball to soccer to fishing. There is an abundance of natural wonders of discovery almost everywhere, as guides will take you on tropical trips of bird watching, hiking trails, and horseback riding. There are marlin fishing charters, and several other angling excursions to partake and indulge in. With beautiful lime green hues, the warm, clean, clear waters offer excellent snorkeling, and scuba diving adventures of discovering red and black corals, and an exotic array of tropical fish and sea life. Cuba's sandy-golden beaches and clear blue waters are some of the best to be found in the world. There are many roads for avid bicycling, and motorcycling routes, that await you like many of those found in the guidebook, *Motorcycling Through Castro's Cuba* by Christopher P. Baker, which are in keeping with the country's energy conservation program. Fuel prices are relatively high and the gasoline per gallon ranges from $2.85 to $3.45 as of this writing (2013).The subsidized rate is lower priced, going as low as $2.45 per gallon.

In sports, Cuba's continuing coaching and training regimentality has made it a world-class training ground for athletes of all sports. Beisbol (Baseball) goes way back to 1874 as the first recorded game to be played in Cuba. The passion to play it has grown ever since, throughout the country. The flow of players between the U.S. and Cuba followed starting from 1959, when Tommy Lasorda played five seasons in Cuba; and in that same year, 1959, he pitched the national team into the Caribbean World Series. Its numbers of Olympic medals, and general participation-per-capita, for a country of this size, are nothing short of extraordinary. Cuba's educational system places top priority on scholastic achievement, sports participation and health care. In today's Cuba, track and field Olympic gold medallists are on the greatest training grounds in all of sports. Their domination and training regimentality for a country their size is, simply put, *nothing short of outright astounding achievement.*

It is a country of unparalleled riches in natural land resources; sugar cane, coffee, and tobacco harvests, and other agricultural wonders. The fertile soils and abundant waters of Pineapple Town produce vast amounts of the harvest, and also the sweet and juicy Espanola Roja, *my favorite*, along with bananas as well as grapefruits. Taking into account the production of vast amounts of sugar cane, tobacco, and coffee... it is also remarkable, *considering its overall landmass and size*, that Cuba's citrus crop, which continues to flourish in quantity, is one of the largest harvests in the world.

The Zapata Peninsula is the best known of Cuba's wildlife havens. Two hundred species of birds, including the Bee Hummingbird and the Cuban Parakeet and Pink Flamingos can be seen everywhere. The crocodile was nearly hunted to extinction, but the population is making its comeback on crocodile farms, like those in Playa Larga. Along with the ancient wildlife of the Zapata Peninsula, there is also painful U.S./Cuban history. The Bay of Pigs–also known as Playa Giron, is a beautiful landscape for diving and snorkeling, with its black and red coral reefs and abundant sea life. Here in Zapata, charcoal is made the old-fashioned way, by covering huge stacks of wood with dirt and letting it burn inside-out to create charcoal.

Like a random woodpile of charcoal in the Zapata, or an *abandoned shoe* of sorts... my discovery process made its way *here*, in finding the Beachcomber's range.

The dawning location of *The Beachcomber* is based in Campechuela, Cuba. *Campechuela* is surrounded by history. It is the territory of the revolution, via the two towns found on either side. Eight miles to the north is LA DEMAJAGUA, home of Carlos Cespedes Sugar Estate, who freed his slaves and called for a rebellion against Spain on October 10th, 1868. And just ten miles to the south is MEDIA LUNA, home of the revolutionary heroine of Sierra Maestra, Celia Sanchez, who was born on May 9th, 1920. Her father, a local doctor, was a devoted follower of Jose Marti. Celia and Fidel Castro united over twenty years in the revolutionary fight, and in life, until she passed away from cancer in 1980. It was this loss more than any of the others that would go a long way to harden the wire within the soul of the leader of Cuba, *to continually sustain* the singular course of Cuba as *disenfranchised* from all its former ties to U.S. politics, prevailing over the next 50 years.

Lost and In Between the Towns of Historical Majesty
And in a Town Near the Pathway of Revolution

It was here in Campechuela, a town described at best as of modest importance, that the idea burned inside of me, that a lost soul of Cuba could meditate alone for a decade on his own. It would be unwise not to say that *The Beachcomber* was tendered to grant my passage one day to there, and traveling through this beautiful country, *beachcombing* by quietly, and respectfully walking, and watching, and learning, and preserving the past, while keeping all my hopes and dreams of Cuba in the future, a separate vision left for others to guide.

I know Cuba is a place that many people from the United States would like to get to know, and definitely many people *from all over the world as well, too*. It has been a fifty-year *time warp* since 1960, and the Revolution of Fidel Castro. Cuba shed its veil of the Trade Embargo, and the feigned, rigid, archaic, odd militarism of the U.S. travel restrictions, which finally ended recently under Barack Obama's administration... with Beyonce and Jay Z walking the streets of Havana to mark the beginning of the new era in U.S. and Cuba relations. *Things finally changed and Cuba now welcomes all U.S. visitors. It took a half of a century to manifest but the change now has come.*

Cuba's tourism with hotel construction, and investment planning in the millennium will become *eventually* the largest capacity in the Caribbean. If the U.S. embargo falls, a tourism gold rush could open up, and a potential five million people could visit annually within just a few years of the repeal of U.S. travel restrictions. The future of U.S. tourism into Cuba is on an economic level, an ever-present torrential outflowing grand well of highly prosperous wealth (that Cuba truly needs at this time) that hopefully nobody can continue to ignore. *The future of this well is waiting to be tapped.*

As Cuba awaits its destiny, Americans are now anxious to begin the exodus of *the yanqui tourism invasion*. The goal is to then double-up or top that plateau and to jump in 2015 to over 10 million tourists. All of this to be done in the realm of, as Ry Cooder put it mildly, "without turning the country into a bunch of baggage handlers like Hawaii." This is a humble beginning of our journey into Cuba, to reflect the type of miracle and perhaps some of the sadness of the irony of what's shaping the whole modern state of affairs with regards to Cuba. I'm opening with 1920 through 1961. Cuba has had many sailors, slaves, and peasants, and dictator presidents and dictator pirates, and also one dictator who rules the region like a true king.

There is nothing in these writings about Cuba's history since 1961. Having been alive for only forty-three years as I penned this, I decided the old history was a less contested manifest, and acceptable fare for a novice of even my own limitations to delve into. The rest of my story is modern fiction. (The exception being the Kennedy file, or the Missile crisis, and the Bay Of Pigs, all of which are matters of true accountable records.)

In some places, I found it necessary to lace in segments with my own commentary to juxtapose the past with the present. In spots I changed the format back into Screenwriting to heighten the clarity between characters. In writing this way, it helped me to understand them. However, in the best essence most of what follows is true in the Long Ago Tales of Cuba. Anything after that is more like life and, *The Beachcomber* can only be... what we ourselves make of it... It should be noted that this is not the traditional classic novel found in bookstores across America. This is a true amalgamated and mosaic text "time capsule condensed," and some would forecast, inherently correctly, it is an abomination placing the abutment, or the bridge between the 50 year long abyss of formal contempt, which links old Cuban history with the 2506 Brigade—Bay Of Pig's CIA-led invasion fighting soldiers—from the late 1950s to the planning, and the execution, and assassination of John F. Kennedy... on November 22nd, 1963. Clearly, this is not the first time that the connection to the CIA power echelon hierarchy has been linked to the JFK cold case, nor will it be the last time—as history has proved this to be reality over the last 50 years. Joe Esterhaus said: "I fell in love with words." With my own life I cannot explain delays or timing and the postponements over several years. My dear departed friend, George Carlin, he would tell you that any creative process... no matter your station in life or where you come from... the creative process; it just takes its own sweet time.

Worse yet, undoubtably, there was a decade long delay from when this book was originally written—2003—until printed in 2013. In the rigorous sojourn... numerous ruthless and worthy houses alike passed on this unique project... and many a handful of editors too were to reject it with contempt for language/content/syntax and/or the sweeping social science it contained in its vile subject matter of philosophy and conspiracy. In that declaration of the journey above mentioned, a property exists via two of its devout saviors. A rare gifted hand, Leslie Sears, resurrected it and saved it by wrestling bravely, while remaining undaunted, editing it together. And, then with book shepherding it into its final form, Mike Rounds. The company he founded that helps new writers, old ones too, through—Rounds, Miller Associates.

A herculean task via my undertakers—my thanks to Leslie Sears and also Mike Rounds for hanging in there during the journey fraught with many an obstacle in the way... with so many of those being found underneath the umbrella and caught in the sheer bowel of an upgrading storm... with the first-time Writer. I insert the salvo of one of my favorite author's lines— William Goldman's lamented chant nearby at the start of my efforts:

"May all of your scars with this trail be only of the littlest ones."

The material was passed down generations on this cold case by far more greater talents than I; including distinguished works from literary majestic writers Anthony Brugioni, Claudia Furiati, Jim Garrison, Jim Marrs; and coincides with the textbook-recorded findings of Fletcher Prouty (and continued now by Len Osanic) and the writer and filmmaker Oliver Stone, writer/historian Howard Jones (The Bay Of Pigs), and the authors Lamar Waldron and Thomas Hartmann. Photographic evidence has been presented in images from Robert Groden in *The Killing Of A President*, Jim Garrison's *On The Trail Of The Assassins*, and in Oliver Stone's film *JFK*, 1991, Warner Brothers Pictures. It's The Story That Won't Go Away.

Not only breadcrumbs but a direct hand rises all the way up to the top in the CIA leadership, and as succinctly as that film's director assesses the facts, JFK WAS KILLED BY HIS OWN GOVERNMENT.

Many a man, and many a committee, and several thousand others have unsuccessfully tried to solve the crime of the century. Winding through the shifty shebang of all the Casablanca-like fog, in the labyrinthine mystery has been a journey, filled with inexorable pitfalls, and self introspection, (one must gather all available faculty or reserve in questioning the United States Government, and its official national + state authority) it's a journey fraught and filled with the usual tightrope of defining infinite wisdom; the government's line or the government's lie. What is the best way to validate the truth? That is the question I have asked myself for the last 30 years.

I went to the wishing well—put my two cents in, the coins flew 22 years dropping down inside a deep hole 50 years deep, until I heard the penance of my two pennies hit water at that depth of the well's bottom. Standing nearby looking over my shoulders now awaiting the crackles of rifles firing the same shellac of bullets flying… Jack was hit clearly by an ambush of multiple rifles spraying, and, firing a volley of bullets 11/22/1963… I await my destiny with those same bullets 11/22/2015.

Somewhere in America I am safe and sound, being of sound mind and body. I hear the voice of JFK calling out to all of us in the times of scarcity in the molten murderous melting pot in a unique place known as our once grand United States Of America, which is always a good place to start.

"Ask not what your country can do for you—

But what you can do for your country." AMERICA…

I have and I will, my brothers and sisters, and I promise that this American countryman will never forget my dying king. Our long-departed president, countryman, citizen, father, author, and true leader… my friend and yours, the leader who truly had your back… John Fitzgerald Kennedy.

THE BEACHCOMBER

A TALE, A SHORT STORY, PLUS SOME ASIDE COMMENTARY BY MICHAEL GERING, as it was started July 26th, 2001... and composed through July 26th, 2003...self published November 22nd , 2013. Expanded to include more material not previously available at our press time as the rights were received afterwards when several publishing houses closed up shop and were acquired...to be self published down the road... the extra 15 years later until it was ultimately completed—November 22nd, 2015.

One must pause when it comes... to the crime of the century... and upon personal reflection, it's more like leavings, breadcrumbs left behind. The Posthumous Rendering's Evidence, And Identity. Yes, someone was here... once truly was here... And these kinds of things were left behind in random reckless disorder, riddled thoughts; these were... in the immortal words... of the late great genius of Mr. George Carlin, my dear departed old friend... in whose company I mourned that great loss... and in his way of those color-filled descriptions and good humor of that good stuff or what he prestigiously referred to in his lifetime succinctly as—

"My Brain Droppings."

The author of this book was a failed screenwriter. In over twenty years of writing screenplays... without a sale, he decided... to create a new format the world had never experienced until now. He used the format of percentile of selling stock in the shoe business which generally translates to this particular credo.

You normally sell 20 percent of your stock 80 percent of the time.

And he created a new book form called–THE CINEBOOK.

Which is 80 percent book and 20 percent screenplay.

What follows is a work of fiction layered in history which is the real truth, gathered for primarily a short story, with some additional background and peripheral circle-talking commentary. At the outset, The Beachcomber's journey evolved from a graphic novel's imagination since there is no penance to grow from such and uncourtly underworld place.

Amalgamated photos and portions of texts are used in a permission's context. In all areas of pictures and words donated and borrowed from previous works, the permission for usage was sought from the Publisher. The pictures we reference are found in the historic collection of Robert Groden:

THE KILLING OF A PRESIDENT, Isbn# 0-14-024003-9 In Blue Cover; A Complete Photographic Record Of The JFK Assassination Conspiracy.

FIDEL'S CUBA, Osvaldo Salas / Roberto Salas, Isbn#1-56025-245-6; A Revolution In Pictures Maroon Cover—Fidel Castro—Che Guevara

THE KENNEDY LIBRARY—Maryrose Grossman—Baileys Beach Photo

The Beachcomber Santiago...
A fictitious character in a Graphic Novel by Michael Gering.
THE KENNEDY FILE,
The Bay Of Pigs

NSC 5412	S—Group—40
FRD / MIRR	MRR / Alpha 66
AM—WORLD	Manual Artime
AM—TRUNK	Carlos Soccarras
AM—LASH	Rolando Cubela
Richard M. Nixon	E. Howard Hunt
Bernard Barker	Joseph C. King
Desmond Fitzgerald	Gordon Campbell

William "King" Harvey   **Robert F. Kennedy**

MONGOOSE	C—DAY
Richard Helms	Theodore Shackley
PLUTO / RESCATE	JM—WAVE / OP—TILT
Z R RIFLE	A—MOT
Lucien Sarti	Pedro Diaz Lanz
Michael Victor Mertz	Herminnio Diaz Garcia
David Atlee Phillips	Anthony Veciana
Howard Hughes	Robert Maheu
Frank Sturgis	Rolando Masferrer
Eugenio Martinez	David Sanchez Morales
Johnny Roselli	Tony "Nestor" Izquierdo
Tony Varona	Orlando Bosch
Sergio Arcacha Smith	Loran Hall

The Cuban Missile Crisis...
Nonfiction, documented, recorded in history.

Table of Contents

INTRODUCTION

A Sugar Boom in a Sexy, Tropical Setting

Corrupt Kings and The Quajiros Dreams

"A Slow Dance on the Killing Ground Behind a Regime with the Dance of the Millions."

The Sugar Boom had preceded the Batista Regime. "The Dance of Millions" it was affectionately dubbed. The peak lasted five years: 1915 until 1920. Sugar prices had climbed up to 22.5 cents a pound. Like the rise and fall of the stock market in 1921, the *crash* came hard when the price dropped to 3.6 cents a pound. In 1924, still producing a high quantity crop, Cuba made 4.5 million tons of sugar, and in 1925 it produced even millions more. With the market glutted, the price of sugar sold for less than one penny a pound. In 1924, having made his millions, Alfredo Zayas declined to run for re-election.

A cattle rustler, Machado Morales Gerado stepped into the breach. The Great Depression of Sugar in 1925 sparked off riots directed against President Machado Gerado, who had more or less consorted and manipulated his election in 1928. But, like the others who were corrupted by the level of capital to be gained, and who forgot about their people, *he just made so much money that he refused to leave office.* Cuba's history is filled with *the king must die follies syndrome.* All along Cuba and the hardworking Cubans at the bottom suffered.

Army troops were called upon to break up the unrest and dissuade the striking workers (the poor). Any demonstrators against the regime were gunned down. They hired thugs to double-whip the people's chances to speak their piece for a bigger piece of the pie, who were known as "*porros.*" The porros systemically thwarted the will of the people by abductions, tortures, and brutality, thereby making *disappearances* of the so-called enemies of the regime. It was the time of Corrupt Kings Killing Quajiros Dreams.

Machado, using periodic tortures by a police force of 15,000, became known as The Tropical Mussolini. The country was in vast levels of unrest and on the verge of a civil war as the workers united in 1933 for a GENERAL STRIKE. The whole country was brought to a halt, Machado Gerardo finally read the writing on the wall, and on August 11th, he hopped on a plane to Miami, supposedly armed to the teeth with his own weapons and stealing as much cash and gold as his free other thieving hands could carry with him.

In the ensuing chaos, an enterprising figure began to take control of the army. A young army sergeant, Fulgencio Batista, organized within the army a revolt of the lower officers. A mulatto of, by all accounts, humble origins with a wining smile which worked well for him, he quickly promoted himself

3

to Colonel, and from that level, he rose higher until he had the full control of the Army. Batista became the major player in all of Cuban politics, managing the government through a long and steady string of puppet presidents.

The Batista Era had begun in 1934 and after running the country through others he decided to run for president himself. It is generally believed he was fairly elected in 1940. I wonder if ever there was a fair election in Cuba. It's hard to say for sure. A tremendous political fabric of a blanket covers the Cuban horizon with a Casablanca-like fog of both mystery and intrigue.

Batista himself was a puppet whose masters lived in Washington. The Americans, perhaps feeling their interests secure, then rescinded the Platt Amendment that guaranteed the U.S. its power of intervention. Aided by the lease that was negotiated for the 99-year deal of their naval base at strategic Guantanamo, the Americans felt assured–the little island paradise was safely within their grasp.

Although Batista ran the show almost all of the time, he could also fade into the background if the mob, or U.S. political pressure, sometimes required it. It was a little of both during the time President Grau was being maneuvered, and put into the Palace spotlight. It was also a sizable gift of an inducement (a combination of bribe and payoff), that was personally hand-delivered by Meyer Lansky of some $250,000.00, which helped convince President Grau to later step aside, and on March 10th, 1952, Batista moved back into the presidential palace.

Havana, wrote Julian Barclay, "is filled with milkshakes and Mafiosi, hot dogs, and Jineteras–whores. U.S. Yankee Doodle had come into this town, and they are having their own wild times doing the old Martini-drinking competitions at the Sevilla Bar." When the U.S. Naval vessels entered Havana Harbor, the narrow harbor mouth beneath the Morro Castle was *jammed with rowboats full of clamoring prostitutes*, all fleeing with calls and vivid hardcore enchantments catering towards every visiting sailor's fancy or fantasy. It was at this time that the city became known as the Prostitution Capital of the Western Hemisphere.

To say Batista ruled during a time of prosperity is an understatement of epic proportions. Havana was a city where fabulous sums of money could be made from booze, drugs, gambling and prostitution. The Cuban Mob came first but the American Mob soon followed them.

Actually, Batista invited them by giving an invitation to Meyer Lansky to take over operation of two casinos and a racetrack at Havana's Oriental Park. Ironically, they were being brought in to *clean up the places*, which had the reputation as being crooked. Lansky quickly brought in his own pit crews to replace the Cubans and soon had the places *reformed*, and the business flourished. In time, more casinos followed with regular kickbacks to Batista, who put the American Mob to work for him. It was all appropriately legal, which was even more glorious. It was a time of gangsters running hotels and the levels increased dramatically as they took the foothold they had gained during the U.S. prohibition, and stepped into Cuba with their eyes, ears, and arms, and legs and noses, knees and necks deep in it. Havana at night became the smorgasbord of the U.S. elite. From all over the world people flocked to its nightlife of booze, gambling and raw sex, like moths to the flame; and all to an erotic Mulatto-African Cuban rhythmic beat.

In Cuba anything and everything was permissible: gambling, pornography, drugs, and prostitution; which created a colossal market of corruption, and the business of self-enrichment a virtual boom town environment. Organized crime became one of the three power groups in Cuba, the other two were Batista's corrupt military regime and American business groups. Together, all three combined to establish in Cuba what became known as the decadent debauchery festival of a complete criminal state.

The country was bartered and quartered and turned literally into a flagship state of ultimate piracy. So many villains and notoriously infamous seedy noir-like characters of diverse and unruly profit and motivational greed ran the place as professional misfits of dubiously ranging intentions. It was like a circus funhouse, full of raw Moulin Rouge pleasures, of the sinfully exotic and erotic adult indulgences. The booze and the drugs, the sex and the rhythmic pulsating music, all combined with the freedoms of prostitution, gambling, and games, and the world knew that Cuba had become The Ultimate Playground.

It was a haven for the pirate souls of men from every place else in the world.

A collection of four families ran the show fraternally and collectively ruled the roost. The first, headed by Cuban-Italian Amleto Batistti, controlled heroin and cocaine routes to the United States and also ran an emporium of gambling from Batistti's base at the Hotel Sevilla. The *family* of Amadeo Barletta organized the *Black Shirts* in Havana. The third *family* was headed by Tampa's Mafia boss, Santo Trafficante, Jr., who operated the Sans Souci Casino and Nightclub, plus other casinos in the Capri, Comodoro, Deauville, and the Sevilla-Biltmore Hotels. Watching over them all was Lansky, who ran the Montmarte Club and the International Club of the Hotel National. Meyer Lansky's greatest investment opened on December 10th, 1958: The 14 million dollar ritziest and gaudiest hotel in all of Cuba, The Riviera. Everyone heard the story regarding the outcome. The revolution raged on outside and everyone scattered as the help left the kitchen and the gaming floor, and left old Meyer and his wife serving drinks and dinner for their guests, oblivious to what was going on outside. All the mob bosses were arrested and kicked out of Cuba as undesirable aliens. Meyer had sunk himself *all in* and gambled everything he had, and he was the biggest loser. He said so too, "I gambled it all in Cuba and I just crapped out."

Havana had degenerated into an immoral sinkhole where visitors flocked to carouse with the glamorous, lithesome Latin lasses or "jineteras," black-eyed and brown-skinned senoritas, languorously, enticingly, shaking and swaying to the mambo beat. Such were the words that appeared on the

5

vintage brochures advertising Nighttime In Havana. And, in living up to that billing it was once known as: The great adult playground for restless souls.

The traveling business men could choose their mulatta at the airport via a photograph and then could drink as much and fuck as much and gamble as much, on the lottery, roulette, dice, horses, and whatever that they could win or lose, and indulge in as much pussy as one's libido and wallet could plunge its way into. They welcomed American yanqui-dollars, and the rate of exchange and value over there (in the days before Castro) always carved a huge pathway into the Cuba experience. In the 30s and 40s and 50s Cuba truly invented today's old phrase of that strange secret indulgence created for modern days in Las Vegas: "What happens in Cuba stays in Cuba." Or if you do go fishing down there and whatever the waters quarry or quandary of yanqui mojo, be careful, since if it's ever for the truth… God forbid "you better not catch anything." A pirate's booty unshared goes only to the pirate.

America in the early 1950s had yet to emerge from its shell of innocence. Television in the 50s, with American shows like *Ozzie Harriet*, and the correct morals of *Father Knows Best*, or even Sid Caesar's *Your Show of Shows*, were all squeaky clean. Even the cranky, portly old bus driver Ralph Kramden couldn't drink on TV. (A bus driver… no less?) The mid 50s shows ushered onto the set *separate beds* for all the married couples. Somehow the U.S. audiences still clicked as *I Love Lucy*, starring an amazing talent, Lucille Ball, and for the first time a youthful Desi Arnaz, as the equally talented Bandleader/Cuban husband, who would become America's first legendary comedic- television sweetheart. America was in the lead of righteousness, everybody liked IKE, and both Playboy and John Kennedy yet loomed in the distance to awaken some of our political landscapes.

It's easy to understand how Cuba's mystique unlocked and provided the necessary needed escape from the good old USA and the United States' old predilection of puritan sensibility. Just off the coast of Florida, a tropical paradise awaited–CUBA, *which unleashed many a taboo and the libido*.

Everything was on the menu, from young teenaged girls, and/or boys, with a minor surcharge for virgins. It was a staggering level of hedonism unparalleled to almost anything that the world had known. The excess here at its worst point was actually unfortunate, but things are truly unique in the Cuban culture, which latched onto Spanish heritage and the 15th Birthday- *las fiestas de quince*, or the quince party for a young Cuban girl, although the U.S. culture has a different more. Here at age 15, traditionally things tend to happen at an earlier time frame when turning from youthful to sexually active. The Cuban children are always smiling and they always appear in such brightly colorful school uniforms that it prompted author James Michener to say, "it reminds me of *a meadow filled with flowers*." In the mid 50s through the mid 60s, Cuba was a very young country. Some 35 percent of the population was below the age of sixteen years.

The celebration of las fiestas de quince–the birthday party held for 15-year-old girls, is a direct legacy of the Spanish Heritage for a young Cubana girl to celebrate. The parents will save money from the day the girl is born to do her right with a memorable fifteenth birthday party. It is also the day on which the quinceanera may openly begin *her sexual life* without any fears with regard to family recrimination. A tradition that's completely unrealistic or unfathomable to any U.S. customs. (Some would equate it to abject parental suicide in the U.S.) It's as if we are somehow far wiser in that traditional westerner's philosophy in this country.

As far as the party is concerned for the Cubana, a whole arsenal of pageantry might be involved from the hairdresser to the dressmaker, to even a good photographer to capture the auspicious occasion. And also, of course there is the classic American car with a driver-chauffeur to take the youthful Cubana girl to the eventful celebration of adulthood, along with all of her close friends to accompany her on her welcomed journey into *early womanhood*, on her way to the big party. It's a simple, natural and expected freedom period for girls. You could argue that with this kind of celebrated tradition, unlike in the United States, it would appear as though Cuba's Spanish Heritage, and its demystifying sexuality towards its younger populace with its *youths truths*, seems to be telling the same thing to the girls as they do to the boys. Sex is viewed as a worthy, healthy activity for both sexes. It is expected that both women as well as men get to participate in it, and indulge themselves, and even be allowed to be happy about the fulfillment of indulging in sex. A novel concept as it relates to Western morals, and they provide *state run hotels*.

As with any jury duty a man or a woman sitting in judgment understands that Cuba was Cuba. Where the intersection of the damn bitters in the reality resides, truth must be then viewed first (where that country exists) as seldom heard but nevertheless in the likely coveted inconsequential burial grounds.

Even Hollywood added to Cuba's sex capital image in a watered-down version with "<u>Guys and Dolls</u>." Sky Masterson would bring his young *virgin*-Salvation Army Love down to Havana to be ultimately seduced. Aboard luxury yachts, Hollywood stars like Errol Flynn, Gary Cooper, Clark Gable, and Marlene Dietrich, all sailed into Havana to have themselves a great time. The greatest singers and entertainers flocked to Cuba to perform: Nat King Cole, Harry Belafonte, and Maurice Chevalier, were all the headliners of the day. It was the western hemisphere's uniquely divine version of the greatest show on earth.

Santo Trafficante, Jr.'s personal VIP guest, George Raft, was the quintessential film star gangster, a part owner and also a full time host of the Red Room at the Hotel Capri. Frank Sinatra, accompanied with Ava Gardner, was flown in to sing. The New Jersey crooner came with two of Al Capone's cousins and a gift of a gold cigarette case for Lucky Luciano. It was a safe place to discuss mob business and in the year of 1946, the big meeting's agenda was to do with Benny "Bugsy" Siegel. The meeting ended with a grim note, "There's only one thing to do with a thief who steals from his friends," and on that note dapper Benny "Bugsy" Siegel was gone by next year. He was put to bed with "bullets and a dirt nap" thanks to Virginia Hill (Bugsy's girl) dipping into The Flamingo's till.

In the lure of the tropics, Cuba's contribution of limitless sensual pleasures, lawlessness and corruption, along with the sordid Casablanca-like Bogartian dangers, exerted an almost irresistible fascination for the many writers, artists, and modern adventure-seeking non-bourgeoise. Those liberal thinking, nefarious, nectarine, nocturnal, non-neophytes who liked to walk among, and also talk among, the hybrid sexual conga-mambo beat thrill seekers, found their ideal nexus within Cuban culture and the Cuban peoples' hip-swaying, swinging lifestyle. Living on this island, indulging in its riches, a man could be a king.

Ernest Hemingway and Graham Greene, among so many countless others, explored or romanticized Cuba, but their contributions were more of a socialized and civil point of view, their cultured stories were set in Cuba. Hemingway's staunch Midwestern morals kept him from losing himself, since he realized early on he had to stay out of its politics to continue living there. He loved the marlin fishing and his favorite bar and daiquiris, and stayed married to his writings, centering only selected works on the familiar old surroundings of Cuba. He was smart, too, to do so, in carefully preserving his forever assurance of *being welcomed* on his adopted island home.

It was very clever to set *The Old Man and the Sea* Man-Boat-Fish-Conflict off Cuban soil–that's a pretty safe subject rather than exposing the trade businesses and political business of Cuba (goings on that he was aware of), which, at the time, would've certainly made more meaty and salacious copy. Hotel Ambos Mundos of Old Havana was the place where Ernest Hemingway wrote, in room 511, *FOR WHOM THE BELL TOLLS*–the epic about the Spanish Civil War, of which even Fidel Castro sung its praises, and read to learn more about the activist and artistic community in Havana, and also its recipes with regard to Guerrilla Warfare. And it was noteworthy that while he had been so vocal in his attitude towards the Spanish Civil War twenty years before, he wisely chose to remain either silent or kept private his thoughts on Castro/Batista, and the movement in his adopted home. He wrote one friend privately, aroused by the drama of the guerrilla war and its characters of Fidel and Che: "This is a good revolution," he said and went on to rightly proclaim idealistically, "it's an honest and just revolution."

During the Hemingway Fishing Competition of Havana, 1960, Fidel won an armful of prizes and Ernesto awarded the trophies. Here was *papa yanqui* standing toe to toe with Castro, and yet he had enough guts of glory under his belt. He left the revolution alone, and distinctly and wisely so-protected his welcome on his island paradise. I would have to agree with Hemingway's great friend and fishing guide for over some thirty years, Gregorio Fuentes, who claims: "I have truly never met a more intelligent man than Papa Ernest Hemingway." Truth abounds in his statement. And had he lived longer, I wonder if he would have come out of the daiquiri-retirement phase and segued his focus to a few other books, and perhaps even one with the revolution as its backdrop. One just pauses to wonder what a glorious work it could have been.

In the void of the vacuum of the real *papa daredevil*, a second-hand daredevil dove into the ever-impending forces of the fracas of intrigue–a man who wrote a story about another type of vacuum, a vacuum salesman-turned spy, Mr. Wormold, in 1958's *Our Man in Havana*. Far more unrestrained, the Englishman Graham Greene had a more decadent thirst and quenched it well in the seamier side by indulging in vivid blue movie and pornographic art films of the sexual exploits of Cuban bronzed-skinned thespians. He found the Cuban capital a place "where every vice was permissible and every trade possible." It is said he lapped up the sordid brother life, "the spinning roulette wheel in every hotel, the fruit machines spilling out jackpots of silver dollars, and the Shanghai Theatre, where a buck-twenty-five cents would get you into a nude cabaret of some very extreme beyond vaudevillian obscenities, with the bluest of blue films at the intervals."

Greene, Mr. "<u>Our Man in Havana</u>" even became caught up in his own minor intrigue when he flew to Santiago in hopes of interviewing Guerrillas in the Sierra Maestra, carrying a suitcase of clothing and also some supplies. He then hopped aboard a plane with a TIME reporter whom Greene decided (on his own) was a CIA spy. There were surreptitious meetings with some revolutionary contacts but Greene became *worried and convinced* that he was now also being followed. The interview then later fell through and in the strain of the *spy spotlight*, and being concerned for his own safety, he finally had to leave Cuba soon afterwards.

Clearly, Graham Greene had entered the fray and obviously Hemingway knew better than to dissolve or dispose himself to such similar quandary of fate. You have to wonder if, during the fishing competition, any ideas of chronicling the old and the new history ever came up for Fidel Castro, being the fan of Hemingway that he was. I lay odds that they likely did. Fidel Castro has told some people about their second meeting. He'd said that he'd been invited out to the writer's home, Finca Vigia, and he accepted and spent hours out there talking late into the night. I wish I could tell you what they talked about (it would've been great to be a fly on the wall at Hemingway's place that evening), but now it's only Fidel who truly knows.

For many years Ernest Hemingway lived rigorously and wrote ever courageously some of the most popular and best prose of any twentieth century writer in English, and created a style of writing which moved Norman Mailer to refer to him as the *literary father* of all current novelists. He was the writer who made the short declarative sentence an ideal for nearly every writer who followed. He was in frontline action in a handful of wars, and he had the injuries that were consistent with being a prizefighter or a town's wrestler from living such an active adventurist lifestyle. He survived four automobile accidents and two airplane crashes (on consecutive days in January, 1954), and it was there the most damage was done (in the latter airplane crash he broke the window's glass with his head to ultimately escape the burning plane). He also had another scrape; he was badly clawed in the head and gashed on a hunting expedition as he was posing over a "kill" for a photograph. There was also the accident where a poorly attached sky light fixture fell from a roof and landed on his head.

Hemingway was a very strong man who took a lot of lumps on his skull over the years but was always able to rely on his journeyman's journalistic old stubborn fighter's resiliency to make a comeback from any kind of a knockdown.

His risk-taking included placing his personal life in jeopardy unnecessarily during World War II when he decided to outfit the Pilar, his yacht, with special electronic gear so he could hunt down and patrol for German submarines out of Cuba. As with the theme in *The Old Man and the Sea*, by going too far out he loses the marlin to the sharks. Here, Ernest Hemingway was clearly risking more than he needed by hunting U-boats and submarines on his own private yacht.

He challenged himself to the limits and heartily wrestled with life and he chronicled it in fiction like a lean and mean daredevil journalist who was high on courage and stretched the boundary of what regular men call fear. He liked the battle and toiled fiercely in those treks in which his characters were ever so rawly tested. And whether it was deep in the front-lines of battles or on the safari hunt for dangerous game, or the battle tour into the ring via the bullfighters, or the challenges of the marlin fishing contests, Hemingway wrote about the metaphor of men being alive in that their inherent hope and confidence was never gone out of them. In all of this bravery he added the old narration which shows us and tells us "that a man can be destroyed but not defeated." It is in this "courage on the brink to be reduced or shattered into nothingness or nearest to death" that Hemingway would bravely go in life, vigorously and courageously, and similarly in fiction, with boldly written testaments that examine life more closely for all of us about a man's faith in himself to be a man. For so many years luck, and courage, and that faith he possessed had never failed him until the very end of his life.

It's clear the man was complicated with multiple ailments, both physical and mental, suffering traits similar to those his parents had, from blindingly bad headaches, to insomnia, high blood pressure, diabetes, depression, and paranoia. There were various eye and ear problems, impacting two of the three most important senses in the hunter, or the hunted, which are vision and hearing; the third being instinct. Add to it the family history of five suicides in a family of eight and losing his father early in 1928. It was clear that Ernest Hemingway felt these complications of heredity more after the two consecutive plane crashes added physical trauma to an already intensely pressured skull, having difficulty with his own demons of depression and coping with his life.

They came like a calling from *For Whom The Bell Tolls* and the white whale of *Moby Dick* thrashing the hull of Ahab's vessel. It was as if the culmination of the lifelong adventures of chasing the swells finally struck the atoll, and the vessel forever rolling upon these waves of adventure was *then collapsed* with the shattering of the hull, which was the eclipse of his own intellectual faculties. Faced with such ultimate sacrifice and his inability to save himself, he chose to go down with his ship, a noble pilot and clever captain who was unequalled, unerring and unending, like the old man and the sea, and the other daring sorts of legends from the Atlantic.

To be at ground zero facing the Cabo Blanco of Ernest Hemingway was to come in and undermine an already unduly undulating soul. And that the death to him, was truly unearned of this undying man, for to lose the power of man's self, over his own mind and for himself to recognize that loss was more than any man could face.

When John Kennedy asked him to write for his inaugural speech, with hepatitis, anemia, and diabetes along with extremely high blood pressure to go along with his depression, Hemingway struggled to write a speech for John Kennedy. After barely being able to construct a single paragraph, it was clear that his once reliable mental state had deteriorated (with the consumption of up to a quart of whiskey a day) into a level impairing his ability to think clearly, or to ever write again.

He realized his mental fate; one of the truly great great writing wells had finally gone dry, his capacities now empty or drained. It had been the healthiest and most spirited of minds, and for him to be no more of this was to be faced with being nearest to the edge of nothingness for a writer. He was faced with the ultimately awful realization of his inability to tap any veins of the infamous well, and the bitter futile mortality in that unfamiliar and final devastatingly-cold *death call*, which was forever knowing he would no longer be able to write.

Some viewed this undoing with their own sentimental rendering of a eulogy by stating it in many different ways, from Norman Mailer, Ray Bradbury, and John F. Kennedy. Many who understood his last act in life believe that he may have displayed courage in carrying out the last option left for a man who spent so much time defining himself in life, fiercely living it throughout, living closest to the edge. People say a lot of things about Hemingway. His style was very minimalist, but his canvas was truly very large.

We will all forever miss that old man "*papa*" and perhaps that last great book that just wasn't meant to happen in the creator's plan. He left us on July 2nd, 1961. He was 61 years old and the most popular American writer of the 20th Century. He passed on after living a life of productivity and adventure of the sort few have ever known. Hemingway, for most aspiring writers, was the 20th century's noble and driving force who challenged us all with the lean and mean "*put it against the grille and see what it's really made of.*" His is truly the greatest voice, living on vigorously throughout all of the worldly trials of his characters in his literature.

PART I

ONE

The Rise of the Revolutionary Hero

Fidel Ruz Castro–The Leader

Not long after 1953, Graham Greene wrote of the Batista Dictatorship that "the president's regime was creaking down dangerously towards its end." Castro's plan included street protests and legal challenges to Batista's Regime. (The basis for justifying the planned revolution was that it was a *legal act* against an *illegal regime.*) He kept his movement's ploy simmering in the minds and hearts of the people who were literally, day by day, becoming more and more intolerant of Batista's treacherously brutal police force and their killing, torturing, and public daily hangings from the trees of rebel-collaborators or suspected opposition members.

Castro's personality and ideals drew the politically estranged Cubans, who longed for the day of the toppling of Batista's ruling secret police, into his fold. In his oratory and protests he was completely focused in the vision of Cuba's future. His magnetism and convictions made his eventual coup somehow seemingly preordained and the Cuban people believed in him, that he would act. As Tad Szulc wrote of Castro's destiny: "Fidel is now personally at war with the Batista Dictatorship, and Fidel Castro is a man who will never relent."

The Attack on the Moncada Barracks

At age 26, Fidel Castro launched his revolution on the day of his favorite number, July 26th, 1953, with the attack on the Moncada Barracks in Santiago de Cuba. Castro's plan was to seize a cachet of arms and ammunition. A simultaneous attack was planned on Bayamo Barracks using only thirty men. They acted on surprise, using the Carnival as a factor, relying on the fact that most of Batista's troops would be occupied on weekend passes. Also since Batista's reinforcements would come from Holguin, he was figuring to counter by blowing up the bridges over Rio Cauto, thereby isolating Oriente Province as a so-called liberation zone.

It was a well-designed sneak attack. Meanwhile, the other members of the movement were to seize key radio stations and use communications to appeal for a national uprising against Batista.

It was a dawn attack at 5 a.m., with 125 men crammed into 16 cars. Fidel Castro rode in the fifth car with Raul Castro (who was leading the second unit) in the third car, which made a wrong turn, arriving after the fighting began. The force was reduced to 105 men after another vehicle had a flat tire. The rebel-commandos stormed into the barracks and took the sentinels by surprise, but an army patrol quickly appeared and gunfire erupted all over the place as the alarm bells were sounded.

In a hail of extreme spray rounds of automatic gunfire, the rebels were forced to retreat. The battle lasted for less than thirty minutes. The rebels lost eight men in combat while Batista's troops lost nineteen men in the fighting that early July morning.

The idea was to sneak attack to "cease armaments" and the weapons the rebels had were less than stellar to start with. One machine gun, a couple old 44 sawed off Winchester rifles, several sporting and hunting rifles, and only one M-1 rifle and only one single Browning submachine gun. Batista's story of Moncada weighed in the rebels at a force strength of between 400 to 500 men who stormed the barracks with modern weapons.

Batista's propaganda placed atrocities upon the rebels. In fact the reality was the sixty-four captured men were tortured and brutally murdered by Batista's forces, which was recorded by photographs.

Photographer journalist Marta Rojas, who worked for "Bohemia," smuggled the film of the murders to Havana. Five days later the photos of the sixty-four tortured Fidelistas were printed and released exposing Batista's lie, and unleashing a wave of disgust among the Cuban people.

The horrible assassinations of the sixty-four rebels was plain for all to see, as the evidence of the gruesome pictures were published. A wave of revulsion swept through the land, and the hearts and souls of so many Cuban countrymen went out to those 64 brave men who had died for change.

Thousands of Cubans attended mass for their fallen countrymen who had given their lives, dying for a worthy and noble cause. The mass that was held in their honor marked sixty-four martyrs for the Cuban people to think about, plus all of what might've been had the uprising been successful. It took the Catholic church into the forefront when the hierarchy of the church ministers stepped in on behalf of the rebels, and negotiated a guarantee for the lives of any remaining or future rebels captured. It remained clear that the hearts and minds of Cuba's people were mostly following along with the rebels, and their rebel leader Fidel Castro.

Fidel Castro was captured by an army detachment, whose commander, the tall 53-year-old black lieutenant Pedro Sarria, disobeyed orders to kill Castro on sight. He took Castro off to Santiago jail where he was safe from murder, since he had risen throughout Cuban culture as a national cult hero figure. Press reporters interviewed him from prison and Castro told them in detail the rationale for the attack on Moncada Barracks. This proved to become a massive public relations coup that sowed more of the seeds of manifesting a future scenario of the revolution's eventual victory.

Appearing in the courtroom and acting as his own pro per attorney, he immediately demanded his shackles be removed. The judge agreed and right from the start of the trial, Castro showed a remarkable knack for the look of a winner. It was, he argued, the rebels' duty to overthrow the illegal Batista dictatorship. Fidel Castro never spoke of any of the charges leveled at him or his fellow rebels-at-arms. He attacked the deplorable record of the Batista regime, in an accurately processed, methodical, and dissecting dissolution with a candid account of the regime's horrible track record, and its disregard for the well-being of the Cuban people. When Castro was asked who was the intellectual author of such convincing arguments? He answered back with "Jose Marti," the response brought him an ovation of applause.

The judges met with increasing pressure put on by Batista to resolve the case before any more of the convincing rhetorical remarks of Fidel Castro's oratory could do more harm to the dictator's ever-receding hold of the *slippery footing he held* with his position inside the presidential palace. Fidel Castro, this rascal Rebel Leader, kept pushing with his valid reasoning for the *revolutionary visions of the eventual toppling* of Batista under the rebels' revolt.

During Fidel Castro's sentencing, the prosecutor spoke for only two minutes. But on October 16th, 1953, possibly suffering from an ailment from tainted food, at the behest of Batista's guards acting on orders to weaken the rebel's strength, a weary Fidel Castro put forth an exhaustive mesmerizing oratory in which he devastatingly denounced the severe invalidity of the suppressive Batista regime. In ending with over 3 hours of a righteous passionate testimonial anthem, with the liberation mantra phrase, just like the words of Patrick Henry, "Give me liberty or give me death," Fidel Castro went to jail with the words: "Condemn me it does not matter because history will absolve me."

The Moncada Attack became the milestone marking history, but it was the brilliant defense speech that was the thought-provoking watershed of clarity for the Cuban people. Fidel Castro was for all Cubans, and the immensely popular revolutionary had earned the support of his people with his day in the courtroom. He now had acclaim and national sympathy for his cause, and he was led away in handcuffs amid cheering throngs of supporters to serve fifteen years in jail on the Isle of Pines, which today is known as Isle de la Juventud (The Isle of Youth). He was sent to the very same prison Jose Marti was imprisoned in, which gave him even more weight towards legitimizing his destiny with revolution. He also put together and organized the Abel Santamaria Ideological Academy to teach history, philosophy, political economics, classics and languages to his fellow revolutionaries languishing idle inside the prison.

During a Batista visit to the Isle of Pines, Fidel Castro led the prisoners in singing a revolutionary song in the face of the dictator, as he walked the stone floors of the prison in February, 1954. Placed in solitary confinement for his defiant attitude at several junctures during his stay there, Fidel developed a secret sign language communications network with his fellow revolutionary inmates. He even managed to smuggle out a copy of his *"condemn me it does not matter because history will absolve me"* speech using lemon juice extract as an invisible ink. Even prison could not challenge his interminable will to fight on.

He filed three separate lawsuits against the Batista Regime. Media coverage continued to mount with each day as the revolutionary's stature gained nationwide circumstance, and it was followed by a "free Castro" campaign, which was ever growing among the masses of the people all over Cuba who sided with the young rebel.

After the rigged Cuban election of 1954, Washington quickly embraced and sanctioned the now tainted but supposedly "constitutional" Batista regime. In May of 1955, bowing to mounting public pressures, a "signed U.S. Amnesty Bill," forged even further sentiments which were then passed by U.S. Congress. Congressional support and the amnesty bill put heavy pressure on Batista.

Later, Castro and the rebel band of his Moncado Attack prisoners were finally freed. When the steaming freedom train reached Havana, he was hoisted high up into the air by an overwhelming throng of supporters. Upon the hands of the people, Fidel Castro was carried as a Hero through the streets of Cuba.

Batista grew more tense and intolerant of the rebel leaders' anti-Batista rhetoric, and the speeches that Fidel would give each time out. Batista banned the rebel from making anymore public addresses or receiving press coverage that his newspapers had printed. All the doctrines of the presses of the Castro revolution were immediately shut down. Fidel was forced to keep in constant motion for his safety, and on July 7th, 1955, he boarded a plane bound for Mexico. Once he had stepped aboard, his message to Cuba's people came back: "From trips such as these, one returns with the tyranny beheaded at one's feet."

In keeping with his proclamation, Castro would certainly return to unfinished work. During Castro's exile, he had but one singular goal: to assemble, prepare, and train a guerrilla rebel army to invade Cuba. Fidel's enthusiasm and optimism were so great he managed to talk aged revolutionaries, such as Alberto Bayo, hero of the Spanish Civil War, into giving up careers and businesses to train Castro's core group of insurgents who were now known as MR-26-7 (Movimiento Revolucionario 26 Julio) in the tactics of rebel-guerrilla warfare.

In yet another brilliant coup of triumphant maneuvering, Fidel sent a powerful message to the Congress of the Ortodoxo Party. He called for the 500 delegates of the party to systematically reject working with Batista's regime. Asked by Castro to take to the higher road of the revolution, the delegates jumped to their feet chanting the call for a changing of the old guard. "Revolution! Revolution!" They shouted the proof that Fidel Castro had won over the will of the entire organization.

Castro also authored the movement's "Manifesto No. 1–to the People of Cuba." Laying out the revolutionary program in detail: the outlawing of the latifundia; distribution of the land among peasant families; the right of the workers to a participation in the profits; a drastic decrease in all rents paid by tenants; construction of decent housing projects for the 400,000 families who were crowded into huts, shacks, and single room dwellings; an extension of electricity services to almost 3 million people living in rural and suburban area sectors who had none at this time; confiscation of all the assets of embezzlers acquired under all past governments. It was a very lengthy list of changes for the Cuban people.

It was also at this time, during his exile in Mexico, in July, 1955, that Fidel Castro met up with Ernesto "Che" Guevara, an Argentinian doctor, provocative intellectual, and revolutionary. The two men's lives and their parallel destinies in revolution merged together with their ideals and ideology.

The Granma Landing, November 25th, 1956, must have been a real morale buster for both Fidel Castro and Che Guevara, but it is remembered and marked in history nonetheless. It was a tribute to an "honest revolution" to have recorded such grave beginnings for change in Cuba. As disastrous luck would have it, the leaky secondhand 38-foot boat overloaded with an 82-man, heavily armed guerrilla force, was battered for a week with huge swells, periodic engine failure and the food supplies running out. For the final forty-eight hours during the last leg of the journey, the revolutionary crew had neither food or water. Finally, two days overdue and landing off the target area, the boat ran aground in the mud at Los Cayuelos, near Niquero, almost one hundred miles west of Santiago.

Forced to abandon their heavy armaments and strategic supplies due to the muddy terrain, the 82-man army waded wearily ashore through dense mangroves. Che Guevara called the landing more of a "shipwreck."

On December 2nd, 1956, suffering one casualty who drowned coming ashore, the 81 men struggled to make it to safety to take on an army of Batista's that numbered 40,000. The boat had been spotted earlier and the planned corresponding uprising in Santiago de Cuba had failed two days prior. It all provided ample warning time for Batista's forces to brace for the assault and be fully mobilized in readiness. It was quickly becoming an exercise in futility.

On December 5th, after an exhaustive march through arduous terrain, the 81-man contingent rebel column halted to rest at Alegria de Pio. They were betrayed by their guide. It was here that they were ambushed by Batista's waiting Rural Guards. The rebel army was annihilated in the bloodbath at Alegria de Pio on that day. Seventeen men survived the ambush, including, miraculously, Fidel Castro, Che Guevara, Raul Castro, and Camilo Cienfuegos, together with other key revolutionary leaders of the movement.

Castro's comments afterwards would sound like he was making a joke, but at the height of such a terrible loss and in defeat he remarked to himself of the battle of Granma Alegria: "There was a moment there where I was only the commander and chief of myself and two others."

Next year in 1957, the rebel army was comprised of 29 men. Soon, more and more peasants began to join in the rebel army. It wasn't a peasant revolution, although guerrilla warfare with peasant support lay at the center of his plans. Hiding out in the Sierra Maestra mountains, he needed the support of people whom he could most rely upon, and the peasants sweating in the fields working for oppressive wages during the coffee harvests were his neighbors. It was an important relationship for the rebels to begin to cultivate.

The rebels respected and honored their peasant hosts in positive ways and "this was the basis of confidence that they had gained." They further cemented their relationship by working side by side with the Quajiros by helping them out with the May harvests of coffee in 1957.

Batista had alienated the peasants with the bloody continual torturing and murdering of randomly picked innocent civilian fieldhands. Any guerrilla actions were always met with a litany of deadly atrocities against the lowest income level Cuban people. Regular sorties of B-26 bombers and P-47 planes swooped periodically and strafed the Sierra Maestra's countryside in Batista's effort to kill Fidel Castro, and his tightly-knit little band of a fiercely loyal rebel army.

One singularly dynamic presence became the rebel army's best kept secret weapon of "goodwill" among the Sierra Maestra local peasantry. She organized the peasant support network which supplied arms, food, and volunteers to fight alongside the Fidelistas in the guerrilla revolutionary war. Her name was Celia Sanchez, a profoundly loyal middle-class revolutionary.

It was Celia Sanchez who is credited with guiding the New York Times journalist Herbert I. Matthews into the Sierra Maestra for his infamous interview with Fidel Castro that broke like a bombshell when the story reached the United States February 24th, 1957. Castro put on a very flamboyant, masterful showing of guerrilla theatre in the mountain terrain and so impressed the journalist that he wrote: "From the look of things, General Batista cannot possibly hope to suppress the rebel movement of the Castro revolt."

The CIA was now playing both sides, channeling funds of at least $50,000 toward Fidel Castro's movement, but at the same time awarding the head of General Batista's Air Force with a "Legion of Merit" for its steady Sierra Maestra bombing campaign (that was using U.S. supplied weaponry and armaments to thwart the rebels).

War in the cities and countryside began to spread as sugarcane fields were set ablaze. Army posts and the police stations and houses of Batista's order were being vandalized and destroyed by mobs of angry Cubans. The culmination of all this unrest came on March 13th, with an attack on the presidential palace in Havana by the Students Revolutionary Directorate, acting independently of Fidel Castro and on their own volition. 35 students died in this attack. Sensing that some of his overall control was slipping away, on July 12th, Castro committed himself to "free democratic elections" in a move designed to assuage the ever-growing new levels of separate uprisings that were diversifying the ranks into a leadership crisis. Fidel Castro was stuck out in the mountains of the Sierra Maestra. The less strategic Cuban revolutionary movement of "urban wings" was right smack dab in the middle of the cities. He had to keep unity with the students allowing for strictly "he and his rebels" to be doing all of the fighting.

That spring the rebel Fidelistas controlled almost all of the mountain regions of Oriente Province. The rebel army evolved into the cutting-edge fighting guerrilla force of the Social Revolutionary process. Castro's ideal was that of a "social revolution" and also a "true revolution." To forestall a deal that was about to undercut his power as the tide was about to turn radically, Fidel Castro appointed the movement's choice of a then respected liberal judge, Manuel Urrutia Lleo, who would head the provisional government after Batista's fall. Manuel Urrutia was forced to leave for exile in the U.S. While there he was instrumental in negotiating Eisenhower's decision to stop arming Batista publicly. (Washington kept on shipping arms secretly anyway, directly to the Batista regime.) The practice infuriated Fidel Castro to go dead-set and sour on all United States' snake-like double dealings of strategic political policies.

Castro had 300 men-at-arms and on April 1st he declared a total war on the Batista regime. He told the Cuban people to refuse to pay their income taxes. A General Strike followed on April 9th, as the whole country once again came to a horrendous halt. Batista decided to go for broke with a mass murdering spree by his police force, showing the Tropical Mussolini was still at large and still in full retention of his power. He slaughtered over one hundred Cubans as the strike was collapsed, and gone by the wayside. With it also fell the last "tendered potency" of any attempts of moderate elements possibly finding any chance of working out for Cuba. Castro prepared for the toppling of Batista, and again he reorganized the movement's top command by leaving himself all alone up at the top spot. The line drawn in the sand by both men reached the apex.

Batista was a stubborn deadly sucker of a conniving Dictator. He would desperately remain in the presidential palace and refused to go without a final flurry of Mussolini-like treachery. He met the increasing storms of the revolt with rampant degenerate violence, as his henchmen police force murdered some several thousand Cuban civilian people. It was far more lives than had been lost in literally two full years of guerrilla warfare in Sierra Maestra.

In Batista's last ditch effort to wipe out the Fidelistas, he mounted an all out offensive into the mountains of the Sierra Maestra, sending out fourteen solid battalions and over 10,000 men for Operation FF (Fin de Fidel). The 320 men of the tag-team revolutionary guerrilla army beat back the massive seventy-six day offensive assault. It was the ultimate "David versus Goliath" BATTLE FOR ALL OF CUBA. Castro broadcast Radio Rebelde through loudspeakers that were tied into the trees to break the morale of Batista's troops. The rebels captured two tanks and huge quantities of modern weapons during the all-out offensive. It was the guerrillas who wore down the will of Batista's forces until the army gave way to the revolution. As Castro's army moved westward, many of Batista's forces defected to the guerrilla movement. It was time to join with a legitimate leader for Cuba.

In July, Fidel Castro, along with eight leading opposition groups, signed the Caracas Pact, an agreement to create a civic coalition, and calling upon the U.S. to cease all aid to the deadly Batista regime. The writing now on the wall, Washington began its tentatively pensive negotiations with Fidel Castro, while also trying to maneuver to keep him from retaining power.

In September, Castro, fueled by massive contributions of both finances and arms from the Venezuelan Government, led an offensive to take Santiago de Cuba. Then on December 30th, 1958, Che Guevara captured Santa Clara, the scent of victory was now prevalent in the air.

Beginning in 1952, at the age of 25, Fidel Castro had now risen to become the most outspoken leader against the corrupt Batista Government. His rise to prominence secured his position as the president of the future. From there it's been more than fifty years, and still-running fairly strong, if you take away the economic woes of the special period. It is, any way you choose to evaluate it, a remarkable reign (for a one man show) of retaining power and leadership in the 20th century. It is a phenomenal tale of modern political dominance.

––––––––

Santeria (saint worship) has been deeply entrenched within the Cuban culture for over 300 years. It is a fusion of Catholicism with the Lucumi religion of the African Yoruba tribes. It is believed that an Orisha (saint) has control of an individual's life (bringing either good or back luck), and thus must be placated (but humans can't talk to them). The Santeros or babalaos (priests) acted as the "go betweens" to honor the saints and also interpret their commands. These old superstitions are appeased by statues in the homes of most Cubans, who profoundly believe in Santeria. The statue represents a god, nearby a full glass of water is placed on the table to thereby appease the spirits of the dead.

Fidel Castro's triumph on January 1st was also known as the Holy Day of the Orishas. The Red and Black flag of the revolutionaries was that of Ellequa, the God of Destiny. On January 8th, 1959, as Fidel Castro addressed the crowds of the nation from Camp Columbia, suddenly two white doves flew over the audience and circled the brightly lit podium. And then, miraculously, one of the doves alighted on Fidel's shoulder and perched there. It was a defining moment for every Santeria-believing Cuban to witness.

The crowds erupted in euphoria with crescendos and shouts of Fidel! In the pandemonium, the white doves became symbols of Fidel Castro's chosen destiny. In the sanction of the doves and "obatala," the symbol of being chosen, like the Son of God, his destiny to lead Cuba, blessed by the Santeria, had now made him into the Maximum Leader. The Chosen One.

––––––––

The Beachcomber

March 17th, 2003

His domination of Cuba's political landscape has been inordinately resilient and truly phenomenally everlasting. It has been now over half a decade since Fidel Castro delivered the people from oppression, making his mark on history in ruling the political horizons of Cuba. Few will admit the awe in such a grip that one man could bring that kind of solo political leadership to Cuba, "his country."

———

The Beachcomber

November 22nd, 2013

The iron fisted leader. The iron fisted curtain remains. It's drawn across the border—covering the Cuban landscape now, for over a half a century.

———

The Beachcomber

July 20th, 2015

Recently, the catalyst for change finally won out over tradition. Now it's okay to visit anywhere inside Cuba that you might wish to go—and to go to see the historically majestic, timely humble emerald jewel of the Carribean. The Cuban embassy is open now, on this date in Washington D.C. A major step forward in diplomatic relations. It's an open road—to all the U.S. Travelers... Havana is waiting for you...

———

In writing your lead in to Cuba, it is a special setting in itself: to unveil it from a lengthy crippling 50 year trade embargo, which was lifted recently (although the great Minnesota Governor Jesse Ventura defied it and traded with Cuba back in 2003; in basic things farming and food goods, under the radar to the political consternation of the Bush administration). Without a doubt you're setting yourself and your book "behind the eight ball." One arrives at the intrusive vibe that you're not supposed to be there back in 2003. A family member warned me with aggravation, and incredulous surprise (after praising me first by saying I wrote like Quentin Tarantino) before she insisted on the condemnation that I should not have chosen that location at the start. It had a lot of rumbling back then, prompting many heavy snoots and sours at the out set.

One respected voice felt that these first 25 pages could've been aborted. I took him aside and I explained that not everyone was as well traveled as he. This guy's name rhymed with rascal. He said "pop the clutch & get on with the story."

Another journalist remarked; "it's an unusual book." I thanked John Schwada, who branded it this way, knowing that George Carlin would have loved that comment. It was David Milch, who read it in early drafts and later commented with its first appraisal and he sanctioned it with, "it's an ambitious book;" since, he went to college with Bush back in his day...it was his voice that carried me...as these pages survived being cut out.

The levels of imagination with Mr. Carlin's voice, and the levels of ambition with David Milch telling me that "you're a writer." I went forth unrestricted, unrestrained, with a high calypso of inexperience; both traits I over-spent, and such is boundless calamity with a first time Writer.

And, it was a truly humble voice... a guy who when I first met him reminded me of James Brolin (the actor) but in person was just as handsome, if not better-looking and maybe even tougher in a street fight, from my p.o.v., the marvelously talented writer of *Son Of The Rough South*, Karl Fleming, who said it best, when he said to me; "everybody's got a story," with the signature trademark of some righteous beliefs.

He believed that even my voice, (and) my writing should be heard, (and) I am blessed or I am thankful for that wisdom from one of my generation's best reporter/journalists.

Encouraged by those greats and the past masters, it's the best that my ambition, my emboldened stocks of the unfiltered wisdom, could muster that betters with hearty imagination.

TWO

A Forgotten Place... A Forgotten Man

CAMPECHUELA

Campechuela CUBA, a town of modest importance described with low houses dotting the railways of the past, now abandoned with faded decrepit rolling stockyards of the better days gone by. So little has been written in travel books about the forgotten city that its only claim of notoriety rating it a mention on the map is the fact that it lies between two of the more historical towns in Cuban history. Traveling eight miles up to the north is La Demajagua, the town of infamous sugar estate owner Carlos Manuel Cespedes, who on October 8th, 1868, rang the freedom bell to free the slaves as he led the rebellion in the fight against Spain. The original National Anthem, Himno la Bayamesa, and the treasured flag of Cespedes are kept in the old house that today has been restored into a museum, open 24 hours a day. Just ten miles to the south is Media Luna, which is mostly dominated by Centrales–sugar fields. However, it is also the town of the revered heroine of the Sierra Maestra, where Celia Sanchez was born on May 9th, 1920.

It is inside this simple green and white modest home, next to the Cabaret Salon Azul, where all people are welcome. There is a mahogany tree in the backyard that was planted by the members of the Venceremos Brigade: a group of U.S. citizens who make annual pilgrimages to Cuba to work in the fields. The many surrounding *fruit trees* symbolize *the wealth* of Cuba's soils and also seem to showcase Cuba's ability for agricultural self-sufficiency (to live off the land's fertile qualities), which was how the Fidelistas had to do it themselves, *managing to survive* in the mountains and trees of the Sierra Maestra.

The Forgotten Town In The Middle...

It is here, centered between La Demajagua and Media Luna, that lies the forgotten city of Campechuela. Once slaves of plantation owners *cut cane* during the late 18th century, and carried on through the great sugar boom, or the older sweetly remembered times of "The Dance of Millions," which layered on over and up into the early 19th century, and up to 1925. Today, the good old days of the sugar boom have all but gone. Campechuela, population 200, has faded into history with the rusted out old irons of the abandoned railway, and the random stockyards filled with the aging shanty huts, "*bohios*" (modest former slave dwellings) dotting the dire landscape, along with the broken and rundown sugar mills of the better days.

It was here that leathery bronze-skinned quajiros toiled in the blood, sweat and years of the glorious sugar boom, under the raging heat of a burning and unforgiving Cuban tropical sun. And it was here that the blackened bodies of these tough, strong men of *cane harvesting quajiros* swung the shining and mighty slashing machetes until the day's torturous sun finally went low, and the day was done.

Then their bodies collapsed from the *grueling work day that was over,* and they would vanquish their souls by stowing away in the empty boxcars or their thatched *bohios* to sleep, gathered with all they owned on their backs. A wide brimmed white skimmer straw hat, dirty boots, and the machete, *the sword of the working class.*

THESE WERE THE TOOLS OF THE TRADE BACK IN THE DAY

Seaside campfires smelled and crackled with sweet roasted pork and fried beans, as these men sat up at night overlooking the golden sands of the shoreline. Silky-looking waves of green cane rolled fluttering, gently swaying, in the evening's long-awaited rustlings of the night's tropical breezes. Disappearing into a sparkling clear blue ocean was a ruby red and fully golden bloody-eyed pirate's liquid sunset of glory, an orange and reddish-hazed ball of fool's gold.

All of that was *soothed in the spirits of 80 proofed rums,* an elixir that helped to ease their aching shoulders and wrinkled grits of cheekbones, as the bent and spent backaches of tired men's souls of all but *swung out and deadened limbs* settled into a mind-numbing rum's buzz, wearily fading off to sleep.

So as the sunlight slowly burned down, the burnt-out Quajiros faded away on down even further, going dimmer, whilst drinking themselves away, off into a hazy evening's oblivion, an ending to a truly back breaking and soul-exhausting day.

It was in a town of history like that where the saga of Beachcomber began.

THE BEACHCOMBER

A TALE, A SHORT STORY, PLUS SOME ASIDE COMMENTARY BY:

MICHAEL GERING

July 26th, 2001

As it was being composed through

July 26th, 2003

One must pause when it comes… to the crime of the century… and upon personal reflection, it's more like leavings, breadcrumbs left behind. The Posthumous Rendering's Evidence, And Identity. Yes, someone was here… once truly was here… And these kinds of things were left behind in random reckless disorder, riddled thoughts; these were… in the immortal words… of the late great genius of Mr. George Carlin, my dear departed old friend… in whose company I mourned that great loss… and in his way of those color-filled descriptions and good humor of that good stuff or what he prestigiously referred to in his lifetime succinctly as—

26

"My Brain Droppings."

The author of this book was a failed screenwriter. In over twenty years of writing screenplays... without a sale, he decided... to create a new format the world had never experienced until now. He used the format of percentile of selling stock in the shoe business which generally translates to this particular credo.

You normally sell 20 percent of your stock 80 percent of the time.

And he created a new book-form called–THE CINEBOOK.

Which is 80 percent book and 20 percent screenplay.

What follows is a work of fiction layered in history which is the real truth, gathered for primarily a short story, with some additional background and peripheral circle-talking commentary. At the outset, The Beachcomber's journey evolved from a graphic novel's imagination since there is no penance to grow from such and uncourtly underworld place. Amalgamated photos and portions of texts are used in a permission's context. In all instances of pictures and words donated and borrowed from previous works, the permission for usage was sought from the Publisher.

The Beachcomber Santiago...

A fictitious character in a Graphic Novel by Michael Gering.

THE KENNEDY FILE,

The Bay Of Pigs,

The Cuban Missile Crisis…

THE ASSASSINATION

November 22nd, 1963

AM WORLD / AM LASH / MONGOOSE

J M WAVE / C--DAY / ALPHA 66

Desmond Fitzgerald   Gen. Robert Cushman

William King Harvey   E. Howard Hunt

David Atlee Phillips   Bernard Barker

George Johannides   Rolando Masferrer

Guy Bannister (FBI)   Clay Shaw (CIA)

George H.W. Bush (CIA)   George De Mohrenschildt (CIA)

Howard Hughes   Richard Milhouse Nixon

Allen Dulles (CIA)   J. Edgar Hoover (FBI)

Nonfiction, documented, recorded in history.

PEACEFULLY ADRIFT, YET NOT UNDULY WAYWARD, HIS DIRECTIONAL GUIDANCES BECAME NATURE.

THE BEACHCOMBER

A homeless *drifter* has lived for ten years on a coastal strip of land in Cuba. He was formerly a Sergeant in the Cuban Army, but these days he's left his first life to find a different level; an equalizer to pain of past paths, an outlet from what's unresolved into a minimalist survival, roaming and beachcombing south from Manzanillo, nearest to the small town of Campechuela, sitting on the sand and living off the land, seeing every sunrise and sunset, *watching the sky's colors that mark the passage of time.*

To wake up to the birds and the dragonflies, the sand crabs, and passing dolphin pods' morning feedings, yet to be engaged to a glorious setting sun; to sleep with the sounds of the bee hummingbirds and mini frogs (Cuba is a uniquely blessed tropical island to claim two of the world's smallest creatures), with a lively chorus background of cricket-beats, and the colorful night birds' callings, while in the darkness the giant sea turtle plows and digs along, scratching through the sandy beach, hiding preciously-laid eggs by the hundreds. The Beachcomber knows full well the perils of life and senses so much of nature's sensitivity, that his whole sustenance and humble existence is his redefining of a meaning, to find answers to his own lost faith in the one above, who took one soul away.

He looked like Robert de Niro from the film *The Mission*, adding the years up to age 67, with a flowing Jesus beard, large hands and a fully employed heart. He had worn-out tattered shorts covering his loins, no shoes, and a eucharistic antiquity of a shirt. He looked like he was on his way to Bethlehem, with his trusty earth-tone-colored, weather-beaten knapsack. He would make a portrait of Johnny Appleseed, *a farmer*–if you dared to mock such a curious-looking figure and sketched a pot upon his head.

A bronzed tough-skinned forehead, which was enlarged with a Caesar's destiny, narrowed his dark orbs with shutters at half mast, for sunlight made hard furrows of lines that trailed his rugged face's landscape from ear to ear. His mouth was a wide, straight, flat line, and it hid many yellowed teeth rarely seen, except when he bit the fruit of Eve.

His shoulders were broadened naturally by learning the craftsmanship of his father's home furniture-making trade. His hands were large and very rigorously strengthened with the trades of both soldiering and sergeanting, and furniture making and sculpting the bulky stalks of various timber wood. The only things lacking on this wayward beachcombing Christ-figure were the holes in his palms and the infectious piercings of a *halo of thorns* across the weary and long-uncropped, bushy and graying brows, that displayed his age's indignity.

In the value of what's important to him is his oneness with the earth and nature, and also a true oneness with himself; in the heartbeats of nature's sounds, our old humbled Beachcomber can feel *the heartbeats of his soul becoming one of nature's own sounds.* His truths vital to his mental stability, rested within this quest for ultimate privacy to be alone. And yet not truly alone, since formulating his partnership to sounds, he once didn't have time for them, but today these sounds are his only friends, and for now the only signs of *the smaller voices of the ones he chooses to hear.* That's all the tendings Beachcomber needs. He was taken by the poetry of Nicholas John Lennartson,

Hello Ocean this is Lover of Land

Come to cry over your silver sand–

When all my people go away,

Your abundance fills me up, finds me my way.

When friendship is just a word,

even loved ones don't love anymore–

As my walls of fear grow taller, your entity is the spiritual wave,
on which I can rise away from my mind–

Till the moon-dust blows the tears from my eyes

Oh Blue-ocean you are love. Like an eternity

unending replenishes the spirit needing, never a day
condescending–

Your love is always forgiving.

Oh Blue-ocean you are love.

So I'll just lie here and wait, I may be cold and quiver, but never
alone–

I'll just build a fire to keep me warm...

Ocean, bring me the new day.

To the Beachcomber, the subtle words of this little, obscure, poet he had discovered in the early 1980s while on a sightseeing trip through sunny Ocean Beach, San Diego, wrote such a sonnet of soothing imagery it brought him great pleasure through the simple heartfelt words. And for how it just happened–that a poet in his 20s could capture the essence of *Beachcomber's life* with those simple words, he knew better than to wonder, *for this Petaluma-born California Native Poet must've not known either* when he found either the time or the wisdom to impale such tranquil dreamy tales of imaginative scenery upon the yellowed scrolls. Even old men like Beachcomber/Santiago could be moved by the heartfelt poetry of a 20-something writer, Nick John Lennartson.

Beachcomber liked to collect and boil clams every once in a while but did so rather infrequently since it was a meal that required a great deal of time to collect, assemble, prepare, cook, and also eat. At least he thought so.

A much more Hemingway-like trait was born within him in that he loved to fish. He had a rod with a deep-sea reel tackle that had a 75-pound test line. A giant Marlin beached itself after it dragged the rod until it expired–after battling a Miami sportsman's charter boat, with the man who could forever *tell tales about the one that got away.*

It's well known that Cuban Marlin don't jump, if they do, it's very rarely, but at any rate this particular Marlin got tired of the hook stuck in its gullet, and with its gills flooded, simply decided to land itself in the shallows somehow, and was rolled ashore by the tide. And with that unlucky Miami fisherman's tackle gear in his capable strong hands, virtually anything at all that Beachcomber could hook, he could reel in.

He fished only sparingly since he wanted not to become jaded of its thrill. He became an environmentally-sound man, who in the decade living by the water was completely in tune with nature and the sea. And for him, just to be looking forward to the task, and the enchantment of that pure peacefulness that his father passed on, that always brought a welcome interlude, or the reminders of a simpler life that provided a rendering friendly solace... in that solitude to him.

His father had shared with him–telling of the old story–wherein you give a man a fish, you feed him for a day; you teach a man to fish, you feed him for life. The Beachcomber learned early how to fish and treated it as something of a special event, like a form of worship. In keeping the a ritual of the glorious gift that it was to him, he chose to only do it once a week in a tribute of timely rationed quantity. It reminded him of his father, fond memories of the man who taught him the glory of the great beauty and the great bounty of the sea.

He gave up smoking cigarettes; he felt he could more safely absorb tobacco with a good chew, and still preserve his lungs to breathe in the fresh sea-breezed air. Cuba was so rich in good tobacco plants and varieties of rich sustenance, Beachcomber could walk to a place nearby to pick out the best of the crop, like Juan Valdez (the Columbian One Man Coffee Harvester of U.S. Commercial Television) selecting himself his own private stocks of leaves to dry which he ground up himself. With a careful process by hand, utilizing a large barnacle-covered seashell with a cylindrical stub-like peen shaft hammer stone, with a rounded studded-end–to pound it out and grind it up into a good, fresh, chewing tobacco mulch.

Food was ever abundantly plentiful at the Beachcomber's jungle spot: he had only to walk two miles inland to catch the edges of a sugar cane farm where he would pick a few stalks from time to time if he had desire to nourish his sweet tooth. But mostly it was the berries, bananas, and fruits that were his staple for a *daily healthy diet,* which kept him very fit and tuned up and alert, and heartily alive in vigorous internally resilient form. With fresh fruits within walking distance, the Beachcomber enjoyed a very good diet. His favorite treats, however, were the lobsters that would occasionally wander into his special lobster crib trap. He fashioned it out of wood, and tied it off to the tree in the bend of the coastline where the ocean's waters flowed into a cove. It wasn't always often, but if he checked his trap just once in the span of a whole week, he could boil up a crustacean cachet of meaty tender morsels of very rich high proteins, spoiling himself in a deliciously splendid delight of ocean fresh red lobster feast.

A SAILOR FROM SPAIN DISCOVERS AN ISLAND

An Explorer from Spain Finds a Paradise

Many say Columbus discovered America, whereas it is likely more apropos that Indians, who were already there, did actually discover North America. Tribes who migrated north from the belly of Mexico, and South America, got up there and discovered it first.

Ancient Chichen Itzan Maya Indians or the Amazon Rain Forest tribes, in my view, were the formulation of the *cradle of civilization* in the modern West. It's true that also most accept the tale of the "European Scroll," of where the cradle of civilization actually exists. How was it so that this tribe from Chichen Itza could fly up in the air and paint markings on the ground that could only be made with the indulgence of aerial flight? Likely, it is plausible for us as human beings to accept the possibility of sundering simple mathematics, that credits the European scroll. This is trusted. However, all I am suggesting is this South American culture uniquely left evidence of flight.

Clearly, the thesis is simple. If you can as beings come from above—as in "the heavens"—wouldn't you leave those bones of your culture up in "the heavens"?

The Maya Indians built an immense plaza at the center of Chichen Itza, and with skill constructed the tall limestone pyramid with a temple on top. They dedicated this pyramid to Kukulkan, the feathered serpent-god called Quetzalcoatl. Not even the great ancient Egyptians could master flight as early Mayans in Mexico did. I agree those Egyptian structures are impressive feats of engineering and craftsmanship, and the cradle of civilization is accepted as Bethlehem and Babylon, which is considered the accepted European scroll. My belief is a viable cradle also exists in both Chichen Itza, Mexico, and in the depths of the Amazon in South America. It is completely possible that, as both history and cultures, and their evidence, persuade us, perhaps it's likely that it is possible for us to accept that *Two Cradles Exist... it's in space... because of evidence they've mastered flight: these bones, could go also as far back as Europe's. This author's humble p.o.v. anyway.*

I also furnish the possibility here that two cradles exist. It is a matter of both science and equity (for all of us to consider the evidence), as to argue which seeds developed first. That's okay to argue about, but I believe that both of these cradles *could've simultaneously existed in our world. One might be older as well?*

31

The Mexican-Mayan and South American Cradle.

(alongside the favored scrolls of also)

"The European-Mediterranean Cradle, Our Bible."

Anyway, it is also written throughout history books that foster the idea of the belief: that it was Columbus who discovered Cuba, November 27th, 1492.

It was there in Holguin Province at Gibara where he first dropped anchor and began charting Cuba's shores. It was in the bay that Christopher Columbus named Puerto Santo: He described it by its distinctive tall, flat-topped mountain, which Cubans call El Yunque (The Anvil). According to legend, he left the wooden cross that is found today in Baracoa. "They are the best people in the world," Columbus wrote and recorded of the Indians of Cuba, "they are without knowledge of what is evil and nor do they murder or steal." He went on to write, "all the people show the most singular, loving behavior, and are gentle and always laughing." As early as 3500 B.C., the first indigenous people (cave dwellers), arrived in Cuba, having migrated over from South America.

Maybe the earlier American Indians were also their descendants as well, and if not as happy on the U.S. plains, were likely just as much (as Columbus encountered in Baracoa) both proper and dignified, and also equally similar, and un-savage-like, and it could perhaps also be said "the best people in the world." In any event, it's just as well that also history books provide us the story that—the square-shaped mesa formation in Puerto Santo (which Columbus described) is accepted as El Yunque, or THE ANVIL. However, some believe it was the similar flat-topped mountain which is near Gibara, further west. In either case, Columbus dotted expeditions to all points, jotting and logging its coastal mappings of distinction in his Log Book of Cuba land discoveries.

Several Cuban cities claim distinction of his discovery and mark their city's spot appropriately with dignity and historic pride. When he landed in the cove of Bahia de Cochinos, he wrote of his visions in June 1494, in sighting "naked indians carrying in their hands a burning coal, and with certain reeds for inhaling their smoke." He was not that far off in his record of scripture.

For the people this charcoal-making art was the craft of their impoverished tribe, they used it for cooking, fuel, and also for trading. The austere hard-working Indians or *Carbaneros* axed nearby marabu and mangrove branches of lengths at two feet, then stacked them into a teepee-shape (horno de carbon) which was a charcoal oven made of straw and earth, hollowed at the center. The branches were then covered in grasses and ash, and then lit and left to burn slowly for a week or so. The smoldering wood was then *just at the right moment doused with water.* The Indians, *Carbaneros*, covered in blackened-soot, would trek, barefoot, the freshly created charcoal *on their backs*, all the way to Cienfuegos for market. They earned literally just a couple of cents per load for their intensive earthly creative efforts.

It was dusk, at the height of the Cuban three to five month dry period known as *La Seca,* when Beachcomber/Santiago encountered a Carbaneros-breed who was trekking over his beach way, his encampment area upon some territory of his range. No matter how unlikely, this five centuries old tradition was still today somehow a trade plied by at least one lost soul.

THE BEACHCOMBER

The History and his story, as it continued–

Exhausted by the humid, dry heat of April 4th, 1990, he lay down his loaded sack of charcoal and walked into the lime-green-bluish cool ocean water to lower his body temperature. He was nearly exhausted by the intense heat, his load-laden back sore from the sixty pounds of freshly made Carbaneros charcoal. He had been hiking up the coast with his bundle sack of harvest fuel on his way to sell it at the markets of Cienfuegos.

His name was Che Ortiz Jiang, born in 1982, of half Chinese, half Indian origin and shunned in shame by both parents of the improper union. His dry cleaning business owner father took off for Miami in 1986. His fruit picking migratory working mother died of tuberculosis five years later, at the age of 29, when the boy was only nine years old.

He grew up in the bush, migrating with the Zapatas, with no education or parental upbringing, just a child laborer and peasant of very modest income and lowly origin. The Carbanero boy grew up into a wiry legged, thin torsoed, Chinese-Cuban-Indian young man. Very dark brown oily skin covered his earnest peasant face, and the marks of blackened charcoal dust heightening the other marks on his soul, some curiously crossed racial liaison of indignity.

Beachcomber/Santiago couldn't help but surmise the parallel of infamy both of them shared. The Carbanero's blackened Indian pirate soul versus his own sunburned and bronzed leathery pirate skin of his transcendent castaway soul.

When Columbus described them, or when Beachcomber described them, it mattered not, for the many years past, for the art of the Carbanero, will always be thy woeful underclass below • peasantry. Beachcomber concurred, *they are the best people, without knowledge of what is evil, nor do they murder or steal.* It is pure then and now, that this tribe is humble and holy like the blackened earth they've bred by the soil. It is out of nothing they make something, then they sell their harvests and go back to nothing, and then they go on and make something once more.

Naturally, the harshness of truth came to be later sanitized for the making of the theatrical version. Beachcomber's tone or vision was curtailed or distilled out into a more suitable folklore-like tale of plausible and tolerable entertainment.

It would be a more theatrical retelling.

It would go like this for the legend.

THREE

The Legend of Carbanero

"They are the best people in the world without the knowledge of what is evil, nor do they kill or steal."

Christopher Columbus, November 27th, 1492.

On hot summer days, the Beachcomber would see his only living human visitor. He was a Carbanero-boy, the Indian/Chinese charcoal maker who three times each month would haul his sack of freshly-made charcoal to the markets in Cienfuegos. They talked from time to time, but like anonymous souls, never called each other by name. It was midway through Beachcomber's self-imposed exile; the boy with no name had grown into a young man, age fourteen, embittered with his own history and shame in his past. It was an act of God that these two exiled experiments of hazard and wayward drifters, Beachcomber and Carbanero, would cross paths over five years, talking to each other and visiting each other completely anonymously.

After sharing some of the lobster tails with his Carbanero-Indian friend, the Beachcomber offered with a big smile, "This is the best that Cuba can offer." The Carbanero-Indian looked upon him with an even greater smile, like he had a secret. He then went on to say to him, "Come with me tomorrow and I will show you, o.k." Beachcomber nodded that he would go and then the Carbanero said these words just before he went off to sleep and whispering quietly, "We will go before the dawn and take a walk and I will show you something that you've never seen before."

The sun dropped into the sea and after a good peaceful sleep, both men got up extra early, before the sunrise, and they began to trek southward towards Zapata Peninsula. After two hours, walking by the moonlight on the shoreline, they approached a final bending of the coastline and stopped. So it was then that Beachcomber felt this must be it to himself, not knowing what it was he might see at this particular spot. Then the Carbanero boy waved for him to follow, they both climbed up onto a large rock.

In the moment looking over the lapping waves, he backed up his viewing and his eyes made out the shape of what looked like a man-made stone fire place oven, built on the shore thirty yards away, out in front of the huge rock that they were sitting on. The water was receding in the calm ebb of low tide, at the brink of sunrise, when *suddenly* the waters rippled as hundreds of giant crabs began swarming the beach as sunlight began its fluorescent orange and yellowish lighting of the shore. The numbers were shocking to behold and yet somehow *sit still to witness*, the whole coastline rolling towards you *a blanket of legs moving, thousands, hundreds of thousands, of giant land crabs*, advancing *storming up* on the shore to mate. It was a mating ritual.

The Carbanero left the safety of the rock and climbed down onto the sand, walking over the crabs as carefully as possible to avoid injury to his uncovered bare feet. He made it to the stone oven, pulled his sack of charcoal from his shoulder and filled it with freshly made coal. He lit the fire and took from its sheath a buck knife and plucked two giant crabs, using the length of its twelve-inch blade, spearing them both and waving them high up for the Beachcomber to see. He then placed them onto the oven's *top* taken from a metal pipeline's fitting cap's end of a spillway-screen, which formed *the grill*. He speared two more of these giant crabs and laid a total of four creatures cooking on the grill. While they were still alive, a couple managed to scatter off the grill. He opened his bag and cut four sticks of thatch wood and skew-pierced each crab. He stabbed them right into the whole where the knife blade sliced and cracked through their body's shells. This anchored them, prone, to keep them on the grill and helped speed up the cooking all the way through to their midsection and the abdomen area. He then humbly and quietly *walked back and sat next to Beachcomber on the rock,* watching the sunrise. They perched on the rock face for hours after feasting on their deliciously fresh crab festival feast, while the coastline was still enshrouded with hundreds of thousands of *fucking crabs*.

CHE ORTIZ CHIANG: This is the best of Cuba, my friend.

BEACHCOMBER: Yes, this is... the best of Cuba.

CHE ORTIZ CHIANG: You see, my father left me... (points to the Florida Keys). I was left behind. My father gave up and he fled the Fidelista regime...

(beat)

You can't make money in Cuba dry-cleaning, he tells me, and when I woke up the next day, he was gone. He went to Miami to get rich.

BEACHCOMBER: What about the rest of the family?

CHE ORTIZ CHIANG: Nobody left, only my grandmother and me. She gets wasted on the rum, and the cigars,sick all of the time, see... well her mind is gone.

BEACHCOMBER: You cannot save anyone from that.

CHE ORTIZ CHIANG: No one can save you from yourself.

(beat)

When it goes it goes, you know?

He taps upon his own temple and in his ample disgust with it all, just tosses a crab leg. The Indian, wise beyond his years, an abandoned, bitter, self-reliant realist, went on to speak very softly about his loneliness on his island, offering the words

CHE ORTIZ CHIANG: You can only do that because no one can do it for you.

Touched in this truth by his only living visitor in the last decade, Beachcomber nodded in that truth. On his way to the markets in Cienfuegos to sell his charcoal, the young man imparted all his truths to the one soul who probably most needed to hear of such kindred spirits and random selections of wisdom. God was apparently now from above looking upon him with a gift of a younger one, or a visitor of kinder youth. God began to whisper feelings with telepathy of what the wayward and devoid of hope Carbanero was thinking... It captured Beachcomber off guard for he had never been spared the ear to read one's mind. He heard clearly as this Santeros (spirit voice) spoke to him, mind to mind and spirit to spirit-

BEACHCOMBER (*channels to Che*): Here was another abandoned soul (and) it's one thing to be Chinese, it's another to be Indian. And it's another thing all together to be a Cuban as well. And it's another thing to be blackened by the smoking flames of charcoal production.

But this mind wondered with more, to be all of those things combined together.

BEACHCOMBER (*continues*): Cuban, Indian, Chinese of bronze skin, Carbanero, who became an orphan peasant boy that was totally discarded by both of his parents.

A passing dolphin pod splashed offshore in the distance to break his concentration. He points to the leaping dolphins just a short distance from the shore and offers to step out from the temporary Santeros babalaos (the priests) who for a minute were *go betweens*.

BEACHCOMBER: That to me is God's version of his best work of both beauty and freedom.

CHE ORTIZ CHIANG: Sometimes I feel God and Fidel and my mother and father let me go.

BEACHCOMBER: I see what you mean, losing both of your parents like that.

CHE ORTIZ CHIANG: This is the rock of Cuba. We can see the freedom of yanqui Miami in the distance. This is the best it will ever be for me.

(beat)

I'm a blackened Cuban-Chinese-Indian-Carbanero. The shades of slavery still mark my soul. I know of no future... nothing.

BEACHCOMBER: You are not nothing. You have a friend, amigo. You have something. You have a friend in me.

CHE ORTIZ CHIANG: Si, amigo, me compadre, me amigo.

He tapped the stick to beat the rock just as a crab had crawled up along the rock and just as he appeared in Che's sight right behind Beachcomber's backside only a few feet away.

CHE ORTIZ CHIANG: Do not worry, we're safe up here. This is ours, the rock of freedom.

BEACHCOMBER: I hope so because I just ate up his whole family for dinner.

Suddenly he takes the stick, rising up to his bare feet and makes a mighty whack of a baseball slugger's *swing at the crab,* sending it flying towards centerfield shoreline.

CHE ORTIZ CHIANG: Maybe I go to Miami to play baseball.

BEACHCOMBER: So you're sure... it's safe here?

CHE ORTIZ CHIANG: We'll be o.k. up here. A Fidelista crab just tried to scale my freedom rock.

BEACHCOMBER: You almost knocked a Fidelista crab all the way back to yanqui Miami.

The afternoon sun glinted on the massive orgy of giant Cuban land crabs. The oiled-up hues of their brick-grayish joints and ceramic-white underbellies glowed, as the fury of red sheets of crabs crawled, layer upon layer, thousands upon thousands of crabs. It was a creepy-crawlers' convention of epic and mind-freaking dimensions, sprawling everywhere and spanning all over. The entire beach became a mating orgy playground. It truly was a sight to behold of a very real part of Cuba's unforgettable nature.

Ironically, a similar scenario was eliminated from the film version of *DR. NO*, in the *final cut,* which unnerved *Ian Fleming* to his wit's end. As the story goes, scenes were filmed with Ursula Andress strapped into a nuclear reactor's cooling chamber near Crab Key, Jamaica, but unfortunately for the filmmakers, most of the captured crabs died during the filming and the survivors were less than enthusiastic to crawl onto Honey Rider. Cuba has the same island's *ritual sexual* Crab Festival.

With abundantly clean, clear lime green and sparkling blueish waters off the sandy golden shores, only footsteps away from his glorious view, everyday was a visualization of everlasting beauty. It was the dolphins, however, that were the most fascinating fancy for studying by the Beachcomber, and they easily held the top spot as his favorite species of animals to observe in the wild.

He would never tire of the wondrous pure joy it gave to him to watch those splendidly fine creatures in action. They were always smiling in gaiety which brought an equally similar vein of a happy smile into his soul during his ten years in observation of them. Over this amount of time the Beachcomber had become quite a naturalist, observing dolphins and becoming familiarized with dolphin behavior.

He was *stunned when he first swam with them* to try to understand them, and was completely surprised by their returned interest back towards him. He went on to make friends with them so darn easily it almost resurrected his soul, uplifting his heart's forgiveness and giving him hope with these very special new friends.

These air-breathing mammals that once walked on dry land, that had in thousands of years somehow evolved into such dynamic, powerful spirits of flight, cruising through the vast open seas, were to him, without a doubt nature's finest form of an immaculate creation. If anything else were to possess a Spirit and ultimate greater power of intangible flying glorious beauty, he knew not of it. It could be said for Beachcomber, in his long observance and reverence: The Dolphins were *the true gods for him to worship*, at least as far as his humble mind was concerned.

The attempted encounter he tried to have happen wasn't easy at first. Over at the bend in the coastline the water formed a cove of abundant sea-life and plant life, the dolphins loved to fish along the shallow shores at low tide. It was there that he decided to make the *first move*, swimming into the three foot deep area to meet with a few members of a playful dolphin pod. At first they circled him and then in a few moments just went out to the sea, leaving the shallow waters of the cove. While he went back to the shoreline, the dolphins splashed off the coast at thirty yards, in the deeper sanctions of the sea. The slaps and sounds and rolls seemed to gather more dolphins to come in towards the shore, but staying around and close enough to him at just five to seven feet of water, just a short distance out with the open ocean behind them. The tide was low, with breakers of two to three feet. Somehow, though, then, the Beachcomber felt summoned by their activity, and bravely he swam back out to meet with them... yet again.

Maybe they were just being cautious, knowing they could freely and easily move away from the confines of mobility within the low ebbed waters of the cove. They had to feel more freedom with the open sea behind them should they then decide to leave his tender and curious company. Naturally, it could be their curiosity, too, that caused the stir with them, that alerted the dolphins to arouse and gather the whole pod to see about him. This time, the dolphins stayed close by, however, and a big male, _splashed a lot of showered waters_ toward the Beachcomber. Wisely, the Beachcomber stopped swimming forward and towards, and then he just decided to calmly bob himself off the bottom sand, up and down, with his head above the water line. He held that vulnerable position, bobbing in neutral fashion, steadily. It was then that several of the members of the dolphin pod began to come towards him.

They swam by him. They swam around him. They touched him with their lengthy bodies, rubbing him on the backside of his legs. It was truly a remarkable and a curious eventful day. And as they gained each other's confidence, as they became even more acquainted, the Beachcomber reached out an open hand and rubbed the water's coating of smoothness of the dolphin's skin in a luxurious long gentle stroke of faith. Not even the slickest snake's skin was as exciting for him to feel *in the context of the under-the-water-touch. (It's a tough skin in a dry rub.)*

He had had a similar experience some ten years earlier. It was such a marvelous interlude for him to *partake in*, that this event encapsulated him. In just that moment he reminded himself of when it all started, like it was yesterday. He began to release *some tears for awhile* in his new discovery of dolphin family company. And the dolphins helped him to let it go, and at certain times, achieving the epiphany (being tuned into Dolphin spirits) to release those tears, *but after it was over*... the tears had stopped. The encounter would leave him with a smile in his heart.

And to observe the dolphins in leisurely study was a genuine unique pleasure.

It is truly a natural wonder of nature—*perhaps its best kept secret.*

A Spiritual Uplifting Dolphin Encounter

THE BEACHCOMBER LOVED THE DOLPHINS

Within the ties that bind and the kinship he shared and experienced with these *go betweens as spirits* through these fascinating social creatures, he learned to *love something again.*

He couldn't return to the people just yet, but he could love the dolphins. It was a step towards recovery,

And a journey to *Himself*.

It was an astonishing compliment towards the dolphins, creating that Spirit, revisiting him, to come back to him through his Soul. It helped the man, for he knew he could love something. And yet he chose to live quietly though, still in seclusion with his secrets; and *his secret dolphin friends*...

For Here and Now, to Go On Forward,

After the Captivating Day with the Dolphins,

After that Day, He Would Not Be Alone.

One of the newer stunning fishing habits that the Beachcomber witnessed off the coast of Campechuela, Cuba, was one the dolphins had developed recently. It's called, oddly enough, *"Scupping"* on the shoreline. It proved them to be the most extraordinary architects, so smart and inventive, and is so very rare to observe few of us have ever seen it before. And for those of us who haven't, we should be so lucky. Here's what happens:

A dolphin using a type of sonar "echo location" locates a target school of fish. In single solo-scupping, he will drive a manageable herd of twenty to thirty fish, or as many fish as he can keep together by himself. The dolphin maneuvers the herd into the shallows using the shoreline as the border. At breakneck speeds, with his head barely submerged by the water's surface, the dolphin speeds up in the chase, overtaking them. The dolphin then hurls his body, after *passing ahead* of the herd. By using the full length of his body (eight to ten feet of his form). He collapses the school by beaching himself up on dry land, sweeping the herd onto the sand.

As the dolphin lays outstretched, the fish flop around helplessly, trying to make their futile attempted way back towards the water. The dolphin mammal waits until the fish *flip-flop up and down* and *fall right into the mouth of his* snout.

39

It is an awesome display of herding and corralling, and then scooping them up off dry land. It's called scupping, like what a scupper does, until they scupper their fill of fish down into their long snout's gullet. Then, its cachet of fish scuppered into its mouth, and laying prone on the sand, it flaps and leans off its powerful body, its side flukes flat, body writhing, to slide its way over to pull itself back into the water.

Solo shoreline *scupping: it's a unique visual treat.*

However, The Dolphin Pod's scupping is even more dramatic. In open waters the dolphin pod *echo locates* a school of fish, up to a thousand roaming fish, or an even larger number, depending on their luck.

They use a similar herding technique, but with several dolphins blowing bubbles making swift passes of sounds and flash bubbling, to scare the fish into a swarming ball, hundreds of fishes all in one *massive moving mound of meat.* They keep the herded ball all swimming together in one massive floating free-for-all, like a virtual *splurge ball smorgasbord* of a school of fish feast.

Then one dolphin swoops underneath while the other dolphins continue managing with the herding process, and this solo dolphin flows through the herd to feed. The dolphins then trade off positions until all of the dolphin pod is fed their respective fill of the feast. This communicative process of the dolphin pod scupping with several dolphins is truly a magnificent feat of nature to witness in the open seas.

Seeing it the first time was magic, if you want magnificent... the dolphins' pod-scupping, or solo-scupping... the dolphins are the true magicians of the open sea.

In the ten years that passed for the Beachcomber, he learned nature, living off the land's and the sea's bounty. Also he learned to be a part of the animal kingdom, his survival, his stealth, and the ability to be quiet. Humble heartbeats made him one of their own for he was one with the birds, dragonflies, and crabs or passing dolphin splashes of sun's risings, and to the cricket beats, nightbirds and the giant sea turtle of sun's setting. The feral cats with longer ears, and less fur, and longer legs, living wild in the colony (held over as society's sentry against the rodents of sugar cane crops, during the plantation's harvesting days), the old Beachcomber befriended them. Two wild things living off the land in harmony.

Usually, the rails and the ships met at a place in proximity to where the harvest was stored. In the island's geography, water was nearby as was rail to move the cane.

However, rats would converge on the stockpiles and growers turned to feral cats as the dominant sentry force to expel the unwanted rodents feeding on cane crops.

The colonies dug a series of deep tunnels and a vast network of holes, keeping the cats warmer during the winter, and also cooler during the searing summer's heat. The Beachcomber had a few cats he was on friendly terms with where his camp intersected the range of the feral cat colony. Some of those feral cat friendships had actually lasted since his decade journey began. He lived with them.

As four legged friends went, they were the animal most like him. He watched them. They watched him. They interacted respectfully as he always let only them initiate moves. At times his eyes monitored the ring leader cat. (Both day and at nights.)

The lead feral cat understood him to be a "friendly" after he stared right back at the lead cat in the moonlight. He bonded with the lead cat as not an enemy or any danger to the colony... as time would go on... down the road over a period of time: the friendly stance made him an honorary member of the feral cat colony.

A slower four legged creature that he met occasionally, and curiously identified with, was the lumbering, and humblest of slow-footed creatures; the sea turtle.

The turtle's belly crawl, or the evening's beachcomb, a combing sound across the wet sands of nightfall, with something to bury and hide and forget. To return to the ocean, to leave and forget years of solitude. The years became a necessity for the Beachcomber, needed to restore a soul. This man was on the coves of being gone away forever, until yesterday.

This nightfall the Beachcomber noticed a greater belly-crawling sound over wet sand, for even the three hundred-pounded sea turtle was not this large in her four heels' flukes flapping, to bury her eggs. This was a greater sound, one of the weight and type that scored wet sand, back and forth scratches that sounded like sandpaper in the furniture maker's hands on a baby crib finish, to ensure safe passages of smaller hands.

This would go on all night, the sandpaper's strokes across the baby crib frame, and all through the darkness the Beachcomber could not return to sleep as this reminded him of his father's home furniture-making business, where he was offered his first job at fourteen. The Beachcomber would wait until tomorrow to see what landed in his path come first light.

The morning's tide sun-rising, the birds, the dragonflies flying over a man-made arrival thing; and the crabs that now would have to belly crawl around this man-made *wish, wish, scratching* noise of a newcomer, too. All the while the dolphins splashed offshore knowing secrets of what came ashore that moonlit night. For it's being *a creature* like the Beachcomber to be for a *decade* on nature's timetable cycle, to sense or to feel the dawn of an orange pastel's coloring of a *waking morning's light* is truly nature's most magical event.

FOUR

Just a Couple Days Back, Only Forty-Eight Hours Ago...

A FOOTBALL TEAM–STATE CHAMPIONS 1990

Most of the team (players in their late twenties) were the guests of their host on this trip; their former coach (who had risen to become a very prominent high-ranking divorce attorney), Harvey B. Goldenberg, of San Francisco. Fifty percent of all marriages end in divorce, and such odds can keep a "good practice" divorce attorney in plentiful coin.

It was on his dime and was his own luxurious gift to them, that former team he coached all the way to the state championship: to go on a six-week cruise aboard an eighty-five foot yacht to celebrate their ten year reunion with the summer excursion of the Bay Area High School COMETS (the State Champs of 1990). Being the top divorce attorney in San Francisco was one thing, but to H.B. Goldenberg, being THE COACH of the Bay Area Comets, who became State Champs in 1990, a decade ago, marked for him what was his true zenith in his life.

It was two things: He was the coach, but he also had twin sons on the football team.

Joe Elliot Goldenberg, a burly 6'5" 235-pound tight end, had the size and the coarse curly hair of ex-Raider-turned broadcaster, Todd Christiansen, plus long sideburns like Elvis Presley.

A star wide receiver, Charlie Jay Goldenberg, the 6'2" 195-pound speedier wide-out, had great hands and quick feet. "C.J." was the most gifted athlete and was carried in reverence with all of this team's pride since he had game-winning touchdowns of such spectacular valor. His clutch catches and ability to deliver with the game on the line always amazed them.

The second thing with them was Harvey Goldenberg's leadership and passion for the game, since he too was once a great college prospect and a player. After suffering a torn ACL, his knee injury sidelined his collegiate football career. He altogether dropped his prospects for turning pro and changed his focus to law at UC Davis, but he was able to, via coaching, fulfill his old dreams of athletic greatness by vicariously tendering his passions, and also re-channeling his energy and guidance through the twins within the context of the Great Team Sport of Football.

His coaching period was four years, and he was himself such a well-known athlete and a *great motivator* that he was able to win the job of coaching his twin sons simply by merely suggesting it to the schoolboard. It was at a gathering of locals, inside the auditorium, meeting to discuss the future rebuilding of a new football field for the Bay Area Comets, the old field having been burned out and all but destroyed by a suspicious fire.

It was rumored that a group of individualists within the high school known as the Devoid Division, or "The Devoids," a hyphenate antisocial group of teens, despised all the sports and all their whole community's impassioned devotion which was forever so rooted in the High School Athletics Department. Some schools' identities, all across the country, are defined by football. Depending on where you go, perhaps in some states, it is the whole community's pride.

The jocks always fetched in and hooked up with the best girls, while this zippo collection of iconoclast misfits were ostracized or prematurely isolated from the "in" crowd. The "geeks" decided to form their own clique society of about two dozen members. All guys that excelled in computers and math and yahoo-like hijinks, and also hacking. Basically, they were disenfranchised white teens and Gen-Xers with the patterns of arbitrary behavior to the so-called norm.

One so-called "Devoid" founder, an Egyptian descendant named Andre Motollah, was the son of a fireman who got a hold of some bolt cutters and four portable acetylene torch welders. He gained entry to the high chain linked, fully fenced-off facility by severing through a series of heavy gauge locks.

The Devoids were briefed by a survivalist booklet they generated from computers' information on how to construct pipe bombs. They used those devices, along with a sizable quantity of over thirty whiskey-flavored rags of Molotov cocktails to set off the whole entire structure into an inferno's incendiary mammoth blaze.

Halloween, 1 o'clock in the morning, the Bay Area Comets' field was an awesome display of a tinderbox on that crisp fall evening. The pipe bombs used by the Devoid's members obliterated the box office's booth and completely disheveled the team's thirty-five foot-tall electronic scoreboard into a useless pile of rubble.

The meticulously fiendish crew *lit up* the old stadium's wooden bleachers and stands. The whole entire structure was fully destroyed and devastated along with ninety percent of the acreage that once was the football team's field of glory. It was furiously raging and burning out of control before anyone could get there to put the hoses to the awesome inferno.

It was a mighty keen ploy, fully planned and schematically sound, a well-executed mad demolition of the entire facility. In the old days, kids would just *light up a single roll of toilet paper* in a stall in the men's room. And then run like hell thinking that was some grand dangerously dubious *wild shit* to pull off in a government-funded facility. Today's kids are just more of an internet educated multiplicity-induced group, both *rebelling* and *destroying*. *Multi-tasking*, a hybrid-bred two-fold, too-detailed non-civilian-like destructive sort of breed.

And a lot like the signature trails of the kids from Colorado and the Columbine High School Massacre. This was their own significantly respective version of a telltale sign that they were rapidly encroaching upon the verge of some later or greater hardcore dire consequence, but *the bloodbath* was long off from then. As with these fledgling future zealots, they were just getting warmed up with this Stage One Showcase. Generation X at work or at play on a natural young man's *man-made* Disaster Project.

———

In a tangent thought a little bit peripherally outside the sphere of Beachcomber, but clearly within the realm of life,

An Aside Commentary

(Notation of the first: 2/26/1993 Egyptian Terrorist Attack on World Trade Center. This attack claims the lives of six people, and numerous injuries from smoke inhalation.)

Then… Somewhere… In the belly of the United States, who created a woeful beast?

In 1995… barely two years later, Americans themselves are acclimated in terror.

In the Midwestern belly of the United States, along came a woeful beast…

A two-ton bomb created by American terrorists is detonated in the United States.

It came to pass that minds like these somehow extrapolated their soul's wisdom and spawned the future generation's next Timothy McVeigh, who would, with helpful agents and accomplices, blank out his own nation and score it with a black eye so bloody, so red, and so deep, *it just rocked the core of a nation's faith.* In its own sovereign backyard or somewhere in the heartland of the good old U.S.A. it would grow such a hardcore, heinous and nefarious infectious mind.

As it forced upon us to fathom belief–it could suffer…

A killer so grotesque, a killer so gargantuan in scope, *a killing killer ground groveling* beyond the belly-crawling or asinine depths of infinity, who created with an unholy and abominable gall (a world now paused to wonder at such an awful bad undertaking.) Here it was in a period of American disillusionment: we struggled to grapple and grasp its shattering faith-testing beliefs, to believe that it should suffer such a blast from one of the damnedest of souls.

And, from one of her own homegrown wild seeds.

In a similar vein of building off the planes of disturbing phenomena, with the over-swelling burgeoning legions and icons of hail Mary yahoos and graduate X-ers' logic taken to the 39th parallel in degrees of anti-societal displacements of almighty grand dysfunctional dysfunctions and degenerates against World Order.

All paled beyond compare as one emerged from deep within the folds of the indecent. Unabombers, Terrorists, X-men and X-ers, the free men, the

Branch Davidians, Nazi influenced ultra Klansmen, and erstwhile zealots of all kinds, including the dysfunctional disenfranchised abandons of survivalist right wing stingers (who keep quiet smartly): The FBI, CIA, and Interpol or Special OPS, be they the Army, Air Force, Navy, Navy Seals, or Marines. No one expected such a dejected rejects unconscionable debut, what is this evil force who had come so wayward and forth, and what hath he so brutally, unbelievably wrought?

Along came a manmade scorpion with a deadly sting, who led the crusade to eradicate some one hundred sixty-eight human beings from the face of the earth. It was the worst on-U.S.-soil terrorist attack to date.

Not only this writer encountered depression, but seeing the world around me, including economic woes forthcoming; a person not close to me but he was my neighbor a few doors down; the neighbor decided to quit the living.

There was a man who shot himself in September 2000. His name was Michael Fox and he was still yet much too much a younger man who just ended his life. An old man tried to make sense of this tragedy for me.

A man from the old country who for thirty years swept the floors and carpets of the high rise, and had to clean up the ending closing carnage, put it in his own perspective and with South American wisdom... Ricardo was his name (he said), his old-world understanding came from Livingston, Guatemala. He spoke spoke in English, articulating the fresh translation of his philosophy in the language of his new country, "The father can't help the baby or understand the baby because" (emphatically pleading), "He make the baby. He make you!" He was telling the father that his son's death was not his fault.

Back to these Bay Area Comets, and the misfits who would thwart their high school's football field of glory. Ironically, it was due to Andre Motollah's "DEVOIDS," who all shared a fanatical preference to the rock music of the famed 1970s super group, Led Zeppelin. And it was all Andre's idea to mount the destruction campaign with a suitable identity, so they deigned it such and called it fittingly:

"Smoking Zeppelin's Balls."

The metaphor fit both the the American blimp-shaped football, and the gas-filled hot-air stoked S.Z.B. members, high on the herbs of many toked and smoked blunts, in preparation for the dubious and doobie-filled event. These were the nerds and non-jock types who could never make the football team, and this was the rebellious way these devoid-types could get wasted while destroying school property, their "nefarious hazing activity." Leave it to a smart-assed Egyptian who must've taken a page from Colorado's legendary folklore with infamous Rocky Mountain Oysters. The runts' leg-boys showed some pretty brassy balls on S.Z.B. night. All disciples of similar youthful ilk, these yahoos and knuckle-headed fools, corkers with cork tree for brains, got away with the erosive expletive job, and kept their wits as well as their big cajones intact.

Somehow our society is building a franchise of some disenfranchised wayward youth, that's just an infamous hard-on for everything in sight: Government/education/happy people/cops/doctors/nurses/computers/or overworked social workers/postal clerks/writers/journalists/and teachers... the list is endless. Somebody better tell someone to just stop the anger mill from cranking 'em out, we're all about just completely overwhelmed with so many misfits of dubious invention.

There's nothing left to be Devoids of or about on this blue planet. Tell them that really everyone's fucked up everything already. No need to go all out, barn bred and all of this chicken haywire nuts, and yahoo it up even worse than it is now.

It was also during the compilation of the short story *The Beachcomber* that multiple school shootings continued to crop up in the town where Nicholas John Lennartson had hailed from as well, San Diego. At Santee's Santana High School, fifteen people were shot March 5th, 2001, and then at Granite Hills High in El Cajon, five people were shot at. Charles Andrew Williams was tried as an adult for killing two students, Randy Gordon and Bryan Zukor, and for also wounding thirteen more in the Santee shooting spree. Jason Hoffman, age eighteen, injured five students and caused several heart flurries of fear and adrenaline within the souls of everyone involved, just like the incident previous to this one. Santee, El Cajon, San Diego, and the country are mending, but the signs on the walls are threatening that this could only be the tip of the iceberg.

We're in a new stage of alert and readiness in all forms of *intention protection. Were living life differently. We try to hide among our will of safety,* but a larger looming foreboding cloud of reality continues to precipitate our fears. In some ways these dark clouds and the treacherous uninspired youths of this whole generation (if we can call them X anymore), are fostering a budding future lifestyle amid some more terrible people, with a sarcastically juvenile insane-like indifference to life. The "*I have a few problems and I'm going to kill something or somebody,*" mentality is suddenly reaching far too low in the youthful track of a teenager's psyche *to manifest itself* in the otherwise fertile minds of this generation's hopes and dreams.

Everyone around the landscape of the whole lot of them is just wondering where that sick candidate of an *irregular sick rebel,* with humans as targets ready for the scope of his crosshairs, who is about to turn degenerate yahoo, will just blow off some rounds at other suspecting or unsuspecting mortals of the regular human beings. Somebody needs to tell them killing in any capacity or reasoning or motive never made anyone happy, or better, or solved their problems... ever.

Even revolution, or war for that matter, often times when it is either necessary or unnecessary, did more damage to the human mind and psyche than anyone could have imagined (anyone who's been in one knows they're never the same afterwards). The old veteran's term for it, *greatly affected by it* seems only hardly sufficient in hindsight. It is a legacy to those legions of men who will remember the experiences, who remember that time or that place or that hill, that village or that beach, that fallen comrade or that fallen adversary, *who died at the hail of gunfire*, or those mortar shells of a bombing raid of bombs blasting in the living nightmares of the past or a previous war's time...

Those Who Remember It All... the fallen soldiers of Military Casualties; men, women, and children in wartime are Civilian Casualties. If they dare to relive it and rethink it, they do themselves more harm than good. Alas, it's truly PEACE, as John Lennon told us, that is life's greatest treasure.

On June 10th, 2001, in the early hours of morning, a man who was tried and convicted by the judicial process of the system, was put to a permanent rest. Timothy McVeigh was executed for his actions, killed for the killing of so many others, one hundred sixty-eight human beings. When it was done and over with, you know that to him the addition of himself gratified him to the total of one hundred sixty-nine.

Without sketching foreboding times ahead or what will follow in our world's next chapter, or anyone's upcoming chapters, in life we must prepare for the times ahead.

It's interesting to me how we all will go ahead on, and do just that...

———

Dec. 14th, 2012, a deranged young 20 year old, Adam Lanza. fatally shot 20 children and 6 adult school staff members killing 26 people in Newtown, Connecticut.

At Virginia Polytechnic, April 16th, 2007, Seung-Hui Cho, another deranged person, shot at and killed 32 people and wounded 17 others in Blacksburg, Virginia. The death toll was 33 bodies including the madman perpetrator. The Aurora Shooting.

July 20th, 2012; The Century movie theatre during a midnight screening of the film The Dark Knight Rises, a gunman dressed in tactical assault clothing, plus gear, shot into a crowded audience killing 12 people and injuring 70 other movie goers. James E. Holmes was arrested and charged with that multiple murder.

Feb. 14th, 2008, Steve Kazmierczak shot at multiple people on the campus of Northern Illinois University, killing 5 people and injuring another 21 people in DeKalb, Illinois.

The Amish School Shooting occurred October 2nd, 2006. Charles C. Roberts shot 10 girls, killing 5 students at West Nickel Mines schoolhouse in Lancaster County, Pennsylvania. My friend and creative colleague Greg Champion directed the touching documentary nonfiction film based on that event: "Amish Grace."

While editing the second edition of this book, June 29th, 2015: The Beachcombing Massacre, Sousse, Tunisia. A shooting terrorist attack was carried out against civilians on a beach killing 38 people.

———

Everyday now we see these events in the Post 9/11 World. I had to find a name for these news stories.

I.E. In like the father son sniper team story. I.E. In like the shooter at University Of Santa Barbara. I.E. In like The Boston Marathon Bombers-All These Stories In Our Cities-All Across Anywhere U.S.A. or, in this world.

I decided on a name. I coined it the acronym I S S I R Y. Idiotic Sick Sociopath Irregular Rebel Yahoo.

We're into the news story era... the ISSIRY of our misery... it seems.

From this day and forward it will become: "A news story of the I.S.S.I.R.Y. within our midst today."

Copyright—August 1st 2015—Michael Gering; Author, *Beachcomber*

COMMENTARY

It is not the world I remember that I was growing up in. It has changed.

Mental health. Political Suicidal Zealots. Freak Murderers. Militant Suicidal Terrorists.

And when these four ideology clashes occur in the post 9/11 world, bad things happen.

In San Bernadino, California, very nearby where I live. In Paris at a popular nightclub spot. In Istanbul, Turkey, at the airport, where free people meet to travel the free world. In Orlando, Florida, where free people meet and attend gatherings at a popular nightclub gathering spot. All I can say truthfully, looking at the world today, at my age, and at my station in life; talking about this climate of all of these... violent and recklessly deranged shooting incidents now: This is not the world that I am used to living in. It has changed. We live in a time of a different wired new world. I classify it... as we sit here today, a time of: "The I.S.S.I.R.Y. of our misery."

———

FIVE

Ten Year Reunion and Vacation Cruise

THE BOAT

The boat they were on was an 85-footer. She had six week's manifest and abundant rations and supplies to last up to sixty days for the many passengers she carried. There was a plethora of sportsmen's gear on board, a bounty of deep sea fishing rods lined up in rows of long poles, and several strong pulley reels of 120lb. test line. The boat was stocked with ample diving equipment, several wetsuits and large air tanks, capacity capabilities of up to 400 pounds of compressed air pressure, and fourteen tanks available to be used.

A deep-sea dive was a rite of passage for this team. It was provided by Harvey Goldenberg's very reputable equity, his own dime. The Team looked forward to the yearly trips to Mexico, and all the players were certified Naui/Paddy, except for one who'd had an encounter yhe previous year off the coast of Cabo San Lucas in lime green waters of glorious beauty with an assortment of beautifully colored little fish and one infamous 300-pound grouper at thirty feet down, hiding among the high branches of corals lounging and flexing his gills silently, with eyes the size of a Chevy Impala's hubcaps, bulging on either side with a *jaw dropping* cavern of a mouth that could swallow a human.

It was only last year in Baja Mexico, on a south-of-the-border excursion, that Cassius (the team's strongest player) had suffered the heart-stopping fright of his life. He began the long arduous ascent, then abruptly expelled huge amounts of his oxygen thirty feet up after seeing this massive monster 300-pound grouper. In the suspended watery animation of the menacing-looking ugly beast nestled in among all the stalks of the brightly-colored corals, he thought he saw a hungry Moby Dick's cousin Devil.

He reached the deck and threw off his equipment as if visited by a horrifying ghastly ghost. He disgustedly vehemently swore off forever the sport for fear of becoming a casualty statistic in a holy writ's text of The Story of Jonah.

He was captain on defense and a ferocious hard-hitting, middle linebacker who could bench 320-pounds on wide grip, but the wide grip of the mouth of a giant-swallowing *Moby's cousin*, the mighty-mouthed, groping grouper, was one inordinately huge bunkering humpback of a damned fish that he just couldn't ever fathom to tackle.

The course they had set was to travel south through the Yucatan Channel, past the Cayman Islands' fishing grounds south of Jamaica and Kingston to Haiti and onward to Santo Domingo and then Puerto Rico, to the St. Croix Coves with some of the best, cleanest and purest waters for scuba diving in the whole world.

They were passing Cayman Brac, between the Cayman Islands and Jamaica over into the area known as the Cayman Trench, which is in the deeper waters of a spiraling current that can swirl between Montego Bay and Cabo Cruz. The boat was going fast, traveling at night to make up a day's time since they were delayed by the airlines strike–controllers coming out of Oakland forced the specially-chartered plane to leave 24 hours behind schedule. The late start broke up the trip's mood and left the team in an anxious, anti-climatic state from the very first start.

The team edgily slept their intermittent forty winks, their cascaded bodies were all legs and limbs scattered across three separate rows of chairs inside the terminal bays, which was just like being locked up inside the locker room and off the field of play before finally, the next day, mounting up on a Miami-bound 737 to begin the adventure of a so-called reunion vacation cruise.

There were four scuba tanks in the boat's cockpit cabin area, lashed together with several tough tight ropes of bungee cords. The tanks were to be topped off in the morning by a compressor that was housed in the B-deck birth, below the ship's wheel and accessible by a drop of six stairs. It wasn't safe practice to have tanks up in the wheelhouse where the captain was steering the vessel, but in a quest to make up some lost time the captain's oversight was simply happenstance, and a commonly made one at that. Also, H.B. Goldenberg used the compressor every time he filled up a special *airbed,* on the doctor's recommendation for his backache and bad knee. He had had enough athletic injuries and old weekend warrior's bones on his body, and in that practicality, he also had to follow his doctor's advice.

But H.B. Goldenberg was a fearless and intense leader and as rogue captain and the coach of his team, a true leader in the self-made (I can do anything I want) Machiavellian-mode. He would keep the fearlessness of this pace, and the boat continued to churn the ripples of the dark sea at a task of 26 knots to make up the lost 24 hours. He was determined to deliver on what was promised to his team, *the St Croix Coves Dive* would be made to happen on schedule. It would occur as he originally had made the plans for it to. He would see to it. He pushed onward all night to make it to the St. Croix Coves, considered one of the purest and most glorious dives in all the world, next to the spectacle of beauty of Australia's Great Barrier Reef and Madagascar's Cave.

He would blaze towards St. Croix like the aggressively strident captain of the notorious Titanic who *sped up the screws* on his watch to steam for surpassing a record 24 hour *day arrival* ahead of schedule to impress the press in New York, and shock the world with the White Star Lines Trans Atlantic Ocean liner's folklore of 19th century-amazing-ingenuity, thereby making history by markedly beating the hourglass' sands of time.

It would be Christ's luck, or just overall phenomenal *buzzard's luck* ,that a downed Soviet Spy Satellite had lost its orbit in the ninth hour yesterday causing it to *hurtle towards earth at a rate of 400 feet per second* until it pierced through the earth's cumulus atmosphere and sailed right across Cape Canaveral's launch pads and Castro's Cuba, which inspired its Soviet brothers-in-arms to launch the floating monolith Daedelus. The satellite was named Polotsky's 11, some thirty years earlier, and its chipped, pot-metal aluminum shell fell directly into the path of the rapid cruiser with its American payload of the winning State Football Champs.

As the downed Spy Satellite floated gently on calm waves, a substantial portion of its buoyantly rocking 26-foot long cork-like cylinder was in harm's way of the 85-foot cruiser's course. It was just there floating like the iceberg of some similar past fate. It is documented in records that at least one satellite of space junk has fallen from the earth's atmosphere every single day for the past forty years. It is as regular as everyday that interestingly *"satellites rain down from the sky."*

The Soviet's space satellites that were launched into outer space orbit like the Polotsky-11 were at the time largely experimental, in a special way, with a built-in retrieval recovery feature. Specially designed equipment injected helium gas into its inner lining of environmentally sound, fire and heat-retardant materials; a man-made sturdy steel belted tubular lining inside its barrel shaped fuselage kept it buoyant in the event of an ideal water landing, whereby the Capsule of the Bird could be then preserved and studied once it was recovered later on.

We had the satellite advantage over the Soviets but were behind the Russians in the race to actually get a man on the moon. Even though the U-2 could out-fly anything previously built, and photograph geographically the entire Cuban countryside, we also had the capability to read the collected spy plane's picture data. It wasn't enough because it was our <u>invisible lead</u>. John F. Kennedy wanted the United States to go to the moon before his Russian Soviet adversaries made it there. It would then become a *visible leap, and a lead ahead*.

Kennedy was not a fan of the space program for any other reason than he insisted to the head of NASA, "We have to beat the Russians to put a man on the moon. Being second just wouldn't do and all the other budgetary concerns for different programs, I'm going to refuse to fund." (So all the other programs had to wait.) The goal was to put a man on the moon *now*, ahead of the Russians.

It was a unique milestone for his presidency, if indeed it was to be his post presidency. (July 20th, 1969… <u>"One small step for man… one giant leap for mankind."</u>)

Few people remember it but it might have been this president's most far-reaching achievement. And so it became in history the *"visible lead"* to the whole world.

With the sizable advantage in Satellite Intel over his Soviet adversary, one of Kennedy's favorite things to do at foreign policy and tech meetings was to read the latest data of U-2 spy planes. Sitting in his favorite chair designed to ease the pain in his ailing back, he reviewed satellite-provided pictures and reports of Castro's Cuba as the CIA brought them in to the White House to examine. And in liking the James Bond books by Ian Fleming, John F. Kennedy loved the spying game like a vaunted U.S./Soviet chess match played between two men of long term arch rivalry. Khrushchev was a worthy foe of an opponent to him and it was Kennedy's crucial intended goal to outwit and to outsmart him at every possible turn of the contest. It was his obsession to be always one step ahead of the Soviets. The debacle of Playa Giron, THE BAY OF PIGS, was his administration's earliest blunder and uncorrectable miscalculation.

However, the Achilles was to later on become a U.S./Russian showdown and stand-off during the heady Thirteen Days of the Cuban Missile Crisis, where he thwarted both Castro and Khrushchev on the world stage and somehow also miraculously dodged catastrophic consequences for both sides.

But with less money to spend and every launch an educational science experiment *for them,* the Soviets built in a strategy to cover their costs. Their engineers wanted to study their old rockets and find out with subsequent retrievals when and why (MAINLY WHY) so many of their birds' missions *aborted and just went wrong for them.* It was the back up recovery system built into Polotski-11 that kept it preserved and intact. And there it was, just stubbornly floating in the Caribbean, in the path of a pleasure boat.

Like a child in toilet training sending shit up into space, the poorer financially-challenged Russians had to get over *not getting their shit back all the time.*

The floating Daedelus Polotski's-11 satellite of great Soviet ingenuity had a very sharp edge. The yacht was traveling at 26 knots when they collided. It took a lean scored gash on the starboard lower, which quickly flooded the lower deck's quarter in a period of less than twenty minutes. The boat's hull was shattered with a hole the size of the front end of a 76 Chevy Nova.

The boat took a 35-degree down angle and the deck's nose was only three to six feet above water, and her rear bow was rising high. The team's fastest receiver, "C.J." led the call to abandon ship and man the single lifeboat.

The satellite was struck with such force at 26 knots it tipped over the four scuba tanks in the wheel house and in their tumble, one tank fell upon the regulator header and broke the top off.

The tank rocket shot like a missile and pierced the control panel of the ship's communication relay radio. The metal tank shorted and arced inside the wiring and it quickly caught fire and blew up with the loud popping noise, like blowing out an amplifier at a WHO concert. And thusly, this drowning boat, from whence it came as a "Magic Bus" became a "Momma's got a squeezebox and daddy never sleeps at night." In this now nightmare, the Atlantic became a creature that would swallow the accordion box that once was a dauntless and resilient boat driven by an ambitious and driven football coach.

Ship to shore communications had no back up to function and the crippled ship could nary harken a distress signal. The team fought to drill a scrimmage and skirmish into the safety launch, hampered by their sleepy drained eyes and groggy-legs of dawn to manage their way into the small lifeboat.

The nightmare's worst sight was both twin sons' stillness while the rest of the survivors crammed into the lifeboat. Cassius looked over the shoulders of Joe Elliot and Charlie Jay, as they looked upon the lifeless form of their father H.B. Goldenberg. The sons were stunned, Goldenberg's skull cracked and both eyes open. He died instantly when the boat collided with the satellite. It was a frightened death on his face.

Charlie Jay Goldenberg, C.J., knelt as Joe Elliot just stood, completely shocked stiff at the sight of an even stiffer body, his father's now lifeless shape. Once so resilient, and once of so many strengths, reduced down to a rumpled and puddled-up ball of flesh.

Without words, praying unto himself, C.J. gently touched H.B.'s face with an open palm to his jaw and circled his chin. He grasped his father's shoulder, steadying his nerves, and let out a tumultuous body waves-jolting-quake-like upheaval and surge in his own heartfelt to the soul's loss. As this sigh cried out of his body, he gently closed his eyes towards and into the seas own continued eternity. "May you rest in deep sleep," C.J. whispers. "It's time for you to go. Now it's time for you to go." He embraced him as he wept.

Joe Elliot pulled him away and Cassius helped both men but it was C.J.'s legs that were the most staggered stiff trudging heavily with steps into a kind of sleepwalking slow motion. Cassius took control of boarding the launch by ordering THE TEAM'S players to dump all their larger duffle bags and take only one smaller bag per each man, and to "load that sucker up with all the food you can manage to cram up into it." And then he added, "Who knows how long it will be before they find us out here."

Arm in arm, the three left the man as they trailed off to board the safety launch boat. The yacht sank in the twenty-ninth minute, a mere half hour after striking the Soviet-built floating Daedelus who flew too close to the sun. The boys just watched her in agony without ever launching a flare of glory. It had all happened so fast in an *instant tragedy*. A reality-now, H.B. Goldenberg went down with the ship. Several team members solemnly bowed their heads to pray for Harvey who was their coach and held the higher heir to a pulpit status, for his way was the only sermon giver they held reserved. In earnest reverence, half of them cried; thankfully the darkness had hidden their flowing tears for his soul.

H.B. Goldenberg's head struck the cabin's teakwood varnished facing with such a force he was killed instantly as if Billy had stricken Claggart.

Naturally, H.B. was deservedly revered in greatness. In the old naked sense of Thomas Kineally, "It was a good death."

H.B. instantly shot up like a rocket into heaven.

SIX

The Beachcomber's Discovery

The Beachcomber finds a writing journal kept by one of the young men. He reads on through the small pocket notebook, a diary that might've been from the hands of a future writer not unlike Richard Basehart's character in Moby Dick. .

And from his point of view examining both the journal and the crew he could assess the launch boat came out of Key West and belonged to a yacht named "Alimony."

The safety launch left the sinking yacht with twenty-four survivors aboard, it was only suited to hold fifteen people at normal capacity. Those twenty-four boys of that surviving team all climbed in, overloading the launch boat. They drifted in the circle of a swirl current for twelve days. The rations expired on day number five, so for another whole week they became nearer to exhaustion and famine collapse before finally drifting ashore at Campechuela, Cuba.

The old Beachcomber studied them in dawn's light. They looked like a sports team, he gathered, from their ages and body contours and shapes. Those twenty-four members had all been in good physical condition, but some men had expired from heat exhaustion and the famine collapse.

There's one thing ole sergeants never forget: the aged and cooking, fleshed-out, raw meaty-smelling stench of death.

He could see that a few clung to the boat, then belly crawled up to shore across the sand. Two had managed to leave a trail, some giant sea turtle scrimmage it must have been, some thirty-five yards, and these two guys had to be the two strongest; ultimately the leaders of the team in some capacity.

The Beachcomber knew from the faces, charred and sunburned, that a rescue search plane was eminent. Even in their haggard peaks of expiration (nearly off the charts of survival if help wasn't given to them right that moment he found them, they all would finally eventually expire and perish, since even the two strongest used up everything they had to belly crawl up to the spot they were at now), he could see these were all American U.S. citizens. Their backgrounds were of more than mid-level income, there were a few thoroughbreds within this mixture. Some of this team clearly came from some high finance if the roots were traced to the family tree.

The Beachcomber thought about the ramifications momentarily before he put himself at risk to be catapulted out of his insular existence and forced to inherit the status of something he didn't want, a hero. In his mind, all of that had altogether long since passed him by, for his days with Castro in the 60s long ago. He once had his own moments of valor, as a man in his twenties he lusted to be a Hero. It was in that valor Cuba put down the Bay of Pigs attempted coup, but what remained behind in the forty years *since* still left a lot to be desired. Cuba was not, in his own mind and in the mind of her people, better off because of that crisis resolution to Castro's Cuba.

It wasn't those reflections that moved him in his decision. No, they were more basic than that. The Beachcomber needed to know that a man as separate from all society (as he was, whatever the circumstances) would do the right thing that he knew that he would have to do. For these faces he saw this morning meant something to others–the fathers and the mothers and the families. If he *let them die today, it would haunt him even more so than* the beloved wife he lost, and the daughter he hadn't seen for the last 10-years of solitude, living away from their lives.

In the morning's sounds, the boat vicariously rocked back and forth across the wet sand as the hull wished and washed with the risings of each tide's recessions, repeating… ssshhh… wissshhh. Again for him that old familiar sound, like that of his father's sandpaper strokes made across fresh wood shapings of a baby crib. The birds, the dragonflies, the sand-crabs belly crawl, or passing dolphin pods feeding, the Beachcomber's protective insular world would be penetrated by the wedged-up onshore vessel, the launch boat whose sound like fresh sandpaper woke him up . He would begin with the two who came the furthest and appeared to be the strongest of this group of exhausted, emaciated young faces of puffiness.

The Beachcomber wore two sashes: one was red, which was, in his mind, his war reminder, and he tended to keep it hidden around his waist, or in his trusty knapsack. The color red was best if he ever sustained cuts or a wound that need not shade or show any damage on a sash made out of a "blood-red" Red.

His second sash was blue and was more or less the last keepsake to remind him of his wife. He had a wedding ring and even had mementos stashed in a chest but he had buried it ten years ago, for even pictures of her sent him into despair. The blue sash was once worn by her, and before her by *his mother Mary*, and its imprint of God *for him* kept him tuned into her faith as a sash or cloth of Veronica. It was his most treasured reminder of his beloved. He worshipped her more than the almighty which may have accounted for his tendering of a normal life in exchange for his beach bum's kind of an existence in an abnormal one.

Before his foray into battle for the survival of the sunburned, heat-stricken seafarers, he wrapped his forehead with his blood red red bandana, then began his work on the shipwrecked lot of United States' cargo; some very weary, come to old Cuba, new Cuba… American immigrants.

SEVEN

Two Good Dudes and Two Counter Souls, Two Bad Dudes

THE TWO STRONGEST MEN

The Beachcomber revived the *two strongest men* in the next twenty-four hour period, bringing shade, rations, and water to them around the clock. As the two men mended in physical condition, they help the Beachcomber with the remaining survivors until each was off the critical list. Two twin makeshift survivor *recovery huts* were built together side by side, using driftwood and tree branches and foliage to house the once near-dead. With this village made it gained a semblance of the living, even if just barely, as thinner ghosts, or shells, shells of boys who are men amid sorrow for the nine others who died out there in a freak accident that put them in a Robinson Crusoe-state time warp in this humble island country, just outside of Campechuela, Cuba.

The two good dudes, Cassius and Joe: Cassius Morman, a Creole with solid broad shoulders, was a quiet man who went about his duties, dutifully, like an officer of law following his father's footsteps. In his mind he would do what Pops would do. He kept silent like the timber of a man he was. He worked nightclubs as a bartender in San Francisco and came out from behind the bar if a fight broke out. But his main thing as a handsome bachelor and a brother of color was the babes and the skirts, or as he liked to call it, "Peace, Love and the American Dream of scattered-ass all around me." He could join the Force anytime but after the break up of his marriage, now he'd just go on and keep being single and have fun.

The other good man was Joseph Elliot. Once his chores were finished, after helping everyone all day up until sunset, he would make his evening's pilgrimage to the shoreline. The Beachcomber had seen the look in his eyes; the knowledge that he had left one out there.

For the Beachcomber knew best, he had already dragged all the others far enough away (their bodies covered up), to not to distract the living survivors for *seeing a dead soul* only served to kill the spirit of the living. This former military sergeant tidied up, and morning's tide brought hope to the man *Joe Elliot*. Waking up near the shoreline, Joe could, at least in this way, give thanks to the Beachcomber, and maybe keep his dream of seeing his brother again alive just a little longer.

When you speak of the two strongest men, certainly Beachcomber/ Santiago was one of them and of course Fidel Castro was definitely the other one, but this part of our story is not supposed to be about them. The exception however is for this one particular act that warrants a special honorable mention. It was one of the things he did to ensure his forty-year tenure that involved *"his complete and total control over the army."*

Here is some background that led up to this one particular act of Fidel Castro.

EIGHT

National Revolution Day

With the attack on Moncada Barracks and Garrison, 7/26/1953, Cuba marked the beginnings of Castro's revolution. The Beachcomber/Santiago was just nineteen years old and also one of the natural choices as a leader of men. He built some baby cribs for a family that was connected to Celia Sanchez's father. He made a deal with members of the revolutionary front to stay in business *as the furniture maker* who would upon occasion build *special projects* for the soldiers. This worked well for both parties as a secret ally to members of the revolutionary front. One comes to understand quickly that the average age of men serving in the rebel army was mostly younger. Beachcomber/Santiago was ranked as sergeant and, unbeknownst to almost anyone, created certain hand-made special devices for the rebels.

Keep in mind that beginning with the attack on Moncada Barracks, it took some seven long years until the triumph of the Victory March.

On New Year's Day, 1957, the rebel army was composed of just twenty-nine men. It was always a task to gather enlistees to take to the cause. It was mostly the peasants or the quajiros who had nothing to lose (or any young man who could be talked into it). They began joining up spirited on by a charismatic Fidel Castro's beliefs and their own desperation with the oppression of the Batista Regime. It was an easy choice, *albeit beset with its dangers,* to go along with the young idealist Castro who seemed to be the natural-born leader of the freedom for Cuba movement.

In a period of three more years, the brutal guerrilla war waged on while Fidel Castro's rebels chipped away at the far superior numbers of Batista's forces, using his vast knowledge of the jungled forests and mountains of the Sierra Maestra territory.

The rebel forces continued expanding and their numbers grew to 329 men before Batista launched Operation FF, *"fin Fidel"* to wipe out all the guerrilla rebels and the crafty revolutionary fox of a leader at its core. Batista dispatched fourteen battalions and armed forces numbering over 10,000 men to finish *Fidel Castro forever.*

With loudspeakers of *radio rebelde* hung from the trees broadcasting propaganda boasting of revolutionary pride, the 329-man rebel army, Fidel and Che, in <u>76 days of battle</u> wore down the fighting will of a far superior force.

After the shooting quelled in the mountains of Sierra Maestra, Che Guevara led the forces and took Santa Clara, while Fidel Castro led the offensive to take Santiago de Cuba. And now having won the will of the people to overtake Batista by beating back the entire army in the jungle... *the scent of victory was in the air.*

All of Cuba flooded into the streets to join Fidel Castro in the celebration of ending the long 25 years of brutality and torture by the corrupt dictator. The reign of the second coming of the Tropical Mussolini was finally over (Machadas being the first). All of Cuba's hopes and future rested squarely on the revolution and on the shoulders of its born leader, Fidel Castro.

At midnight on New Year's Eve, with his closest followers and supporting allies by his side, Fulgencio Batista quickly boarded a plane bound for the Dominican Republic, carrying the spoils of corruption along with him to the tune of a whopping $300 million in cash. Some reports say he had twice that amount, over $600 million on the plane that night. In either case, it was the motherlode. He eventually settled in Spain and lived the princely life as one of the world's wealthiest men until his death in 1973. He came a long way for a mulatto former cane-cutter from the sugar fields.

In the ultimate aftermath, the immediate bust was on the gambling and mob casinos. All of the gangsters and the mob were *booted out of Cuba as undesirable aliens.* The Tropical Gold Rush of the 1950s for the mob families had ended and with Castro's revolution firmly in place, it was now officially over.

Faced with a faltering economy and rampant disorganization everywhere, Fidel Castro nationalized the CTC–The Cuba Telephone Company–which *marked the beginning of confiscation of U.S. properties in Cuba.* Fidel Castro was invited to the United States but President Eisenhower, on a golfing vacation, left then-Vice President Richard Nixon to meet with Castro. Fidel Castro was warned about the dangers of any further confiscations. But the sweeping changes of the revolution were promises to the people of Cuba that Fidel Castro intended to keep. Eisenhower's snub of leaving Nixon to deal with Castro had its own price.

It started with all the U.S. banks, and then the umbrella included all the U.S. businesses, and later *the most dramatic land distribution*–among all the working classes, *radically altering ownership of large estates and sugar plantations.* The changes were vast, including everything from housing being constructed for the poor, to the additions of electricity and health care, and also education, and all of these things of course, would take some time. (Embittered rich Cubans became instant deeply-embittered poor Cubans.)

The Soviet Union set up a *huge commercial aid pact,* granting Cuba a 400 million dollar loan. It was set up after they had agreed to buy a million tons of sugar each year for the next four years.

The dealings with the Soviet Union continued to creep deeper into the political horizons for Cuba. Fidel Castro, in his speech on April 16, 1961, referred to their revolution in Cuba as *"socialist."* Then on December 2, 1961, the era of a *"socialist construction"* evolved into Castro's statement that he *"absolutely believed in Marxism,"* and that he *"had for quite some time."*

During those seven long years of the *impossible hell* that the guerrilla fighting war was for the rebels who fought so bravely in the Sierra Maestra, and since its beginnings at Moncada 7/26/1953, Fidel Castro was riddled with the belief that the United States would surely be back any day to invade Cuba, and take the country out from under him.

He swore to himself and to the people of Cuba that he would not let the imperialists take back what he and his revolutionary brothers had fought for, and died for, for so many oppressively arduous long years.

In order to prevent this from ever happening, and in seeking out a mighty helping hand, his full allegiance had now turned towards Soviet Russia.

Wrapping himself in the safety blanket of *Red Soviet Socialist Russia* and with the veil of Communism lurking about in the future of Cuba, Fidel Castro found himself safely hitched underneath the parental wing of Khrushchev and the Soviet Union.

It was under this wing that Fidel Castro would tactically plan to retain his control over Cuba and *total control over the army.* A part of that resolve also included liquidations in the Cuban Rebel Armed Forces. Here is what one of the strongest men would do to insure his control at the top spot.

After the January 3, 1959 victory march to Havana, there was a cleansing period, "Botar a Todas Los Osciosos."

Some of the older recruits who were leaning towards a challenge of Fidel Castro's leadership control had other ideas in mind for the future of Cuba. It was via a clandestine faction that the order was to be carried out and several members were kicked out of the Rebel Army, forcing them into exile or into trafficking and then later on into becoming Mafia Dons or the country's untouchables.

It was the *"cleansing of all the rotten eggs"* as it was referred to in English.

Many of the really rotten eggs were executed.

One such would-be head Don *in the making*, whom Castro expelled from the army, was named Juan Carlo Farshottia. He moved himself to Havana, leaving his two sons in Bayamo Oriente with their mother (who bitterly divorced him after his discharge under the scandals). He was a military washout who needed to go away and lay low for awhile, to wait for a new press to take over. It was like a whisper for those who dared to remain in the country who were known outcasts. Here was a man that was always endowed with a ploy and ever-present plans.

The two bad dudes: Two sons, two counter souls. Both Juanito and Roberto Farshottia were good looking Cubans. Their father's thick and dominant eyebrows, the prominent nose, and the lurking shoulders he possessed were endowed within both of the sons' body structure. They were always hungry looking, poised like reptilian monitors waiting to strike. It was born into their nature, inherited from their father.

They had a look that said *we are reptiles and we need to feed.* You automatically went on guard in their presence thinking you could possibly be their next meal.

It was the same hungry look that was the signature recognition factor often attributed to movie actor Lee Marvin.

Roberto Farshottia Jr. and Juanito Farshottia Jr. both grew up wild but it was Roberto, *the oldest* and the more ambitious, who was more fiercely determined toward winning or getting his way over the other kids in the neighborhood. He never missed an argument or a challenge or a confrontation to prove himself.

As for Juan Carlo Farshottia, his evils were mostly delegated to loyal underlings since he was a man who knew how to cover his own ass. His far reaching Army Intelligence and his roots of connections to sources left him prepared for multiple scenarios and eventualities. He plotted his deeds and covered his tracks. Juan Carlo was well acquainted with the coming changes in Cuba. He also had a hand in orchestrating some of them. Carefully, in his snake's belly-crawl he learned to *slither away after a kill or an action* that was carried out for him by his *"Juniors."* In his playing both sides of the revolution, he would go on to bigger and better deals. He planned for his own survival in case the American influence somehow failed. Whether or not Castro was overthrown, *he had a long-term plan* for staying in the game. And staying below the grid, off the radar.

Their mother wasn't much versed in the ways of teaching the boys any discipline. She was half Columbian and to her *it was a man's job to raise the boys.* Girls she could handle, but since the stork delivered her these two bad apples instead of oranges, she resented the boys as fruits of a poisonous tree. She left the two wily souls solely dependent upon their father's hand for upbringing and to know right from wrong. And Juan Carlo Farshottia was none too pleased or keen to do much about them for he was away quite a lot dealing in clandestine business; he was at best a patchwork of a father figure. The boys learned to wait till their father left, then they always proceeded to do whatever they wanted, which was the latent pattern for them almost all of the time.

Juan Carlo felt the Columbian blood from "her" side of the family was to blame whenever Roberto lost his temper and flew off the handle, which he did repeatedly. After awhile, the *"blow ups"* were becoming a pattern, and became even more frequent as time went on, blow ups unchecked. Roberto gained more *"madness clout"* than any of the other adolescents in the entire village of their neighborhood.

Pop-pete-toe blamed Moma-cete-toe and on and on it went, spiraling continuously more and more, and round and round as Roberto Farshottia Jr.'s head case temper became a recurring headache for Juan Carlo Farshottia Sr.'s tolerance levels, which kept on shrinking with all the evolving feculence with his dill pickle of a sour son.

Juan Carlo Farshottia Sr. eclipsed the point to where he thought he could mend the young rascal's turkey-tempered hardhead. His brick brain could never be molded into a shiny marbled tile of reason. He called his son by the name of *"The Percolator."* The phrase fit him well, named after the percolating Coffee Pot.

He blew his stack so frequently with the neighborhood kids, even kids bigger than he, that before long nobody dared to cross the Roberto Farshottia Jr. boy. Nobody wanted to see his top blow off at any given moment of aggravation or testing. No one wanted to deal with the half Columbian, blood-boiling pressure pot of little Roberto *The Percolator* Farshottia Jr. who was known as a virtual Cuban-Columbian Firecracker of a Kid.

His most famous *temper explosion* came at a baseball game at nine years old. The pitcher, who was ill-advised of his storied anger, *beaned him on the head,* and the hardball pitch hardboiled his numbskull to a fever pitch of contemptuously wild fury. Roberto stalked out to the mound with all due quickness and attacked and bat-whacked and whipped the pitcher down onto the ground, as the entire team tried to pull him off. When his sweat work was done, he put the kid in the hospital for six weeks. The other mothers took their sons home after that *too terrified* to let the game's outcome unfold. They had seen enough unbridled carnage on the baseball diamond. It was a Junior League performance of Al Capone at the dinner table.

Even though Juanito was the younger one, he was taller than Roberto. He was passive to the action, and and wore his hair uncropped and longer. It was in his eyes, too, and it seemed that nothing too much was going on behind them since he was not bothered by anything.

Here was an interesting paradox, whereas Roberto was the altogether percolator bothered by everything, with an explosive temper, Juanito was much more of a complex kettle to read.

Having been there every single time, and as a monitoring witness to his fierce brother's blow ups and brew-hah-hah episodes, he just learned to *arch an eyebrow of approval,* at whatever deed his crazy brother had done.

Standing there beside the acts of anger, what people could read and see of him was his devil-may-care *arched eyebrow of approval.* This trait made him an accomplice to his brother's bravado.

No one dared to cross either of them, even though, perhaps oddly enough, the percolator's brother, Juanito, never got into any of the fights or entered into the fray. He never had to prove himself; with a gay arch to his brow over any decadently mad behavior his brother would display, he was feared for his lack of passion. It was as if he had no feelings or remorse to the violence.

At least Roberto showed what his passions were at every chance. But like a stubborn barn owl who is sitting on the fence, Juanito didn't care one way or another. He was on his brother's side but all he had to do was watch.

Whether or not he had the cajones nobody knew, for his scrotum sack rode very close to the mantle.

———————

It was only a matter of time as the rescue planes had communicated with the ground patrols, and in a rare display of cooperation between Gitmo-Base Rescue and the Cuban Army, a battery of trucks and personnel carriers and heavy field equipment was dispatched, and finally descended upon the football team. As their new-found Hero, the Beachcomber had to smile a bit since he revived them and had literally taken them back from the brink of extinction. It was a bit of a linguistics nightmare as the Gitmo Base Rescue contingent tried to take all of the Americans to Guantanamo Base, but Lieutenant Juan Cortez used his sly amiable best self to influence the Marshall of the MPs (this particular Marshall had been to Havana before without his khakis and fatigues...ok. He knew J.C. better than he would admit to). A luxury hotel reception with liquor and booze flowing free and aplenty was a far better homecoming for the rescued team than just heading back to base camp barracks. Besides that, Juan Cortez was a very powerful persuasive personality.

It was a ploy to get the Americans; the MPs, who were only a party of about a dozen men (which was dwarfed by the Cuban troops' numbers), and Juan convinced the leader of the MPs to see it their way and cooperate with them. They had to because of those odds. But mainly, the calming force of Lt. Juan Cortez convinced the Marshall of MPs (plus that other secret aside) that they would chaperone them to the luxurious hotel where they would enjoy an open bar and some of the local color (and the ladies as good friendly company), which proved to be the extra nudge of a little bit of unzipping pleasure, or the final clincher of inducement *to get some pussy to go with their drinks*.

This time the Cuban side (not the U.S. contingent) would *run the show*, and would be the subsequent heroes' side of the story. I guess they learned with the Elián González immigration that they needed to control the emergence of the press from their point of view with regard to these American Castaways. It was an amazing millennium coup d'etat. It was time for Cuba to rate a few headlines again for a healthier story in some of the American newspaper presses. Cuba deserved their natural pride with a Cuban hero.

The Beachcomber and yacht survivors are rescued–his life had become changed. Beachcomber was thrust from Beach Bum to being absorbed in the annals of town–*A hero* from what was virtual obscurity for ten years, suddenly snatched out... and then, absorbed back into culture: *A folk hero of Cuba*. Everyone came to see him, from Castro to his former C.O. Lieutenant *"June"* Cortez (his mother named him), and although the Beachcomber knew him as June (his closest friends were permitted to call him that) the armies he still commanded knew him as Juan Cortez... the two men went way back.

Lt. Juan Cortez Ortega was of the highest caliber of reputation and respect and, perhaps one day, a possible successor for government office, if Castro chose it for him. Lt. J.C. Ortega had already refused higher office and rank as one of Castro's favorites. He preferred to contain his power to Lieutenant for his thirst to rule Cuba (one day) was not a job that he wanted for himself. He was a man who believed the country should rather wait until after Castro's passing. He was a man who believed the country should change for the better for her people, too. Hence he declined Castro's offers. He remained a favorite, even though he kept his mouth shut about Cuba's future, and his own future.

For himself, a true Patriot and a War Hero like the Beachcomber was always willing to *await his own destiny,* he knew it would be forthcoming in due time. So many of the Bad Dictators and False Kings of the past had too much blood on their hands. Castro was an important catalyst and right for Cuba in 1959, but forty years of Castro's ideals and his policies of trade and economics had forced many to believe that those ideals and also ideals of older passionate Marxism/Communism now needed to be "modified" to fit the current and more modern ideas of the century in trade and economics, to be more "world open." Many people now wonder how much more decaying the facades on these older buildings can take if the sad ideas or the repression lingers on more years.

A true leader of Cuba's people in the New Millennium would in fact have to be of the people and for the people, for Cubans and the Cuban quality of life would have to be improved in order for Cuba to thrive. Her people must be free and her leaders will have to find a way to bring the open free trade market back to Cuba. It's not anything at all to do with the past or what's been taken out of Cuba. It's to preserve what can be put back into Cuba and the Cuban people, to improve the quality of their lives and get into the pace with a more advanced and modern world of free trade. The reality of a Cuba that was to be frozen in time… must come to pass.

Cuba is a proud land of very hard working people and people who love life very much. The biding question among Cubans is, why not put more free enterprise back into Cuba? Let the people determine how much freedom *works in the modern world,* with a free trading economy, and travel access allowing her people to flourish in that trade. Fidel Castro can bring that prosperity while still remaining in the hearts and minds of Cuba's people (he could be a part of it). The doubt should be erased, *a clean slate is possible… as is his living within that policy,* to see that free trade and an open market works best for everyone.

It is a choice that only Fidel Castro can make. He controls the destiny and legacy for Cuba in the New Millennium. Cuban people fear <u>more of the same things are coming,</u> versus the arch of a growing prosperity of change. There is a long way to go, it looks like Cuba stopped and froze in 1959, forever riddled with buildings of decay. The road looks even longer… walking it today.

The American families came a few days afterward, their talk was always the same. A hero and their prayers, their embraces, the ever constant "thank yous" with warm handshakes and gripping hands of praise finally reaching out beyond their fears. It was overwhelming to the Beachcomber. His picture was in the newspapers and on the TV's evening news.

This celebrity wore thin quickly, but from his own past as a leader of men he knew that when so many lives were affected, it was the same as long ago, today's shadow of affection was the mirror of yesterday's similar shadow of affection.

He smiled throughout all this barrage of interest for he knew he would try to escape when the time came for him to do just that. It would come soon enough but the smiles he felt his own face reflecting were as real as could've been realized upon him, *for he hadn't worn one in many years.*

The Beachcomber saw no one and talked to no one for over ten years. He enchanted himself to harken back into a déjà vu of a recalling of his childhood, for this was an awakening, a rediscovery of people. He became the child in the crib again who watched his father making baby furniture all day long, seemingly to never tire. This experience was relit in his mind and came in through his eyes, as he watched the fathers and the mothers of those survivors... For he saw in them the same reflection, and although these were different lives, U.S. born to Cuba born, the emotions felt were the same.

They saw with eyes of understanding, they saw the light of a true hero. One who brought their children home from the brink of disaster. This was an eyeful of love and true emotions, *it's rare enough to see the love in their eyes.* The Beachcomber felt them all in a deeper place, for his own life resurfaced before him on these beautiful father's and mother's faces, parents of U.S. born children.

June Cortez, later that day, raised his glass and with all of the Lieutenant's epaulettes of signature glory, said what must be said: "Today I celebrate the legend of Santiago Dominguez, today a hero, forty years ago a hero. He was saving the lives of Cuba's people when we fought together on the beaches in 1961."

FLASHBACK INTO HISTORY

PART II

NINE

Playa Giron, La Victoria

BAY OF PIGS

NSC 5412 Special Group Forty S-GROUP 40

Manuel Artime / Carlos Prio Soccarras / Tony Varona

THE FRD / MIRR / OPERATION RESCATE / ALPHA 66

THE U.S.A. THE CIA BRIGADE 2506

FROM PLUTO TO MONGOOSE

In mid August 1958--three years of training concurrent with the 13 million dollars budget that was approved by Dwight Eisenhower--the CIA had 60 to 80 guerrillas infiltrated on the island, and CIA Operation Mongoose trained for air strikes out of Nicaragua--concentrated for targeting Cuban Military buildings. Once the invasion began, these strategic military buildings would be hit from the air in an effort to overwhelm the Cubans on the ground, the massive firepower would then scatter Castro's militia--leading to a wave of the Cuban soldiers defecting, which was crucial to CIA victory. The attack was planned for a Sunday in the middle of April 1961. To compliment the plan, the Eisenhower government would announce publicly the break off of diplomatic relations with Cuba on January 3rd, clearing the way for the invasion. In the Whitehouse, the most enthusiastic supporter of the plan was the republican Vice President Richard Nixon, recently defeated by the energetic young future star, democrat John F. Kennedy, in his bid for the presidency of the United States.

Gathering steam in six years, the Special Group Forty, group NSC #5412 (in existence from its inception March 15th, 1954) was blessed in its secret formation with herculean vastly unlimited financial backing. It did not have to answer to anyone. And, more importantly, all of its agenda meetings were without limits. The proof of this is dramatic when you google search NSC 5412 and read their concept manifest, the power base was vast under Allen Dulles and John Foster Dulles, with unlimited funding through Howard Hughes, Prescot Bush, and George Bush (a businessman at the time of its formation). Richard Nixon, Richard Bissell, General Robert Cushman, and Colonel Joseph C. King, Tracey Barnes, Ted Shackley, and Gordon Campbell, Gary Droller, and, also backed up by Frank Bender (General Boulding), Jack Engler, Jack Crichton, along with David Atlee Phillips, and

E. Howard Hunt. James Noel (CIA in Cuba), H.L.Hunt, Clint Murchison, George De Morehnschilt, and D. H. Bird, along with future members in George Bush's Administration Robert Mosbacher, and James Baker.

In the NSC 5412 nest: Richard Nixon was owned by these huge corporations. The massive financial base specifically included Pepsi Cola, Ford Motor Company, United Fruit Company, CTC--Bell Tel. Company, ASR American Sugar, Anaconda Refining Company, Standard Oil, and Zapata Oil (also CIA). Robert Bennett, Howard Hughes, Richard Nixon, Allen Dulles (CIA), Prescot Bush and George Bush (CIA). Richard Nixon was was directly connected to Carlos Marcello through his campaign manager Murray Chotiner. Richard Nixon was directly connected to Santos Trafficante through his Florida banker, Bebe Rebozo, which is the layer connection to Florida real estate, The Keyes Royalty. The Keyes Royalty was a CIA front company that also laundered its funds to these CIA agents and to their Cuban mercenary soldiers. In no particular order they were Eugenio Martinez, Bernard Barker, Frank Sturgis, David Atlee Phillips, David Morales, Orlando Bosch, Raphael Quintero, Rolando Masferrer, Johnny Roselli, Anthony Veciana, Pedro Diaz Lanz, Herminio Diaz Garcia, and E. Howard Hunt. (Frank Sturgis, Pedro Diaz Lanz, E. Howard Hunt, and also Bernard Barker, were the partners in Cuba.) The above mentioned lot had one goal, win back a billion dollar business and to overtake control of the Government inside Castro's Cuba.

In *Z R Rifle* Claudia Furiati reported information from the Cuban Secret Files (Ocean Press 1994) from inside this Cuba base, the political leader evolved, and Manuel Artime was chosen by E. Howard Hunt, and David Atlee Phillips as political director of the invasion. Page 17, and Page 18, *Z R RIFLE*; "At the Miami base the Revolutionary Democratic Front (FRD) was formed. And, among the political figures heading up this exile coalition were: Manuel Antonio de Varona, one of the leaders of the Partido Autentico Party (Authentic Party) which was in power in the two administrations preceding the 1952 coup by Batista (those of Ramon Grau San Martin, and Carlos Prio); and Manuel Artime Buesa, founder and head of the organization called Movimento de Recuperacion Revolucionaria (Revolutionary Recovery Movement, M R R). Howard Hunt chose agent Bernard Barker as his principal assistant for coordinating the F R D, and setting up houses for clandestine meetings. Barker was a U.S. citizen of Cuban origin who had served as a spy in Batista's police force, and had been the link up with Manuel Artime. Also on the Miami base was Frank Sturgis (Fiorini), a special CIA agent. He had struck up a friendship with former Cuban President Carlos Prio, who was linked to the U. S. citizens who ran the gambling casinos in Havana and who now lived in Miami, and was eager to return to power. Through Carlos Prio, Frank Sturgis had infiltrated Cuba at the end of August 1958, in the company of a Cuban pilot, Pedro Diaz Lanz.

His plane was destroyed and the following month he was able to slip back off the island with the help of the U.S. Vice Counsul in Santiago de Cuba, the CIA official Robert Wiecha. Preparing for a new trip in November 1958, Frank Sturgis and Pedro Diaz Lanz were detained in Mexico. The tide had turned inside Cuba, and gaining ground now it was Castro's time to rise.

A few days after the triumph of the 1959 revolution, Pedro Diaz Lanz was named the first head of the Cuban air force, and there is information which indicates that Frank Sturgis then attained the rank of captain in the same branch of the service. In September 1959 Sturgis fled Cuba, and the following month he returned to bomb the city of Havana, alongside the deserter Pedro Diaz Lanz. In April 1960, Frank Sturgis began direct International Anti-Communist Brigades, a phantom organization that ran a network of safe houses, some naval operations, clandestine infiltration on the island, and training the anti Castro Cubans in weapons and explosives. In August 1960 after all of this--the company was pushing hard now--for two years and not gaining enough momentum to inspire a popular uprising, and then, finally deciding instead to emphasize the external factor--the formation of the CIA expeditionary Brigade-- based in Guatemala. What gave way and occurred during the early days of Fidel Castro's revolution was the type of espionage counter indicative and counter revolutionary tactics from CIA men like E. Howard Hunt, Bernard Barker, Anthony Veciana, Frank Sturgis, and Pedro Diaz Lanz. Multiple in-fighting and disputes were ongoing among all these participants, who were in this all consuming battle, jockeying for their political positions while plans are being laid, so the CIA began to assign posts to these men linked to Antonio Varona and Manuel Artime, naming them with assignments so to speak, for the structuring, or the restructuring, and the coordination of posts, to emerge--inside Cuba once they took back-- their beloved country.

As odd as it may sound, Manuel Artime's M R R, a force of 160 Cuban mercenaries, were part of a highly dubious pre-planned attack on the U.S. Naval Base at Guantanamo, under the command of Higinio Diaz, who had deserted Castro's rebel army. The militia men who were being used were trained in New Orleans, Louisiana. They were going to disembark in the area of Baracoa, pretending to be revolutionary troops, and stage a false flag operation by advancing on the base with "on island organizers of the attack." The force grew in size to number between 600-750 men who were getting stale (even with brothels to keep the men inside these camps), having been in preparations now over 2 years. This became the sizable portable detonator force under the command of Nino Diaz. The manpower trained by CIA in New Orleans was what was to become the counter revolutionary track force similarly like the republican guards, that would then unite with Cuban exiles, once the over throw of Fidel Castro was under way. This group was separate from Brigade #2506 forces that numbered some 1,500 men, who were to be led by Pepe San Ramon during the Bay Of Pigs invasion against Fidel Castro. To keep the American involvement under wraps with FRD / Alpha 66 members undisclosed--names were changed and false identifications were given to any Americans--however to be later found out or captured--whom were all-- embedded with either group. This U.S. hand, no matter how hard they tried to deny it, was clearly in the hundreds. The breakdown went as follows: 750 Men FRD / Alpha 66, 1,500 Brigade #2506 Men, 70 Para Troopers, 86 Men under Raphael Garcia Rubio (CIA trained in Panama), 100 Air America pilots trained by U.S. / CIA. In all, the CIA was now directly responsible for the lives of all these militia, numbering some 2,506 Militia Men, that would be the mercenary CIA trained armed forces, landing on the beach at Playa Giron once the invasion began. (Two extreme forces were at work boiling up in a pressure cooker, the army was set ready to explode and go off.) This is an extreme firecracker and bandits secret militia FRD / Alpha 66 on the ground inside Cuba, and then the other CIA right winged mercenaries (run exclusively by the CIA interests, directly from room #5412 inside of the Whitehouse... Richard Nixon's / Howard Hughes / Allen Dulles... Special--Operation Group 40). That same group (he feared trying to control them as did a lot of others involved,) was referred to as The God Damned Murder Incorporated In The Caribbean, historically by Lyndon Johnson, at that time.

To move things forward in a speedier time frame rather than wait on the coordination in the bickering factions inside the FRD and Alpha 66 because Cuba was becoming very hard to manage and train and in building any rigid foundation, or the alignment... with shifting sands of time, and still keeping within the shrouds of any secrecy... on the islands exile members, since Fidel Castro was paranoid; and he truly had his Cuban, and Soviet spies, plugged into the streets and he had spying eyes and ears on everybody, everywhere.

The accelerated process began. Richard Nixon took the defeat in a very close U.S. election very hard. He had made commitments to some very powerful people who had spent millions funding his 1960 election campaign. Nixon now owed them all some of that money back. The mafia connections tied to getting Havana gambling and huge corporate interests. (Cuba represented over a billion dollars in lost revenue if indeed the rebel fidelistas, or the fly in the ointment--Fidel Castro's led regime--was not eliminated, before it had any chances to gather up any more of a foothold, or any roots and any head of steam.) Nixon's entire financial backing would surely dessert any losing politician...they would all certainly leave him forever if he could not find a way out of his debt to these men. Therefore, Nixon, was owned by these powerful corporations, Pepsi Cola, Ford Motor Company, United Fruit Company, Standard Oil, Zapata Oil Drilling, The Howard Hughes Corporation, Anaconda, and A.S.R. Refining Co. Nixon had to put his foot on the accelerator or his political career would be cancelled, since he could not ever get elected again with John Kennedy getting a possible second term, or his brother Robert Kennedy, following up with his terms as the president. He re-joined with his CIA partners Allen Dulles, John Foster Dulles, Howard Hughes and Prescot Bush, who appointed the former Vice President Nixon and the former CIA action officer--Nixon to the head of a more powerful position than any U.S. presidency: the leader of The Special Group--40. The NSC #5412. (Richard Nixon was available to run a post that was actually more powerfully connected than the United States presidency.)

Arguably this was a fact. As a CIA proponent. As the head of Special Group 40. The leader of NSC #5412. The post had benefits of his financial backer's whims. (He was paid handsomely well with nobody to answer to either.) Hence the evolution of the secret--Special Group 40 / Committee 5412 / NSC 5412. Nixon now ran the powerful elite force...this major group inside the Whitehouse...where they all met inside the Room #5412. "First things first," Nixon's first order of business was " we got to get rid of this son of a bitch rebel and that communist Fidel Castro." [Executive Action Began].

The handwritten memo--under the stewardship of the Special Group 40 / NSC 5412 / Richard Nixon--directed Mr. Richard Bissell, supported by Allen Dulles who quickly approved of the mid-December recommendation by the head of the agency's Western Hemisphere Division, Joseph C. King, to consider the elimination of Fidel Castro. All of this is readily confirmed by Nixon's closest military aid--General Robert Cushman--who essentially, named Richard Nixon as the S-Group Forty / NSC 5412 / Committee #5412 defining Nixon as the said projects CIA action officer in the Whitehouse. "We've got to get that damned--bearded rebel leader, who hypnotically attracts all of the masses--down there, in all of Cuba." Also present with Mr. Nixon in room #5412 were General Robert Cushman, Richard Helms, Allen Dulles, Desmond Fitzgerald, Charles Cabell, and also the General Lyman Lemnitzer.

Dwight Eisenhower witnessed proceedings that were once cautious in the beginning, but as soon as IKE left his Whitehouse seat in office, and as soon as JFK was later sworn in, these Nixon directives changed into some brash "fiercely proactive activities" as it was reported later by Colonel L. Fletcher Prouty. Under orders from the "S-Group #5412," from room #5412--through Nixon to Bissell--came a Military mission from both CIA Richard Helms, and top brass Desmond Fitzgerald--wherein he piloted a light plane, an L-28 Helio Courier that only needed 120 feet to land, to transport two Cubans home with a high power snipers rifle, with a telescope which was to be used to kill Castro. To Richard Bissell, Fidel Castro's assassination offered a realistic solution to a very major problem to the Agency. He said in his memoirs, "the last two or three years in the agency... that my philosophy was very definitely... the end justified the means." Keep in mind that the CIA Task

Force--would report to Richard Bissell--as the head of the clandestine operations. He was answerable to the CIA Director Allen Dulles, and also to Richard Helms, and his deputy director, General Charles Cabell. And, the CIA was answerable to the new president JFK, who at this point in time had not even been sworn in yet. In effect the CIA had been rolling their thunder ball of a plan since 1958. Kennedy had met with the Cuban leaders at his beach house in Florida. He had whipped Nixon in the last TV debate which focused on foreign policy, and also on Cuba. But he was ill prepared for what Nixon, and Bissell, and Dulles were planning the invasion, against all odds; they had to take over Cuba, or they stood to lose over a billion dollars. (Nobody wanted dealings with this guerrilla leader who had spent the last 4 yrs. in the Sierra Maestra Mountains.)

Supply ships had been loaded. Some vessels traveled and moved into positions closer to the targeted areas. And as all this went on under clandestine operations the vessels were quietly moved into position without drawing any attention to the manifest of arms, weaponry, and, their military cargo, that they held stowed below the decks. As with the movement of amphibious hardware. A businessman at that time, George Bush, had financed three of the ships to be used during the invasion. In the early 1960s the cost of putting all of these guns and hardware and equipment was in excess of 46 million dollars. Next with that aspect, and these ships sailing or already in motion, Colonel Frank Eagan was sent down to evaluate the troops, and he quickly declared that "the militia possesses adequate leadership and training." Even though roughly only 20 per cent of these Cuban forces had actual military combat experience. They were buoyantly confident that the massive firepower they had (packed away inside these supply ships were over 25,000 weapons in reserve guns and ammunition, to arm possibly 25,000 defectors, once the fighting began) it was the largest combat and military transport ever undertaken to a landing in Latin America.

The CIA believed that the overwhelming equipment and this firepower deployed, would scatter Castro's lightly equipped guerillas and lead to a wave of defections crucial to victory in Playa Giron. To the CIA planners like Richard Bissell, and General Robert Cushman, and General Charles Cabell, and Tracey Barnes, Colonel Joseph C. King, and CIA top men like Desmond Fitzgerald, Gary Droller, Edward Lansdale, and, General Lyman Kirkpatrick, and Frank Sturgis, carrying exactly 25,000 in arms to the CIA / Brigade 2506 invasion forces, all these numbers made a lot of sense, since estimated numbers inside Fidel Castro's Army were just about the same in the Cuban Army... that they were matched up against enemy-wise. The CIA estimates were believed to be in alignment with... a numbering force of about 25,000 men, in Cuba's army. (Ideally enough weapons to arm all the Cubans whom CIA believed would join up with them once... their on the island landing... invasion began.)

Not just the two dicks up at the top of the impending future CIA fiasco, along with Richard "Dick" Bissell, and Richard "Tricky Dick" Nixon, the entire CIA apparatus went ahead with the plans which were long odds, or, dicey at best to say the least (maybe it went downward towards 50/50 for the odds against invasion's success at the outset).

In the wrap up stage prior to invasion: The men directly involved with NSC 5412 / S-GROUP 40 / Nixon's Secret team were: Howard Hughes, Robert Maheu, Sheffield Edwards, General Robert Cushman, Desmond Fitzgerald, and Allen Dulles, Prescot Bush, George Bush, Bernard Barker, J. Edgar Hoover and E. Howard Hunt. Hoover and Nixon's alliance was cemented at numerous rendezvous meetings held annually at the Hotel Del Charro, in La Jolla. Alongside in the NSC 5412 "nest" were the names associated with Nixon during his presidency, all the way up through Watergate until his untimely departure and resignation. Frank Sturgis, Virgilio Gonzalez, Eugenio Martinez, and also E. Howard Hunt. The other men connected to NSC 5412 / S-GROUP 40 directives inside Cuba, and during the Bay Of Pigs are David Sanchez Morales, David Atlee Phillips, Pedro Diaz Lanz, Herminio Diaz Garcia, Raphael Quintero, Thomas Eli Davis, Tony Izquierdo, Anthony Veciana, Rolando Masferrer, Orlando Bosch, Eladio del Valle, Manuel Artime, Roland Cubella, Tony Varona, Ted Shackley, Felix Rodriquez, Joaquin Sanjenis, George Johannides, and Santos Trafficante. (As reported in *Z R RIFLE*, Nixon referred to this group... on the Whitehouse tapes... as "The Cubans.")

The Money Men Behind This Secret Team Were: (some names are repeated here in this no-controls-whatsoever huge cash operation) Mr. Prescot Bush, George Bush, Howard Hughes, Tracey Barnes, Joseph C. King, backed up by Frank Bender (General Boulding) with CIA's William King Harvey, Edward Lansdale, Guy Bannister, Clay Shaw, Jack Crichton, Bobby Baker, Jake Engler, D.H. Bird, H.L.Hunt, Clint Murchison, John Foster Dulles, Robert Mosbacher, James Baker, George de Morhenschildt, and General Charles Cabell. (As reported in *Z R RIFLE*--Nixon referred to this group... on the Whitehouse tapes... as "The Texans.")

Z R Rifle Program / The Task Force W / Operation Mongoose / Also Operation Rescate / Pluto. William King Harvey was the original organizer. The CIA went into high gear with assassination plots; flying assassins into Cuba (who failed), developing a poison capsules plan, and an array of attempts to kill Fidel Castro before the invasion. All went awry (as we know). Under the CIA's direct orders from Richard Bissell, Robert Maheu contacted through his mafia connections Johnny Roselli, and, Jim Oconnell, and, Sheffield Edwards were all meeting regularly Santos Trafficante, and Sam Giancana. Joseph Schreider developed the poison capsules and it's through Joseph C. King and Tony Varona (FRD) Authentic Party. The last president of the Cuban Senate, who was part of the administration during Carlos Prio Soccarras (1948 through 1952). It's been reported over the years so many times and the story never gets better with each retelling. The Boom Boom Room/ Tony Varona/ Alberto Cruz Caso: met with Johnny Roselli, Robert Maheu (the CIA liaison through Sheffield Edwards and with Jim Occonnell) as the Floyd Patterson versus Ingemar Johansson (3/11/1961) boxing match went on in the background. Santos Trafficante and Sam Giancana present, Maheu took the cash payment from a suitcase giving $10,000 dollars to Varona, who took the poison capsules and the cash. Oddly as these steps were played out the same mafia men had already given Varona, one million dollars? Rescate would find the right person and there were the flights... from Miami to Havana every 45 minutes... and to get it right to the correct cell, into one of the proper hands of Santos Trafficante's employees, at the Havana Libre Hotel Casino. Plan's details told them: Fidel Castro regularly visited "The Peking" and the "Hotel Libre," attending to important guests. The plans failed miserably. The nights of both April 13th and April 14th, calls from Maheu to Roselli were dispatched but Varona had been ordered to confine to barracks the new government of Cuba to avoid leaks and have them on hand (in these events confusion, by not being able to communicate with Opalocka, Roselli could not find Varona) the agency strategy of compartmentalization, the security of plans, contributed to the collapse of Pluto and Rescate.

To Commence Battle With Fidel Castro The CIA Would Go To Its Deepest Depths: The Bay Of Pigs. This event was the nightmare moment for CIA.

Along with the men Pepe San Ramon would lead the brigade 2506 (there were militia support that would raise these numbers to more than 2,500 men, that were going to be engaged on the ground inside Cuba) and it was a secret invasion; a covert operation which was going to be extremely dangerous, and filled with peril. The investments were to win back the country, and to win back control of a billion dollar empire; the stakes were very high, along with the risk for failure which was not on the minds of the CIA officers based in Miami, New Orleans and Washington D.C. Alpha 66 / Brigade 2506 / The FRD / NSC 5412 / S-GROUP 40 / Richard "Dick" Nixon / Richard "Dick" Bissell. William "King" Harvey, Richard Helms, Allen Dulles, David Atlee Phillips, E. Howard Hunt, Frank Sturgis, Anthony Veciana, Orlando Bosch, Manuel Artime, Tony Varona, and David Sanchez Morales, Bernard Barker, Pedro Diaz Lanz, David Ferrie, Guy Banister, Clay Shaw, Jacob Esterline, Grayston Lynch, Joseph C. King, William Robertson, Herminio Diaz Garcia, Tracey Barnes, Cord Meyer, Edward Lansdale, Gen. Lyman Kirkpatrick, and Desmond Fitzgerald. The consequences were high for this group of formidable men "they were destined to win and of course failure was not an option."

"The Pigs and the President End Up In the Basket"

The Bay of Pigs is likely the one greatest flukes in history and is perhaps improperly named and remembered in U.S. history books. The battlefield was Playa Giron. If you take away the translation, it was a counterrevolution backed and conceived by the United States and the CIA. In Cuba, the Cubans refer to it as The Battle of Playa Giron, or La Victoria *"The Victory"*.

It was the brainchild vision of Richard Bissell, then Deputy Director of the Central Intelligence Agency. The plan was for a force of anti-Castro guerrillas to infiltrate the island so that they could link up with Castro's domestic opponents. "The Program of Covert Action Against the Castro Regime" called for the creation of a Cuban Government in Exile, and "covert action on Cuban soil," and also a *"paramilitary support force outside of Cuba, for future guerrilla mercenary action."*

Back in August 1958, then President Eisenhower approved a $13 million budget with the provision that: *No U.S. Military personnel were to be used in combat status*. The CIA recruited Cuban exiles and set up a training ground at an abandoned Naval base at Opa-locka, outside of Miami, to train the brigade. The cost was much higher than this figure, of course, but the costs were spread out and ballooned over the next three years. The trainees were later moved to U.S. military locations in Guatemala (replete with brothels to keep the men in camp), and also in Puerto Rico, in violation of U.S. laws. *"The Government In Exile"* was chosen from within the Frente, an uneven but dedicated group of political exiles prone to feuds and conflicts who were between extremes in ideals, including some corrupt souls on the right wing who longed for the old Batista Days. This rebel brigade would later on be transformed into a provisional, if makeshift, government once they gained their foothold on Cuban soil. The brigade became a force of 1,500 mercenaries that were... mostly Cuban exiles now based in Miami.

On January 26th, 1960, Kennedy met with the Joint Chiefs of Staff to discuss his options and review the plans of the invasion. There were two scenarios: the so called *"Trinidad Plan"* which was scrapped in favor of the *"Playa Giron"* based attack, where the brigades would land at three beaches some twelve miles apart, surrounded by swampland. The belief was that a great percentage of Cuban Army officers were ready to rebel against the existing government at any given moment, and would take their troops with them to desert Castro's regime, and join up with the invading Cuban exiles.

Kennedy was ignorant of key aspects of the operation: according to the CIA's plan, the brigade was meant to be little more than a portable detonator, and would be insufficient by itself. The internal support for the invasion on the island of Cuba had been knocked out, dictating that air attacks by U.S. forces would be indispensable. JFK was also kept in the dark about the biggest secret of Operation Zapata, in place since Pluto: that CIA operatives were to dispatch the brigade at any cost, since the military chiefs at the Pentagon had guaranteed military action after the invasion. They deduced that, faced with the pressure of the moment, Kennedy would end up authorizing military support in order to avoid humiliation.[1]

In photos by U-2 spy planes, the CIA's intel-interpreter identified what he thought was seaweed offshore. A frustrated brigade member, Dr. Juan Sordo, told the man *"they are the coral heads."* He continued to plead with him, *"I know them well... for I have seen them... myself."* Another brigade member agreed with Dr. Sordo and basically told them, "the water's too shallow for a landing." But the CIA had their plan and presidential approval from John F. Kennedy. Asking for more time to come up with another idea, or plan, was risking... that John F. Kennedy would scrap the entire junket... altogether.

Castro knew the layout of the terrain intimately. In November of 1960, he visited the locale of the Giron site for a possible development of a New Community Center that included also a hotel and recreational facility. At that point he turned to a Cuban journalist and said, "you know this would be a great place for a landing... I think we should place a fifty caliber machine gun here... just in case." Castro, ever the quick-thinking military-minded leader, had the weaponry in place and it later fired the first shots of defense against the US-backed invasion force.

In the weeks leading up to the invasion, the site had been flown over by reconnaissance missions *so regularly,* Castro knew that something was amiss. His restlessness resulted in round-ups of suspected counter-revolutionaries and those suspected of activities on the ground. Ironically, four days before the U.S. backed invasion, Castro ordered a battalion moved to Playa Giron, but the order wasn't processed and it took too long to be carried out, and the battalion didn't arrive. The U.S. invasion relied on eliminating the Cuban Air Force–U.S. planes with Cuban decals painted over their markings bombed the Cuban Air Forces–on April 15th, *two days before the actual invasion*. Castro was forewarned and ironically only *five Cuban aircraft* were taken out in the bombing raid.

Castro's Air Force still had three Soviet-made T-33 jet fighters, and four British-made Sea Fury attack bombers. The Air Force was still active, thus making the next phase of the operation almost academic; it was literally the last chance for Meyer Lansky, Santos Trafficante, Carlos Marcello, Amleto Batistti, and Amadeo Barletta to ever return to mine the fortunes they had built up in Cuba.

Batistti and Barletta would move on from here but Meyer Lansky, Santos Trafficante, and Carlos Marcello were feeling betrayed by their own U.S. president. The Rebel brigade was the only chance they had to make a comeback in Cuba. Joe Kennedy's previous ties to the prohibition trade of rum-running gave reason for this old guard of Mafia bosses to believe they could exert force upon those channels to the president's father; by possibly

---

[1]   ZR RIFLE pg#28, Claudia Furiati; Ocean Press, Talman Company. 1992—Paperback Edition—Cuba Open's Secret Files.

reminding him of who helped him out in the past *getting him rich in business,* during those prohibition years, etc.

The U.S. Navy's aircraft carrier Essex and five armed destroyers were to escort six freighters that were loaded up, carrying all the Cuban fighters and their supplies. The whole force moved in radio silence. The landings began about 1:15 a.m. on April 15th, 1961. The landing crafts (LCVPs) were now roaring towards the shoreline of Playa Giron–The Bay Of Pigs–but just before they got there U.D.T. scuba diving frogmen in lifeboats ran re-con on the beach, led by William "Rip" Robertson, who was active in CIA executive action Z.R. RIFLE programs inside Latin America against foreign leaders. The CIA hand, and Nixon's hand "all in."

Keeping in mind Allen Dulles had the green light from Dwight Eisenhower, and JFK inherited the impending CIA covert operation (beyond the programs 13 million dollar opening budget, and its projected 46 million more dollars for Brigade 2506 in its aftermath costs); it was Richard Nixon's "all in" gamble. He was S-GROUP 40 / NSC 5412 / along with Allen Dulles the leader of CIA in concert with Richard Nixon, and Allen Dulles, and also with Richard Bissell (the CIA was attempting the most audacious covert clandestine enterprise... ever attempted in Latin America... to grab back control from Castro over a billion dollar Cuban economic empire). The men who were in it with Nixon and Dulles were as formidable a group ever assembled in military history. William "King" Harvey, Charles Cabell, General Robert Cushman, and Desmond Fitzgerald, General Lyman Kirkpatrick, and, Lyman Lemnitzer, Joseph C. King, and Tracey Barnes, and Gary Droller, and Ted Shackley, Raphael Quintero. The deepest waters requiring the CIA's best soldiers and operatives, like Edward Lansdale, E. Howard Hunt, Bernard Barker, Frank Sturgis, Grayston "Gray" Lynch, William "Rip" Robertson, Herminio Diaz Garcia, Pedro Diaz Lanz. Along with the background men in support below Thomas Mann (the Mexico Ambassador–United Fruit Company–UNFCO), Anthony Veciana, Rolando Masferrer, Tony Cuesta, Gordon Campbell, John Martino, Bradley Ayres, Orlando Bosch, Eladio Del Valle, David Sanchez Morales Thomas Eli Davis (ZR Rifle), Manuel Rodriquez Quesada, Gilberto Rodriquez Hernandez, and Nestor Tony Izquierdo. The level of players including CIA and Alpha 66, and Brigade 2506, and Air America was a very lethal mix of mercenaries and extremely... deadly shooters... Richard "Dick" Nixon's NSC 5412–S GROUP 40–CIA link; the CIA action officer, whose in charge... whose sole job was to get rid of Fidel Castro... by any means necessary.

The proof of this leadership by Dick Nixon with his connection to the Bay Of Pigs / Brigade 2506 / Alpha 66 / and the CIA is well documented in numerous visits to Cuban mercenary militia men. Also, several well documented Nixon visits with Cubans and Frank Sturgis in Miami at various hotels. In *THE BAY OF PIGS*, Howard Jones wrote that prior to The Bay Of

Pigs Invasion; "On April 13th, at Puerto Cabezas, a man referred to as "Mr. Dick" joined Colonel Frank Eagan, and other Americans, at the last briefing of the doctor's and the brigade's staff, and all of the battalion leaders... just before the embarkation... for Cuba. "

"Mr. Dick had been there at least a couple of times before, clearly the highest person in charge." Under a steamy morning sun, they sat at two wooden tables before a blackboard, to go over final details with the tall and angular man in glasses–Richard Bissell as the Cuban's had suspected it was. After a second round of meetings, in the afternoon Pepe San Ramon had declared that Frank Eagan "assured us, that we were going to have protection by sea, by air, and even from under the sea." The U.S. Navy, the Brigade forces were convinced, would support this invasion. "Most of the Cubans who were there," Pepe San Ramon asserted, "because they know the whole operation was going to be conducted by the Americans, not by me, or anyone else. They did not trust me, or, anyone else. They just trusted the Americans. So, they were going to fight, because the United States was backing them." (Nixon and Bissell's presence guaranteed that Pepe and his comrades weren't going to be alone during invasion.) It's now known...today, Nixon was there.

Incorrect CIA-gathered intel was to reflect a vastly different battlefield at the Blue Beach, and for the special forces soldier Grayston Lynch, who was a WWII Normandy veteran, and also a Heartbreak Ridge warrior over in Korea, known as "Gray" to his men. The 2506 / Alpha 66 / CIA led landing site was lit up like Coney Island. The first sign of the CIA's faulty intel had caused men in the clandestine operation to shit a brick, "they were seeing this construction crew–and their families were building this vacation mecca resort–who were all stationed there." In Playa Giron they were living on the site, where multiple buildings were scheduled to be opening up in summer. To add insult to injury, far worse was that on the very night of the landing a party was ongoing that was spilling out onto the beach they were invading... booze and music blaring... and a bunch of drunken Cubans partying away.

Gray and his U.D.T. landing frogmen team had to drift further from the original site... and soon his boats were hitting the coral heads... forcing him and his team to paddle or wade their way over the shoreline obstructions in the rough coastal terrain. Previously the U.D.T. had installed marking lights which started blinking and suddenly turning on. The strobe lights "attracted attention from shore." Two militia men in a jeep and a young teacher were looking over the tourist area under construction. Gray ordered his men to lay flat on the raft, but the jeep had aimed headlights to the unknown raft in the dark, attempting effort to aid or to help... the floating drifter; thinking as if it was a strayed fishing boat, or a surviving defecting Cuban who didn't surpass the currents–on their way--to Miami. Then combat instincts took over. Gray pumped his BAR, firing with a barrage of bullets at that jeep's location... the first shots onto the Cuban shoreline of the Bay Of Pigs were fired at the vehicle. The firing rounds wounded the teacher. The two militia men actually escaped injury. Both fled the beach to warn their superiors. (Later.) Within hours the word reached the top. And, from that point on Fidel Castro was alerted... the CIA led invasion had started. The mark of how badly things could go only escalated with every single hour of The Bay Of Pigs CIA invasion. Gunfire, triggered this earlier warning to Castro which put an enormous pressure on these landing forces... to move further inland... before the enemy combat would severely cripple the movements of arms, equipment, and men.

The Cubans called him "the alligator," based on his rough sun-dried scaly skin, even more daunting was his real name, William "Rip" Robertson; he was the leader at the Red Beach landing. A Texan. A Marine. A WWII Vet. A military man with combat insurgency expertise, with multiple CIA executive action missions under his belt. The truth being told, written by Howard Jones, *THE BAY OF PIGS*; As at Red Beach. As at Blue Beach. The first person hitting the beach was an American, who engaged in a firefight. But involvement in Cuba was not new to "Rip" Robertson. A month prior to the Bay Of Pigs invasion he had participated in a sabotage operation on a cuban oil refinery. Bissell had told the president the truth. There wasn't "a white face on the beach," (there were two). The Red Beach landing struggled at the outset. Only 270 of the 399 men in the 2nd Battalion made it ashore because of enemy fire combined with mechanical and planning problems. Machine guns sprayed "Rip" Robertson's reconnaissance boat, killing one of his men. Seven of nine landing craft developed engine trouble, leaving 2 boats carrying nine men in each to repeatedly make the twenty minute run to the sand and, after another mishap, only one boat left at the end. The boats were not the type needed, bitterly complained one officer. "They looked like speed boat's made for water skiing."

None of the 5th Battalion's men had made it into the water. All 180 forces remained on the Houston, ordered not to land by their commander, Montero Duque. Like his men, he stood frozen in fear, pointing to engine troubles in the aluminum landing boats and preferring to await until daylight. When "Rip" Robertson hurriedly boarded the ship and hotly demanded an explanation, Duque just as hotly responded, that his men lacked enough ammunition, that his landing craft were not reliable, and that Castro might have artillery. "Look Mister," shouted Robertson in disgust, "it's your war and your country not mine. If you're too scared to land and fight then stay here, and rot." And, Montero Duque would not budge. Nor did any of his men.

Thus the invasion at Red Beach posed no real threat to Castro's legions. Small in manpower, it carried only two days' worth of supplies that included four 81-mm mortars, four light machine guns, and four 57-mm recoilless rifles, along with rocket launchers, grenades, and BARs. Furthermore, Castro had been aware of their landing, beforehand. Close to the beach sat an abandoned radio station with the switches on and the apparatus still warm. The Brigade angrily destroyed the entire network, although knowing all along that it was too late. Contrary to intelligence reports, Castro's communication system extended to the beaches around the Bay Of Pigs. The CIA had been wrong again.

As daylight broke, Castro's air assault at Red Beach began with a flurry. A B-26 machine gunned the Barbara J, disabling two engines, and coming close to sinking it with another burst, before retaliatory fire downed the plane on its third pass. Another B-26 swept by several times, its bombs missing both vessels, but a Sea Fury followed, strafing and firing rockets that hit the Houston close to its waterline, killing two while wounding five. The worst news was yet to come, however, for a T-33 jet zoomed onto the scene, this time surprisingly firing rockets that barely missed the Barbara J. but twice struck the Houston. The Barbara J. however, had suffered a split seam from the rockets' percussion and took on more water, and the Houston lost its steerage and started to sink. Fire broke out on the Houston, raging out of control below and threatening to kill everyone aboard. The crew could neither put out the fire nor escape. The ship's fire hoses had been torn apart by the enemy's machine guns, and one of its only two lifeboats had rotted from disuse.

As another Sea Fury resumed the attack, the captain frantically struggled to maneuver the burning hulk toward shore while gas seeped into the water and surrounded both ships, in what would soon become a deadly ring of fire. About a hundred yards out, many of the more than two hundred men jumped overboard in life jackets; up to twenty of them were killed in the water by strafing, while another ten or more either drowned, or fell victim to sharks. The Houston ran aground over on the western side of the bay as its survivors frantically scampered onto Red Beach, only to confront a storm of militia fire that scattered them into the swamp. Montero Duque and his men had finally made it to shore–though--not by choice.

At this point, the focus shifted back to Blue Beach, where three hours later a Sea Fury closed in to three hundred feet and fired four rockets at the Rio Escondido. Three missed, but one hit its bridge near two hundred barrels of aviation gasoline on deck, setting the ship afire. The missile also shredded the fire hoses, making it impossible to put out the gasoline fed flames, rapidly licking toward twenty tons of explosives below. Ignoring the danger, rescue crews from the Blagar rushed in aid and somehow managed to save everyone aboard, just before the Rio Escondido became fully engulfed in one-hundred-foot-high-flames and exploded... in a mammoth fireball the shape of a mushroom cloud... seen sixteen miles away at Red Beach. "Gray!" radioed Rip Robertson. "What the hell was that?" Upon hearing the stunning news that the Rio Escondido had exploded, Rip replied in shock, "My God, Gray! For a moment over there, I thought Fidel Castro had the Atomic Bomb."

The Rio Escondido sank close to Playa Giron, taking down ten days' supply and ammunition and the communication van along with all the other vitally needed goods. The brigade's forces at Blue Beach had little ammunition and truth be told could not communicate... with their needed, or expected air cover. Castro's luck was now in favor of turning the tide on hitting that cargo.

The men who made it to Red Beach fared no better. They inched northward for four miles, but Castro's forces were moving into position and they quickly swarmed into the area, preventing them from reaching the southern end of the road they were to block. Fighting continued all day, with a dozen tanks arriving mid afternoon, and artillery shelling the area in an unbroken barrage. Militia forces likewise steadily pounded the landing site, suffering numerous casualties and extensive tank damage, but continually depleting the brigade's ammunition and forcing its withdrawal to Blue Beach.

Events at Red Beach north and east of the Bay of Pigs ended just as badly for the brigade as those above at Blue Beach. Fourteen miles north of Playa Larga, paratroopers seized the road to Central Australia, but they could not hold it for long because their heavy equipment missed the mark during the drop, and disappeared in the swamps. One other group got lost in the marsh, and still another missed the drop zone. A contingent of brigade forces occupied Playa Larga, until they ran out of ammunition and had to retreat in the face of a wall of fire from enemy tanks, rifles, mortars, bazookas, and automatic weapons. To the east, the brigade put up stands at San Blas, in an area close to Covadonga northeast of the Zapata Swamp above Blue Beach, and on the road below Yaguarmas east of Covadonga. But it had to withdraw in a battle providing what one young Cuban student soldier termed his "baptism of fire." When the tank commanders finally called off the assault, "we heard the yelling of the wounded," he recalled in horror. "There was a concert of the dying."

The roads at Red Beach as well as Blue Beach lay open to Fidel Castro's steadily advancing forces.

The CIA had no choice but to follow the original plan–though belatedly–by ordering... all remaining ships... out to sea to await dark. Then the ships would return and unload. Pepe San Ramon, either unaware of this arrangement or choosing to ignore it, angrily rebuked the Blagar's U.S. commander for making "that withdrawal against my orders to hold position and fight." Military principles... made it clear that "the commander of the support forces takes orders... from the commander of the supported forces." The U.S. commander crisply replied, "A higher authority has ordered to the contrary." Gray too was reluctant to withdraw... until he read the last part of the message declaring that the "Navy will provide cover at the 12–mile limit." American help at last? The three slowly trudging LCUs went first, followed by the freighters Atlantico and Caribe, and then the Barbara J. and the Blagar, but not without incident. The convoy encountered another B-26 attack in which the Blagar's guns hit the planes' fuel tanks as the pilot unleashed with a second round of rockets, causing it to explode in a swirling ball of fire, and a Sea Fury inflicted additional damage on the Barbara J. before their return fire chased it off. Further out to sea, the Blagar's captain saw two U.S. destroyers and radioed for help. Captain Robert Crutchfield sent a crushing reply: "My heart is with you, but I cannot help you. My orders are not to become engaged in any way." Fear turned into contempt over Captain Crutchfield's cold reply.

Problems continued to plague the convoy's departure. The boarding of the Rio Escondido's badly shaken survivors onto the Blagar had demoralized its sixty crew members, leading two of them to join new arrivals in arming themselves and refusing to return to the landing site. (Not a full on mutiny, but united in a stance of stating that they wouldn't go back.) But the captain's forces quickly subdued these two mutineers and convinced the others of their responsibilities to the twelve hundred comrades stranded on the beach. The two freighters carrying the ammunition, the Atlantico and the Caribe, ignored the Blagar's directive to meet at the rendezvous point and continued south, the first making it more than a hundred miles before deciding to turn around, and the second more than two hundred miles, at which point a U.S. destroyer fired a shot across its bow and forced a reverse course. The two ships' late return further undermined the invasion operation. The Atlantico did not get back until the late afternoon of April 18th, and the Caribe failed to reappear until after the battle was over.

As for the assured Navy support at dawn, the jets had not appeared, but word arrived that they were still "on the way."

By the close of D-Day, both beachheads were on the verge of collapse. Many forces at Red Beach were nearly out of ammunition and had to turn back south. During the night, four C-54s and two C-46s tried to replenish the supplies. Five drops at Blue Beach were successful, but one arms cache at Red Beach drifted so far out in the water that the landing party could save only part of the load. Fletcher Prouty contended, "the ammunition ran out."

The air cover operations had gone badly. Brigade B-26s launched thirteen close-support strikes on D-Day and four more that night, but they were not effective. Nearly panicked over the deadly effectiveness of the

T-33s, the CIA now realized how badly the D-2 air strikes had failed, and asked Washington to authorize a pre-dawn bombing assault on Cuban airfields while Castro's jets were on the ground. Surprisingly, the request won approval, leading General Charles Cabell to believe that the nation's leaders were "a thoroughly scared bunch."

But everything went wrong with this rapidly assembled, jury-rigged operation. Six B-26s were to hit San Antonio de los Banos on D-Day night, but two planes aborted on take off and the other planes could not find their targets through the low clouds and dense fog. By early dawn of April 18th, three more planes headed for the target, but one failed at the takeoff, and the other two once again could not locate the bombing target points through scud and lingering haze.

Castro's forces won the first day's air campaign but at heavy expense that again points to debilitating impact of the president's decision to call off the D-Day air strikes. (There will be caveat footnotes below, that accompany this event.) Rebel B-26s sank one of his gunboats and hit several hundred of his ground forces at Red Beach, and anti aircraft fire brought down two Sea Furies and two B-26s. But his T-33s proved devastating. Downing four B-26s, and forcing the remainder to seek refuge in Nicaragua or other friendly airfields. Richard Bissell and many other CIA strategists had erroneously assumed that the so-called "T-Bird" was merely a lightly-armed training plane, but they were wrong, dead wrong. Fidel Castro's engineers (or perhaps the Soviet bloc technicians in Cuba) recently fitted these jets with rockets under their wings, along with a pair of .50 caliber machine guns–each capable of firing–seventeen hundred rounds per minute. The T-33 shot out of the sun with such blazing speed that the only warning of its presence was the sound of rockets already whistling towards their target. The outcome could have been worse. Had Fidel Castro's planes launched concerted attacks... rather than sporadic assaults by one or two planes at a time, they could have inflicted even more damage... while not exposing themselves to as much concentrated fire.

And, as for the CIA's predicted outpouring of popular support for the invasion, nothing of the sort took place. The landing spot of course was less densely inhabited than that of Trinidad, which made the pool of potential assistance inherently thin. The CIA had failed to establish a tight network of communication with the guerrillas in the mountains, who were not aware of the timing of the invasion and they were a prohibitive... distance from... the beachhead. Castro had clamped down on dissidents days before the invasion, putting a hundred thousand in prison and further diminishing the sources of indigenous help. The five hundred guerrillas the CIA assured were nearby to help the brigade never showed. Fidel Castro telephoned his forces over at the Covadonga Sugar Mill, about fifteen miles north of Blue Beach, inspiring them and others to resist the invasion. Operation Peter Pan had meanwhile taken priority among many families, with the first five hundred children removed from the embattled area by the end of March, and the balance of a total of more than fourteen thousand in a mass exodus that lasted until October 1962. The result was that only a small number of citizens and militia helped the brigade by transporting supplies, nursing the wounded, providing food and water, and joining in the fight. Whether too frightened to break with Castro or simply loyal to the regime, most Cubans stayed out of the battle, leaving the brigade alone on the beaches.

In an appropriate epitaph to that one day in April, Pepe San Ramon radioed "Gray" on the Blagar–pleading for reinforcements. "Gray, the enemy tanks are already into our position in Giron. Right here very close to us. You can here the guns. I am ordering the retreat."

"Hold on," Gray responded in ignoring the administration's restrictions. "We're coming, we're coming with everything." Pepe asked the following wrenching question, "How long?"

Gray honestly told him, "three to four hours." "That's not enough time. You won't be here on time. Farewell friends. I am breaking this radio now." According to one sailor on the scene, then these Americans; started crying. Howard Jones, *THE BAY OF PIGS*.

––––––

History was not accurate when it came to any post discussions on John Kennedy and the legend regarding air cover. What was missed and what was also recorded in few accounts... until Jim Rassenberger / L.Fletcher Prouty / The Zapata Report / and in the testimony above that got it right... as in the correct account by Howard Jones, *The Bay Of Pigs*; John F. Kennedy ordered the final air strike--to eliminate the remaining--Castro jets that survived the bombing raids. At about 9:30 p.m. on April 16th, 1961, Mr. McGeorge Bundy, Special Assistant To The President, telephoned Gen. Charles Cabell of the CIA to inform him... that the dawn air strikes... the following morning should not be launched until they could be conducted from a strip from within the beachhead. Mr. McGeorge Bundy indicated that any further consultation with regard to this matter should be with the secretary of state. General Cabell accompanied by Mr. Bissell (CIA) went at once to Secretary Dean Rusks office, arriving at about 10:15. There were only 10 aircraft in the CRAF Cuban Air Force, seven planes were known... to have been destroyed. John Kennedy made the provisio "the three planes remaining must be destroyed, and they must be taken out immediately."

They launched four B-26s to take out those airplanes. In a terrible miscalculation, in mishandling JFKs order: Mc George Bundy had changed the timing when he telephoned General Charles Cabell (due to terrible lack of any better explanation... than anyone can think of) nobody informed Adlai Stevenson, what to expect at the United Nations; he was getting publicly humiliated on the world stage, or lambasted at the U.N. He was damn furious with the exposed CIA false defector's scheme going awry. Adlai Stevenson insisted any more air strikes had to come from on island and or they had to originate, and be launched off, on the Cuban airfields. This is confirmed by McGeorge Bundy, as he told Dean Rusk "I got to go to see the Vice President." (Asked why: he responded sounding thoroughly entrenched by dryly adding in the soiling caveat) "I have got to go. I am off to go over to hold the hand of Mr. Adlai Stevenson." Fletcher Prouty stated clearly, "Kennedy had ordered the remaining Castro's three jets had to be taken out immediately." Whereas history was not so kind in retrospect to JFK. They forget: The CIA plan had no air cover to begin with in it. The original plan had no air cover. All Castro's planes were supposed to be taken out. CIA stated: "the air will be yours." When the Zapata Report was released, these facts were all confirmed.

The brigades exposed in daylight of 04/16/1961 were butchered in the rolling abattoir... like a slaughterhouse:

"Mr. Mc George Bundy, the CIA leadership. Dulles, Bissell, and Cabell, need to take some roads of the blame in this fiasco." And, perhaps to re-examine the role JFK has been plagued with, despite the actions of Nixon's NSC 5412 / OP 40 Brigade.

(This so being the humble opinion of this particular author and, L. Fletcher Prouty, and, also a few other selected noteworthy historians.)

———

The pummeling was brutal. Fidel Castro had gotten close enough to the battlefield. Photographs show, he jumped into the front. Fidel Castro: He was seen riding atop a tank, and he was seen directing his troops. (As multiple photographs recorded it.) Using the headquarters of the sugar mill, Fidel Castro continuously directed The Cuban Defense Strategy–using both radio, telephone and handwritten communications. The brigade managed to unload WWII Sherman tanks and they fought in the Battle Of Rotunda against Cuba's equally outdated Stalin tanks. Then the terrible truth of the invasion: Ammunition ran out. "It was a blood bath. Men soaked in bloody fatigues lying in a swamp, so many already dying from the lack of adequate medical care."

Despite CIA projections the local Cuban people armed with M-52 Czech rifles wrote Peter Wyden in *Bay Of Pigs*

The Untold Story, defended their homeland until the first Cuban battalion of *900 student soldiers arrived on busses*, although half were delayed when their convoy was attacked by B-26 bombing raids. But the reinforcements from Cuba's forces eventually poured into the fray and, both by outnumbering and out-maneuvering, *encircled the invasion force's brigade*, and the fight and the battle became a fracas to whittle away at the unsupported lame duck exiles.

U.S. jet fighter squadrons flew reconnaissance over the fleeting invasion, but were forbidden to engage the enemy in combat tactics. Kennedy was warned as the situation worsened without additional sorties (*or yet even more airstrikes* than those that he had previously signed off on). By day number three, the invasion had become much more bleak for the Brigade #2506 and the Alpha 66 Cuban exiles... still fighting for their lives, on the ground. As per Howard Jones' account (and Peter Wyden's, or Claudia Furiati's), recollecting on all smattering levels of what was going wrong, and with what was going right: a lot of wrong, especially as the air drops to resupply the brigade ammunition were missing their target. Kennedy had agonized over three days. He got sand-bagged by overwhelming bad news. Whether he was in "salvage mode," or the fourth quarter of the big game that was just out of his reach; he found he was at a crossroad, "*shall I dig in any deeper into this mess?*" In a crossfire, or at a crossroad beyond this threshold point, it turned into enough. Therefor he decided to cut all of his losses, and abort the brigade men *by finally pulling out*. By Tuesday many fearful "*Brigadista Pilots*" were begging off the task tempting their fate, flying any combat sorties, because CRAF Pilots In Cuba; they firmly held... the upper hand.

Hence, the CIA authorized its own last ditch efforts to save the invasion forces on the ground. In the battle's final hours, four of the six pilots who flew over the fleeting invasion were shot down and killed. The Cubans recovered one of those pilots and found his dog tags. It is reported that his body remained unclaimed in a Havana morgue until 1979 when his daughter claimed it, and he was laid to rest back home in the United States. That U.S. pilot's name was Thomas Ray. The futility of the invasion was clear to both sides; the brigade would try to now withdraw from the beach to safety.

Two amazing things happened that are uniquely remarkable in irony and hindsight, but as Wyden recalled it, "The military-CIA faction assumed the president would order U.S. intervention." But the president assumed they knew he would flatly "*refuse to escalate the miniature war.*" Both sides were unsure of one another's resolve, and Kennedy ordered the Navy to: "*withdraw the brigade forces from Playa Giron.*"

Fidel Castro knew that the fleet of U.S. destroyers were coming in for an "extraction." He allowed the U.S. Navy's approach for the coastal shore to proceed with the evacuation. If the Cubans fired upon them, the lie was going to be "they were merely on exercises patrolling international waters." It was the luck of Fidel Castro's *proper choice to go with restraint*. In the end, there could've been dire and ever foreboding transcendent consequences. The Soviet Union guaranteed it would come to the aid of Cuba in the event she was attacked.

The destroyers picked up the Brigadistas who had made it back to sea, and then sailed away home. They left other survivors to fend for themselves. The brigade of mercenaries lost 114 men. The Cuban forces lost 161 men (the casualties were vastly under-reported), solemn concrete monuments rising from the bush terrain attest their sacrifice for Cuba in Playa Larga. In all, 1,189 men were captured. Later on they were returned to the United States in exchange for 63 million dollars in food and medical supplies. It was basically a ransom amount Fidel agreed to for returning the members of the brigade to the United States.

Feelings ran high among the returning Cuban-exiled Brigadistas. At a ceremony at Miami's Orange Bowl Stadium, President Kennedy, in attendance (perhaps a brave acknowledgment in itself, it seems), is said to have remarked to Eduardo Ferrer, "You didn't get any help from us." (Each Brigade member received a cash payment of $300.) "No, Mr. President," Ferrer replied, "but I truly will expect your help on *the next time.*"

The president jovially chimed in with conviction, perhaps to save face from the disastrous results, *"You better believe there's going to be a next time."*

Although Kennedy made an indelible impression with his speech to The Bay of Pigs survivors by lashing out at communism in general, and Fidel Castro in particular, he became caught up in the political atmosphere when he accepted the Brigade's flag and made a noteworthy pledge:

"I can assure you... this flag will be returned to this brigade in a free Havana." Most of the men present that day truly believed in this statement of a continued commitment to overthrow Fidel Castro. But all the future events that came to pass ultimately proved otherwise.

Less than a month later, the Brigade members received mimeographed letters advising that no further compensations would be paid out or be forthcoming to them in their effort to overthrow Fidel Castro. It was a bad draw of the straws for these men. The U.S. Government had washed its hands of the whole involvement with the Cuban Exiled Brigade they had used in a bad covert action of a now forgotten war. It left the entire exile community feeling doubly betrayed.

Failing to choose a next time turned out to be a bad draw for Kennedy.

Che Guevara made the most poignant comment afterwards, when he talked with the opposition at a conference abroad. Even if it was just commentary delivered to mock the United States with some indignity, it was prophetic:

"I thank the United States for the true leveling of the playing field for us."

It was here in Playa Giron where Cuba went toe to toe battling a U.S. superpower and came out victorious. Che Guevara said of his U.S. nemesis, with all due... but rather displaced respect, in essence "thank you for the prestige."

On the world stage, it effectively, permanently, stamped the promise and providence of the Cuban Revolution with a worldwide resounding national pride celebration.

The forever remembered... Day of La Victoria–Playa Giron.

THE VICTORY OF PLAYA GIRON.

After the Bay of Pigs drastic failure in agency policy, CIA officers got a feeling that there was no more carte blanche in Cuba the CIA agency's armor was damaged.

E. Howard Hunt recalled the ill feelings by describing the few officers who were remaining with the CIA, in his book; *The Night Watch* (1977). He wrote it was if the scene there was like: "moving up and down the halls... like attendants... at a sepulcher."

(Sepulcher directly translates to a burial vault.)

THE BEACHCOMBER

In Howard Jone's remarkable veracity in its forward assessment–*THE BAY OF PIGS*, or even inside the fine pages of the chronicle of this event in Jim Rasenburger's *A BRILLIANT DISASTER*, and in the other retelling accounts with regard to this bungled fiasco wherein the CIA invested 46 million, plus another 13 million dollars, to lose it all in seventy two hours. In the 3-day operation the CIA blew 60 million. The ships and weapons sunk were millions more.

The hardest lessons were yet to come for JFK. Worse in every retelling was how the cover up ensued with this all being a clandestine black C.I.A. operation... nobody could tell the truth about it to hide the embarrassment for the terrible failure. The casualties had to be skewed and misrepresented to make both sides appear unscathed (in hindsight the lies were to be rottenly forthcoming on either side of this ugly conflict to avoid a humiliation... in ultimately grim numbers); it was falsely reported. Period.

Assessment ranges were more in tune with the following reality. "There were horrific under reported casualties numbering some 3,650. There were 1650 deaths." Over 5,000 or in some accounts 5,300 Cubans were injured... so when Fidel Castro compares this awful incident... to Pearl Harbor, from his perspective the truth being told, "he's damned right about it." The Americans, the CIA government's story on who died on that beach... this untold number is in dispute until this day. If indeed Fidel Castro had lied about the casualties (in proclaiming 161 Cuban deaths), in the public forum to match up to our own (CIA led brigades numbered 114 deaths); this author's opinion intending and assertion, this number is false. It seems impossible– to imagine with 1650 deaths, 5,300 injured out there... and somehow on our side we lost only 114 men... in this battle?

The wrap up. Post WWII capital and the cold war ideology, and the emergent world stage in 1960, meant that IKE and/or the Truman legacy, and, American military strength was still high in the forefront or ran still deep in everyone's mind. And, nobody dared make any moves politically, that would screw that inherited status off of it's peak. United States, and this imminent merging war capital, was very high at that time. Therefor, any president could ill afford to blow it all to hell and gone... in less than 72 hours... in a combination false defector's scheme... and a CIA clandestine invasion... that would be exposed, and then mocked by the casting of aspersions world wide, as a devastating or drastic... and or such a horrific catastrophic failure.

Che Guevara sent a direct message in a note to president Kennedy to the Whitehouse secretary, Richard Goodwin, which read; "Thanks for Playa Giron [The Bay Of Pigs]. Before the Bay Of Pigs CIA invasion the Cuban revolution was weak. From now on, this Castro-Cuban revolution is stronger than ever before. JFK thanks to you"–signed by Che Guevara.

TEN REASONS FOR THE FAILURE OF THE BAY OF PIGS

#1.) Richard Bissell's plan was changed from the original Trinidad landing to the Playa Giron landing. The plans original intent to incite the insurrection on the populace was taken away. It was the Gen. Jacob Esterline who said afterwards, "there's nothing there but alligators and ducks." A night time secret landing could not unite anti-Castro Cubans to join up into a fight to overthrow Fidel Castro.

#2.) Multiple plots to assassinate Fidel Castro failed. Maheu / Edwards / O'Connell / Roselli /Trafficante and the Juan Orta plot that had failed. The Roselli / Tony Varona / Caso plot failed. Rooftop assassination plots failed. Rather than admit failure, CIA's Walt Elder through Gen. Charles Cabell lies to McGeorge Bundy, to say that in a CIA written false flag UPI article that explains this fabricated defection of Juan Orta. (This was a crucial paramount element in the Richard Bissell operation that preceded the whole invasion.) Any bad news, had to be "spun, and it had to be eliminated."

#3.) General Jacob Esterline (CIA) and Colonel Hawkins (Marines) failed to realize the hour time difference between Nicaragua and Cuba which sent the air strikes timing into a chaotic interval to the invasion. Add to this oversight a new administration that had less than 60 days to get to know each other. In its infancy, it was 77 days into the JFK administration. In its early tenderfoot stage of these men working in sync with complete concert and trust... having yet to find its bedrock... in its formative foundation of trust.

#4.) Richard Bissell had undersold the president on the reality of the CIA operation. Clearly he had lied about the chances of the popular uprising, inside Cuba, and the ability of the Brigade to escape into the Escambray mountains some 80 hard miles away. The notary scholars I talked to saw this as being the ridiculous assumption: It should have alerted the president's team that the plan should be scrapped. (It would take the mercenaries a full week to make it through to deeply—enough into the safety of the Escambray mountains.) One such scholar, who confirmed this; Prof. Maurice Zeitlin.

#5.) Castro had imprisoned 20,000 suspected indigenous traitors, who would have joined the invasion. Invasion was to conceal the American hand. It lacked the dramatic flair. It was less likely to stir up a general uprising so vital to bring about Castro's fall. Invasion offered the greater prospect of "the military success," but it greatly reduced the chances for the CIA to claim its "plausible deniability." Reiterating #1.) and, #2.) It was clear if they didn't kill Fidel Castro prior to invasion: The plan's doomed to its internal failure.

#6.) A brigade member (Dr. Juan Sordo,) told the CIA at the outset it was impossible to land at Playa Giron due to the coral heads. Juan Sordo said "I know the area very well and I have... seen them... for myself." Richard Bissell lied. He down-played what Juan Sordo, told the CIA. He dismissed whatever was detrimental to his plans by saying it would not be a problem to the 2506 brigade landing. In squelching anything that was a terrible flaw, and denial of weaknesses, by lying down and lying up. He would say anything to keep all of these plans rolling ahead pushing the young JFK administration, forward no matter what came up as the down—sides, in any conversation.

#7.) Richard Bissell cut the D-2 air strikes plans in the number of planes from 16 aircraft down to 8 aircraft sent to destroy Castro's–Air Forces–In Cuba. A full on better game plan. If the CIA sent 36 airplanes it would have been sufficient to destroy every plane in Castro's forces. If they had to cut the plane's number down and the plan still needed to be successful, the plan could stand a cut down to 24 in number of planes to fly. The number 24 was the "doable minimum option." They scheduled twenty-two aircraft in the original operational plan. The number was cut to 12 planes that went on the mission. Here the CIA went too far in trying to reduce the noise... by crippling it... by cutting back severely and going on with only 8 aircraft.

The odds were impossible against 8 aircraft taking out Castro's air forces. Men who saw it coming, this disaster, realized it was not enough planes... and they sought to stop... the impending slaughter. General Esterline from CIA and Colonel Hawkins from Marines had seen the disaster forthcoming April 9th, 1961 (Esterline and also Hawkins, went to Richard Bissell's home, to resign). Also, thereby in doing so... they insisted on this caveat in follow up protocol... by vehemently informing Mr. Bissell that he should do the right thing, and also inform JFK, and the Whitehouse, to save the humiliation of the United States and the president and justly call off the CIA invasion.

The pleas were swept under the rug. Bissell kept the resignations private. Bissell had presidential approval–and he refused to reevaluate the plan– asking for more time would have caused JFK to scrap the junket all together. Bissell talked these men into keeping quiet, and staying on sticking it out. Richard Bissell was determined to keep it going forward and to keep the plan active. He was lying down he was lying up. He was stabilizing plans that he knew realistically that they now know, were less than 50/50. (More than three officer's knew it...and he knew it too...it was a sadly doomed invasion.) Howard Jones, "THE BAY OF PIGS," was generally the announcer on this information.

#8.) April 15th, 1961. The false defectors scheme "began." Returning from their flight missions, the CIA pilot Mario Zuniga lands in Miami, jumps out of his plane in his khaki pants, white T-shirt and his baseball cap, with all Cuban labels, puffing on a Cuban cigar, while enthusiastically boasting that he and others had defected... after strafing and bombing Castro's planes... as part of a widespread Cuban revolt and insurrection. (Early on in the ploy briefly there were hints that the CIA plan had a possible chance of it working.)

The CIA doubled down. They launched two more confederate defector's, landing in 2 more cities. The CIA gambled more... would be better to prove that Cubans were rebelling against Castro's forces. The fraudulent second one was in Key West. Just in case the earlier one (over in Miami) had failed. The third and final one...the real defector...had landed 340 miles north, over in Jacksonville, Florida; as well too.

Then when reporters deduced the facade and exposed that the entire invasion was a hoax "the jig was up." By pointing out the clear differences between the Jacksonville airplane (the genuine defector) and the other two phony planes that had already landed in Miami, and landed in Key West. Shit hit the proverbial fan in a truly major way. "The Cuban B-26 bore a recent paint job and its guns hadn't been fired." The hoax CIA scheme had been exposed, now Adlai Stevenson was being ridiculed by Raul Roa, the Cuban foreign minister at the United Nations. The proof was now on display for the world to view. The B-26 had a metal nose for its cowling: "Hence it was all American." And, the U.N. Cuban minister Raul Roa, publicly sneered of foul play at the damn-American-CIA hand for launching such an unwittingly foul lie to the audience of the world nations. Fidel Castro's B-26s bore only plexiglass fronts over their plane's nose, and over their cowling. The uproar continued to snowball and intensify now as the Soviet U.N. Ambassador Valerian Zorin threatened, "Cuba has many friends in the world who are ready to come to its aid... including the Soviet Union." Adlai Stevenson was being humiliated worldwide, being part of a false flag invasion. (This first-time let down absolutely hotly infuriated him.)

#9.) The 168 men led by Nino Diaz (trained in New Orleans) didn't have the nerve to land in Baracoa, and march ahead to the Guantanamo Base. The diversionary landing did not take place due to poor leadership. They were unable to get to the landing site in time, hampered by a sizable Cuban army platoon and division of patrolling ground forces, led by Raul Castro. Waiting for 24 hours they heard several more jeeps, and trucks, arriving, "they're waiting for us" declared a battalion officer who reported to his senior officers who believed him, even after the next days delay; the panic of knowing that a large military battalion was already in the vicinity, the group of 168 men, then decided to flee from the area. Raul Castro had been there since early April in command of his troops, and an anti aircraft battery consisting of a half a dozen, four mouth machine guns. And, he had spotted the Santa Ana that was waiting for nightfall. The ship withdrew, taking all the concert sound equipment intended to simulate the sounds of this great invasion, and leaving Castro to singularly concentrate on his defenses... on only the one front... over at Playa Giron, The Bay Of Pigs. No diversion force. And, also no back up landing. They had chickened out.

#10.) Adlai Stevenson was publicly lambasted at the United Nations. He was sand-bagged by the phony false defector's of the Cuban Air Force. The entire CIA invasion plan, was now exposed as a CIA jigsaw, made-up-mess, of a straight up hoax.

Adlai Stevenson hotly called over to the Whitehouse to bitterly complain to McGeorge Bundy, and Gen. Charles Cabell, and to the president. The end result of that was the biggest mistake of the entire invasion.

Colonel Fletcher Prouty contends that John Kennedy had ordered the air strike on April 17th, to take out Castro's remaining three T-33 jets. However the calls to the Whitehouse by Adlai Stevenson... had an impact on the way JFK's air strike... was to be postponed, to lower the noise. In these concerns "political concerns, outweighed the Military necessity concerns." Mc George Bundy called Gen. Charles Cabell and told him not to fly the airplanes until they could take off... from the beachhead, the next day. "The dawn air strikes will not be launched until they can be conducted from a Cuban air strip on the beachhead." (It would doom the landing to a slaughterhouse failure, thereby catastrophically forcing the entire brigade to wait on late airplanes.)

To get the full story, one must turn to the most prestigious factotum to date of The Bay Of Pigs invasion, *A BRILLIANT DISASTER*, 2011, author JIM RASENBERGER; (Scribner Books). A Great Document. (Check Out PART III, in paperback pages 113 through 309.

La Victoria (the Victory), the Battle of Playa Giron, directly led to the next chapter in U.S.-Cuba history: The Caribbean Crisis aka The Cuban Missile Crisis.

The movie *Thirteen Days*, New Line Cinema (2001), chronicles the period in 1962 when nuclear war with Russia seemed likely as a result of escalating tensions. U.S. foreign policy, and perhaps U.S. government's business interests in trade relations abroad, combined with our own ideals of which countries should be deemed as appropriately worthy trading partners, escalated the tensions during the height of the Cold War.

The Soviet Union was deeply threatened by the American deployment of intermediate-ranged ballistic missiles on the Turkish border with the U.S.S.R.

The Bay of Pigs facilitated the provisional "outlet opening" for the Soviets to establish a similar nuclear threat at equally close range to the United States' borders.

The intention was to use these bargaining chips of ballistic missiles *too close for comfort* (just some ninety miles off the coast of Florida) to force the United States to either rethink its policies, or to back off in Europe, and bring a reduction of the missile build-up going on in Turkey.

Fidel Castro feared a U.S. invasion of Cuba and the Soviets confirmed his fears, therefore prompting Castro's insistence to formally request aid in the defense plan with a nuclear package of strategic defense weapons. The Soviet Union quickly began a covert military build-up in Cuba in early 1962. Cuban ports began a pattern of being closed at night with certain restrictions and curfews. Everyone in Cuba knew that clandestine military cargo transport activities were brewing under the cover of darkness.

Upon returning from a spying snapshot session over the Western Cuban landscape, a U-2 plane now had pictures of missile launch sites. Immediately President Kennedy demanded that they be removed. Khrushchev, in return, promptly refused to comply. The Thirteen Days of the Caribbean Crisis began. See the book by author Anthony D. Brugioni, *EYEBALL TO EYEBALL*.

The first issue President Kennedy raised was whether the U.S. dependents at Guantanamo should be evacuated. At the time there were about 900 families that all totaled would comprise approximately 2,800 women and children living on the base. Secretary of Defense McNamara stood up at a meeting between Admiral Ward and Paul Nitze. "Mr. Secretary, you have your instructions to get the dependents out of Guantanamo Bay, now, please, carry out those instructions for me."

Mr. Nitze felt that they should replace those dependents with Marines to avoid any possible misunderstandings between the Russians and Cubans. Orders were given dispatching both airlift and sealift combat Marines to Guantanamo Base.

Friday and Saturday, October 19th and 20th, four separate ships dropped anchor in Guantanamo Bay; transport, Upshur (TAP-198), Duxbury Bay (AVP-38), Hyades (AF-28), and Desoto County (LST-1171). Kennedy wanted the evacuation completed before his address to the nation the following Monday night.

On Monday just before 11 a.m., October 22nd, the morning routine for families at the Guantanamo Base was interrupted by news delivered by both phone calls and messengers. The kids were driven by busses from schools to either transports or to piers and waiting ships. Around noon, ambulances and trucks began moving all hospital patients to the airfield. By 1 o'clock, it was a madhouse at the loading dock.

Admiral Edward J. O'Donnell, who was the Commander of the naval base, ordered that all processing cease, the dependents be taken aboard as quickly as possible, and that further processing be done at sea. Loading was completed shortly before 4 p.m. The Upshur was loaded to capacity, with 1,730 passengers; the Duxbury Bay took on 351; the Hyades, 286; and the Desoto County, 92.

Before the ships departed Guantanamo, Admiral O'Donnell read the following messages over the ship's loudspeakers:

"To you who have had to leave your homes at Guantanamo, I send my deep regrets. I know you do so with sadness, for some of you also leave behind your husbands, others, your fathers–your jobs as well as your homes. It is my most earnest hope that circumstances will permit your return. I send my warmest greetings and best wishes to you and those you leave behind.

(Signed) John F. Kennedy"

O'Donnell then read another message:

"The calm and serene manner with which you have accepted the threat of possible personal danger while living at Guantanamo has been viewed with admiration and respect. Now our judgment dictates that you should leave the scene of an increasing danger to your safety. I am sure you will accept this action with the same fine spirit that has been so obvious throughout your stay at Guantanamo. Rest assured that we will do all possible to provide for your welfare in the days ahead.

(Signed) George Anderson"

In Norfolk, Rear Admiral James C. Dempsey, commander of the Amphibious Training Command of the U.S. Atlantic fleet, was preparing to receive the dependents. It was decided that the Little Creek Amphibious Base, on the outskirts of Norfolk, would be the reception and processing area and that some of the four ships would dock there and the others at Pier 12 at Norfolk. The chief of naval personnel, Vice-Admiral W.R. Smedberg III, was dispatched by Admiral Anderson to Norfolk to assure that activities in the Norfolk area regarding the dependents were being coordinated.

It was the same day, October 22nd, President Kennedy ordered the U.S. military to go from Def Con-5 state of readiness to Def Con-3. On national televised broadcasts John Kennedy made the announcement:

"I have directed... initial steps to be taken immediately for a strict quarantine on all offensive military equipment shipments to Cuba."

The statement went on to highlight that:

"It shall be the policy of this nation to regard any nuclear missile launched from Cuba as an attack by the Soviet Union on the United States, requiring a full retaliatory response back upon the Soviet Union."

It was during this betting of wills that were being dispatched that also 54 Strategic Air Command bombers were being dispatched to the air. The fleet of Polaris submarines were put to sea. The (SAC) bombers prepared 136 Atlas and Titan ICBMs for possible launching. The United States Naval Task Force set out to intercept all Soviet vessels and blockaded Cuba.

The volatile exchanges between Kennedy and Khrushchev heightened as worldwide tensions began to mount. On October 24th, the United States military ticked down to Def Con-2. (It was the only time in our ardent military history.) The world watched and waited apprehensively on Armageddon as the super powers verged toward enlightening upon a full-scale nuclear showdown.

October 26th, the United States launched an ICBM from Vandenberg Air Force Base. It flew across the Pacific and hit the missile test range on the Kwajalein atoll in the Marshall Islands. It was an ill-advised provocation shot. The game of chicken had Khrushchev composing with grave prophetical commentary on possible outcomes for U-2 spy planes daring picture sorties over Siberian air space. "They could easily be mistaken for nuclear bombers, which might push us to the next step of engagement." The Air Force deliberately had their pilots baiting flights to go beyond-turnaround, into the territory of Soviet air space.

Whereas the United States citizens were altogether bracing for the conflict of a nuclear war, most of the Cuban citizens were bemused with the radical patriotism of in-differential defiance. Seemingly, nobody in the country knew whether or not an atomic bomb would come to fall on their country.

To the average Cuban it was absurd—no one comprehended the damage or cost of a holocaust in nuclear weapons. It wasn't part of the psyche in the educational background of the Socialist system. If you're not educated to know about what nuclear weapons can do to you… then: "*what you don't know can't hurt you.*"

Very few people in 1962 accepted the likelihood of the theory that we had enough weapons presently deployed to destroy the world. It was not a unilaterally accepted belief in the United States, for that matter, either.

Some people knew for sure we had enough bombs in the world to destroy the world, but at that time not every single citizen of either Cuba or the United States could truly take that theory to the bank. It wasn't the *belief of everybody* anyway.

To Cubans: The invasion and the revolution both were guerrilla wars fought in the countryside of Sierra Maestra and Playa Giron. The battles were fought with Quajiros tools, their machetes and bayonets, and older M-52 Czech-rifles, and pistols, and knives, and Cuban cajones. The additions of strange ICBM missiles were a secretly-injected equation (to most of them) with the outcomes uncertain with things like nuclear blasts. They simply *just clearly* didn't fully understand.

Cuba is a very rural country with humble workers like the hardworking quajiros, cutting cane in the sugar fields, or harvesting the vast citrus crops, or curing the tobacco leaves on tobacco farms, and making fine Cuban cigars. The coffee harvester's and Cuban rum producer's transportation across the land is by horseback, or by oxen carts, or on old trucks, or even older railroad trains. Things are done by hand by these men and in the old-fashioned ways. In 1962, through no fault of their own, by spoils of dictators full of greed who were unwilling to provide an education to their countrymen, only a very limited amount of Cuba's citizens (in 1962, mind you) were literate.

Regarding the impact of nuclear bombs, even the Nobel Laureate Gabriel Garcia Marque reported back from the Cuban front that, "we on the other hand are quite calm, over here in our neck of the woods." That was quite balls out bold.

The Cuban perspective came back in an irreverent arrogant manner, defiant of the impending disaster or quagmire the people were really fixated in. Since it was unknown consequences (to them), they responded with: "After all, the atomic bomb doesn't hurt." The average Cuban had too much balls or big cajones to fret dangers concerning war.

There were millions all across the country, legions of gullible radical Cubans who would bravely and loyally (without question) go out to fight to the bitter end, and *roll with the punches*, and blindly follow along with their leader Fidel Castro.

No Cuban parents told their children, "Oh, by the way there are enough nuclear weapons on the planet now to completely destroy the world." Not too many American parents, even those in the military, *chose to tell their children either*, that we had such capabilities to destroy the world with the firepower combined between the U.S. and Russia. Why complicate matters and create more unstable insecurity with what most parents knew as the truth about the world's nuclear uncertainty in what was supposed to be a secure world? A lot of people were left to learn it on their own. These truths were not shared by most of the parents in a lot of cases, since it would create more questions and doubts about the freedoms we have to share in this sometimes imbalanced and delicate world.

Thanks to the Batista regime, and other corrupt leaders in Cuba's past, some seventy-five percent of the population was illiterate and millions of Cuba's people went without school.

This was all prior to Fidel Castro's reforms with 1961's "literacy brigades," and the year of education for Cubans. It was at this time high school seniors and college students dispatched education, fanning out over the countryside with the goal of the revolution to teach every single Cuban to read and write.

Within less than two years the regime added over 10,000 classrooms. By the end of the first decade, the number of elementary schools had doubled from 7,567 in 1958 to 14,753 in 1968. The number of teachers tripled from 21,806 to over some 68,583. Fidel Castro's revolution would radically change Cuba's horizons.

In a salute to Fidel Castro and his Fidelistas regime, "The Cuba" that the whole revolution triumphed for was truly evolving for the masses at the time of *The Year Of Education*. It was providing the program of leadership in "literacy brigades."

But in 1962, the reality was that the people simply couldn't comprehend a catastrophe such as the holocaust, especially if the people of Cuba just didn't understand what the famed words between the two leaders Khrushchev and Kennedy meant.

And to the Cuban people at that time, perhaps one could argue that their bemused tone of natural instinct or mundane ignorance was the bliss to form a basis for a behemoth of cajone-ridden Cuban National Pride in total *Yankee defiance*.

There was an air of celebration in the city and Havana was brimming with proud Cuban-Yanqui defiance. The people were ready to face their nemesis foe with "Patria O Muerte." The revolutionary indomitable fiery Cuban spirit was an irascible son of a bitch that flat out refused to shake in fear of the U.S. giant.

The country had all gathered together in pride and remained steadfast and pure in its resolve, and stood up dauntlessly resilient in the face of death. And here was their leader, Fidel Castro, equally as reckless in his gambler's bravado trying to taunt his enemy of deadly formidable U.S. forces, with a myriad of weaponry in its arsenals to annihilate him, poised at Def Con-2. But Fidel Castro kept on pushing the giant, like David versus Goliath.

On October 27th, a U-2 spy plane was shot down on a fly-over mission. Major Rudolf Anderson, the U.S. pilot, was the solo single casualty, as we approached the brink of war. It took NSA several hours to sort their data to conclude that the U-2, piloted by Major Anderson, had been downed by an SA-2 missile. Fidel Castro boldly egged his men on by making fierce prognosticating remarks spitting towards the smoldering U-2 plane crash, "Well, let's see if there's going to be a damned war, or not?" (It's rumored that Fidel Castro pushed the button which launched the anti-aircraft missile himself.) Whether or not he did push the button, the U-2 plane was shot down, and how we (the U.S.) averted the fate of an all-out war with the Russians at that point... was some miracle of wonder... to marvel about. It was not until 1989 that a former Soviet ambassador to Cuba admitted that the downing of the U-2 was the result of a "trigger happy Soviet air defense commander."

The fate of the world now firmly shouldered by two men, Kennedy and Khrushchev bargained their way out of a nuclear holocaust showdown by guarantees to Khrushchev (unbefitting to Fidel Castro) that the United States would never "try" to invade Cuba. When the Soviet Union backed down, both of Cuba's most passionate anti-American leaders were apoplectic with rage. Castro and Che Guevara thought it would have been better to take the conflict to the end.

Che was more uncompromising than Fidel Castro, and even if the war was now averted, one could argue that Cuba had held its own against the super powers. It was the last straw for Che, and he left Cuba soon afterwards heading for Africa.

Fidel Castro had, as history has proved thus far (in a postponement posture), correctly calculated that the grandstanding results from the nuclear countdown-conflict, would save him from a second forthcoming event of a non-nuclear subliminal or sublimational CIA or United States-inspired invasion against his regime. Whether Castro wanted it to or not, all the United States could do now was sit back and watch from the sidelines, and he has had deliberate control over all of Cuba's future events since 1959.

With the conclusion of the Cuban Missile Crisis now clearly behind him, Kennedy could continue the Eisenhower embargo and he escalated it further by tightening the grip and promising that, *"We will build a wall around Cuba."*

Of course, the day he signed the bill he had his aides purchase 1,000 Havanas for his own *personal cigar indulgence* of Cuba's fine tobacco-producing industry.

––––––

The CIA and the mob now simultaneously had an ax to grind with Fidel Castro. The botched Bay of Pigs invasion was literally the mob's last shot to make a comeback into the gambling palaces they had once built and restored to make flourish during the tropical gold rush. It was the goal of the mob bosses to plot their return to mine that tax-free gambling oasis in Cuba, and it was proven when they put a million dollars up for a bounty on Castro's head.

The White House and the CIA were forced into an uneasy cooperative alliance. Now the CIA had to kowtow to the president's brother after blowing it with the Bay of Pigs debacle; they were coerced into letting Bobby Kennedy become a "Mr. Fix It Man" whose job was to tidy up and finish what Eisenhower had started in 1959. (Both Bobby and JFK would now be keeping a closer eye on things, and be directly involved in covert activities that involved all the Cuba policies and operations.) The resulting operation became known as Operation Mongoose.

The Operation Mongoose event spearheaded by Bobby Kennedy mushroomed to involve 500 caseworkers handling 3,000 anti-Castro Cubans, at an expense which ballooned to over $100 million a year.

These are facts, the undisputed truths with regard to Richard Bissell's vision to overthrow Fidel Castro.

At the Bay of Pigs (or Playa Giron Battle, as I prefer to call it), there were CIA point men and operatives who were at the battle to report, monitor, and guide the rebel brigade to victory. After all, this clearly made sense since it was… "their plan." The operation cost a fortune in planning and training and military hardware. Costs were in excess of $100 million in 1960s U.S. dollars. April 17th, 1961: the plan failed when John Kennedy backed off when it came time for the needed support of air cover. (CIA point man Gary Lynch observed, as well as others, that Fidel Castro was slightly more prepared than U.S. intelligence, and the CIA, had originally planned on.)

There was a contingent group, subsequent to this loss of the project at Playa Giron, who felt bitterly betrayed by the president. Watching fallen comrades being captured and overtaken in hostile territory and giving up on the troops they had trained for the last three years was not a part of their military ideal. Some of these CIA operatives at the field level or ground level also had a stake in Cuba's future from the gambling casinos (a sorta mob reward if you will, for winning them back their businesses). They were a definable and defensible delegation, a short list of mercenary agents with defalcator fingers into a piece of the pie. They were looking for the type of money that goes unreported to the IRS (tax free), much like the kickbacks Batista had gotten, that were promised to key field CIA operative personnel. It wasn't ownership, but it was a substantial enough reward or inducement for these operatives to be looking toward the bonus pay off, and the collection of it. When the air support never materialized, these CIA operatives were pissed off with their commander-in-chief's actions.

Now both scenarios had tallied under John Kennedy's leadership to cost his new administration and the U.S. government over $100 million each time out; the cumulative cost of Playa Giron since 1958, extending over three years up to April 17th, 1961, in ships, planes and vehicles, arms, and military hardware, including the brigade's training, plus the personnel involved with the coalition's movement through channels of the CIA. The second $100 million incurred with Bobby Kennedy spearheading the retaliatory "Operation Mongoose" plan. If you added up the cost of the ransom paid to Fidel Castro's revolution to buy the brigade back, the total cost of the Bobby and Johnny Kennedy Cuba plan, kit and caboodle, was a towering figure of $263 million. There was also an additional $27 million spent to fund the U-2 spy plane and deliver all the photographic-intel with those high altitude fly-over missions. Add 10 million to maintain a technical crew of pilots, also fuel, and the ground maintenance team to keep the U-2 plane airborne since its maiden voyage on August 1st, 1955. Kelly Johnson at Skunk Works, with 29 engineers delivered it, remarkably, in only 8 months time.

These four totals added up:

Playa Giron-Bay of Pigs, $100 million +

Operation Mongoose, $100 million +

Brigade Buy-Back, $63 million

U-2 Spy Program, $37 million

The U.S. outlaid some $300 million. About the same amount that Batista had fled with (U.S. $300 million) when he boarded the plane for the Dominican Republic.

If you take into account Gus Russo's latest book *THE OUTFIT*, he states quite candidly and clearly that Batista's kickback was 30 percent. You do the math and multiply this +300 or up to 600 million times the other 70 percent.

Always, Cuba was about vast sums of money, much of it (in gambling casinos) both coming or going protecting and preserving it. Then add to the fact that all this money was tax free, which made it very rich and extremely alluring to the Mafia bosses.

Here it became clear with repeated attempts on Fidel Castro's life by both the CIA and the Mafia that the chance to return to mine the casino fortunes that Santos Trafficante and Meyer Lansky had built up, ended at Playa Giron. Boom and gone: "POOF" with John Kennedy's failure to provide air support that the brigade members needed to win at the battlegrounds during the Bay of Pigs.

A second planned invasion by the CIA was also scrapped by JFK.

Then Bobby Kennedy's failed Operation Mongoose plans (that were going nowhere) opened the door for and led the administration to contract an outside equalizer, known as the Mafia. After several botched attempts on Fidel Castro's life, the CIA, who had failed so miserably, desperately turned to the mob to finally get the damned job done. Several assassins were handpicked by Johnny Roselli, who was acting on behalf of his mob boss Santos Trafficante. Johnny Roselli had run the Sans Souci casino in Havana. The killers he selected were ironically the focus of Bobby Kennedy's organized crime crackdown against the syndicate, they had made both lists: Bobby Kennedy's syndicate figures target lists, and the FBI's 10 Most Wanted list.

Here was an interesting paradox in history as the United States government's ties to organized crime were clearly enmeshed inside covert operations and the plots, where both entities shared a "mutual objective." The CIA made a secret deal with the Mafia, involving them to do a job for them and put out a contract hit to assassinate Fidel Castro.

Fidel Castro had his own back and he had surrounded himself in an impregnable bearded, green-fatigued military-fighting guerrilla Army Force of intensely loyal and dedicated rebel Fidelistas. The revolution was not going to be undermined according to Fidel Castro's new goal. He correctly assumed the CIA would hire assassins whom he considered inefficient. He was of the mind set that: "An assassin does not want to die and he's only waiting for money, so he takes care of himself."

The Fidelistas had invested their lives and souls for the revolution, which meant so much more when you "stake your life to the cause." The MR 26-7, the rebels' movement, was more important than money. A paid assassin was like a fly in the ointment and about as bothersome to the slippery Fidel Castro as something stuck to the bottom of his combat boots.

It was clear that Fidel felt that he had to be ready for any paid singular efforts and mercenary actions, and he was right. The marksmen who were entering Havana disguised as "Marx-men" were caught and immediately executed. The Fidelistas were an impenetrable and fiercely loyal group of guerrilla rebels and they always recognized the Mafia hit men every time out; plan after plan and attempt after attempt failed miserably.

Several who tried were caught and executed, and some made it back to the United States, but in the end the uncollected bounty remained against all odds.

Nobody got to Castro: Neither the CIA or the Mafia could get a shot at him. It was easier, it turned out, to kill a U.S. president than a small island's dictator.

The battles between the White House, the CIA, and the FBI were exacerbated by the botched job of the Bay of Pigs, to the point where (2 months 11 days later) on June 28th, 1961:

NATIONAL SECURITY ACTION MEMORANDUM NO. 55

The memo showed that President Kennedy planned to transfer covert activities out of the hands of the CIA over to military jurisdiction, where clearly monitored under a new very highly defined complete system of checks and balances. The CIA, feeling strapped and rebuffed, was now going to be taken off the field of play by their commander-in-chief who had (in their minds) undermined and collapsed their planning schemes.

Here it was, the absolute conflict:

The president blamed the CIA for the absolute failure of the Bay of Pigs.

The red flag went up to the CIA, they were in trouble with the president.

The CIA wholly believed and totally blamed the president for not providing their plan's desperately needed *air support* which caused the whole plan's failure.

Both the CIA and the Mafia shared a mutual interest in retaking Cuba. The Mafia wanted to return to mine their gambling fortunes and the CIA would restore American business interests and the strategic military interest (by removing a pro-Soviet Fidel Castro). Both groups were into it for the obvious reason: And…when all else fails all you need to do is *just follow the money*.

Increasingly, as John Kennedy's press conferences answered more questions about the Bay of Pigs with considerable underlying tensions, the same equal underlying tensions escalated with mounting questions about military movements and actions with troops (more and more activity and increasing numbers were being sent to Vietnam). This trend began to take a downturn in President Kennedy's willingness to defend its *"provided justification of that Military Solution."* Both the CIA and the Pentagon eagerly, purposefully, wanted to dynamically increase its commitment, and their overall involvement in this region.

In July 1962, in the face of increasing demands of U.S. and world public opinion, Kennedy resolved to withdraw from Vietnam. He instructed Robert McNamara to begin a plan to pull out the advisers, which was to conclude by the end of 1965.

The plans were to be kept private... until shortly after JFK's reelection... in 1964.[2]

NATIONAL SECURITY MEMORANDUM No. 263, October 11th, 1963, one month and eleven days prior to President Kennedy's death, proved that the president's increased underlying tensions meant that he would clearly go on to *slowly* back out of Vietnam by Christmas '65 starting *that year*. It was clear to the older moneymaking war machine of the CIA that they were losing their grip on some very *highly substantial and lucrative contracts* for military hardware.

The Bay Of Pigs affair had been treated the world over as a fiasco and a serious political setback for President John Kennedy. It ended the careers of two of the intelligence committee's most distinguished men, Allen Dulles and Richard Bissell. Do not discount the fact that these were two brilliant minded career men. Allen Dulles, the great white case officer, was known as a man who would've stayed on with the agency *until he was carried out*. Allen Dulles and Richard Bissell's demise as casualties of the botched Bay of Pigs made them very much complete enemies of both Kennedys. They had damaged the agency's armor. Allen Dulles resigned November 29th, 1961. He was forced out, to step aside. In reality he was fired.

One day later, November 30th, 1961, JFK initiated through the National Security Council (NSC) that Bobby Kennedy and Max Taylor would begin to over see Mongoose.

Max Taylor recommended Edward Lansdale to unify plans for PROJECT CUBA: Some 32 tasks were to be carried out by the CIA's Richard Helms William King Harvey. These three men were a formidable alliance.

The president appointed Alexander McCone to director of the CIA and his principal objective was *"to stabilize and refloat the vessel."* McCone selected his team: Richard Helms, deputy director, plans; Ray Cline; deputy director, intelligence; Robert Bannerman; deputy director, support; Lyman Kirkpatrick, Jr. executive director; Lawrence Houston, general counsel; Sherman Kent, Office of National Estimates; and John Bross to handle interagency coordination problems.

McCone used his personal friendship with the Kennedys, especially Bobby, to reestablish close communications between *the Agency, and the Whitehouse*. Unlike most cabinet members, McCone was afforded easy, frequent, and direct access to the president. At a typical meeting with the

---

2   ZR RIFLE page 92. Claudia Furiati, Ocean Press, Talman Company; 1994.

president and the National Security Council, McCone would introduce the subject of the meeting and then call on his experts to present the evidence and details. Carefully choosing his words, he would often summarize their presentations and then dismiss the experts. When questioned by the president or any council members, he would sometimes take positions oblique to the intelligence presented. In so doing, he would always qualify his remarks by indicating that he was speaking as John Mc Cone: *"private citizen."*

While McCone was becoming acquainted with the Agency, the covert war against Cuba was continuing under the leadership of William King Harvey, who headed up the important Task Force W in the Agency's Directorate of Plans. Harvey was a huge man with a massive head, a frightened shock of hair encircling a near-bald pate. He had a gnarled brow, and cold protruding eyes set into a red face. When he moved about, he wheezed and grunted like an animal. He was also a man of extraordinary personal ambition. He had transferred to the CIA from the FBI and become one of the Agency's outstanding case officers. He was hard-drinking and possessed of an enormous ego and a Jekyll/Hyde personality, but his brashness and flamboyance were counterbalanced by a certain tenderness and propensity to help the underdog. (During his Berlin assignment, he would work long hours carefully planning covert operations that would ruin the careers of KGB officers. In contrast, walking home from his office, he often encountered destitute children for whom he would compassionately provide food and clothing.) A gun fancier since his days as an FBI agent, he often carried two loaded pearl-handled pistols in his belt. Frequently, he would place them on his desk, or point them at subordinates or visitors, *to emphasize* a particular point. He reveled in the planning and execution of covert operations. He had the imagination and audacity to carry out bold covert plans but also was fully aware of the countermeasures his adversaries might employ.

Harvey quickly established his reputation in the Agency. Early in his career, a flood of East European and Russian defectors to the West provided compelling information that the British intelligence services had been penetrated by the Soviets. It was Harvey, not James Angleton, who fingered Guy Burgess and Donald Maclean as British agents in Washington working for the Soviet Union. He also pointed to Kim Philby as *"the third man"* when Burgess and Maclean defected to the Soviet Union. But it was in Berlin that Harvey enhanced his reputation as a covert operator. Using a radar station as a cover, he was the man who masterminded the digging of an eighteen-hundred foot tunnel from West Berlin into East Berlin. It was about twenty-five feet deep; all the dirt was removed in small wooden boxes. The tunnel provided access to the main Moscow-Berlin underground communication lines, and taps attached to those lines for nearly a year provided thousands of tapes which kept translators busy for several years.

In 1960, Harvey was brought back to Washington to head Task Force W. He was given responsibility for intelligence gathering, propaganda, and sabotage raids against Cuba. He was also made chief of Project Mongoose, or *Operation Mongoose,* which was an elaborate plan to unseat Castro. The failure of the project was first disclosed publicly during a 1975 Senate investigation. Edward Lansdale had touted Harvey as the modern-day James Bond to the president and Bobby Kennedy. From their first meeting, there developed a hate relationship between Bobby and Harvey. Harvey looked suspiciously at Bobby's suggestions as those of an amateur and openly questioned Bobby's judgment.

Harvey's propensity for drink and his tendency to speak his mind often generated hate and animosity toward him from his superiors. Professionally, his plans were thorough and detailed; however, he would never reveal the whole plan, allowing for what he termed *"a freedom for action of the operators."* He was not a friend or sympathetic to those in the Agency concerned with aerial photography. "He looked upon us almost as adversaries, spying on his operations. As a matter of fact, we could often see that he was lying about the success of his operations. Repeatedly the aerial photography conflicted with the statements and the data Harvey was dictating back to us. When time and time again we continued to prove him wrong, Harvey demanded that we send photo interpreters to brief his Miami office." After the abortive Bay of Pigs invasion in April 1961, President Kennedy placed the control of U.S. covert operations in the hands of the Washington Special Operations Group that was augmented, headed by Bobby Kennedy. This included Operation Mongoose, among others.

Harvey and Bobby Kennedy continued to be at odds not only on operations but also on methods. King Harvey would maintain to his superiors that Bobby was trying to conduct covert operations with little knowledge or experience, while Bobby would complain to the president that not enough covert action was being taken to unseat Castro. Bobby Kennedy had an office at the CIA headquarters building at Langley and would stop in that office several times a week...on his way home... to nearby Hickory Hill. Frequently, he would chat with Mr. McCone, but more often he would want to discuss the latest covert operations against Cuba with officers in the Directorate of Plans. Bobby had become so intrigued with covert operations that he was insistent on talking with Cuban exile leaders directly involved.

This brought him into violent disagreement with Harvey. Harvey argued unsuccessfully that someone of Bobby's stature and position should not be known to the covert operatives, much less be seen with them. After one of these meetings, Harvey came storming into his office stating that Bobby was carving a path-- in the operations so wide-- that a Mack truck could drive on through. One participant in these discussions would later claim that Bobby could "be charming one moment and could be a complete bastard the next." General Maxwell Taylor would remark, "I don't think it occurred to Bobby in those days that his brazen temperament, his causal remarks that the president would not like this or that, his difficulty in establishing any tolerable relations with government officials, or his delight in causing offense, was doing a lot of harm to the JFK administration."

Ray Cline, the deputy director for intelligence, was "convinced that it was Bobby's original objective after the Bay of Pigs fiasco to dismantle the covert part of the Agency." It soon became evident, however, that Bobby grew unalterably intrigued with the power inherent in intelligence operations and began to exercise it, much to the chagrin of those trying to run the operations. According to Cline: "Both of the Kennedy brothers, and *particularly Bobby*, felt they had been booby-trapped at the Bay of Pigs, and it became a constant preoccupation, almost an obsession, to right the record somehow. And I remember what people have said about the Kennedys in other contexts, that they learned from their father's wisdom, *"Don't get mad... Get even."*

Harvey had undertaken three types of operations against Cuba: The first was the infiltration of agents; second, the logistical or cache operations, i.e., delivering provisions and equipment for indigenous groups opposed to Castro; and third, sabotage operations. It was the last that were most encouraged by Bobby Kennedy, with the hope that, through the sabotage of certain key Cuban industries, Castro could be brought to his knees. Harvey had assured the Special Operations Group that such operations could and would be conducted. There were a number of industries singled out for sabotage: the ESSO oil refinery in Havana, the Moa Bay nickel-mining operations, the oil refinery at Santiago de Cuba, a number of large railroad bridges, and a number of oil and gas storage installations. While the infiltration of agents was going well, along with the placement of agents, the most important sabotage operations were going awry; and of course, the failures of those operations could be seen in pictures of aerial photography. More often than not, secondary and tertiary targets were being hit. The oil refinery at Santiago de Cuba was to be sabotaged, for instance, but (when it was discovered to be defended), a lumber mill was hit instead, and Bobby Kennedy was furious.

Anthony D. Brugioni, *EYEBALL TO EYEBALL–The Cuban Missile Crisis*. Edited By Robert F. McCort: Random House--Publishing Group.

Our visits to Harvey's office were growing more frequent and always, with more bad news. On one occasion, I accompanied photo interpreter Ray Gripman. He looked at me and said, "You know we are going to be about as popular as the proverbial fart in church." I said I knew, but perhaps a better analogy would be that of the messenger bringing the bad news to "King" Harvey. Although operation after operation against Cuba was going sour, Harvey continued to blame Bobby. He began to refer to the Kennedys as "fags," in an implication that they were not physically up to the task demanded of them and that they remained in the closet instead of confronting Fidel Castro.[3]

Harvey was not the only one discontented with the Kennedy administration's foreign policy, especially toward Cuba. U.S. congressmen and senators began to criticize and make suggestions, much to the consternation of the Kennedys. Senator Fulbright delivered a long speech in the Senate on May 9, 1961, entitled, "A New Approach to the Latin American Policy of the United States," which was regarded by the Kennedys as an appeasement to Castro. All of this was going on at the height of the Soviet build-up of arms going to Cuba. The Kennedys were disemboweling the actions of the CIA, and were meddling within CIA affairs to possibly circumvent their current efforts. As smooth as McCone was at the top of it all (in both Bobby and the president's ear) on Capitol Hill, and in the White House, it didn't matter because the president's list of mortal enemies grew into echelons of the highest powers, the likes of the CIA, and the Military Industrial Complex, and they all were imploding-now, and continuing to multiply in number rapidly.

The CIA felt the country was going to hell in a hand basket, especially with the appearances of: #1) Memo #55, and #2) Memo #263, "they're being pushed out."

Then an uncanny parallel in the mutual planning of four of the president's worst enemies came into the picture: Allen Dulles, William King Harvey, and Richard Helms. The acting FBI Director *(after learning of the plot he later helped with the cover up… then in background support)* J. Edgar Hoover. Between these four men the inner workings of a conspiracy was set up which involved the Mafia grouping of Santos Trafficante, along with Carlos Marcello, Meyer Lansky, and Sam Giancana, to eliminate the arch enemy of all of those men. It would take the cooperation of certain set agents on the ground, especially on the grassy knoll, which led to the hill with the cement wall and the wooden fence, which leads to the railroad tracks and to the freight yard. The CIA was in position on the grassy knoll, and it was from up there that the president's murderer operated.

---

[3]   The relationship between Harvey and the Kennedys continued to deteriorate, and after the missile crisis, the president asked that Harvey be replaced. In January, 1963, Harvey was removed and sent to Rome. He was replaced by Desmond Fitzgerald. Harvey's problems with drink continued. On one occasion, he was driving home at night at high speed when he was stopped by an Italian patrolman. Harvey got out of his car, drew his pistol, placed it at the patrolman's temple and asked, "what's the problem?" The uniform patrolman, with eyes bulging, thought he had stopped a Mafia chief and was going to die meekly. He said, "Nothing." Harvey said, "That's what I thought," and got in his car. and drove away. He was the type of a man who would and could sooner or later arrange his own planning to later get even…with both of the Kennedys.

ZR Rifle was the code name given the CIA operation directed initially by Allen Dulles, Richard Bissell, and allegedly also later by Richard Helms. William King Harvey was the original organizer of the whole operation. In the first months of 1961: Bissell entrusted William Harvey the task of creating ZR Rifle.

ZR RIFLE, The Plot to Kill Kennedy and Castro, pg. 128; Claudia Furiati:

> The "kill shot" was from the front, and the bullet passed through the president's skull, killing him. Three men dressed as bums and another shooting team also fired from the Texas School Book Depository.

The Mafia was handling, "monitoring those that were on the grassy knoll." Jack Ruby had to report back to Trafficante that the job was a success, which he did. Ruby kept tabs on these Roselli-picked guns who did the job.

Of those five men up there, one was dressed in a business suit with a fairly large girth, and left a coke bottle on top of the wall. The second was an important witness who climbed the cement pedestal attached to the pergola structure and scanned the parking lot behind the fence. This man witnessed what happened to the fleeing group. He has never been identified and he has never come forward or ever been questioned about the incident. It was a very complex detailed effort, that I will explain, *as clearly as I can* in the chapter: THE KENNEDY FILE.

Railroad dispatcher Lee Bowers, sitting up in his tower observation post, saw the three men disguised as bums moving towards the trains. There is only a limited amount a man is willing to testify to, or swear to, which *included a flurry of activity* he noticed near the stockade fence. He also gave testimony to the Warren Commission in which each time he tried to describe just what he had see in the parking lot, the interviewer led him away from the subject (trying to avoid certain particular facts of vitally important information that he might reveal to the Commission and the public). Afterwards Lee Bowers said in accounts with other unbiased researchers that: "*there was some unusual occurrence--a flash of light--or smoke or something which caused me to feel like something out of the ordinary occurred there.*" Lee Bowers continued to scan the fence searching for the cause of the flash and those noises that he had heard over by the stockade. Shortly afterwards, Lee Bowers noticed a train moving, the departure of which he had not authorized, pulling out of the yard.

He then transmitted the order to stop it. Police found and then arrested three fairly well-groomed tramps or vagabond bums who were hopping a ride on a freight train. Then the mug shots, and also the fingerprints that were taken along with any records of that arrest went mysteriously missing, for 27 years. It is what it is, and that's just some very uniquely clever and classic CIA subterfuge.

In the remarkable book, *The Killing Of A President* by Robert J. Groden, see page 69, pictured is one of the shooting teams that fired on JFK's limousine. Focus on the man trailing the officer heading for jail. In my opinion seeing him in those photographs he has the look of the fiscal finality of the sharp-shooting military eyes of a serious calamitous contractor, that in my view had just recently taken out a target. These three men being led by Robert Maheu were all employed by the CIA, conspiring to assassinate John F. Kennedy.

They were not without accomplices–see chapter: The Kennedy File.

The bullets they used were tainted. One frangible bullet tore a huge bore into Kennedy's skull and blasted him into the ultimate *dirt nap*, as the bullet passed through...on its way... into the streets of Dallas. The FBI handled the Texas School Book Depository, and various background collections and the droppings of various key articles of evidence. After hearing the crack of a high-powered rifle shot, Officer Marrion Baker's attention was attracted to the Depository by the startled flight of pigeons from the roof. He left the motorcade to investigate the building with his gun drawn. Baker, and building superintendent Roy Truly ran up one flight of stairs to the second floor, where they encountered employee Lee Harvey Oswald in the lunchroom drinking a Coca-Cola. Oswald responded calmly while Baker questioned Roy Truly, "Does this man belong here?" "Yes," he told Baker, "this guy's okay, he works here." There he was, arousing no suspicions or even breaking a sweat at this time. Lee Harvey Oswald nonchalantly left the building, unhurriedly, and quietly boarded a bus. Stalled in traffic, Oswald got off the bus and then took a taxi ride. Richard Randolf Carr had watched the procession of the motorcade from the new Dallas County Government Center. During the assassination, Carr caught sight of a heavyset man who was wearing a tan sports jacket, as well as another man *who wore a hat and black-framed clear glasses up on the sixth floor* of the Depository building.

When the shooting stopped, Carr saw these two men run from the Depository building, jump into a Rambler station wagon and drive off, away from the scene north on Houston Street. After leaving his vantage point, Carr saw the heavyset man again hurriedly leave the plaza. I will go into details, with the identities of the members of this team that handled the depository in the JFK chapter of *The Beachcomber*, THE KENNEDY FILE.

Without going any further, the pattern emerged that there were two teams of five men each. It seems like it was done in the pattern of a basic field operative military style: 3 shooters, 1 spotter, and 1 watcher. Both on the grassy knoll from the stockyard fence and in the school book depository building. It's very clear that a team of men was up "on point" firing from the knoll, and up in the building of the Texas Book Depository. Oswald never picked up a rifle on that particular day.

What's equally interesting is the *conduct of the* FBI, who would try (for whatever reason) to gloss over Jack Ruby's involvement with the Mafia. Lee Harvey Oswald knew Jack Ruby, and both men were seen together by numerous patrons and witnesses that had frequented the Carousel Club. It's also true that everybody acknowledges the Ruby, Oswald, Shaw, and Ferrie connections.

David Ferrie was Lee Oswald's superior officer when he was in the Civil Air Patrol in New Orleans. Also he was known to have managed the Carousel Club at one time. And, added to that, he and Oswald were also often seen together. Beverly Oliver asserted on record that she had observed both Oswald and Ferrie together numerous times. The mob would tie up all the loose ends in its part of the bargain. Jack Ruby with the help of the Dallas Police Department was ready to take out Lee Harvey Oswald. It's true, and also indisputable factual accounting by many sources that after Fidel Castro had taken over the Cuban government in 1959: Jack Ruby traveled there to meet with mob figures whom Fidel Castro had both exiled and imprisoned. On one of those trips to Cuba, Jack Ruby met with Meyer Lansky who was known (to Jack Ruby) under the moniker of "Mr. Fox." Since the CIA and the FBI were calling the shots, the Mafia did the government's bid. If I had to say by dividing the conspiracy groups into a three-part set-up:

#1.) The FBI, Texas School Book Depository; The B-Team, in the Background.

#2.) The CIA, The Grassy Knoll Shooters Group; The A-Team, Hit Squad.

#3.) Ruby, Shaw, Marcello, Trafficante, Lansky, Roselli, Giancana; Field Personnel.

I think number one was the worst that day and the most disorganized not knowing which kind of damned rifle to pull out of the building. I have to admit also that even if it was sloppy work, they still managed to pull the whole thing off. Then… letting Oswald escape from the building, and maybe causing the plan to almost collapse. It required some *heavy troubleshooting* and hustle work to frame Oswald for another killing of a Texas police officer, J. D. Tippit. Lee Harvey Oswald was framed twice in one day. And, remarkably, he never pulled a trigger or fired a shot on the afternoon of November 22nd, 1963.

I suppose that the most blatant attempts to cover up the advancing ideologies of the war-making machinery of the military industrial complex occurred when Lyndon Johnson had the evidence contained in the presidential limousine soon afterward, even before the blood had dried, *washed and dismantled.* If ever there was a symbol to come out of this crime of the century, it was in those words and in the orders from the future president: *"have that car washed and dismantled."*

The president's brain was dealt with in a similarly crude fashion. Here it was removed, and placed in a stainless steel container, filled with formalin solution, so with the standard "forensic testing" it could be sectioned and examined a short time later. The brain, belonging to JFK; got mishandled later.

The key tests would have shown clearly the trajectory of the bullet's pathway through the brain, however, there is no record or indication that this critical work was ever done. If the tests were performed and the shots or the bullet's trail indicated a shot fired from the front, from the location up on the grassy knoll, from the fence overlooking the railway stockyards, it would brand the event a conspiracy: The key evidence was purposefully suppressed by the United States Government.

You need the help or the additional hindrance of some mighty powerful segments of government to tell the country you've lost your own slain president's brain at the facility of Parkland Hospital in Dallas, Texas. To send the whole thing even further along into the abyss, or to make matters worse somebody had the gall to put <u>Allen Dulles on the Warren Commission,</u> along with Gerald Ford who was also continuously leaking out vital information to the FBI and J. Edgar Hoover.

The directives of the commission's investigations focused solely on Lee Harvey Oswald. There never was *any other suspect* on the commission's agenda. Arlen Spector and Gerald Ford both supported the theory of the lone assassin and the remarkably ridiculously false theory of the single magic bullet. When the report was released and printed and backed by the majority of the press coverage, it sort of quelled and obscured for awhile the existence of outright conspiracy.

The newly sworn in president, while at Parkland Hospital, said the immortal words of instruction: "have it washed and dismantled." Literally, the leadership and now the direction of the country were notoriously changed by the conspiracy that took place. America and its true leader as the commander-in-chief, had been radically washed and dismantled on November 22, 1963.

Bobby Kennedy's involvements with the inter-meddling within the CIA covert operations policies caused several stirs inside the secret agency. Memo #55 and Memo #263 and the agency's blunder of the Bay of Pigs spread writing on the wall that everything had been changed. Bobby Kennedy had completely pissed off "King" Harvey who described the Kennedys as fags... and scoffed at McNamara, calling him... his bagman at the CIA. Boiling hot bad blood was abounding.

They had fired two of the agency's most important people, its leader Allen Dulles, and Richard Bissell. (Dulles and Bissell resigned in theory, but in reality both were forced out.) And if the Kennedys' enemies list wasn't large enough, they had increasingly angered the Mafia's--business affairs-- in the United States with the McClellan Committee Hearings. The Mafia lost billions with Castro taking over in Cuba and the money coming into the U.S. mob business was already tightening up once the Joseph Valachi--testimony was airing on U.S. Television during--October 1963. In a public fallout afterwards, there was going to be a forever shrinking pie, for the mafia to salvage.

(General Charles Cabell was also later fired in Jan. 1963, by John Kennedy.)

Both Lyndon Johnson and J. Edgar Hoover were knowledgeable men and they knew if Kennedy could *dismiss* the director of the CIA, and a man like Allen Dulles, and Richard Bissell, <u>ANYONE COULD GO.</u> And with a re-election swiftly approaching the rumors were amiss about Kennedy soon dropping LBJ from his ticket. Certainly Kennedy would let J. Edgar Hoover fall by the wayside the earliest chance he got after his reelection was over. He would've quickly replaced the old deadly little FBI *wing nut* that so squarely despised him.

The CIA, the Mafia, and to some equal extremes Bureau Chief J. Edgar Hoover of the FBI were direct enemies of the president: All of this was added to tensions of the Cuban Missile Crisis and the possibility of the troops being withdrawn in Vietnam.

John Kennedy made a vital concession in the agreement with Kruschev at the conclusion of the Cuban Missile Crisis. He agreed to cease the U.S. led CIA assassination attempts against Fidel Castro and to *not invade Cuba.* All of this was in exchange for the Soviet Union (in their part of the bargain) following through to: Outright <u>remove all of the Nuclear Missile warheads from Cuban soil.</u> Behind closed doors missiles were being secretly wiped out or eliminated gradually, but this part is kept completely out of view, off the table; <u>in a back door deal Missiles were also removed or re-deployed, taken out of TURKEY.</u> The agreement hindered The Military Industrial Complex, and forced the military to decrease its *direct pressures* that were already *active and working* and also currently effective and in place: The Brigade training camps, and the funding of several units of mercenary groups on Cuban-soil, working to overthrow the pro-Castro regime.

Suddenly things drastically changed and the Military had to walk a fine line to keep both Kruschev and Kennedy satisfied that they were going to honor the agreement, which gave the fledgling Fidel Castro two concrete things:

#1.) It allowed Fidel Castro more time to solidify his governing position, forming his people's allegiance to the revolution working with the guaranteed postponement in delaying the U.S. Military's and the CIA's planned second invasion on Cuban soil.

#2.) Cuba would thus remain under the protective wing of the Soviet Union even after all the missile warheads were eliminated. And, Fidel Castro could still exchange missiles for manpower, which was his strategic planned *alternative* towards solidifying his military position. Nobody knew about the missiles being removed in TURKEY.

(*The missiles gone in Cuba, secretly going gone in Turkey; as the Cuban army vastly grew in size with more and more numbers of Russian advisers.*)

Not only McNamara, but all of the U.S. authorities and Kennedy collaborators at that time affirmed that they were not going to invade Cuba, independent of the crisis or its consequences. But there were contingency plans and the covert actions of Operation Mongoose, which projected a direct invasion.[4] (Kennedy seemed more concerned in the global context with Russia and Berlin… and how close he had gotten himself…into a nuclear war.)

Now Kennedy had to rely on the economic blockade and Operation Mongoose working. Even with the blockade in place, Kennedy had made a deal with Kruschev. No matter *how small this agreement seemed*, to Kruschev it was paramount.

Since Kennedy had already authorized Bobby to head up the Operation Mongoose plan, John Kennedy was truly handcuffed to make good on this one promise. JFK was *still stinging very badly* from the CIA's mishandling of the Bay Of Pigs:

The plan could not succeed unless the invading forces were to link up with more military support that he (JFK), in the heat of the battle, steadfastly refused to provide. By not informing him of all the details, the CIA had wholly counted on JFK (duped by proxy) deciding in immediacy, in battle as the commander-in-chief of the military's armed combat forces on the ground in Cuba, to act or fall in line with the CIA's desperately needed air support.

Post the Bay Of Pigs fiasco, post the Cuban Missile Crisis, John Fitzgerald Kennedy was aptly now more than ready to clearly distance himself from the Cuba problem.

The Defense Department also made its contribution to the assault.[5] According to instructions in the National Security Decree No. 100, the Pentagon prepared military contingency plans with a view to a possible confrontation with its adversary. In fact, in April 1962 (one year later), the U.S. military carried out a rehearsal for the invasion, dubbed "Operation Quick Kick" on the Puerto Rican coast facing Cuba, involving 83 warships, 300 airplanes and 40,000 men.

This D.O.D. exposure of such an audacious about-face to what JFK was trying to weave into domestic foreign policy post the disastrous Bay of Pigs fiasco, sent the wrong signal to JFK as he hotly responded and sent his signal:

When the president caught the CIA's top military brass trying to ignore his memos Number 55 and Number 263 by dragging their feet in carrying out his new policies to cease all plots against Fidel Castro, JFK sent the FBI and local law enforcement in to raid, shut-down and *eradicate* all the CIA's secret military training camps on Florida's No Name Key in the Everglades, and also the same operationally connected camps of Lake Ponchartrain, The Ponchartrain 11's brigade groups of mercenary soldiers, who were training in

---

4   ZR RIFLE: The Plot to Kill Kennedy and Castro, pg. 61.

5   ZR RIFLE: The Plot to Kill Kennedy and Castro, pg. 43.

the New Orleans Louisiana corridor. This move by JFK was the straw that broke the camel's back.

The idea in Kennedy's mind, other than finding the CIA/Mafia's collusion deplorable, at this time was simply to back off for awhile after resolving the potentially horrendous consequences of the showdown of the super powers in the United States versus Russia/Cuban Missile Crisis. Kennedy needed this time to cool out and rethink his strategy. JFK's own thought process was that he needed to regroup after the CIA had put him through the ringer with the Bay of Pigs debacle. He felt that he was just lucky that he dodged the bullet and survived the Cuban Missile Crisis, and he had to back off of Castro, and concentrate on pressing economic and domestic civil rights issues. Cuba and Castro were put on the back burner, because it was time for him and the JFK administration to focus more squarely on his upcoming reelection. JFK's infamous line to the CIA to go "swing the ax elsewhere."

John Kennedy had truly antagonized the network of organized crime, since the president and his brother were in the midst of conducting a very powerfully sweeping and intense–and successful–war on the mob; obtaining several key indictments, convictions, and also deportations. The president's decision to back off for awhile and not to invade Cuba a second time meant that all of their hope to return to mine the fortunes they had created in Cuba with the syndicate's highly profitable casinos and prostitution operations which Fidel Castro had shut down upon coming to power… now would remain permanently… shut down.

The CIA, and the military industrial complex, and the Mafia, were completely dumbfounded with all the loops and hangman's nooses JFK was interconnecting: *tying up both their hands and tying up both their feet,* on every *possible* alternative move necessary for them to succeed in getting back into Cuba. Those holding power in the U.S. intelligence agencies, and as well as organized crime, now hated Kennedy more than they hated Fidel Castro.

Such hatred evolved within both *the ranks* and *the leadership* of the CIA in groups like TASK FORCE W, OP 40, Brigade #2506, AM LASH and also MIRR or Alpha 66 and Ponchartrain 11. It evolved to conclude with the plan designed *by the CIA that collaborated with the FBI and also with the Mafia,* to eliminate the 35th president of the United States. The uncanny parallel of the two men: Allen Dulles, *and* William "King" Harvey (both fired and reassigned by JFK), started the ball rolling. In time, later on, J. Edgar Hoover came on board to aid with cover up of the CIA's Plan. Allegedly: General Charles Cabell, Gen. Maxwell Taylor, and Edward Lansdale, and also Colonel Frank Eagan, of the military industrial complex "M.I.C." Contingency Group, along with the contributions of the Mafia that were secondary to the CIA's objective, provided the support team and some additional field personnel (this so being *the view* of this particular writer). Below denotes exceptions, or those men on duty or following orders acting on behalf of top of the chain of the command, in the CIA leadership, underneath Allen Dulles.

Maxwell Taylor, Colonel Frank, Ed Lansdale acting on prior orders. Not one of these three men who knew of this plot said or did anything to stop the acts of the traitors... therefor they were co-conspirators... in this tyranny.

(Maxwell Taylor was removed from complicity but must've known about it. It is impossible for this author to believe that Max Taylor did "not know." Maxwell Taylor is one of JFK's most capable and reliable officers.)

NSC 5412

THE WHITEHOUSE ROOM #5412

What Made This Room The Omnipotent Control Room

Although there had been some covert U.S. operations in Indochina during Harry Truman's administration, as set forth in NSC directives 10/2 and in 10/5, which had been controlled by Dwight Eisenhower, the approval of NSC 5412 on March 15th, 1954 marked the official recognition and sanctioning of a much larger program of anti communist activities in Indochina and also throughout the world. These so called "covert" and "clandestine operations" began with black operations (black ops) and forthwith the CIA's branding of what later on after 1974, became known as "the cult of intelligence."

THE CIA AND THE CULT OF INTELLIGENCE

A Book. Written By Victor Marchetti and John D. Marks

1974, Alfred Knopf, New York

"For in this country this secrecy.... has become a God in this country, and those people who have secrets, travel in a kind of fraternity.... and they will not speak to anyone else."

In chapter one: Senator William J. Fulbright, Senate Chairman, Foreign Relations Committee; 1971.

"All activities conducted pursuant to this directive... which are so planned, and, executed that any U.S. Government responsibility for them is not evident to unauthorized persons, and that if uncovered [later on] the U.S. Government... can plausibly--disclaim any responsibility--for them."

"Specifically, such operations shall include any covert activities related to: propaganda, political action, economic warfare, preventive direct action, including sabotage, anti-sabotage, demolition; escape and evasion and evacuation measures; subversion against hostile states or groups, including assistance to any underground resistance movements, guerrillas and refugee liberation groups; support of indigenous and the anti communist elements in threatened countries of the free world; deceptive plans, or operations; and all activities compatible with this directive--necessary to accomplish all of the above--all of the foregoing, all inclusive."

In chapter eleven: (CONCLUSIONS) Malcolm Muggerridge wrote in the summation--May 1996.

"In the eyes of posterity it will inevitably seem that, in safeguarding our freedom, we destroyed it; that the vast clandestine apparatus... we built up, to probe our enemies' resources and intentions, only served in the end... to confuse our own purposes; that the practice of deceiving others for the good of the state, led infallibly to our deceiving ourselves; and that the vast army of intelligence personnel we have built up to execute these purposes were soon caught up in the web of their own sick fantasies, with a lot of disastrous consequences to them and to us."

AND, YE SHALL KNOW THE TRUTH. AND, THE TRUTH SHALL MAKE YOU FREE. (John, VIII: 32 Inscribed on the marble wall of the main lobby at CIA headquarters. Langley, VA.)

The special group NSC 5412 was blessed in it's most secret formation with a truly herculean unlimited- financial backing: "It did not have to answer... to anyone and all of its agenda meetings... were without any limits."

The financial power base was vast under Allen Dulles and John Foster Dulles, and Prescot Bush, and Mr. George H.W. Bush (a businessman at the time of its formation), Howard Hughes, Richard Nixon, Richard Bissell and Tracey Barnes, Gary Droller, and Colonel Joseph C. King, backed up by Frank Bender ("General Boulding"). E. Howard Hunt, Frank Sturgis, and Jack Crichton, H.L.Hunt, and D.H.Bird, and Clint Murchison, and George De Mohrenschildt, along with two future members of the George H.W. Bush administration including Mr. James Baker, and, Robert Mosbacher. Richard Nixon was owned by the Pepsi Cola company, the Ford Motor Company, also the United Fruit Company, and the Prescot Bush, George H.W. Bush Zapata Oil Company. Robert Bennett, and Howard Hughes, and Robert Maheu, and Richard Nixon, and Allen Dulles (CIA). All this above out of NSC 5412. Mr. Richard Milhouse Nixon got his backing from everywhere, including the mafia. He was easily, the most strongly linked of all past American politicians to the mafia. After he lost the election to JFK in 1960, he owed all those backers even more... since they gave to him multi millions in the lost cause of backing him. Richard Nixon was bought by Carlos Marcello through his campaign manager Murray Chotiner. Richard Nixon was also deep pocket bought by Santos Trafficante, through Florida Banker Bebe Rebozo--The layer connection to the CIA's front company, which was based in Florida real estate—to Keyes Royalty. The Keyes Royalty, Eugenio Martinez, Frank Sturgis, Raphael Quintero, and, Bernard Barker, with

Orlando Bosch, Howard Hunt, and William "King" Harvey, and Richard Bissell, and also Richard Helms.

The men who were controlled by the Dulles / Nixon / Bush / Hughes all operating inside the big NSC 5412 nest that were subordinates with Richard Helms included Joseph C. King, Tracey Barnes, Ed Lansdale, William King Harvey, Nino Diaz Lanz, David Atlee Phillips, David Sanchez Morales, Gordon Campbell, John Martino, Bradley Ayres. Frank Eagan, Ted Shackley, Jack Hawkins, and, Rolando Masferrer, and, Eladio del Valle, Gary Droller, Robert Maheu, Anthony Veciana, Lyman Kirkpatrick, Desmond Fitzgerald, and, Gen. Robert Cushman. Thomas Eli Davis, Tony Izquierdo, Manuel Quesada, Gliberto Hernandez, Tony Cuesta, and Herminio Diaz Garcia.

Understanding the real hierarchy and the complicity of the players and the several layers involved in the JFK cold case: Keeping in mind--Nixon is Prescot Bush's man since 1946, with a long hand and a deep major financial commitment and investment. Everything the grocer's son will become...his political career is bankrolled by Prescot Bush. Nixon was the pro War in Vietnam and Indochina politician since 1954. Vietnam, it was his brainchild (Dulles and Prescot Bush were selling this war option with Nixon since 1946); the WWII war making machine was finished and war contracts were highly lucrative to the Military Industrial Complex. Nixon's anti-communist stance as the Special Group 40 / NSC 5412 / being its most ardent supporter with Allen Dulles for major war campaigns moving throughout Southeast Asia. John Fitzgerald Kennedy: "JFK since 1954 had in point by multiple indefatigable undeniable veracious facts opposed this Vietnam war."

Nixon is the one who promised this war to Pepsi Cola, Ford Motor Company, and Standard Oil, and Zapata Offshore Drilling (George Bush's Company), and the United Fruit Company. Then, Nixon lost to John Kennedy in 1960 in one of the closest elections in U.S. history. Chicago went to Jack Kennedy through a big helping hand of Sam Giancana (and the powerful teamsters union, which helped sway the contest there); as Frank Sinatra and mafia ties to Joe Kennedy prevailed there. Nixon had all these fat cats and high rollers, or corporate backing, and business people backing him. After he lost, these debts to all these fat cats haunted Nixon owing them all millions. Jack Kennedy had his family's inordinate fortune, through Joe Kennedy Sr. backing him. JFK had charisma, and also a powerful vibrant people's allegiance. Through television the world got to know this new younger movie-star handsome candidate, and America became enthralled with John F. Kennedy. Nixon was the lesser magnetic figure, the dour looking dowdy politician (The Old Guard). America went with the promise of the new frontier of the shining rising star of camelot (the new vanguard). John Kennedy's ace in the hole was being bank rolled by his family's extraordinary wealth, and since nobody owned him (but his own family) he could do whatever he wanted to for his country, and his people, without the interest of sticky fingers controlling his interests. In the greatest sense, he was the least corporate--influence--peddled president in all of U.S. History.

Top that with the blessing, or possibly the curse, of him being only the second in line of the United States President's who was also an intellectual. (FDR being the only other one.) Of course we know what happens when somebody with big ideas like FDR tried to do too much for the American people he served. There was a coup attempt... by some titans of Wall Street to overthrow FDR in 1934, and they intended... to put a military man into the Whitehouse. The plan was foiled when the man they had selected, Major General Smedley Butler, blew the whistle to congress. JFK did something very disturbing to later undercut the spirit of the old guard, and the cold war politicians. Blazing away, in the intellectual approach to moving away from the arms race, towards challenging the Soviet Union to a "peace race." These peace with the enemy speeches threw the military industrial complex into shifting sands. The peace talks with Russia indicated some upcoming wing clipping in the business volume for the Military Industrial Complex. The crowning moment was he signed in to law the nuclear test ban treaty. Later, to go even further in cementing that more changes were forthcoming, he told the banking industry to return back to the Gold Standard. Kennedy tells the Treasury Department to print its own money... rather than distributing the traditional federal reserve notes, which carried the interest charges. Then, in an unprecedented move towards U.S. Steel: JFK decided to tell U.S. Steel that, "asking for... a price raise... at this juncture [in the early 1960s] is far too greedy." Raising the steel prices up six dollars more per ton would be detrimental to the economic growth, at that time... in history. JFK wanted to put a stop to U.S. Steel price gouging. If all that did not worry big business and big banking, he told Texas oil billionaires the 27.5 percent oil depletion allowance was far too liberal. He wanted to repeal that big tax break for Texas oil. Now JFK had four big enemies that knew that they were on thin ice with this youthful, forward thinking president. The Military Industrial Complex, United States Steel Industry, The Banking Industry, The Texas oil tycoons. The final shocking deal breaker sealing a change to the war making machinery: JFK told cabinet members and selected confidants privately that he planned to back out of Vietnam by withdrawing all U.S. Military personnel after his reelection–before Christmas–1965. (The speaker of the house Tip O'neil confirmed this on record with Colonel L. Fletcher Prouty confirming it too.) JFK, DVD See The Extra's "BEYOND JFK," 1991; Warner Brothers.

These bold steps towards peace–and changing business and big banking and altering big oil barons from getting their liberal 27.5 percent oil depletion allowance–all these big moves were the dress rehearsal for the coming party that none of these vanguard old dogs and older politicians... the anti-communist pentagon war hawks like Nixon or Allen Dulles, and all of the CIA / NSC 5412 mechanics who were working with Alpha 66 and Brigade 2506 underneath (Allen Dulles) Gen. Robert Cushman, Charles Cabell, Colonel J.C. King, Tracey Barnes, Desmond Fitzgerald, nobody in this S-Group 40 / NSC 5412 committee wanted to see any of these bold steps JFK was taking ever make it towards fruition. It was clear to the older vanguard, the war hawks, that it was time to say: "JFK has got to go." (The men connected to the CIA decided to assassinate... their president, John Fitzgerald Kennedy.)

The Pentagon insider who wrote the book *JFK–The CIA, Vietnam, and the Plot to Assassinate John F. Kennedy*, Fletcher Prouty called it succinctly what it is by recording thusly that "a power elite coalesced...and they don't vote or there is nothing on paper...and they just decided this young–forward thinking president–that guy has got to go." After the Bay of Pigs failed invasion the Cuban Missile Crisis, the men in the CIA knew that Jack Kennedy planned to change things and reset the playing field; he began to dismantle the CIA. He started pulling the teeth out of the CIA. The first Memo #55 took the CIA out of covert operations. He later followed with the General Walter Beadle Smith dictum and he told Bobby, "It's time to take a bucket of slop and cover over it. It's time to put these CIA covert operations, under a different roof." (Sept. 1960: The formation of ZR RIFLE-Dulles / Bissell / Helms-William Harvey is the organizer of the operation. Sept. 1963: Howard Hughes / Howard Hunt / David Atlee Phillips. Anthony Veciana saw Phillips directing: Lee Harvey Oswald / Clay Shaw / Guy Bannister / George de Mohrenschildt. Jack Ruby, Bernard Barker Robert Maheu all involved).

It's extremely soluble, in this bitter wedge of good old American Pie–understand the mendacity that these old dogs who pulled the coup de ta–JFK– killing off were the old dogs we've heard tales of corruption about since their passing.

THE OLD DOGS MOST RESPONSIBLE FOR JFK's MURDER

#1.) RICHARD M. NIXON AS THE TOP DOG

#2.) ALLEN DULLES THE GHOST DOG

#3.) J. EDGAR HOOVER THE BULL DOG

#4.) LYNDON JOHNSON THE UNDER DOG

THE MEN WHO KILLED KENNEDY--THE GUILTY MEN

BBC-- Nigel Turner--The History Channel

Recent revelations in numerous books and the exquisite documentary on the history channel TMWKK PART #9.) THE GUILTY MEN–In it Ed Tatro, Bar McClelland, and two other fine writers Professor Walt Brown, and also

Gregory Burnham, reveal a very meticulous investigative narrative story. Ed Clark (known as the secret boss over in Texas) had in theory pulled all of the strings throughout Dealey Plaza–orchestrating the whole JFK assassination–on behalf of then Vice President Lyndon Baines Johnson's orders. As I have interpreted the story, at the concluding wrap up, the price paid was 8 million dollars. LBJ bowed out in 1968. (Ironically it was reduced to 6 million.)

Due to the path of the investigation in the Henry Marshall probe into LBJ's past back door deals involving illegal appropriation of Federal Cotton Allotment Funds through Billy Solesties–in crystal clear legal language, Ed Tatro recollecting or reporting this story, LBJ / Cliff Carter / Malcolm Wallis have a meeting to discuss what to do about the probe of Henry Marshall into their previous–business dealings. In the television recording I watched from that website on that series it is reported that LBJ's orders were the directed neutralization of Henry Marshall. Ed Tatro stated later, after that meeting with LBJ and Cliff Carter, that Malcolm Wallis eliminated Henry Marshall on June 3rd, 1961. (I am paraphrasing the indictment by the men reporting this history. They reported that LBJ said this, quote; "get rid of him").

Afterwards the continuing senate investigation with Bobby Kennedy (as reported by researcher Gregory Burnham) into the Bobby Baker corruption and bribery scandal involved payoffs and contract manipulation with Texas oil man Clint Murchison. It is reported by Burnham that Lyndon Johnson realizes the senate probe into LBJ's contract payoff and bribery deals (with Billy Solesties, talking about all of these secret deals) will result in getting LBJ dumped off of the 1964 ticket. Of course this probe is sent into firey overdrive when Nixon releases that hot news story, as he got it from FBI–J. Edgar Hoover over to Carl Freund, who writes a disastrous headline-JFK MAY DROP JOHNSON-In Dallas Morning news. (Photo Copy: Robert Groden. See Page #6, Arrival In Dallas; "The Killing Of A President").

Gregory Burnham alleges that this is the straw that broke the camel's back. This is what he believes drove Lyndon Johnson to go along with "the Texans" and "the Cubans" or the big oil magnates who hired CIA plotters to eliminate JFK. In order to pursue the lucrative KBR war contracts in the war in Vietnam: JFK had to be taken out to stop the intense probe into the Bobby Baker / Malcolm Wallis / Billy Solesties / Clint Murchison / LBJ corruption scandal. Also to stop JFK from doing away with the lucrative twenty seven and a half percent oil depletion allowance. It also suggests that Jim Marrs' closing line in *CROSSFIRE–The Plot That Killed Kennedy* that these said pointedly strong allegations in books as well as what we can see on the world wide internet in JFK's murder are both liquid, fluent or, conversely accurate. (*THE MEN WHO KILLED KENNEDY*–NIGEL TURNER–THE HISTORY CHANNEL, BBC, LONDON.) The evidence by itself is quite staggering.

In Book One–*THE BEACHCOMBER*–Michael Gering

November 22nd, 2013

On the 50th Anniversary of the JFK Assassination, a naive writer wrote "I Am A Texas Oil Friendly Writer." Even perhaps far worse in my esteemed colleague's eyes, I went on to add that I was a mafia friendly writer damned to that. I have evidence that I believe that, based on the first book. I will go on with my assertion that I'm correct sticking to it. I am recalling what I said in book one. I will add a few names to the NSC#5412 / S Group 40 / Alpha 66 / Z R RIFLE. I added what I learned about E. Howard Hunt, and Richard "Dick" Nixon, and "the Alpha 66 tie ins to the Bay of Pigs" and the threads of the JM Wave Cubans naming names added to ZR RIFLE... adding in the Richard Case Nagell and Abraham Bolden story. Stubbornly with all the evidence that accumulated or is mounting here that fingers Texas Oil and LBJ as the scoundrel, I prefer to state again: Texas Oil sign the checks, they do not pull the triggers. That is the only reason George Bush... would dare allow himself to be photographed standing...out in front of his old friend–D.H. Bird's–Texas School Book Depository. It's on display in multiple websites.

IN NOVEMBER 2003–I WROTE THE FOLLOWING PARAGRAPH– *THE BEACHCOMBER*

There once was this odd headsman headstrong theory. It was right out of the book of travels like a fantasy like that old Elvis film–set in the old Arab Nations the... sensational plot... of a film "harem scarem." (It's truly as far-fetched a plot, that in my-opinion is fantasy.) Nevertheless rumors persist so here goes that theory. The headsman told me the characters before he told me the story. He said the names of all the characters. Clint Murchison, LBJ, and Bobby Baker, Billy Solesties, Malcolm Wallis, and a wildcat oil man, H. L. Hunt. And yet between those six yahoos... you could find enough skeletons buried to make some Texas hay-maker's... hazardous hazel and some hare brained harlotry, that could cause a stampede through graveyards; if those skeletons from the dead were ever allowed to reanimate... and if those spirits could talk some day? It would galvanize us all in God's country... the country would rejoice with the rapture... aint that a pistol? Oh I beg unto thee "don't believe the gospel," the words they speak shall not tumble, off of my elder philtrum. If we look at it their way for a moment even if I do not share their uniquely bazaar point of view: They'll tell you countless times over and over that The Crime Of The Century was so simple in the context of the swarthy "high cabal." Clint Murchison Senior, H.L. Hunt, J. Edgar Hoover, and, Richard M. Nixon and from there back to Nixon to Carlos Marcello, and, the Hotel Del Charro–La Jolla. Over and then, through the ties with D.H. Bird and Bobby Baker–who owned the civil air patrol which David Ferrie is a pilot in. If LBJ, Bobby Baker, Malcolm Wallis, or Billy Solesties were all part of a scheme with Nixon–Marcello Johnny Roselli, Clint Murchison, and the wild cat oil man H.L.Hunt, well I must then ask you, weren't all these men already very fat, and very wealthy, and beyond riches to spend? (Yes?) Also, ask yourself: Would you if you were already that far ahead with your wealth risk a joint venture... with the likes of the above mentioned "lot" and roll the dice, over a "27.5 per cent oil depletion allowance" planning a public murder of a President–John F. Kennedy–of The United States Of America? The answer in my opinion is No.

My stubborn naive plea persisting, I do get the Richard Nixon part of it, but not the Texas Oil men's part in it. Uniquely, as rotten as the excuse... being naive, or in my being a naive Writer; I'm still a Texas Oil friendly Writer. We know that as we sit here today Richard M. Nixon would have never seen "the presidency" had not JFK been "killed." J. Edgar Hoover "would have been retired, put out to pasture, after JFK's reelection," into his second term. Round Up The Usual Suspects–Bogey Would Utter In Casablanca–Hereby So Forth And So On: This too shall pass? Big Texas Oil– They Sign Checks–They Pay People–To Do The Work. A CHECK SIGNER, "watches who he pays." If indeed the reporting was accurate...and if indeed LBJ has Mac Wallace inside... D.H.Birds' Texas School Book Depository. If indeed the pictures prove accurate...George Bush has his hands in pockets...in front of that' old Texas Book Depository. (He could possibly only be there to watch Alpha 66 / NSC #5412 / S-Group 40 / and Cuban shooters, and the hit men doing the work that they were contracted-hired for by William "King" Harvey to do... as the mechanics in the conspiracy... to kill JFK; 11/22/1963.)

We know, as we sit here today the pictures exist that reflect the image of George Bush who is standing outside the front entrance at The Texas School Book Depository 11 / 22 / 1963. It's the opinion of this author along with these various internet websites, that it is reasonable... to ascertain from all of these reflected images. It's to watch and to see, or, making sure the patsy shows up to work that day; to make sure Lee Harvey Oswald came in to do his day job.[6]

LBJ is the pawn in place, the underdog, who will assume the position after the check writer writes the big check. I believe the Top Dog is Richard Milhouse Nixon. NSC #5412 / S-GROUP 40 / Alpha 66 / Murder Inc. The Top Dog.

We turn to Page 149.) *THE KILLING OF THE PRESIDENT*–In the Robert Groden book. *The Bay Of Pigs Invasion*–Run By CIA operative E. Howard Hunt–And, Richard M. Nixon: Hunt/ Sturgis/ Nixon (Spec. Group

---

6   Frank Sturgis, Jack Ruby, Jim Hicks, and David Ferrie, underneath the CIA communications coordinating expert Tracey Barnes (JM WAVE), Robert Maheu, E. Howard Hunt, and also Edward Lansdale. These are the team members with Anthony Veciana, and Johnny Roselli, who were C-CUBE. The C-CUBE stands for the command and control communications center for sniper operations.

5412), Bernard Barker, Eugenio Martinez, Frank Sturgis. (In hindsight we know today Hunt got 2 million from Nixon... to keep the lid on all this. Far worse the scheme got his wife, Dorothy Hunt... killed in the CIA arranged plane crash.) Blackmailing Nixon... cost Dorothy Hunt her life in my p.o.v.

THE TOP DOG LEAVES THE TRAIL OF A SMOKING GUN – ON THE TAPES. "This Hunt, that will uncover a lot of things. You open that scab, there's a hell of a lot of things. This involves these Cubans, Hunt, and a lot of hanky panky.... Just say [tape then erased to become unintelligible] .... it's very bad to have this fellow Hunt, he knows too damned much, if he was involved... [Nixon continues adding to a terrible JFK confession] If this gets out, that this is all involved, the Cuba thing, it would be a fiasco. It would make the CIA look bad, it's going to make Hunt look bad, and it's likely to blow the whole Bay of Pigs thing which we think would be very unfortunate, both for the CIA, and for the country." Nixon resigned in August 1974.

One thing is clear to this author about the Nixon business of this pantheon like Pandora's box of secrets, kept deeply hidden inside the mystery surrounding the whole JFK Cold Case. It's H. R. Haldeman, who makes the assertion in his book "THE ENDS OF POWER."[7] Haldeman makes it crystal clear... that in all of those Nixon references... to the Bay Of Pigs, that he--Nixon himself--was in no minced words; actually referring to the John Fitzgerald Kennedy (JFK) assassination.

NSC 5412 / SPECIAL GROUP 40 / Operation 40 / Brigade #2506:

E. Howard Hunt, Eugenio Martinez, Frank Sturgis, Herminio Diaz Garcia, Bernard Barker, Pedro Diaz Lanz, Colonel Joseph C. King, Desmond Fitzgerald, Tracey Barnes, Gen. Robert Cushman, Howard Hughes, Prescot Bush, Richard Helms, Richard Bissell, Allen Dulles

They were directly involved in the assassination of John F. Kennedy.

They were in on it, with the CIA, from S-Group 40; in room #5412.

TIER GROUP ONE

BASED IN MIAMI AND IN WASHINTON

RICHARD MILHOUSE NIXON

Richard Bissell, Allen Dulles, Richard Helms (CIA), Gen. Robert Cushman, William King Harvey, Desmond Fitzgerald, Ray Cline, James O'connell, Gen. Charles Cabell, Sheffield Edwards, Tracey Barnes, Ted Shackley. MANUEL ARTIME (Chosen by E. Howard Hunt), TONY VARONA,

---

7   H.R. Haldeman with Joseph Di Mona, "THE ENDS OF POWER" 1978 Time Books, The New York Times Book Co.# Three Park Avenue, New York, NY 10016

CARLOS PRIO SOCCARRAS, ROLANDO CUBELLA, HOWARD
HUGHES, ROBERT MAHEU, BERNARD BARKER, Orlando Bosch,
Rolando Masferrer, John Martino, E. HOWARD HUNT (CIA), ANTHONY
VECIANNA (ZR RIFLE), DAVID MORALES (CIA), FRANK STURGIS
(ZR RIFLE), C—CUBE EDWARD LANSDALE

CIA BACKGROUND SUPPORT

Reuben "Rocky" Carbajal

Thomas Mann   U.N.F.C.O

John Martino   JM WAVE

Gordon Campbell   JM WAVE

Bradley Ayres   JM WAVE

George Joannides   JM WAVE

Joaquin Sanjenis   JM WAVE

Robert Morrow*   JM WAVE

* "First Hand Knowledge" Robert D. Morrow SPI BOOKS; 1992

TEXAS SCHOOL DEPOSITORY TEAM
(IN Z R RIFLE THIS GROUP REFERRED TO AS THE CUBANS)

Pedro Diaz Lanz   ZR Rifle

Eladio Del Valle   (CIA)

Herminio Diaz Garcia   ZR Rifle

Raphael Quintero   ZR Rifle

Felix Rodriquez   ZR Rifle

Thomas Eli Davis   ZR Rifle

Jose Miro Cardonas   ZR Rifle

Luis Posada Carriles   (CIA)

———

(TIER GROUP TWO – IN Z R RIFLE, THE TEXANS)

NEW ORLEANS / WASHINGTON / AND IN DALLAS

RICHARD MILHOUSE NIXON (NSC 5412)

GENERAL ROBERT CUSHMAN, LYMAN KIRKPATRICK, DESMOND
FITZGERALD; FRANK BENDER—GEN. BOULDING (CIA).

Richard "Dick" Bissell, ALLEN DULLES (CIA), Richard "Dick" Helms,
George Bush (CIA), Howard Hughes, PRESCOT BUSH (CIA), William

"King" Harvey, CORD MEYER (CIA), DAVID ATLEE PHILLIPS (CIA), Richard Cain, Robert "Barney" Baker, David Yaras, Sauveur Pironti

EDWARD CLARK A.K.A THE SECRET BOSS IN TEXAS

THE MOTORCADE ROUTE — Dallas Mayor Earl Cabell

J. H. Sawyer/George L. Lumpkin

(officers who knowingly gave false information on suspect Lee Oswald)

Eugene Dinkin[8]   Robert E. Jones[9]

THE TEXAS OIL MEN— LBJ's FINANCIAL BASE

JACK CRICHTON / JAKE ENGLER

H.L. HUNT / CLINT MURCHISON / D.H. BIRD

Senator John G. Tower, Texas; and George Brown, and also Herman Brown. (KBR) John Tower brought defector Oswald, back to the US from Russia. A red, white, and blue all American, law abiding and god fearing Texas Senator brings into this country via a brand new cleaned up visa... a red Communist Russian defector... back into the U. S.? George HW Bush, George De Mohrenschildt, C.B. Reitzman, Standard Oil, Lyndon B. Johnson, Neil Mallon, Bill Leidtke, Henry Luce. William Colby (CIA) Clay Shaw (CIA) Clair George (CIA) Oswald's Monitor or handlers James Jesus Angleton, (CIA) David Atlee Phillips (CIA) Nixon's man E. Howard Hunt (CIA) + (NSC 5412); James McCord, Guy Bannister, David Ferry, Orlando Bosch, Jack Ruby, with a fall guy or the patsy as he told the media and all of us watching it unfold what he really was; Lee Harvey Oswald. Johnny Roselli, Anthony Veciana, Frank Sturgis, Pedro Diaz Lanz, Herminio Diaz Garcia, Gerry Hemmings, Charles Cabell. Arthur Mashman, LBJ's Pilot, and Arthur Young, Owner—Bell Helicopter; who married Ruth Paine, Lee Harvey Oswald's employment agent, for the Texas Book Depository. The

---

8   Eugene Dinkin was the cryptographer (communications expert, or code breaker) for intelligence in Metz, France; who actually uncovered the dire SAS plot to assassinate John Fitzgerald Kennedy. William King Harvey, Q J WINN (ASSASSINS), Michael Mertz, Jean Soutre, and Sauveur Pironti. He held a press conference to warn the U.S. about the Alpha 66 / Q J Winn hit team in operation. The hit team inside Alpha 66 / NSC 5412 / through Desmond Fitzgerald... was squelched by CIA. It was also true... James Angleton worked out some classic CIA subterfuge... to appease RFK. The threat evaporated. The CIA left a trail leaving JFK naked in Dallas.

9   George De Mohrenschildt, provided intel to the 112th MIG (Military Intelligence Group) to Colonel Robert E. Jones, and, those files that were released to the national media that had all the information on, Alek James Hidell; AKA Lee Harvey Oswald. "HIT LIST" by authors Richard Belzer, and skillful investigative journalist David Wayne. SKYHORSE Publishing Inc. 2013.

majority were members of the Dallas Petroleum club. (All of these names are written inside the address book of George De Mohrenschildt, who was also known to be Lee Harvey Oswald's--CIA--handler.)

AND J. EDGAR HOOVER (FBI), THE COVER UP ENGINEER.

THE ASSASSINATION TEAM

MALCOLM "MAC" WALLACE (Top Gun plus Watch Dog)

THE GRASSY KNOLL/THE DAL TEX BUILDING

Malcolm Wallace was strictly there watching the CIA hit team.

MICHAEL VICTOR MERTZ, LUCIEN SARTI, TONY "NESTOR" IZQUIERDO, JAMES FILES, CHUCK NICOLETTI, CHARLES HARRISON, EUGENE HALE BRADING, CHAUNCEY HOLT, JOAQUIN SANJENIS, CHARLES RODGERS, LUIS POSADA CARRILES, ROSCOE ANTHONY WHITE, MANUEL R. QUESADA, JACK LAWRENCE, GILBERTO R. HERNANDEZ, PEDRO DIAZ LANZ, HERMINNIO DIAZ GARCIA, GUILLERMO NOVO SAMPOL IGNACIO NOVO SAMPOL

RICHARD CASE NAGELL

THE CIA / ALPHA 66 / INFORMANT

ABRAHAM BOLDEN

THE SECRET SERVICE PROTECTION FOR JFK

THE BOLDEN STORY / THE NAGELL STORY

RICHARD CASE NAGELL (CIA INFORMANT)

ABRAHAM BOLDEN (A SECRET SERVICE AGENT)

We know as we sit here today that there is a clear connection to a cover up through the traceable ties into Alpha 66, Lee Harvey Oswald, and the upper echelons, through Robert Graham, up to Desmond Fitzgerald, and General Robert Cushman, who as we know was Richard M. Nixon's top right hand man, over at NSC 5412. He was recruited to the CIA office in LA by Herbert Leibacher, and Joseph DaVanon (Dec. 1956 through Oct. 1959), Richard Case Nagell had gotten intelligence uncovering a plot, by the deadly Alpha 66 mercenaries who were planning in October 1962 to execute an assassination attempt against president John F. Kennedy. "The Bravo Club / Alpha 66 is in discussions planning for the killing of JFK." Nagell shadowed them: As these plans by Bravo Club / Alpha 66 to kill JFK were in the later operative stages. In June, 1963 Nagell reports that David Ferry (CIA pilot for

Brigade 2506), is using the MK ULTRA "hypno-therapy" on... Lee Harvey Oswald. Later on, in that same year 8/27/1963, Nagell complained to his boss Desmond Fitzgerald about Lee Oswald's impending predicament within the Alpha 66 / S-GROUP 40 / OP–40's / plans to execute John F. Kennedy. Less than a month later, 9/13/1963, Richard Nagell, claimed to have met with Lee Oswald over in Jackson Square, he tells Lee Oswald not to cooperate with the assassination plotters... just in case he was being set up by the company. Richard Case Nagell (we know today) was not able to convince Lee Oswald that the CIA was setting him up. We know today Nagell petitioned for help at the top. We go further along. We can clearly see we can take this to the bank.

Richard Case Nagell made 2 more attempts to inform law enforcement about the upcoming hit by Alpha 66: He wrote a letter directly to the FBI Offices and addressed to J. Edgar Hoover's attention, on September 17th, 1963. He wrote a letter directly to Sen. Richard Russell about all of the same information to the Soviets, on the plot 9/19/1963. Now, fearing that the plot has progressed beyond the talking stages, by Alpha 66 / Bravo Club / Op-40s-Agents; Nagell writes letters to 3 superiors: Desmond Fitzgerald / E. Howard Hunt / Tracey Barnes at CIA headquarters. Nagell named Oswald's handlers, in the months before the assassination, Clay Shaw, David Ferrie, Guy Bannister. We stop here. We know today both Hoover (THE FBI,) and Fitzgerald (NSC 5412;) withheld all this evidence. It's clear to this author that Richard Case Nagell spoke the resilient truth. (In this authors p.o.v.)

In the fine book *DESTINY BETRAYED*, By James Di Eugenio; he writes: When the Nagell letter to the FBI, warning of the JFK assassination was sent in the U.S. Mail to J. Edgar Hoover, Hoover didn't acknowledge the Nagell letter? In self defense, being enmeshed too far, and deeply undercover (he feared, his intel surveillance pick ups would somehow later incriminate him as a possible co-conspirator, and, in the effort to fully detox himself from any involvement) he walked into a local bank, with a loaded revolver; he staged on his own volition, or he then faked an attempted hold up. He discharged his Colt .45 revolver, after firing two shots into the upper wall of plaster, just below the ceiling. He walked outside of the bank and surrendered. He was arrested, and taken to jail. In Robert Morrow's, *FIRST HAND KNOWLEDGE*; Robert Morrow, a contract CIA agent was working under Tracey Barnes during 1963, and, Morrow says, that during the summer of 1963, he was instructed by Tracey Barnes... to purchase a 7.35mm manlicher carcano (not the 6.5 mm manlicher carcano that was found at the Texas School Book Depository.) Morrow claimed to have purchased 4 rifles and he found one to be defective. The guns were picked up by David Ferrie, and then they were flown over to New Orleans. In late September 1963. Morrow says he was contacted by CIA agent Eladio del Valle, who asked him to pick up "four walkie talkies," that could not be traced that were also good up to at least a quarter of a mile, to be used by the JFK hit team. (We can clearly or affirmatively understand and see for ourselves that a four man team... set up with a fall guy in mind... is planned for in multiple cities.)

This dovetails to the known mercenary leaders Gerry Patrick Hemming, and Frank Sturgis... who operated under aegis of the... Cuban Revolutionary Council (CRC) who established a training camp for the Cuban exiles; under the leadership of Laureano Batista. Two of the instructors there were David Ferrie, and Pedro Diaz Lanz. In the camp with Hemming / Sturgis / Ferrie / Lanz with the other leaders were Loran Hall, and also Sergio Arcacha Smith. Also, in camp were Raphael Chi Chi Quintero, and, David Sanchez Morales. And, if the group wasn't lethal enough, within this militia was the deadliest former leader of "the tigres," Rolando Masferrer, who as we know now today trained the group of 53 men, who were all during the years 1960, 1961, 1962, and 1963, polishing up their killing skills... at the ranch owned by infamous millionaire Howard Hughes. This army of 53 men who were called the Bravo Club was also connected directly to Carlos Prio. The connection moves on directly to Tracey Barnes, to Joseph C. King, and, E.Howard Hunt, and up to "Dick" Bissell, Desmond Fitzgerald, Robert Cushman, and, Richard "Dick" Nixon. ZR Rifle pages 69,) through 79,) covers this aspect; very succinctly.

This team was under the leadership of the Whitehouse, and NSC 5412.

It was learned that the Bay Of Pigs exile Brigade members including DRE/ Alpha 66 / MIRR / Brigade 2506, and the minuteman militia in Ponchartrain 11, New Orleans, sent out a formal request to Alexander McCone (CIA) and Desmond Fitzgerald at Langley, to return the Brigade's flag that was presented to JFK over at the Orange Bowl stadium. Added to a public breakup in Washington with the exiles, the second public breakup in Havana, with law professor Jose Miro Cardona, after the April 5th, 1963 meeting, with Bobby Kennedy became the opening avalanche of anti-Castro and Bay Of Pigs rebel faction's–to break off into radical subversive groups that were, "fed up or now turning against Kennedy–seeing him as more of an obstacle than an ally–in the effort to get rid of an enemy Fidel Castro." The getting rid of John Kennedy tide "boiled over." " The brigade saw it as the best way to win their way back in Cuba." Evidence proved this too on July 19th, 1963. Two exile rebel leaders were set to cease a town in Cuba (lacking security and a wide range radio transmitting station). The plan: "takeover the town, and back Kennedy into a corner to force the hand of the United States intervention and to get help in Cuba directly coming over from Washington." The plan led by Enrique Orbiz Llaca and, Jose Santos Andreu–if then, JFK didn't dispatch military forces and if the rebellion would be crushed, the subsequent firestorm–that would be a political nightmare for the Whitehouse. If he abandoned the rebels with the perfect pretext to act. He would be branded a traitor, and, a coward to the rebels and to his word given to the exiles. JFK on all fronts in Cuba, or in Washington, it was clear that he was moving on thin ice. "It was an abundance of rising bad blood abounding in so many factions."

The feelings of contempt ran high on three fronts. John Martino, Johnny Roselli, Santos Trafficante, and also Gordon Campbell, Bradley Ayers, John Martino, and, Rolando Masferrer, Orlando Bosch, David Sanchez Morales; Anthony Veciana. Things became intrusively rotten, when Carlos Marcello was deported. David Ferry flew him back--from jungles of Guatemala. Soon afterwards Johnny Roselli is taped by the FBI saying "Kennedy, is going to be hit." It was beyond the gloves coming off stages... it had accelerated into the ultimate sacrifice stages. "This guy was going to be buying his own dirt nap."

Mary Meyer, the former wife of CIA agent Cord Meyer, was also slipping JFK the LSD drug... under the watchful guidance... of Doctor Timothy Leary while James Jesus Angleton was taping the affair listening to the bedroom, and her telephone calls... for CIA blackmailing purposes, at some desperate point, to slow up the bohemian mind altering self enrichment adopting the peace and love approach to politics... through that mind bending experience (fatefully) someone had decided these bombshell activities were turning JFK into "a dove-ish peace like activism around the globe." Mary Meyer unfortunately through this exploration, was a dangerous woman in certain circles, (to those CIA spooks like E.Howard Hunt / G. Gordon Liddy / James Jesus Angleton–bugging both–the telephone, and, what went on, over inside the bedroom) the bombshell ramifications with JFK on LSD, had to be brought under control, and put to a halt. Someone between James Angleton / Nixon / H. Hunt / Mr. Liddy / David Atlee Phillips, or, Bernard Barker had snapped. James Angleton, the bright, but rebarbative man with a certain genius for making enemies, made one out of Mike Gering, when in my opinion he had his Alpha 66 / NSC 5412 / militia men murder Mary Meyer out on a morning jog. We know this today because police caught James Angleton trying to steal Mary Meyer's diary after the killing.[10] If anyone doubts the cost of just talking about "a peace race," as opposed to building or expanding "the arms race," with the enemy (at that time, 1950 through 1960, the Soviet Union); "To the Alpha 66 / or the Brigade 2506 / S-Group 40 / NSC 5412 / and then up ultimately Richard M. Nixon." Take a closer look at Sweden's Author–OLE DAMMEGARD–The research called CIA Operation

---

10   In *Mary's Mosaic*, Peter Janney, SKYHORSE 2012; he concluded the murder of Mary Meyer had been a CIA operation. The assassins code name was "William L. Mitchell." In the second source, Richard Belzer's *HIT LIST*, it's recorded that; Mary Meyer was eliminated by the CIA in a job that — as Cord Meyers' personal assistant aptly put it..."It had all the markings of an in house...rub out." SKYHORSE--© 2013 Authors--Richard Belzer, and, David Wayne.

40 and JFK, RFK, John Lennon assassinations, Watergate, 9/11: Ole Dammegard. youtube.com/watch7v-209M2dodkio#1-16

In his research it is written or alleged that, "S-Group 40 / Operation 40 / Black Operations murdered John Lennon for inspiring the nation, and the world with his peace activism." NSC 5412 / S-Group 40 / Alpha 66, (Richard Nixon's Plumbers Unit) assassinated John Lennon, while a patsy; a soulless lunatic loner-stalker named-Mark David Chapman, shoots. (Chapman was a fall guy while a standby assassin buildings guard pumped him full of led.)

"THE U. S. VERSES JOHN LENNON " The Documentary Film "It indicates that peace is a dangerous choice...to practice it." (Particularly during an unpopular war, going on in Vietnam.) A superb documentary film.

If JFK had lived, Tip Oneil said, "There would not have been that terrible cost...Vietnam's 550 Billion Dollars in war contracts to Kellog, Brown, And, Root... and the loss of 58,000 American lives, and the 2.2 million Asian lives that were lost between 1965 - 1975. The decade that divided a country.

THE TINDER BOX BEGINS TO HEAT UP IN MIAMI AND CUBA AND IN WASHINGTON: Bircher–type Republicans, Richard Nixon, and Richard Bissell, and Robert Cushman, and Desmond Fitzgerald, led by Paul Bethel who is a close friend of David Atlee Phillips, and, Arleigh Burke, William Pawley, Hal Hendrix, and Claire Booth Luce... wife of Time Life media baron... Henry Luce. John Martino, and Johnny Roselli, and Edward Perez, (Eddie Bayo) William Rip Robertson, David Sanchez Morales, and Anthony Veciana, and, Orlando Bosch. Along with Gordon Campbell, and Reuben "Rocky" Carbajal, and George Joannides, and Bradley Ayres, and Eladio Del Valle. E. Howard Hunt, Pedro Diaz Lanz, Felix Rodriquez, Luis Posada Carriles, Virgilio Romero, and Raphael Quintero. All these men... were deeply connected to... Alpha 66 / Ponchartrain 11 / Minuteman Militia / Brigade 2506 planning. (We know from Robert Walton that David Morales revealed: "he was directly... involved in... the JFK assassination.") (Raphael Quintero said publicly the Bay of Pigs soldier's in 1961 were--responsible for killing-- JFK on 11/22/1963.)

This dovetails to a TIMES PICAYUNE Article, "Hideaway For Bomb Materials Discovered" Aug. 1st, 1963. (9 Cubans Now Exiles / And 2 North American's / are preparing for attacks / inside Cuba.) The two groups were Ponchartrain 11, along with Sam Benton, Alex Rourke, Jose Juarez, and also, Paulino Sierra Martinez, Orlando Bosch, all of them within the (Minuteman Militia,) operating in New Orleans financed by Clay Shaw, Guy Bannister, and, Santos Trafficante, and Howard Hughes. William Jules McLaney, and his brother Mike McLaney, co-founder with Rich Lauchli, along with Eddie Bayo, Tony Cuesta, and also Tony Varona, along with David Atlee Phillips. It was Sam Benton, who was directly involved as the intermediary--with all of the Havana Gambling casinos through Santos Trafficante, Howard Hughes, and Mr. Richard Nixon. The same men tied to Watergate were the known associates tied to--Nixon during the--Bay Of Pigs; Eugenio Martinez, and, Frank Sturgis, and, E. Howard Hunt, and Bernard Barker. Santos Trafficante bought in (over 2 million) heavily to Nixon... through Bebe Rebozo. Carlos Marcello, paid similar monetary contributions to Richard Nixon through his campaign manager, Murray Chotiner. All of this money, was laundered through "the CIA front company," under, Bill King Harvey, Richard Helms, Richard Bissell, and, Allen Dulles. (Nixon / Hughes, "NSC 5412.") Soon after Operation Quick Kick the D.O.D. operation "practice invasion," with 40,000 men, and 83 warships, and 300 planes off the coast of Puerto Rico (which bristled JFK to the boiling point) then after barely coming through the harrowing Cuban Missile Crisis, and, following...William King Harvey being reassigned to a post in Rome. Then newly appointed to replace Harvey (RFK had basically fired him), JFK-Kennedy had clearly promoted Desmond Fitzgerald (CIA) to carry out his policy. As soon as he came in, Fitzgerald had to "rub" some of the Alpha 66 / Brigade 2506 / Minuteman Militia the wrong way immediately. "JFK aggravated a very frustrated group of Cuban's some inconsolable soldiers and some furious right wing CIA agents greatly." Many describe it as the final straw that broke the camels back.

Kennedy shut down three of the mercenary camps, Ponchartrain 11, the Minuteman Militia in New Orleans, and the one in No Name Key, Florida. "JFK had finally snapped." Memo #55, cut out the teeth of the CIA. Memo #263, told them they could not count on getting the major war contracts for Southeast Asia (Vietnam). This was the focus in policy of Nixon's / Dulles / Bush / Hughes. Mr. Nixon, had been the biggest anti-communist who was optimizing, and planning a major war campaign policy on-going since 1954 for the War in Vietnam. And, JFK was pulling the plug on Vietnam. (It is clear we can see how the Nixon tapes recorded exposed what Nagell and Bolden had concretely uncovered... with the plotters inside... Alpha 66.)

NSC 5412 NIXON / BUSH / HUGHES / DULLES (The Conundrum Emerges–The Double Jeopardy–Lose Cuba It's Not Okay–Lose Vietnam: It's No Way In Hell.) Problems emerged wherein Nixon was not going to be able to get the money "he owed back," to his numerous, and, huge investing backers and collaborators that included the mafia Santos Trafficante / Carlos Marcello / Jimmy Hoffa, the teamster's leader. More than two thirds of what he owed was to come from a successful CIA invasion inside Cuba. Everyone wanted that billion-dollar empire to fall back into the U.S. hands... and they all wanted Fidel Castro dead. Then, the fiasco unfolded. There was a huge cover-up of the failed invasion and nobody believed they'd lose upon the landing. Ironically, there were many in the CIA, and within Nixon's NSC 5412, who blamed JFK for losing the brigade 2506. E. Howard Hunt's CIA men stewed in prison, for what they termed as JFK's--cancelled air strikes. Nixon had gotten major funding, from Pepsi Cola, Ford Motor Company,

Standard Oil, United Fruit Company, along with Zapata Offshore. (George Bush and Prescot Bush, and Howard Hughes.) Nixon went to the FBI then asking Hoover what he could possibly do to get the Kennedy brothers to back off of Trafficante / Marcello / Hoffa who were under heavy Mc Clelland Committee "heat" since JFK and RFK were waging war on the mafia. (Richard Nixon's huge investors and closely tied "friendly business associates" who truly had owned his political career since 1946.) Hoover's organized crime ties to these figures like Trafficante / Marcello / Hoffa were well known. All Hoover later could come up with that could possibly hurt JFK, was show the dirty linen to LBJ, what RFK planned to use "to blackmail him off the 1964 election ticket." This becomes clear when you see Nixon's picture when the story broke. Dallas Morning News "Nixon Predicts JFK May Drop Johnson."

Hoover, decided that the only dirt he had on JFK that was something he could use to his detriment and downfall, in making this trojan horse-type of a move... J. Edgar Hoover shows the evidence to Nixon... and Nixon uses it to motivate LBJ "to act." In a strange twist of fate Hoover shows the Bobby Baker / Billy Solesties charges... in the indictment to Nixon. Richard Nixon leaks the story to Carl Freund (Dallas Morning News). Now through LBJ... by getting him to fall in line with the CIA factions who oppose his policy in Southeast Asia... Nixon then uses LBJ to help him...to get rid of JFK, by exposing that RFK is about to kick him off the 1964 ticket. Nixon believes with JFK assassinated... he has some chance... to later repay George Bush, Prescot Bush, and, Howard Hughes /Trafficante / Marcello / Hoffa. And, if his political career has any chance of getting him back into the Whitehouse–it would mean he has to go along, with the plot–to kill John Kennedy. What he later called on the Whitehouse tapes as "the greatest hoax that has ever been perpetuated." Nixon opened a door to LBJ, forcing him to go along with the trojan horse plan. LBJ also became complicit wherein he assisted Mayor Earl Cabell, and Edward Clark with the plotters by opening keys to the security detail for JFK by changing the parade route in Dallas. With the parade route altered to slow JFK's limousine... SX 70 the secret boss in Texas (Edward Clark) made sure... Bill Decker had told his deputies, "take no part whatsoever in the security of president Kennedy;" then Ed Clark made sure that LBJ took care of the secret service detail. You can see it all unfold during the motorcade leaving Love Field, the follow up car tells the two running guards assigned to ride alongside on Lancer (JFK's) running board agents riding with JFK, on Limousine SX-70 to stand down, just before leaving the airfield tarmac. You can see the agents, protesting the move by out spreading their hands, wondering who in the hell... would have ordered the step down.

We know that it was Nixon, who was the king of dirty tricks, who forced LBJ to act in self defense to go along with the Texans, and Big Oil who were all a smaller part of a deadly vastly larger government conspiracy to kill JFK.

Nixon would have never seen the presidency had not John F. Kennedy been murdered, or assassinated in Dallas, on the day of November 22nd, 1963. Nixon's entire political future and career was restarted by that event.

In an interview with Spotlight Magazine, Richard Helms is quoted in nineteen words fingering E. Howard Hunt. "Hunt was in Dallas the day the president was murdered and he was involved in the conspiracy to kill John Kennedy." Marita Lorenz, said she was with Op-40 during a road trip from Miami to Dallas (in a station wagon with the teams who were carrying rifles with telescopes) inside the Dallas Hotel. She saw: E. Howard Hunt arrive there, and passing out... maps and cash to... this "hit squad." She said, "I'm getting out... this is too much for me... I'm going back to Florida." Later afterwards, Frank Sturgis said, "you didn't stick around for the big one, we got the son of bitch over in Dallas." Lorenz said "you're not serious, you didn't kill the president." He said, "yeah we did it, and, who the fuck will ever know." Hunt took Spotlight Magazine to court in a lawsuit for slander. The article was true. So, there wasn't any judgment. It explains Mr. Nixon's paranoia on the Whitehouse tapes, and Hunt's final deathbed confession to his son, St. John Hunt. Hunt tells all the names in previous chapters outlining the conspiracy. In the final analysis THE KENNEDY FILE which follows in the later chapter of this book we will cover all the multiple teams who killed JFK travel the list of the actual shooters and mechanics operating in Dealey Plaza. This is the first pass or my first "run through the background."

MOVING BACK INTO THE FRAMEWORK OF THE ABRAHAM BOLDEN REALITY AND THE RICHARD CASE NAGELL STORY...

In relationship to some of the above paragraphs with regard to Richard Case Nagell, The CIA Informant:

We know now as we sit here today in hindsight that these attempts on JFK were uncovered, the two plots that existed were well documented if we care to now dig into the records. There was a Chicago attempt as well as the Tampa plot. The Kennedy secret service was well aware of these tinderbox elements, especially the hot mess within the Cuban exile community that felt that JFK's handling of The Bay Of Pigs invasion cost them their right to return to their homeland. Essentially, it is a fact. The plans were already set in motion in two other major cities prior to Dallas, and Dealey Plaza. We also know today that ABRAHAM BOLDEN, the first black secret service agent in the presidential protection in United States History... who was personally picked by JFK "foiled one of these attempts." Of course once these secret details of the two previous plots (that part of the story leaked into the press corporations, as it made the headline news.) The NSC 5412 / Alpha 66 / Nixon's CIA plumbers unit designed to plug leaks saw this as detrimental to exposing a hoax. We understand today that Richard Case Nagell informed

Robert Graham / Desmond Fitzgerald / J. Edgar Hoover / and, also RICHARD NIXON.

RICHARD CASE NAGELL – Contacted Oswald in Jackson Square–September 13th, 1963.

RICHARD CASE NAGELL – Contacted Hoover of the FBI, via letter–September 17th, 1963.

RICHARD CASE NAGELL – Contacted Also Senator–Richard Russell–September 19th, 1963.

RICHARD CASE NAGELL – Informs Desmond Fitzgerald / E. Howard Hunt / Tracey Barnes. (Nagell names names of Lee Oswald's handlers–Clay Shaw, David Ferrie, and Guy Bannister.) Keep in mind, this is the ALPHA 66–The group connected to NSC 5412 / Anthony Veciana. We know Tracey Barnes (CIA) had manlicher carcano rifles; picked up by, David Ferrie (CIA). Rolando Masferrer and 53 Cuban mercenaries polishing their killing skills on Howard Hughes ranch? (It's implausible or better stated, it would be totally impossible information, that could miraculously stay completely bottled up.)

The NSC 5412 / Alpha 66 / Nixon's henchmen stepped into action. In this scenario the agent Abraham Bolden... has since been framed by Nixon's NSC 5412 / S Group 40 / special plumbers team (E. Howard Hunt and James Jesus Angleton). He (Abraham Bolden) has been framed, or targeted for attempting to expose these prior plots in both Tampa and Chicago. Kennedy was informed by the Secret Service there was a plot to assassinate him in Chicago. This resulted in the cancellation of his visit to that city due to safety concerns. It is recorded that Bolden and other agents shadowed the suspect due to the report. On March 21st, 1970; Sherman Skionick stated on a program with Tim Weber of WTX Radio Program that the Secret Service Agent Abraham Bolden was falsely imprisoned, to prevent him from revealing there was a plot TO KILL JOHN KENNEDY IN CHICAGO.

THOMAS ARTHUR VALLE was an Oswald lookalike who was involved with four other men who were conspiring to assassinate JOHN F. KENNEDY in CHICAGO, but the attempt was aborted, following a traffic stop in which Thomas Arthur Valle was found to have a concealed weapon (the manlicher carcano rifle) with a scope in his possession. A weapon that the CIA – Tracey Barnes picked up to fly to New Orleans–by David Ferry.

THE BEACHCOMBER. All the tinder box elements factoring it all in.

THE ABOVE STORY – IN SUMMARY – AND IN CONCLUSION

What both stories signify in the JFK cold case: The plot was well in motion prior to Dallas, because we now know today that certain factions (with the 53 Cubans under Rolando Masferrer) were all part of the hit team Z R RIFLE. WILLIAM "KING" HARVEY, David Sanchez Morales, David Atlee Phillips, E. Howard Hunt. CORD MEYER, Pedro Diaz Lanz, Orlando

Bosch, Anthony Veciana, Manuel Artime / Rolando Masferrer / Raphael Quintero, Thomas Eli Davis / Eladio Del Valle / Nestor Izquierdo / George Joannides / Gordon Campbell / Reuben Carbajal / Tracey Barnes / and Frank "Fiorini" Sturgis / John Martino/ Herminio Diaz Garcia /Jean R. Soutre/ and Michael Victor Mertz/ Howard Hughes, and also, Robert Maheu; [FBI.]

(a lethal cocktail or tinder box filled with the extreme right.)

This combination brings about the addition to *The Beachcomber*, hatching the 2015 revision. I needed another pass to add this additional information–more likely, the case required a second pass. And so this author submits the following additional opinion, on the JFK cold case. He alleges Lee Harvey Oswald was being closely monitored by NSC # 5412 (and also Richard Case Nagell had firsthand knowledge "humintel pick ups" indicating that there was a direct connection... all the way to the top, which we know is Richard Nixon); or, through... Robert Graham, Senator Richard Russell, E. Howard Hunt, Desmond Fitzgerald, Robert Cushman, and Tracey Barnes. And all these men inside the Whitehouse room, or inside of the S-Group 40 / NSC#5412 / Alpha 66 / which is including the men training on Howard Hughes' ranch the 53 man "murder incorporated", that made LBJ—Nixon, nervous as hell; the guilt that haunted LBJ into an early grave. (Rolando Masferrer, Sergio Arcacha Smith, Orlando Bosch, David Ferrie, Clay Shaw, Guy Bannister, and David Atlee Phillips, and, Anthony Veciana, Manuel Artime, and, Raphael Quintero.) All these anti-Castro Cubans these upper echelons at the CIA, including Bernard Barker, E. Howard Hunt, NIXON-HUGHES. (All of these men of zeal JM WAVE all of the above were deeply involved inside the plot-- that killed the 35th president—in Dallas, Texas—November 22nd, 1963-- John Fitzgerald Kennedy.)

It is conceivable (or at least possible) the moves that "THE MAN WHO KNEW TOO MUCH" was allegedly making... in saving himself and in self preservation; by staging the fake bank hold up... getting himself thrown into jail–it clearly would prevent him (RICHARD NAGELL) from being tied into the deadly Alpha 66 / NSC#5412 conspiracy–which is the Guy Bannister, David Ferrie, George de Mohrenschildt Clay Shaw connection, to events leading up to 11/22/1963. In June 1963 (six months prior to the confluent assassination) CIA agent NAGELL witnesses, and reports to superiors, that CIA contract pilot mercenary (David Ferry's) using manchurian candidate MK-ULTRA "hypno therapy" on Lee Oswald. He notified the LA Office CIA Agents Herbert Leibacher, and Joseph DaVanon, then it goes up the chain of command that... included Robert Graham, Tracey Barnes, E. Howard Hunt, Gen. Robert Cushman, along with both Nixon, and Hoover. Then for added good measure he then informed a U.S. Senator (Atlanta, Georgia's Richard Russell), what was happening. NAGELL knew that if Bravo Company was openly discussing a planned assassination of John Kennedy: It had to be for real, because Alpha 66 / NSC#5412 was for real. NAGELL knew Alpha 66, and these radical 53 man Cuban mercenaries... were already known as "the murder incorporated" in the Carribean; "Los Tigres" –one of the most deadly feared killing outfits in Cuban History. Rolando Masferrer / David Morales / Anthony Veciana / Raphael Quintero, / Reuben "Rocky" Carbajal, George Joannnides, Gordon Campbell, Nino Diaz, and, also, Orlando Bosch, Frank Sturgis, Felix Rodriquez, Luiz Posada Carriles, Bernard Barker, Porter Goss, and Barry Seal, Manuel Artime, and Sergio Arcacha Smith... in the lethal cocktail of this killer army... financed by Howard Hughes, H.L.Hunt, Clint Murchison, George Bush, Prescot Bush, Santos Trafficante, Jack Crichton, Robert Mosbacher, James Baker, Richard Bissell, Tracey Barnes, and of course Mr. Richard Milhouse Nixon. (Source) Common Cause, The Article March 1990; "Involved with Bush family since 1946." (Source) Freedom Magazine, L. Fletcher Prouty; 1986. "The Kennedy Assassination–The Nixon And The Bush Connection," Paul Kangas; The Realist.(Source.)

HOW IS IT POSSIBLE TO KEEP ALL OF THIS INFORMATION, OR FOREVER ODDITY BOTTLED-- UP NOW FOR OVER 50 YEARS?

When NIXON came strutting into the oval office in 1968 and wanted to obtain any and all documents the CIA had pertaining to the "whole Bay Of Pigs situation" going back to 4/17/1961, he tipped-- his hand-- in the JFK conspiracy. NIXON'S involvement, going back to formation of NSC#5412 dating back March 15th, 1954; and the Bay Of Pigs. Leading the meetings with Richard Bissell (Dick Nixon, the highest ranking officer who was there per Howard Jones); they endeared him to history as "Mr. Dick," and The Bay Of Pigs–Brigade 2506, and the General Robert Cushman, along with the CIA leader Allen Dulles, and, also (CIA) Desmond Fitzgerald–Richard Milhouse Nixon–had a direct hands-on first-hand knowledge and a deep involvement within the JFK conspiracy. Nixon had a direct hand in the clandestine black operations of the S-Group 40 / NSC#5412 / Brigade 2506 / Alpha 66 Cuban exiles who explicitly participated in the murder of John Fitzgerald Kennedy.

Inside the pages of the fine book *AMERICAN CONSPIRACIES* by ex-governor turned author Jesse Ventura, it is covered that there was a major showdown between Nixon and Helms over all these documents related to the CIA involvement in the JFK–Kennedy cold case that were pure dynamite— as related in the preceding paragraphs here. As a Whitehouse aid wrote to John Dean on February 1st, 1971: "Maheu's controversial activities and his contacts in both democratic and republican circles suggest the possibility that a forced embarrassment of Lawrence Obrien, might well later on shake loose Republican skeletons from the closet." In this fine passage of Jesse Ventura's disclosure of our own United States History, it becomes clear to this author and to others looking into our past that Richard Nixon, and Howard Hughes / Johnny Rosseli / Robert Maheu / along with Desmond Fitzgerald, and Gen.

Robert Cushman, and William King Harvey whom were acting on behalf of Richard Helms (and top levels of the CIA interests and also its leaders) to assassinate JFK–Kennedy–were committing high treason. Nixon felt he had to cover all his tracks within NSC 5412 that clearly did show how Desmond Fitzgerald, and Robert Cushman, later in collusion with Bernard Barker, and Eugenio Martinez, and likely with James Jesus Angleton (with Helms) got a presidential protection detail in Dallas cancelled... over the protests of their... unit commander Maximillian Reich. Those are the documents, he fought (in my p.o.v.) with Richard Helms to fork over to him–Richard Milhouse Nixon; inside the oval office.* (A.K.A. In attempting to cover his own ass and also several others...who were all involved in treacherous high treason.)

Furthermore, if anyone is convinced that it's the cracker-jack-minded Texans with LBJ who might be running the show, they need to keep in mind that the ZR RIFLE / S-Group / NSC #5412 was already exercising previous attempts in Chicago and Tampa, that came up before the Texas trip to Dealey Plaza over there in Dallas. So, the plan to kill JFK was already rolling into the highest echelons of that Central Intelligence Agency. (From all the way up to the top of the CIA.)

If Kennedy was killed in either Tampa or Chicago, nobody could or would be whispering these rumors that LBJ cold have anything to do with it. It was later on however justified when LBJ's name kept cropping up since the crime of the century took place in Dallas, Texas. And, yes with the big calamity of the E. Howard Hunt "death bead confession" it is very uniquely compelling, in all of its details, to link LBJ's thirst for power to the hierarchy that made the event take place on November 22nd, 1963. I can assure you as we sit here today in good judgement of these facts and perception of facts: as stated for the entire world to hear on the Whitehouse tapes, it clearly fingers Richard Milhouse Nixon as the dick-dastardly-culprit in the JFK cold case. Nixon's words, on tape: "Because, if this gets out... it's a hell of a lot of things... because this involves HUNT [THE CIA] and, THESE CUBANS [ZR RIFLE] and a whole lot of **hanky panky**, which would be very bad for the CIA if it gets out... and very unfortunate, and bad... for this country."

RICHARD MILHOUSE NIXON – NSC#5412 / S-GROUP 40

The Ardent Anti-Communist. The Ardent Anti-Castro.
The Ardent Anti-Kennedy. *He's the bad guy who's behind it all.*

THE TINDER BOX ELEMENTS WERE ALL AROUND JFK

---

* *It had to come from the top, Desmond Fitzgerald and Richard Helms, because CIA director John McCone was a close personal friend of JFK. It's the only way the Secret Service protection could be dropped over in Dallas, Texas, and the only way that Bobby Kennedy couldn't catch the CIA red handed while they were pulling off the actual conspiracy.*

There have been over 300 separate deaths of witnesses and declarants who saw what occurred in Dealey Plaza in Dallas, Texas, that afternoon. Many were forcibly intimidated, threatened, harassed, and ultimately most all of them were horribly *silenced or killed* in a myriad of dubious, mysterious circumstances. This is a short list in summary of the strangest 17 deaths.

It is statistically one chance out of a ¼ million that all of the 300 accidental deaths that are chronicled could have been, as it has been reported, *all coincidental or either accidental, or of natural causes*. One thing is clear: The mob is tired of doing their dirty work and the FBI had a big hand in this case. By confiscating the bullet that Deputy Buddy Walthers found on the curbing at Elm Street, and thinking that he was giving it to a trustworthy FBI man, the bullet has now completely disappeared forever. In 1969, Buddy Walthers was killed in a hotel room during an arrest. The Deputy allowed the naked suspect to go into the bathroom to dress (not protocol or wise in dealing with a wanted criminal), and when the man emerged he shot Walthers in the chest. This witness along with George Bower's death (the railroad tower's train operator), are both somehow connected in orchestration, since they both had such key testimony. The most outwardly bizarre murder was of Dallas Reporter Dorothy Kilgallen who was the only press member to gain an interview with Jack Ruby. While attending the Ruby trial, she told a friend of her plans, "to break the JFK assassination mystery wide open."

Kilgallen was found to have accidentally overdosed on barbiturates (the autopsy report showed that she had enough drugs in her system to kill at least ten men). Her death was mysteriously listed as suicide.

George Bowers, Buddy Walthers, and Dorothy Kilgallen's untimely deaths, compounded with deaths of Eladio Del Valle, and David Ferrie, and also Clay Shaw's gun-running partner Guy Bannister, added up to a stunning rising body count as numerous others surrounding or connectable towards Jack Ruby died abruptly, like Thomas Hale Howard (friend), George Senator (his roommate), and a cumulative group of a half dozen more deaths of others like Jim Koethe, Bill Hunter, Rose Charami, along with George McGann, Hank Killam, and also Karin Kupcinet. When we look closely at all this, the JFK/Tippit/Oswald/Ruby murders combine to implausible odds.

As Jim Marrs stated so candidly, *"We have to ask ourselves when do these coincidences end and when does the full blown conspiracy begin."* The FBI used their former operative Guy Bannister in the dual doorway entrance offices at 531 Lafayette Street. FBI man James Hosty from Dallas was assigned to keep tabs on Lee Harvey Oswald. It was David Ferrie of the Civil Air Patrol who introduced Oswald to Guy Bannister. In New Orleans, the Mafia connection was Carlos Marcello. Ferrie, Bannister, Marcello, and Oswald were all involved in the CIA's anti-Castro campaign. Clay Shaw is the CIA connected gun runner of the mob, who supplied all the black market weapons sent to Cuba and other Latin American destinations. The infamous Louisiana corridor of arms to the CIA anti-Castro campaigns like Task Force W, OP 40, AMLASH, ZR Rifle, Brigade 2506, and also MIRR, or Alpha 66, and the U.S. militia men of The Ponchartrain 11.

Clay Shaw was the ideal unsuspected spy type for the CIA who was sheltered by his socialite circles in the New Orleans high life, with a queer lifestyle and also an equally queer business of running millions in arms to the Cuban anti-Castro militias; as well as all the CIA mercenary groups mentioned in the above paragraph. It was through this double life as a socialite French Quarter party-host/sophisticated-dweller, that he merged together with the social society connections in business. He knew all of the players and the switch hitters, or as it was in 1963 _swish men_, of the gay underground and the homosexual party circuit in New Orleans, Louisiana. These _"gatherings"_ were legendary.

The umbrella connection of the CIA man, their agent David Atlee Phillips, who often used the alias Maurice Bishop, was the man who controlled the actions of Lee Harvey Oswald. If you read *ZR Rifle: The Plot to Kill Kennedy and Castro*, in that text the plan was coordinated in meetings inside Guy Bannister's offices.

Pre-planning, Op-40 had a plan in place by Sept. 1963. Prior or other previous meetings were to see what Kennedy would do next after Playa Giron 4/17/1961. Sept.1st, 1963, William Harvey; is the original organizer.

It was the *pulling the plug on nearly every operation* the CIA had in place, and the *final straw* of canceling the second planned invasion, which was totally scrapped. All of this culminated to a very bad end when William King Harvey was *"deposed"* to a reassigned post in Rome. Allen Dulles was gone and Richard Bissell was gone. Things got really bad when General Charles Cabell *"was fired."* J. Edgar Hoover knew that he would be next in line for *dismissal*, as soon as the reelection of Kennedy was forthcoming.

The most ardent question is not about operatives like E. Howard Hunt, Frank Sturgis, Maurice Bishop, Robert Maheu, David Atlee Phillips, Pedro Diaz Lanz and Herminio Diaz Garcia (the two Cuban hit men), or the rest of them like Jack Ruby, Santos Trafficante, Clay Shaw, and David Ferry, or even J. Edgar Hoover's men in 1963: Eugenio Martinez, and Bernard Barker. None of these men on their own could take out a president without help. It is my view that the help came from the men JFK fired, or dismissed.

Some ten days after the final hearings of the Warren Commission in 1964, both Guy Bannister and his partner Hugh Ward suddenly died. Guy Bannister was found dead from a gunshot, and Hugh Ward died in a plane crash in Mexico.

The bottom continued to drop out as the Jack Ruby, Oswald, Ferrie, Bannister, Clay Shaw, Carlos Marcello story began to unfold during the second probing, or secondary investigation, by Jim Garrison. There was a continual stonewall that went on as everyone's puppet master became more nervous with the bottle that *kept uncorking* with steady developments of each passing hour of the day three years later as Jim Garrison re-opened the investigation of the case.

The most telling witness who could link it all together for Jim Garrison became David Ferrie who could turn Garrison's case against Clay Shaw.

Members of *two secret societies*, both the New Orleans gay underworld as well as the CIA-operative network of anti-Castro campaigns, it would not be easy to crack the case. When the CIA asked: *"what are we doing to protect our man Clay Shaw?"* <u>The Answer Came back fairly quickly to that question.</u>

The war to stop the bleeding got pretty ugly when it came time to take out David Ferrie and a message had to be sent to stop the security breaches. The first casualty was on the same day that David Ferrie died, when his close friend Eladio del Valle in Miami was shot in the heart and had his skull split open Cuban-Quajiro-style with a machete. Eladio del Valle was a CIA paymaster to David Ferrie. David Ferrie died from a brain hemorrhage on February 22, 1967. With his death went the case Garrison had against Clay Shaw. Grabbing at straws now, Garrison sought testimony from Clyde Johnson, who also knew of the Oswald, Ferrie, Shaw, and Jack Ruby connection. The day before his testimony he was severely beaten. Not long after that he was murdered in a shotgun-style mob hit.

Everything seemed to spiral too far out for the network-net of Garrison's probes versus the highly effective tactics of the Mafia's hands and the CIA's network of secrecy, aided by the FBI. None of the Garrison charges would stick in court.

The most intensive effort ever put down by the CIA to try to eliminate one man was targeted at Fidel Castro. The secret war backfired miserably when the Russians came charging in to increase their commitments and began the build-up of armaments going to the Cuban army and Fidel Castro's revolution. The Cuban Missile Crisis was the classic showdown. We thought that Kennedy had done so well in that crisis. How could we know that the ongoing real battle between the politics of the White House and the CIA, and the FBI, was the larger precursor and or the deadliest enemy danger to JFK?

The Cuban Missile Crisis ended with the United States promising not to invade Cuba. It guaranteed that it would never set foot on Cuban soil. That ill promise was never broken, and Fidel Castro's reign as supreme commander and el presidente of Cuba has entered slowly into its fifth decade.

Both the CIA and the Mafia had counted on returning to business as usual with their vast money-making Casinos. The men seen on the ground at Dealey Plaza in Dallas, Texas, with headsets were agents who were operatives of the CIA, field personnel similar to operatives used at Playa Giron. They were in disguises that day, bum's clothes, with good shoes, and sharp haircuts and earpieces, *coordinating the foreground, and also the background shots;* completing a triangular ambush of a firing configuration to the target. This was a classic military style hit squad successfully hitting a target. Sort of like the Beachcomber, but these agent guys were dressed up, or better yet dressed down, as hobos. They were bums no less, but bums with good shoes.

In effect, Fidel Castro had waited for and counted on the projected outcome. And in a unique way sorta like the Cinematic retelling, with the

Siamese fighting fish in the opening scenes of the 1963 James Bond film *From Russia With Love*, he waits to see who is still standing to make his move in for the kill. In reality, Kennedy became Kronstein in the chess match, and he was assassinated on November 22, 1963. Fidel Castro had matched wits and outsmarted the United States (aka Goliath) for many years, and would for many years to come, he became the unique beneficiary of "I'm untouchable now through a stateless CIA hit team." (A fifty year long reign.)

————

In the early 1960s, we were a young country and the CIA had some pretty unique factions and influences and activity that were *far reaching*, tantamount to United States security, and foreign policy's Sentinel Force. And back then, at the time, a few members were angry. In the 1960s, the mob has some pretty unique factions and their influences and activity were *far reaching*, tantamount to commerce and business throughout the United States as a Sentinel Force... and back then, at the time, a few members were angry.

There might have been one time in history: The last of the Mohicans struck an unprecedented arrangement to continue to do business in the United States. Who else could pull off a story like the lone wolf nut, and the Energizer Bunny of <u>a magic bullet,</u> that could somehow parlay enough girth to liquidate a president?

It will never happen again in history. And it is true that most of the wiser souls admit that (as I do) IT NEVER HAPPENED AT ALL, AND THIS BOOK, *BEACHCOMBER* IS REALLY FICTION. AND THIS ELASTIC THEORY WORKS OUT... *as the true magus.*

A masterful, divine, clandestine intervention, and we're left with a divisionary slice of U.S. history that will remain always and forever and again a clever, mysterious monster U.S. mystery: *Central Intelligence Agency S.O.P.* When it comes to secrets:

That bullet hit the target, and you must understand that we the people... *must never hear the truth...*

In the CIA lobby, just as you enter the building, on the wall it is written:

"And ye shall know the truth... and the truth shall make you free."

Source: *The Bourne Identity*, Chase Brandon, CIA Officer

Universal Studios, California. Copyright UNIVERSAL 2004

————

Back into the story, rejoining the Beachcomber... Flash Forward.

And now today he saves the lives of fifteen Americans. In 2003, *For all Cuba, and Cuban pride*, from here and all the way to American soil. Today Santiago Serna Dominguez, I salute you a HERO *once again*. The whole room erupted in toasts of roaring applause, and soul-rocking cheering.

It was a joyous celebration of Cuban pride.

TEN

Mother, Mother, Mother

Then just happens: the mother of twins is brought in amid this range of celebrating the living. The room quieted with her arrival, her heart beckoning into the room toward only the one son she could see. And the one son she couldn't see, too. One son, he arises from the cushions of the hotel lounge, but just as he rose she dropped to her knees. Her father holds her wrecked and weakened limbs as she sighs to a fainting spell, *hurting upheaval* in a dying harpooned whale's final pain. The sole surviving remaining son goes to her, and all three rise to leave the room. Moments later the distraught son comes back to the bar.

Everyone can see the favorite son was the one lost out to sea. And the twin brother knew she could never forgive him (she knew better anyway). But what's worse was that this wasn't unlucky, for always he had accepted his role. He was happy to be just average in comparison to the apple of her eye, which was reserved, which was fine with him. That in his mind was no problem, he loved her for her love for him, anyway, and so he reconciled himself.

She loved her son C.J. more than she missed H.B. Harvey Goldenberg. As it turns out the Goldenberg's marriage was more partnership than loving friendship. The couple's own private livelihoods were filled with busy active social calendars that each could partake in with many separate network friends to lean on, and occupy themselves with. They were in good standing within upper social circles in San Francisco. The couple maintained this projected appearance through that shelter of livelihoods by being generous with their time with charities and *the arts*: the Opera and the Theatre. It was accepted as a very normal marriage that made more sense to others than even perhaps to themselves. It was a kind of soothing and quietly businesslike quartered sense of ties that bind.

Joe Elliot was the part of the deal that she had the least amount of time, patience or interest in. As a twin pup he just was always the furthest away from *the mother's nipple* since in her heart there was only room for one, and that had to be C.J. This family concept was where she picked up and received most of her guiding light. With two tall strapping handsome healthy boys (nobody knew otherwise), it was easy on the eyes and everything always looked just right to those peeping in on the picture. And over time, with the right picture projected, this variety of marriage was what it was, as it grew to be more and more business-like over time, and much less like the bonds of passion. As Eve, she was a willing concubine of no more Tangos or Entanglements with Adam.

For the sons of H.B. Goldenberg, the most attributable trait he passed on to the boys was pride. And he taught them well on how to accept *the good times in life*. He told them and instilled it clearly with both boys: "go on and live your life. I'll be up in heaven, so don't dwell on the past, just go on and live." It was his way of giving them an *I'll see you when I get there* type mentality. His passion to live out his life as the stout force of a man that he was was the only example that they needed to look to.

For a jewish lawyer, he was truly a modern practical man who left tradition to pursue excellence. And it was in his quest of striving forward diligently ahead that he just devoured truths voraciously every day.

He once leaked out he thought that some social workers were not to be trusted. He also tended to debunk certain psychologists' or therapists' advice for his divorcing clients; he thought it to be hideous, unless they were one of the few that he respected, which boiled down to just two. One, Barbara Brunswick, graduated the top in her class at a Bay area university. The other, an activist and a publisher named Gloria Steinletter, was the greatest women's rights advocate to ever practice law. These two women carried all of H.B. Goldenberg's reverence and respect. On his meaner side, in dealing with psychologists and/or therapists that his cases would cross him up with, he believed mostly that if two people who knew each other for a very long time couldn't figure out their differences, how could you trust *a paid shrink on the clock?* It was to him like *spitting in one hand and wishing in the other.*

He wasn't much for mending fences. It was either that you're in it or you're out of it. His felt that you, yourself, were the best barometer to observe what's up with yourself and spouse and house. To be a man's man and run your own show.

Perhaps he knew that he would get it for his own client. Whoever's side of favor he fought for, to H.B. Goldenberg, his side was a true winning one. So these were just folks in the way of his clients' variable savvy, and he felt only he knew best for keeping all their respective wits about them. And, towards keeping everything in tact (including the pocketbook), and all of that... that ran through him, first and foremost; they needed to remain *tapped into him.* H.B. Goldenberg didn't have the time to wear a yarmulke or fast for a seder or make a pilgrimage to the temple. He was far too busy with his complex world of his highly evolved professional hybrid life. His sons fully understood that. They would know how to move on. At least ideally, he taught them well enough, and you'd think it would be so.

However, the problems with Mom were more complex. A son will cry deeper and fall harder if he can't get his mother's love. It's just a worsening ailment.

Alas, with fathers it's different, and sons can go away for some periods of years. Like the celebrated poet who wrote the Beachcomber's favorite sonnet, Nicholas John Lennartson hadn't spoken with his own father in twenty years. So that harp or violin's bow on his melon was *within the heart of a poet no real smell of fetid vapor.* It's just that for him it was simply a *macht nix's* struggle written within his joint's grasp. And for him he could handle that just fine, because he would get around to him when it was the right time. The brain-droppings of all truly self-made men.

But for Joe Elliot, his mother's distance took its toll. He doubted whether he was worthy of her heart. He soul-searched and questioned why she hadn't taken him in, as she was so taken with C.J., her heart's Porsche... whereas Joe Elliot's stinging penance was that he was just a Ford-lemon. It completely befuddled him. Now the tragedy of being the sole surviving son and the one she didn't want just magnified the quantity of pain in him.

He could never please her and couldn't learn how. He just didn't have it with her _ever._ It was enough of a thorn in his gut that it could fester into a foreboding monolith of a sacred burning cross... And for the better that he should not, for if he dwelled upon its merciless destructive soul-breaking, heart-wrenching power, he could crack under its forces of prophecy, under the hammering weight of his own heart's tendency to fathom his mother's flawed heart's frustratingly darned, negative and damned scrutiny upon and over him.

It's hard for a son to not wonder what's wrong with himself when an instinct as all truly bon vivant natural, like a mother loving her son, just peters out like a flat note of an untuned piano key. There's no tuning, nor tuner's fork, that cures it or can change the bitters on that cancerous soured sore of loathing, and there's no music to be ordained from that harp's sulking vulture's flat note.

It was enough to make one sick, like one of Ian Fleming's characters in James Bond: in drags on about a mantle-filled novel of mojo and pseudo-sexuality, the honorable hangover that was left over his noggin.

"Futsuka Yoi," he called it in Japanese.

It was after a long night out dealing with the old sordid toil, and the horny tales of the feisty and festive festivals of the sordid cathouse....

At dawn's light and in the huntings' mysteries of a morning, "He had to go in low to the bowl... for the Big Spit."

The Beachcomber watched this unfolding within the young man who sat at the bar with a mother's secondary love complex, *the favorite* died at sea. Joe Elliot just sat and the look on his face, for somehow losing *the primary love* of his mother churned in his gut, like the noises of an 18th century train, grinding to end in a stop, or even screeching steel wheels slipping on rails to a start. A moving and ever present train in the pit of his stomach, that somehow he would tolerate for now. He must have seen a solution to this pain since he sat with a stillness, like Beachcomber. It was what the Beachcomber had learned to do to stop his own pain. So, the look on the young man's face, which was familiar to him (in its contempt) of a mighty and torn soul and a stricken with fate, face.

But this tale of woeful-slow dance on the killing ground, mother's secondary love complex, brought what was worse, that he couldn't live with himself for somehow he's owned up to his feeling responsible for taking her favorite son away from her. It was a theme, like in 1980s *Ordinary People*. He'd rather have been the one not to go home. That's how much he loved his brother lost at sea, that's how much he loved his mother, even if she didn't love *him*. I guess that showed how much love he held for her. To *love her, for her love for him* and, so yes, it was a built-in paradox, but one he could fix.

The Beachcomber watched him for an hour and finally went over to him. Most of the celebration was done, the celebrators gone. June Cortez left him a phone number and asked that he should call him up soon so they could catch up on old times. But duty called and he had to talk with the Consulate General, arriving soon in Havana. Or as he put it, "I have to meet the Consulate General from the good old United States." It was a jovial, jolly good laugh with several slaps on the back, when he said it to him, too.

The Beachcomber knew of a story he liked to tell often, but at the right time. This was one of an embarrassment to his family that he could tell it to lighten up the mood a little bit, because it always brought a smile to faces as he told this to them. It was on a Sunday, in a filled church service his parents valiantly visited. They always faithfully went to worship in the House of the Lord. On this day he did not have to go, so he decided to visit them while they sat up quietly in the seventh row, far right side, and next to a beautiful stained glass window. It was his mother's favorite seating place, and she came early and always sat there. If anyone was sitting in her place if she did arrive later, she also knew how to kindly *ask* them to move to another spot so she could retain her special seated position.

Juan Paul Rodriguez was a fine silver-haired priest that had also advised her in confession, and been with the family for many years. His resonant and powerful voice gave to her an inner strength that kept her happily fulfilled within all the answers to all life's questions. Like a father figure, she always admired him. Suddenly, Juan Paul stopped mid-sermon. A boy riding a bike... a Bicycle, rode right into the church and, pedaling very fast, to a specific place to get a specific thing.

His pedals didn't stop as he came all the way down the center aisle way. It was like an eternity of a squeaky-sounding bike's wheels and the bike's odd freak combination of a family's future scandalous nightmare; a public relations debacle-by-a-son. In the sacred bastion of the Holy Church's astonishment of an embarrassment... little tiny small wheels and even smaller feet churning at the rotors to amass a distance of 79 feet, which took forever and ever, in the Church's stunned silence, at this unique awestruck interruption and total uncharacteristic stoppage of God's Gospel Class Lecture. Making the curve with the race car driving precision of Mario Andretti, arduously pedaling the hard left turn, he rode seven pews up, and he stopped at the stained glass window his mother always sat next to. He got off his bicycle, leaned it up against the glass window, and with ready and all due glory put a hand out to his parents, in front of God and the entire Village for his weekly allowance. Beachcomber was shut out and grounded for a month. It was the worst, longest suspension he had ever received in his whole life.

Not too many noticed, however, that the Beachcomber had mostly up to now kept his own plight out of the narrative. With the bearing and building significance of the surviving American tourists, their subsequent family arrivals, the reunification process, the shifting of focus became more apparent to all who were involved. And fittingly, to the Beachcomber, he began to see his way clear to return eventually to the optimum humbleness of an otherwise overlooked drifting beachcomber. He blended into the background of the now highlighted AMERICANS' situation. He was a hero, a true hero, but perhaps maybe, more so... He was an anti hero.

The luxury hotel buzzed with family reunions, and the hype of it all. In a period of forty-eight hours, they drank and revealed their faiths and triumphs and gave thanks so voraciously, with toasts of meaning-filled convictions to the bonds of gratitude. Their lives now beckoned them back into Civilian American life. It was quiet today. The Beachcomber looked around the now vacant-ness in which only he and the bartender remained, he thanked him graciously for all of the free drinks they shared, thanks to June Cortez. It also was clear that maybe his old friend June Cortez had arranged his parting, an exit, so if he wanted to he could slip back into the wild, which he did when darkness fell.

With a smile he shook the hand of the bartender and he parted with these words, "Thank you my friend." He turned away to go and then after he walked several paces he stopped, and then he looked back at him too and with a broad cheerful smile he uttered, "I will see you again sometime." He left.

He would be happy to return to his erstwhile beachcombing amity or animism. Beachcomber chose to stay within the humble nature of *the other world.*

If this whole thing was just a dream, if Beachcomber *was just a spirit*. If you could believe in the pulse of John Lennon's credo " All you need is love." If we could ponder the thought of how Lennon looked at a piece of the puzzle with regards to indemnify indemnity towards defining our being with the Lord.

"God is a concept by which we measure our pain." He probably meant that in one true sense that surely: "God does help the ones who also help themselves." (John Lennon admired the spirit people find with god.)

If I believe that Beachcomber was or is real, I know he would end this dream–I believe he would've chosen this spot to leave us. And go beachcombing into new history, as the wandering spirit he truly was, *the meek shall inherit the earth.*

ELEVEN

Shoeless Joe

AMERICAN PLAYER

Night birds' callings and the cricket beats along with the moonlight had welcomed him back to the spot of the shipwrecked lot he found, but the Beachcomber was like a ninja in the darkness: he knew how to walk with the delicateness of sand crabs' steps through wet sand. He sensed that he was not alone and remained still, watching a figure in the dark shadows that stood facing the water, leaning against a fallen S-shaped tree's trunk that was embedded in the sand. The figure rested its two hands on the trunk of the tree like a track athlete would on starting blocks.

Joe Elliot remained poised to embrace the S-shaped fallen tree as the old beachcomber silently watched him contemplating, and embraced in his mind that tonight he would learn if a man would choose life over eternity. He must wait, and as a purveyor of true nature, *remain still* and see what this man was going to choose tonight.

Joe Elliot removed his shirt and pants and rested them across the S-shaped tree. With steady, determined strides like a baseball player who is walked to first but continues walking to second, and third, he continues to home plate. Joe Elliot, in his own mind, approached his own eternity, and for him now, his own "Field of Dreams." He would join his lost brother and bury his pain in this eternal sea in his departure. The Beachcomber let him take the plunge into the sea, for how can you bring a man back to life if he is not *allowed to believe* he did somehow briefly and sort of accomplish the making of his own death?

The Beachcomber pulls him ashore, turning him over and kneading his upper and strengthened tight V-shaped thorax until the seawater in his lungs is all but wrung out of his body. Joe Elliot, with disgusted grief, belly-crawls away to go sleep off his failed suicide. It is an irony to save another man's life twice: You then begin to wonder what the creator had in store for you, to place a man's twice periled life in your hands. It's some kind of stubborn assistance or a dysfunctional Kismet of a déjà vu.

The homeless man, the Beachcomber, had appeared again and saved his life for a second time. In that period of a time lapse, like a twilight zone, in their odd, or as it now had evolved to, restrained imprisonment, they lived together at the Beachcomber's *jungle spot* of paradise, near Campechuela, Cuba. Like a sordid scientific experiment, the condemned man meets his awkward lifesaver of a cure, and it was not unlike an Island of Dr. Moreau.

Whether or not Beachcomber had a premonition, or that he could be *at times* psychic, it was true his date of birth was on that curve of Pisces, February 28th, 1939. And in his sense for foreboding fate, he took his blood red sash out of his knapsack and carefully tied it upon the stilled body of attempted driftwood, wrapping it around his large self-inflicted, tortured melon of a troubled soul's forehead.

Like one of the many stray cats innocently scampering to cross one of Cuba's busier streets when it was struck by the bell ringing thunk of a '55 Chevy's low hanging chrome bumper's tack, walking around, numb-dumbed and doomed-lame, with its nine lives eclipsed by a fragile cracked skull turning itself into a sort of a suicidal sleepwalking "Hemingway House Whore." It treks beach-ward, wandering along right out into the ocean's waters, drowning itself within the very element it truly despised just to end its permanent misery.

The Beachcomber's saga was equally becoming more disturbing where in this was truly an extolled, extraordinary extradition and also extra mundane (on both of the unpracticed, unsevered heads), mounts, and mantles of bounty. The Beachcomber, by all rights, had evolved into a life-broker, and also an insurance collector's dream type of a disclaimer. He held serve on his own to Joe Elliot's soul's *sole ownership* of a damned mortgage. He became a devout right-to-life extortionist, from wanting to give any peace to a wayward numbskull, his right unto himself, for yet he had held up and held quantity of one man's escaped epitaph.

The stakes here became like the pierced gold doubloon nailed to the mast's tack of the fate-filled ship, as a reward from the mad Captain Ahab, to any man who could have successfully impaled the great white whale in Moby Dick. Joe Elliot couldn't kill himself. It was his destiny just like the infamous famed white whale Moby to sail on into history. And it was Beachcomber's destiny to keep him alive.

Joe Elliot _tried_ to kill himself four more times in that lengthy period of observation, exasperated by their *trying* oddball relationship where each impending suicide is altered by Beachcomber's existence.

By preserving his life, Beachcomber ended up gypping Joe Elliot (or inadvertently jerking him out) of his own private right to suicide. With each attempt washed up, it built up in increments with levels upon the passing of each attempt's failures, cheapening his ownership on his own life.

Joe Elliot figured the cumulative sixth time out nobody could mortgage a man's body (like his), pitifully tied to such a stubborn broker and a *floating leg* like the Beachcomber. In his mind these daredevil suicide efforts made him feel like a dangerous cliff diver. "I might as well have been born with wings," he sighed. His mortal semi-urgent, half a year's worth of yearning for bearing his own cross of an indecent immoral but heartfelt tired wish.

A late 12th century orb cast him, the Beachcomber, into this island's moonlit sphere of a compass of endeavor as part of the treasure of holy Roman emperors. He tried by then acting as Thalia, the Greek muse of comedy and pastoral poetry: as if this *blooming one's spirit* would somehow come back and revive Joe Elliot's spirits. He knew sooner or later it would have to bring a true VENUS, since both grew weary within the battle to make his own death. The Beachcomber feared each coming of nightfall, certain one fine day he would wake up alone in failure.

And once a soldier, always a soldier, the Beachcomber was reminded of this: the oldest of rhymes that his army buddies used to sing for luck, with a bastard's chagrin. It was in times of uncertainty that these young men, who were on their way to battle, would sing a few rambunctious lines of it to lighten up the mood on the road.

This is my rifle. And this is my gun.

This is for fighting. And this is for fun.

(Only a Cuban would understand a sonnet that ends pointing to his own cock's calling.)

Having not seen the Beachcomber act this way in six months it was a measurable silence that came between them. The Beachcomber had no time for any sort of mind games. It was a coming of a concession and conclusion. Both had exhausted one another with a half-year's dependence. So, maybe, the singing was just a way to mock him back for all his suicidal episodes, and cast a few aspersions of madness back to him. Or maybe it was time to grant a condemned man his one last mortal wish.

One wonders why he kept the same spot.

Beachcomber: Why here?

Joe Elliot: I lost my brother here.

Beachcomber: You can't do it here.

Joe Elliot: Why not here?

Beachcomber: This is my watch. This is my post.

Joe Elliot: Just let me die for once, please.

Beachcomber: Not on my watch. Not on my post.

This was at the spot where he was rescued by the Beachcomber. And the Beachcomber and his sergeant's blood was a stickler for minding his post.

Sort of like the Hemingway bat that flew into his villa and cracked his skull when he rammed the wall. He tried with penicillin, liquor and herbal remedies to save the night creature, but all proved to be in vain as the BAT DIED. Hemingway kept the carcass as a reminder to and of both the night creature, and of himself... in his valiant effort as "the widower" to a "wayward bloodsucker."

Valiantly, as if preserving once a nightingale's spirit.

The old Eddie Haskell line from *"Leave it to Beaver."* It came after Wally fell under the spell of a beautiful young maiden, Eddie sarcastically commenting on the loss of his good friend's company:

Once you've flown with the Nightingale

(beat)

You've got no time for the bats.

Beachcomber's could see he was crossing up with a dead man's peace offering: he knew he could not change his forever and so troubled mind, so he recited that poem or rhyme to buy some time and think up a solution of just what he could do for him in a last ditch effort.

"This is my rifle. And this is my gun. This is for fighting. And this is for fun."

For the first time in their weird fidelity of a partnership, just listening to him sing a ridiculous nursery rhyme over and over again, quietly, like he was playing his own little mind game on Joe Elliot, giving him that chord of "I'm about at last wit's end dealing with you, too." Joe Elliot thought that this poor soul's mind was lost far more than he was, which was quite odd unto himself he figured in his reflection of *who's fooling whom* thoughts. Finally they confront each other. Joe Elliot stands before him, facing him, as the older Beachcomber sat, knees raised and his toes into the sand, pleading his case until finally he implores him, ripping away his red wrapped bandana with the cry of the forever damned "just let me die for once, please." He threw up the flag of surrender in battle.

An ode to Beachcomber UNTO HIMSELF HE PRAYED:

"God grant me the serenity to accept the things I cannot change. The courage to change the things I can, and the wisdom to know the difference."

Oddly enough, the vaunted San Diegan Beachcomber's favorite poet, Nicholas John Lennartson, at one point in time of history during the Kearny High School stage play (touring the boards of the auditorium), in December 1977, uttered that very same prayer with some boldness and daring conviction, playing the alcoholic doctor in the William Inge tale, "Come Back Little Sheba." It was completely a mark of true insanity for him to even ever be out there, dangling such a marquee gauntlet moment hanging by a thread, who knows what ilk, or what mess had brought him up there. Ironically it was the immensely more talented and daring bravery of his best friend and high school buddy, Wade Morman (whose far greater performing courage he greatly admired), but it was only through him that he gained the courage to step out on that stage. Today, twenty-five years later (their paths crossed in drama class, 1976), it was dedicated through the pane of this story… Nicholas John Lennartson *thanked him* for his older friend's generous encouragement to nourish his creative dreams, which later evolved into his sonnets and odd tales, and his final renderings of what was to become his writing. Wade Morman was a true Pisces soul and a brother and a great friend born 2/24/1960. (The above paragraph is but another brain-dropping of life, *the author refers to an experience from a high school play.*)

The Beachcomber concedes and he agrees to *part company* with Joe Elliot as it's laid out on his next refrain of those words, "just let me die for once." O.K., he says, but not until I leave and I am gone. "You can die tomorrow night." With relief inordinately abounding, both men left each other feeling *relieved of one another's quarry.*

TWELVE

Leave It To Beaver

The Beachcomber recaptures Catch 22

The Beachcomber goes into a bar. He has a look of urgency on his face, coupled with guilty bitters, as if he knew for whom the bell tolled and which *hellish damned stoned-out rock* he would have to overturn to make the deadline. He was on a mission to save a few souls, himself excluded.

The olden bar, known as Papas Beers at Biamo Oriente: The infamous bar had withstood the test of time and had been in existence for over fifty years. It was rumored Che Guevara had a mistress whom he met here while he and an few rebels were traveling through the area and had some drinks, putting away a few bottles of good Cuban rum during the summer of 1958.

It was also famous among the Quajiros for its Sunday night cockfighting. The staging of such gamely contests between competitive Cubans netted both the night spot and the traveling Quajiros some exciting heavy wagering of gambling earnings to add to their otherwise flat wages that they quelled from the trails of the summer coffee harvests or cane cutting in the sugar fields. The yearly wages for a cane cutting Quajiro, or the coffee harvester, or fruit pickers, have always remained very slim. The cockfights, outlawed in some cities, are still practiced today among the traditionalists like the keepers of the infamous Cuban hangout. Many a Quajiro would come from all over the countryside to partake in the high stakes and wagering of such traditions.

When he first walked into the place the room hushed and was stirred with his presence. It was most of the two things combined: nobody had seen him in person for ten years, coupled up with everyone had seen him on TV as the hero who helped the castaways of the U.S. Like it or not, he was revisited and a re-envisioning type of a spirit. In some rarified fashion, he was this infamous and famous ghost who came back for a spell to walk among the living. People didn't know what to make of this spirit, *their silences confirmed it.*

Then atop the staircase, where no one was looking, a rare breed of beauty with healthy loins and brown hair down to her well-rounded ass, Rita Hayworth from Gilda would describe her best, looked over the room scanning the cachet of men, as if each was a jewel in the pocket. Her body was carefully hand etched by the fingertips of Maillol (Ma-yol): these two unique stars... about the cosmos... then begin a curious orbit.

The Beachcomber is distracted momentarily as the whole bar decides to erupt into uproars of applause and major cheers with what the American newspapers called him. Suddenly the Papas Beers mingling two hundred Cubans on a Saturday night cheered: Compadre de la BEACHCOMBER!!!!

The Beachcomber was given a glass and walked through the ovation. He went to a booth that was on the west wall that gave him a view of the room but also allowed him access to make a tidy exit when the time came for one. The drinks were flowing heavily, the festive moods once anchored by his appearance when he got there were all just castaways galvanized by an Ahab's farewell party to another celebration, as if returning only for one night. For tomorrow's sunrise he would shove off and leave to go back to sea. It was right out of Cuban pride to now a hero's folklore. Beachcomber was a Hero.

The second star captured the limelight in a different way but held an equal share of the celebrity in town, as she descended the staircase she commanded all the eyes in the room. Both men and women felt her moonlit gravity, but her most daring envelope was the fate that she could seal and steal the heart of any man. It's very much an old cliché, but such an applicable moniker: this young raven-maned tart was enough to make the Bishop kick out the stained glass windows of the church.

There was no competition between the two since fame made them about equal. Sure, every man loves a town's folk hero. Some envied him and maybe even wanted to be him. To be condemned to do just one night with this girl for hire would all but *resurrect the soul's erection,* and for one whole week afterwards, after a wicked romp with her ripe ass jousting a whip: Well, let's just say for the record that you'd be high stepping and walking like a folk hero. Often asked, "Is that a new dress?" "No," she'd reply, "I've kinda worn them all." She sat down with the Beachcomber. There was no shame in her game for she snapped her fingers and two men appeared, one with a drink and the other lit her a fat Cuban natural home-rolled stogie smoker. Lips protruded as she *bit and sucked on the straw* of her drink, leaving a heavy trail of wet lipstick. The next move she took such a long drag it burned a quarter of her cigarette, she blew a steamer train's stack of smoke into our Beachcomber's face, and she slurped her drink mirage-desert dry. The performance that she put on was a mock stag-party type, early low budget, decadent Fosse, crossing vaudeville with this noir bewitchingly, bedizen version, like what you'd find in "Send in the Clowns." Wincing before any spears came out he felt the indignity he deserved.

"Here we are, Big Daddy...!" with the broadest voice, "Here we are at Papas Beers. You're Big Papa, so go on Papa, give me another drink." She began a wicked laugh upon and at him for a hard minute. She stopped suddenly as the Beachcomber just looked at her with the earnestness of love, like a father truly would; if his wife's passing hadn't marred all their prospects of the lost years.

Up overhead in the private office, Juan Carlo Farshottia looked to the goings on through a mirrored two-way glass, spying on the bar's pride and prized maiden. The feisty whore went by the name *given to her,* reportedly *Osrah.* He didn't know for certain what her real name was nor did he even care. He knew she brought money to him, and to this club. He also knew that one of his own sons was in love with "Osrah." His son was out of town that night on important business, and that was also good. Who needs an *idiot son* who would fall in love with *a bar whore*. He shuddered and silently mused *the notion* which apparently, somehow, disgusted him anyway.

Now I got a Cuban Hero and beachbum falling for her, too, all right in my own business. But for that he watched as together Osrah, his bar's prize whore, walked out the door with Cuba's latest prized beachbum. His status of fame surprised Beachcomber. As Farshottia watched them leave together, he only thought of his bottom line: more money for himself and the club. Better yet: Osrah runs off with a lucky bum like this. At least with Osrah out of his hot-blooded son's life he could add on an R.B.I. to look at his son with some respect (baseball logic had found its way into evaluations when it came to the boys).

The Beachcomber and his real daughter, all of her estranged beauty of raven's mane and her lipstick's ruby rouge cheeks that she was, dragged along to go to the spot of where the recent shipwrecked lot of this story began. She has to, too, best as she can, keep up with her father; for her *true memory* was that of *how much he adored her*. And despite the ole wretched bravado of her routine back at the club, all of it was just to mask the pain. Her own madnesses began a few years after her father gave up. She lived with her elderly grandmother but when Grandma passed away two years ago, she began a period of decline in her ideals, spiraling out of her control. No mother/no father and a dead grandmother now had all but broken her. Descending and drifting along with no direction or strings or parents to tie anchor with, soon evolved into the club set, the high heels, and face-painted nightlife of the sordid, wholesale who's who types (and seeing what's it like to be really in) when you're running wild with the in crowds.

It was at that time the *hot tempered* Roberto Farshottia was drawn to her.

How she never knew it was he who had driven the car that killed her mom, well, that remained a mystery. It's just bizarre fate that they were linked and destined for bumping into each other again… God was having fun pulling his old puppet strings.

She only had to fuck the son of the owner, Carlito, Jr. This angle left her free to taxi the other men to buy her drinks, and saved her soul's wear and tear. It was also quite well known that fucking into Farshottia's fortune was also rising into a future Don's stellar path. And the money she made was a small fortune for her body of 25. She prospered in the high life, and it all worked better for her until her father arrived in the club that fateful evening.

Less than an hour later that they were at the Beachcomber's little beachside spot. "Listen to me now," as both went to their knees, while he clutched her arm. "I ask you to sleep on this beach. This is where I come to be with your mother in my arms. I want you to spend the night here with her, for just this one night, so you can hear her. Will you do this for me, Deborah Jean Mendoza?" as he shook her body, rocking her soul. Mendoza was his wife's maiden name before she married Santiago Serna Dominguez, the old saddle beachcomber. For if he said it in her honor, it echoed deep into her heart. It always meant, when she was growing up back then, "You better button it up quick and listen up good," and she did.

He placed the blue bandana scarf over her bosom and heart. The daughter Debbie Jean bent back to see it upon her nightclub's dress of telltale gaudiness. Comparatively, it was contrasted by the holy garment, now the blue bandana scarf's pureness of beauty, to behold it like a ship's christening or both things ringing through her soul, simply by bestowing it upon her.

"Daddy, this is Momma's scarf. Oh, it's so beautiful. I remember how she would wave this sash at me when I rode the tire swing." Her praise continued on with all the exalted glory of rediscovery. "It's beautiful, Daddy."

He placed it around her neck as if he had knighted her in honor of her mother's memory. He placed his trademark knapsack down and retrieved from it a thick gray flannel shirt and draped it on the sand. He carefully arrested her shoulders to motion her down, gently, to rest upon it for the night. Softly he whispered to her, "Sleep well tonight and her voice will come just as she has for me at this place, for all these long years." Then quietly he said, "You're beautiful," to the angel Debbie Jean. He kissed her forehead intently, tenderly and departed as she faded quietly away under Beachcomber's hypnotic spell, hoping to see cherished distantly past pastoral visions of Mommy. She exhaled, and went fast to sleep, and even faster into her dreams. It was just like that, an instant spell of past fatherly-magic.

He was 42 when Deborah was born. He loved his wife so much they waited, unlike most married couples in Cuba. He felt he would try to preserve her form for him (and they had a late child). She was all of 36 years old when she gave birth to little Debbie Jean 25 years ago.

Her father left Debbie Jean at the spot, the area just twenty-five feet off to the east, or at the left, behind the fallen S-tree's trunk. But also far enough from it that the darkness hid her form, and *it wouldn't be seen in the darkness* of the forthcoming nightfall. The moonlight seems to comfort her and she beckons her thoughts of Papa coming into the club to rescue her, this simple thought after he had left and been gone for over ten years was such a welcomed event that she herself had long since visualized his eventual return to her life.

She forgave him his absence since she knew how much he loved her mother. That love was eternal and forever sound, like the sunrise and sunset. Her thoughts to have him back now would quiet her in her tears. Papa would be back early and for sure and she was certain, it would be tomorrow morning, because it was, as he promised to her, tomorrow morning. He told her this night alone would cleanse all of her soul of anything that she might have done. The *little girl* was still alive inside of her, and she wanted another shot at being daddy's little girl. He convinced her of this for he had never lied to her, or her mother in her lifetime. Beachcomber, up until her mother's passing, had built a bank deed of trust with both women. Something very few men accomplish in their whole lives. Easily he would grant a mortgage of this trust to buy an extra night to think things through. It was on that mortgage *even 10 years after* to have always been forgiven. It was a measure of how much a man he was that he loved his family more than God and they worshipped his love even deeper in return.

All this, and she would go to sleep and wake up in the morning when he came back; and all that was wrong would become right, somehow. A father can do that for his girl. Up until her mother's fatal tragedy in the head-on collision, he had never let Debbie Jean down. All these factors allowed her to place her head down on her scarf and drift off within the folds of the thick gray-flannel shirt, into a peaceful and hope-filled dream in gentle sleep. Night birds' callings and crickets' beats and her heartbeat went into the tranquility of the moonlit skies and the forever dreams in the infinity of all the shining stars.

The giant sea turtle's belly scraping across wet sand awoke her from a dream. She was dreaming about her favorite time with Dad, which for her was the wide-open flight propelled by him on a simple backyard tree swing. The swing was a 1955 Chevy's tire, tied up by a thick, sturdy, ship-to-shore rope. Her father had built in a set of bike handlebars from a big *motor scooter*, that he had *melted* through the upper portion of the hanging tire. She fondly remembered how she would roar sounds of the make-believe motorcycle as loud as she could, with every push from her proud dad. This simple memory, flying with the big motorcycle-handlebar tire swing, marked her truly happiest time with her dad. What a dream life can be to imagine there are only so few times in your life, you'll marvel at something so simple, to make a child feel her father's love, and to be on a tire swing made by and propelled by his very own hands. To think that was all it took just to do that, to be happy.

She had the warm smile of that dream within her heart as she watched the giant sea turtle coming across the shore to spawn. Life was beginning, she thought, for hundreds of baby turtles, eggs were about to be buried, to later be hatched. Witnessing the simplicity of this natural display, she equated her father (in his own life's trek), to the giant sea turtle's plight.

It was during her peaceful sleep that Debbie Jean harkened back into time with another memory of her father during her adolescence. This story came later along as she journeyed into womanhood, when she reached puberty at sixteen, with a patch of thick pubic hair and underarm hair and a ripe, blossoming voluptuous bosom.

In his Cuban-idealized father-knows-best role, the Beachcomber Santiago felt he had to go outside the sticky rules of Catholic faith. He felt confession needed a more balanced practical answer. The ever-outreaching Santiago Dominguez wanted to counterbalance all these realms of being a woman into more of an empowerment role with what was to him *The God's honest truth of practical wisdom.* He wanted his daughter to have that. He thought it hideously dwarfing in common sense that his private sex life, which was a sumptuous one that he shared with his wife, would end up in a booth of the Catholic church's confessional, with a priest named Juan Paul Rodriguez. (Not that it was ridiculous not at all.) He felt *taking that* to a church to be absolved of a loving marriage, and a healthy sex life with your wedded wife, just didn't make a whole lot of sense. Beachcomber Santiago worried about the frequency of his beloved wife's visits to Juan Paul Rodriguez. She went to him so often with her stories of passion, he feared it might result in an angry uprising in the confessional booth; and end the favorable cleansings or dissolvings with absolution.

He smiled with absurd chagrin *at his own thoughts* of how God might deal with a true Cuban's libido. Jesus Christ might just be saying, "Jesus Christ." It gave Christ one hell of a headache, but for Santiago, one heckuva vain hearty chortle. Santiago Dominguez knew he had a handful of a little girl in Debbie Jean and as he watched her curvaceous nubile figure taking shape, developing both for her wellbeing and, in his own sake's vision, he figured it like: with what's coming, *he had to be honest,* and when it came to sex, Santiago was bluntly frank and would outrageously shoot from the hip if the subject ever was to come up with his own daughter.

Armed with ardent, able, military sergeant's advice about what comes with the territory of becoming a beautiful young maiden (a virtual honeypot to all the prowling males and bears' lumbering snouts, sniffing all about, trying to lick her Venus flytrap's nectar), he never missed a chance to educate her on the delicious, or the deadly, pitfalls of intercourse that truly could later on arise for her. It was too important to leave her in the dark with that.

In creating that frankness with his daughter with regard to sex, he truly hoped he would impart a fairness, *or an equality of some kind of emancipation.* He told her *constantly* what to expect to get from a man. These conversations tempered her, strengthening her with some very clear, candid resolve. And, in her mind he was (in hindsight she reflected), demystifying sex for her.

She admired his honesty, whereas her mother despised it. When she realized she couldn't change the pattern he developed with her, Mom noticed it in conversations that were less animated or lively or flirtatiously honest, when she came back into the room. And she accepted Santiago's binding chemistry with his Deborah Jean. She would be a more modern woman than the pretensions of his wife's traditions of the past. She also, as time went on, began to tolerate his spirit for trying so hard to make her so wise about men, in the worldly ways of life (especially in Cuba), and the ways of the world.

For their constant visits with confessions, both women, Mom and Debbie, went to the same place. Cardinal Juan Paul Rodriguez confirmed it, that for a while Deborah, Mom and Dad had a bit of a quandary. With the two of them in, and dutifully reporting for confession, it became clear to the priest that the father, Santiago Beachcomber, was never, truly actively participating in prayer.

He merely liked the shell game of the whole belief in God. Unfortunately, when he walked into the church, he came with his nuts. And his cajones were not negotiable to Christ or anybody else up there. What was hidden under the third nutshell in the three-way Monte? His magnanimous offering to Christ was to keep him *guessing*, let the Lord figure it out in that cosmic fashion: beneath which of the three nutshells lay a nugget's pearl of wisdom, and which was his true secret faith.

Both women became less and less relaxed about the time that each spent in the home's single bathroom. The dilemma grew into an epic argument about wearing make-up, earrings, and certain more non-conservative, revealing, dresses. So Beachcomber decided on a compromise. He would build a new bathroom, even bigger, and also put a special courtesy lavatory in his wife's room with its own make-up table, vanity set-up table, and lighting, that she would also have to share, at least until both were fully operational. And so, during its construction, one bathroom was completed and that was in Mom's room. While the second bathroom was still under construction, Deborah constantly pleaded with him to finally finish it.

It was still very dirty, with the tile cutting going on and it was about a week before it would be finished. It was one night that for a lengthy period of time that her mom was occupying her el banyo too long. Finally, at her wits end and exasperated, Deborah went to Dad Santiago, the Beachcomber.

Deborah: She's been in there for over an hour now. The new one, can I use it yet?

Santiago: O.K., but if you go in there, watch out because your tarantula could get a little dusty.

They both laughed at the reference of how he made light of the possibility of getting some tile dust on her youthful crop of bush. And such was her memory with Dad growing up, adolescence was always just a happy and wonderful memory with her silver-tongued dad.

Beachcomber's wife's aberrant jealousy caused her to be chronically peeved or ticked off with the constant affirmative attention that the dawning younger and prettier up and coming little Debbie Jean was getting. In her mind Debbie Jean believed too much of it anyway. She felt Daddy's *salty minded guidance* in her upbringing elevated Debbie Jean's stature to top billing as the nubile star female of the household.

SO HE BOUGHT HIS WIFE A BIG DOG.

Beachcomber's wife felt, as the old saying goes: "You never introduce a new power figure into the home." Debbie Jean had *evolved into* power figure status, and her dad had brought her up to arrive at that juncture sooner than most girls since they got along so splendidly well. The dog was sort of a combination gift token and buffer for his wife's peace of mind.

It occurred to him with the dual competing females present inside the home, that he needed to divert some tension. He believed, or at least he felt, that the dog would listen to his wife. And in this ploy it would give her a new pet project of attention that just could *spell her ego a little bit* with this newfound precious pet to supervise.

The dog was a dynamically resilient, handsome colored brown and black German Shepherd, two and a half years old, and good with a household: trained, obedient and a good watch dog that was very loyal to its previous owner who lived a mile away and died very recently of a catastrophic stroke. The owner was an eccentric artist who painted animals, like a poor man's Picasso of Campechuela, Cuba. He fed the dog the treat of peanut butter, a delicacy sent to him by an American art collector who was an avid admirer of his works, who regularly shipped specialty contraband U.S. goods. It was a smuggling liaison, if you like, and kept him in an ample supply of peanut butter. The brand gave this particular dog a very happy name... "Skippy."

Skippy bonded immediately with the family, and in the short span of a month's time, like Kismet, became the favorite of Beachcomber's wife. For all these four weeks, her attentions were diverted to the new pet dog. Seemingly all was going beautifully well as the Beachcomber had planned, until:

Beachcomber: Honey, I don't understand, why?

His Wife: That's it. Santiago, it has to go out.

Beachcomber: You mean outside of the house?

His Wife: No, I mean go away, gone.

Beachcomber: You, we're getting along so well, I thought...

His Wife: I don't care the dog has to go out.

Beachcomber: I just don't know why you're doing this.

The Beachcomber was stunned and stung with astonishment. The argument went on for several minutes. But it ended in finality like a court judge's slamming the coaster plate of the timber-wood gavel.

His Wife: I want this dog out of my house! I tell you, Santiago, get rid of this mutt.

The wife made a heck of a stink about Skippy the dog. It was a strange affair that had abruptly ended. During the Beachcomber's calm questioning of her gallows decision, his wife became vilified of visions and literally scowled some unforgivable horrifying indignity. It was a nightmare so awful that she expelled and excommunicated the dog from the house. She dare not be revisited by the revolting bestial sight of another male species, so happy to see the damned blossoming, nubile thief of hearts. She was fully disgusted.

She just couldn't stand sight of the dog, or something so awful and morbid. She remained in a shocked, steadfast, bona fide denial, miffed state by some four-legged devil's lurid treacherously dastardly demon's deed. It was a mystery.

The Beachcomber was baffled and completely befuddled for a whole two weeks after that episode. It was finally revealed rather quietly in confidence, with the unduly begotten ridicule of embarrassment of innocent shame. But the Beachcomber quickly assured her, ushering his tendered forgiveness, hugging the tearful Debbie Jean as she unwittingly shared the nightmare in a

159

conversation of whispered infidelity, without any fear of condemnation from her father, which was a godsend to help in the confession. To shed some light on the pet mystery shame...

Debbie had gotten her period two weeks ago. Beachcomber knew she slept in the nude, which was O.K. since with the island's lifestyle of hot and humid summers in Campechuela, Cuba, comfort always came before vanity. There's no such thing as a robe in the Cuban wardrobe for that matter, anyway. Alas, that night Debbie Jean had left the bedroom door open when she went to bed, not very much concerned of trespassers of any kind. Usually the house was all asleep by 11 PM, as all of them were early risers.

He knew, too, that always, shortly after Debbie Jean retired to bed, its sanction of resting at an ease of peaceful sleep came quickly for her. It was just very easy for her to fall asleep. It was that she was young and happy in her blissful daily life. Her dreams were readily switched on, equally welcome for her soul to explore.

Sure enough, that evening Skippy smelled the juices of the flowing Venus Flytrap's nectar. Late that dubious moonlit evening, Mom arose awake. She got out of bed hearing the murmurs of some intense, _heavy breathing_ and _moaning sounds_, and a lapping of long laps of something licking up some wet liquefied spill of body fluids. There it was.

All the Mom managed was stupor as she stood in the doorway in shock.

It wasn't that she could touch the dog. It wasn't that she could strike the dog. It wasn't that she could stop the dog. It wasn't that she could awaken Debbie Jean either. It was a horrifying climax of epic consequences. The dog was licking her daughter's mantle and the mother had *a crucial-terrifying mental stress breakdown on the spot.* Instantly, she became dizzy, inglorious, and sickened, all simultaneously. She couldn't contain or control herself as she ran into the bathroom to throw up. Big Fatzuka Yoi! Mom was up all night and sick till dawn. It didn't matter at the moment, but Deborah had her first wet dream of innocence lost. Both she and Skippy got a good night's sleep after it was all over and done with; as far as they were to be concerned of the feast of the nosy four-legged beast.

He couldn't imagine what Juan Paul Rodriguez would do with this confession. Wisely, he stayed out of the church for three months, hoping that with the indignity of older age (a senility clause if you will), the priest would hopefully forget it.

It was not in the Beachcomber's mind to even begin to try to explain this one with the holy-minded eyes of God looking upon him with an arched eyebrow of sinful shame. Man's best friend he joked to himself out loud, and he laughed some more even harder than the first time as he repeated himself once more, _thanks man's best friend._

For Debbie Jean, these emotions were the trials and tribulations of life growing up with Dad.

As she dreamed, everything seemed to be racing through her mind as she fondly remembered the past, but during her dreams somehow the thoughts of a horror flashed past her, as she knew deep down that Roberto Farshottia, Jr., would take after her. One time, one of Osrah's many would-be suitors came up with a sure-fire scheme to awaken her to the two-timing ways of Roberto Farshottia, Jr.'s philandering ways... with several local girls behind her back. He hoped in doing so he could lure her away and spirit her from a bright-idealized prospect and fetch her unto himself (who he believed to be a more ideal partner), to gain her favor; to somehow steal away this Gilda-like goddess.

Well, the mobster's son got wind of this gossip-tongued, snake oil scam and took the man to the bottom basement for creating such a soap opera. He had three men beat the tar out of him. The man had wailed in agony so loud the sound carried through the lengthy channels of ventilation ducts and into Juan Carlo Farshottia, Sr.'s offices. Up above the cellar, Juan Carlo Farshottia, Sr., aroused by the yelping cries, came to see what the fracas was all about. He looked upon the group of three burly bodyguards holding a guy whose face was bruised and bloodied beyond recognition. He stopped at the bottom stairs and he looked upon the battered victim and his rag doll limbs. He wondered for what awful, drastic penance should a man so mercilessly be punished, with such a vigorous and hardcore cathartic cadence?

Farshottia, Sr.: What did he do, my son?

Roberto Farshottia, Jr.: He told Osrah I was screwing around with another girl. (Wipes the sweat off his brows.) He told her I was a two-timing shit! (He backhands a whippingly rude smack to this would be suitors now broken jaw.)

Farshottia, Sr.: And you beat him up for what? (Puts on a smirk) For telling the truth?

He laughed out loud in an uproarious fashion with the most gleeful laugh he had all year.

The three bodyguards who had grasped the battered man's torso, and left and right limbs, released him, his wrecked body collapsed as he plummeted unconsciously upon the cellar's flooring.

The three bodyguards walked towards the stairs, passing the exasperated Roberto Farshottia, Jr., and his raw knuckles of fury as he silently stared at his fallen prey. The bodyguards climbed up the wooden steps and followed Farshottia, Sr. out of the cellar. Atop the stairs, the men turned and began snickering at the horrendous pummeling the suitor took in the name of lust. Their laughter echoed overhead as they exited the chamber, leaving Roberto Farshottia, Jr. standing in the dankness of the wine cellar's quarters with his wretchedly wrecked prey.

Roberto Farshottia, Jr. burned with rage upon hearing them snicker over his intrepid fidelity felony. If only he could have taken the father's jest of rapture in the spirit it was meant to be taken. Here was a bar brothel, the owner's son nearly losing his mind's marbles over a patron who had eyes for one of the young frolics who danced in the club, and told her that her man (the un-idyllic Farshottia, Jr.) had a roving eye and had yet an alternate frolicking affair with oh yet another frolic of flavor other than hers. It was ridiculous.

However, the tragedy in the soap opera took on a new meaning the day after when everyone heard the spaded suitor's tale of how Roberto Farshottia, Jr. alone in the cellar had knifed off his tongue. He could no longer speak of any man's infidelity (nor create any future liaisons of his own), for he became the town's local mute of old Papas Beer' storied folklore. It was one hell of a way to go quiet and keep your pee pee.

Much like the Dude character in 1959's Rio Bravo, he was known as mucho borrachione, the town drunk, who was in pity kept in booze and his own blues living off the townsfolk who tossed him a scattering of coins off the barroom floor for the rest of his tapered-tongue's tripped-up tale of his miserable life.

The storied legend grew from there, and nobody dared to cross Roberto Farshottia, Jr., for all knew better. Like priests they held their zippers with Osrah, for fear some body part or *favored limb* might a tryst with this fetching femme fatale cost a man's piece. Tales of this kind of madness from one soul to the next can only tend to multiply in magnitude with every retelling of this tragedy, known as, "The *fancy fornicating flapper* that cost a man his flavor-savor, taster's trapper."

The thought left her mind as quickly as she dialed into it, *like a wrong number* she quickly hung up on that train of thought. The daughter of the Beachcomber (Deborah Jean), is suddenly awakened by the rustling of feet across dry sand. The steps Joe Elliot took were deep as the grey granulized sand beneath his 6'5", 235 lb. frame, shoveled over his toes with steep heapings with every laden step. He stopped near the fallen S-tree. He put his hands upon the tree like he stood before a pommel horse, preparing to mount.

Deborah Jean sat up and watched him as slowly, carefully and with a delicateness of last will and testaments in life, he began his unholy beckoning towards the restless waters, where he was prepared to finally join his lost brother and perhaps even meet thy maker.

He placed his shirt and pants across the tree. He took off his boxers and stood poised as if in some sort of moment, checking the stars, and in heavenward gaze, thinking how glorious it might be if he could join his brother and father, and how near he was to crossing over (self sacrifice... to die out there at sea), to go away and be back with them.

Deborah Jean looked over his backside and put her scarf over her mouth, as it draped open. She was looking at the backside of a good-sized man, and she was struck with his tall, lean, broad-shouldered form.

Joe Elliot remained still in heavenward gaze.

Deborah Jean began to lean forward and belly crawl on her stomach as she kept vigil on this form that pulled her out of her dreams and into a fantasy. She would crawl up to be closer to view the man's backside in the moonlight. She was entranced by this moonlit Adam figure's form.

Joe Elliot got down on his knees. He prayed at the altar of the fallen S-shaped tree.

He arose and walked into the waters of the ocean, prepared to accomplish the making of his own death. It was something he had six months to think about and his spoiler off his back, *that floating leg*–Beachcomber–was *off his post*, and Joe Elliot believed with each of these steps and final strokes toward eternity that he would finally, peacefully perish without interference. This time for sure he would make it to the other side.

Deborah Mendoza watched in amazement. Her fantasy model male form of a huge Adonis was submerging into the waves of the tides rolling beyond the shoreline, and she finally ran out to try to somehow capture him before he would have disappeared forever.

Upon reaching him, he was already filled with salt water. She wrestled to gain his head and upper torso as she paddled and stroked back towards the shore, until he dragged on the bottom sand as with each wave of water he washed up along and up a bit further ashore. With one more showering last wave and a "final heave," she tugged the man up and finally away from the tide's reaches, turned him over and plunged his lungs. She rolled him over once more on his back and, with an angel's breath, she gave him mouth to mouth resuscitation, and purged the H20 with her own hot blooded, high oxygen until he came back to a consciousness. His eyes fixated on the raven-haired angel's eyes and her bosom of mercy, for he had awoken now into and of a deeper dream of visions of the master poet Kahlil Gibran.

Song of the Soul

> *Sons of my ancient mother, you rider of the tides, how often you have sailed in my dreams. And now you've come to me in my awaking, which is my deeper dream.*
>
> *"Ready I am to go," and my eagerness with sails full set all of us await the gathering first winds...*
>
> *The world's cultural, spiritual, and intellectual treasures; Her true vastness, and experience, we seek to bring in...*
>
> *Only another breath I will breathe in the still air, only another loving look cast backward–And then I shall stand among you.*
>
> *A Seafarer Among Seafarers, As a Writer of my Dreams.*
>
> *And you vast sea, sleepless mother, Who alone are peace and freedom to the river and the stream; Only another winding through this stream I – will—make only another prayer – into this glade, I – will – take*
>
> *And then I shall come to you*

A boundless drop

In a boundless ocean.

How life can change! One single act of another human being of kindred kindness is wonderful. Beachcomber's daughter, Debbie Mendoza, pinch hit for her old pop. Papa's baby girl saved Joe Elliot's life. And lo and behold, she proved of mighty lineage in the spirit of the floating leg of Beachcomber, truly an ever ebullient, buoyant chip off the old block, and yet more so, even a mesmerizing, intoxicating, resilient trophy of sheer lustful beauty.

Joe Elliot was infused the moment her mouth enveloped his, and she blew oxygen into his lungs. With this life-giving transfusion he returned from darkness, having nearly reached the other side. It was a momentous awakening, with her lips on his mouth and her luscious bosom compacting him, both of her angel's wings of fulfilling arms cradling him firmly, but tenderly. He was hooked. It's as if a Ship's anchor had suddenly hoisted his entire soul into the world of her completely magnetic field of total realm.

Destiny was thus fulfilled (thanks to her father's vicariously leading her into a midnight's mercy rendezvous with the wayward ballplayer Joe Elliot). Yesterday's once damned damsel of despair was today's reprieved, fully redeemed, damsel of a sailor's lineage; saving a sailor and being a savior. Yesterday's damsel became a hope for both for a better tomorrow. And the greatest sign attributable to love was born again.

On Love

And think not for you—

Might try and direct the course of love,

For love it finds you worthy;

Shall direct your course.

Kahlil Gibran

People always want to know with books/novels, "What's holding it together?"

Or how does this beget that, and what ties it all up? What's the crux of this story, and what's it all hinged upon? Every modern reader must decide *of the read* what's classified as *the essence* that explains it, or supposedly somehow defines its raw reasons of its existence.

The Beachcomber paused to wonder this, too.

What's it hinging on, and why this dangled lynch pin?

Beachcomber knew what he wanted to be: ALONE. He found his way in that trek. But what happened in his life was that he learned to uphold and embrace the disordered or happenstance circumstances of his life. He knew in the world that existed today, you had to or else you wouldn't survive. (Embrace this fractured energy and disorder in it.)

Even in a humbled humble traditional life of a Cuban countryman who served <u>CASTRO</u> and *his country,* and later earned a respectable living practicing a handed-down trade of his grandfather's livelihood of furniture making, in the baby crib business. All the tremendous hard work and all of the effort he put into it versus what was ultimately taken away: the great love of his life (like pulling the rug out from beneath his feet), stolen by bad fate.

It's when life is testing you. It throws you into the curse of Cabo Blanco, Costa Rica. Some 78 air miles southwest of San Jose, exist high coastal cliffs of natural wonder. Floating birds slam into the rocks, hitting the cliffs to die. Human beings fall out of step occasionally, and fail in the test to come back to evolve on when we hit that adversity of being tested... or like somebody feeling at life, *failed—and...* we just give up and die right there and then—on the face of an old earth stone rock.

Beachcomber needed to go away long enough to mend his heart's ability to cope and reduce the infamy of its empathetic heart-wrenching grief. He had to deal with the loss of his *best times years,* that's what that time with her was to him. And he would spend a decade to find himself since God made a mistake with a fatal eclipse, and clipped the wrong skull. It's a lot of years before you balance your own ship when some of life's storms rob you of the soul's true north.

It's lost forever... and the mind settles by becoming a living fossil of discarded water color faded out beachcombing driftwood...

Until it's either going to molt back, rejuvenated into being worthy of somehow taking roots again before it fossilizes forever. Or miraculously, metamorphosing back into roots of the earth and being reborn into life's chain.

It occurred to Joe Elliot, now, after all that had passed, there on the boat it was clearly evident. He watched as his brother Charlie Goldenberg, overcome and stricken with grief, grasped his father's lifeless body of once steady shoulders. "May you rest in deep sleep," he said softly. He remembered when he closed his eyes in death.

He remembered how he whispered those telling words:

"It's time for you to go. Now, it's time for me to go," C.J. said, as he embraced him, and he openly wept...

It was hard for him to accept it but the reality was both sons loved their father a great deal but Joe Elliot had an even stronger love for his brother. As with the dueling grief which compelled him to try to exit from his own life, he took it upon himself to finally now realize what must have taken place with C.J.

He was, too, one of the strongest but yet he somehow did not make it through the safety launch boat's journey to the Beachcomber's jungle spot near Campechuela, Cuba.

It wasn't until just then he felt the truth had awakened within him, and it was somehow a one truth he had not resolved, however, up to now:

"C.J. let go."

For all his life C.J. was extraordinary. But in the ending of his own life, he became *ordinary*. He wanted to be ordinary. He truly loved and worshipped his father. And that minus... he wouldn't face life without him... so, he made sure that he became ordinary.

Within this final baptism of an unholy act of trying to end his life, Joe Elliot meets and falls in love with Deborah Mendoza, Beachcomber's daughter. And from that day forward, their's was an inseparable union. More than kismet, it was the piece that hinged into and hooked the whole puzzle of his life together, and he could readily *see and feel it fit.* He had a clear picture in his mind now. Whereas Lt. Dunbar of "Dances with Wolves" rode across the battlefield on that horseback with arms outstretched to enter within all God's truly blazing glory, to envelope the heavens within the hail of those Confederates' buckshots, here Beachcomber's daughter became a floating leg of lineage to save a man's soul from a sinful suicide.

Joe Elliot became a sovereign survivor by the sweet angel's lips and to her credit settled in with Deborah Jean Mendoza within the island paradise of Castro's Cuba. A U.S. transplant for life. In trying to trade in his life, Joe Elliot was born again by her kiss of life. He would be with her from here on out, and forever, for here and now.

Later on, after gaining inheritance from his father's life insurance, Joe Elliot able to claim a sum of $225,000 in U.S. currency once all the lawyers' fees were doled out and it was finally then delivered by a courier case. He bought a house of moderate consolation since he loved it mainly for its beach access. In Cuba, a man could live very well on very little U.S. currency, but living good, with a quality in the life of the soul, Cuba naturally brought.

Joe Elliot and Deborah Jean fell deeply in love and soon married in a union of trust and livelihood. She became the betrothed Mrs. Debbie Jean Goldenberg, and November 13th, after a tropical rainstorm marking in déjà vu, with nature's fury of how they had originally been brought together, a son, Joe, Jr. was born. For a few years *a singular soothing spell of happiness* was ever so uniquely coming from way up above... which had been sweetly blessed upon both of their souls.

THIRTEEN

Evil Among The Saints

That day, it just happened–Roberto Farshottia accosted Deborah Jean Goldenberg at the supermarket in the meat section, with all blood-red marbled quantities of rare beef. He walked up behind her and startled her with her Papas Beers moniker, "Osrah." With the shock of not hearing it in four years, she quickly stiffened up and froze for a minute, as chills ran up and down her spine. He's here, a man with a beef, here in the beef section.

This was the man who once cut off her admirer's tongue at the nightclub. His mere stalking presence instilled within her body the chilled stiffness of an imaginary stiletto. This man, Roberto, was a switchblade of evil.

He fondled the back of her neck and he sent chills up and down her spine as he repeatedly called her name over again until finally her son broke Roberto Farshottia's evil ambiance of his menacing vibrato of whispered tones into her stunned ear.

She pulled money from her purse–the little boy Joe Junior took the coins.

Debbie Goldenberg: Go play on the rides, O.K.? (After a heartbeat.) I'll be there in a few minutes.

He scampered away towards the coin machines, the rows of children's rides you find in front of general stores.

Roberto Farshottia picked up a porterhouse steak from the meat section and he touched it to her shoulders, as Deborah Goldenberg stepped back.

Roberto Farshottia: It's O.K., I just needed to cool off a little bit.

He rubs the steak's frozen exterior plastic to the side of his face and on his upper shoulders and neck area to cool himself.

Roberto Farshottia: I just wanted to tell you that I missed you these last four years. (beat) I see you have a son.

Deborah Goldenberg: Yeah, Roberto, I'm settled down now. I gave up that life at the club.

Roberto Farshottia: You didn't even say goodbye to me, Osrah. And that night Papa told me you left me for that beach bum.

(he throws the icy steak into the freezer)

Deborah Goldenberg: That bum is my father. I got married, now I'm a mother. You know... (beat) you get older, and sometimes you settle down, and that's what I did.

Roberto Farshottia: You get older you say, huh? You still look pretty young and beautiful to me.

Deborah Goldenberg: Now I have to wear make up to look beautiful.

Roberto Farshottia: I still miss you, Osrah. I want you to come back with me.

Deborah Goldenberg: I can't, I can't... I'm too old for that life, Roberto. beat) I was 25 then, and it's been four years since then. I'm almost 30. It's time for me to move on. I can't go back. Do you know what I mean?

Roberto Farshottia: Yeah, I know what you mean.

Deborah Goldenberg: Can you understand I can't go back now to that life... (beat) It's over for me now. Will you please understand I gave up that life?

Roberto Farshottia: Yeah, I understand you gave up the life. (beat) We all got to go and get married sometime.

Deborah Goldenberg: So, you're going to let me go?

Roberto Farshottia: It's a small island and I had to find you. (beat) I just wanted to say goodbye.

Deborah Goldenberg: Then this is goodbye... (beat) for the last time.

Roberto Farshottia: Si, Señora Goldenberg. The last time... goodbye.

Roberto stamps out his smoke and he turns away. He is seething with anger but he holds it in. And in deliberate slow-motion steps, he leaves the general store quietly without a word. He pats Joe Junior on the back as he walks past him at the game riding machines. Deborah Goldenberg clutched her neck in terrified fear of dire doings as his hand touched her son's back. Thankfully he retrieved it as soon as he put it to him. Deborah Goldenberg rushes up towards the toy machine ride and grabs Joe Junior and then runs towards the car with a fury of rabbit's quick feet. She roars out of the parking lot, leaving a cartload of groceries abandoned over in the meat section.

As the car speeds away, Joe Junior can see she's shaken and unnerved by the man back at the general store. And as he asks her, "What's wrong, why can't I go back to the ride?" She answers, "I'm sorry but I just need you to be quiet now because Mommy has to drive the car now. We have to go home." He looked at her in this state of shock and he wondered about the man back at the store. "Momma?"

He could see she was very upset and the pair of sunglasses couldn't hide the pain, because there on her cheeks the little boy saw flowing tears.

It was the first time he watched his mother crying.

————

Speaking of sadnesses, on a separate note of sorrow: one of our best writers, John Lennon, was gunned down and blown away, assassinated by a delusional killer in New York, December 8th, 1980. One of the great modern thinkers of *virtual reality enlightenment*... In John Lennon's mind, if the heart believed it, and I mean if you truly believed what was in your heart, if you could think it and feel it, then you could be it. The late 1970s people still yearned to believe in the promise of the peace love generation that came through the 1960s.

One could reason, the 1975 horror classic camp musical spoof of old monster movies... *ROCKY HORROR PICTURE SHOW*'s timely line of wisdom here: It was a spirited feeling prevalent from 1975-1980.

"Don't dream it... Be it"

Well, here was a man who said it, and he was proud of it. He spoke volumes to a generation of souls also when he said: "All you need is love." December 8th, 1980. Twenty years later, Friday, December 8, 2000, this tale Beachcomber was approaching its apex, nearing completion, being written out on the yellowed scrolls. Even though the writer himself was very short on words, and not particularly clever in the body of his work, he had always insisted on tooling with his words on 8 ½ x 14 long legal pads. I guess that you could say he longed for the day he would have something important to say. And that he could have room to express it at length. And he dreamt or imagined that some idea he had to say could be important or of importance. But for what he lacked in talent he mainly relied on the strength of the forces (within and without or throughout that flaw), he knew that he could always make up for his literary limits with his vivid imagination.

Here was a man who possessed both traits; gifted with imagination, and a very important message to impart to the people of this world. It was in this realm that he felt he could translate a miracle. He would mark the day with a tribute to one that always had such an important message, and was truly a special soul that always had something to say. "Virtual Reality Enlightenment."

A memorial at a park in Havana unveiled a JOHN LENNON bronzed, sculptured figure sitting on a bench alone. One arm is resting on one end of the bench, his legs comfortably crossed, and the other arm is relaxed up across the top of the bench. His body is turned to face and listen to any of his potential company, whomever would happen to choose to sit next to him. The index finger of his left hand is extended in an invitation and pointed fashion *to sit here.*

It was fortunate he was bronzed for a moment there, because holding the white sheet during the unveiling, and looking upon him with a curiously odd wonder, was fucking Fidel Castro. The president, commandante, el presidente of Cuba: And, I could hear John Lennon's voice over the transference as it echoed from the Atlantic to the Pacific:

JOHN LENNON: Jesus Fucking Christ! Fidel Castro is staring at me and I'm sitting here in a park with a thousand people around us. All Cubans... and it's me looking at him. There he is, looking at me. It blew my mind... yah know. Yes it did, brother. (he takes another breath;)

Dammit, lad, I mean, you cannot imagine just how unbelievably surprised I truly was, you know what I mean. And there we were. I felt my body was there but my mind had lost it. It was just crazy like that for a second or so until it hit me... (beat) Then my mind caught up to my body. Then it was like a reality to me. There I was in the park there. And everyone in the park is really happy and the mood is in the air. I feel peace and love emanating from the hearts of the people there. Everyone's singing Beatles songs, and we're all smiling and rocking and rolling along in the hot afternoon sun. Well, I thought I must be dreaming but I wasn't because you see it... (he starts again.) And so it is, I mean it really is... what it is... or what it really was.

John Lennon thought: this is nirvana. It's me and Fidel Castro in the park, a thousand Cuban people are smiling, and all of them chanting along singing BEATLES SONGS, CAN YOU IMAGINE?

JOHN LENNON: I've got Castro in the mack, looking over my shoulders at the park. He's looking at me and it's me looking back at him. And it's truly, really *him looking at me...* me looking at him. (beat) And then in this dream I turned to Yoko and I said it out loud as if she was with me:

(gloriously) strange days indeed... most peculiar, momma.

It was in that power of a vision, of a dream of love, a No. 9 dream, and John Lennon breathed a sigh of relief and belief. His spirit was preserved, the message had gone on and it had come through, and now he could rest in peace and love. "Imagine."

There is now in life and as in dreams like Beachcomber a new bronze statue of John Lennon sitting on a bench, in Havana, Cuba. It is really... truly real. The *Los Angeles Times* article December 8th, 2000; FROM LENIN TO LENNON: Cuba Honors Former Beatle. A memorial at a park—named for the member of the once banned group draws 1,000 fans—including, Fidel Castro. Lorenza Munoz, L.A. Times Staff Writer.

(A print copy of the article and the image hangs at the author's home.)

PART III

FOURTEEN

The Kennedy File

Perhaps two of the more extraordinary facts about November 22nd, 1963, the two that haven't been challenged since the day of the event, have a structure that places some unusual occurrences afoot.

1. The media camera crews were for the one rare time in history placed way way back...far away, behind the president's limousine... some eight cars back. As we know JFK was a cameras-front-and-center type of world leader.

This phenomenon itself is remarkably unique as to how it all happened. It's the start of these multiple and unusual pieces to fit into this unique event.

2. The anonymous victim of an epileptic seizure on Elm Street just before the president's arrival. Everyone's <u>focus was altered</u>, as that ambulance then drove to Parkland Hospital, and then the victim promptly disappeared. His name and the dire situation he was in, was expunged and later erased, too.

The list of formidable enemies within the government and private sector that President Kennedy had made in his first 1,000 days in office was a very substantial list, enough to cause great concern for his livelihood. They had grown to include FBI director J. Edgar Hoover, CIA director Allen Dulles, and several echelons of very powerful factions of the CIA and the anti-Castro community. The president was angered with the CIA for the Bay of Pigs fiasco and also equally disturbed by The Agency's direct involvement in "assassination plots" (abetted by Mafia chieftains Santos Trafficante and Carlos Marcello) against Castro. President Kennedy disallowed a *second planned invasion of Cuba* and made a bold threatening remark against The Agency by avowing, <u>*I will smash The Agency into a thousand pieces.*</u> Then followed the president's damning memorandums, both Number 55 and Number 263 that would make matters even more complex as John Kennedy headed into a re-election year where he would possibly conceivably take on a new running mate for vice president. Nixon leaks that story to the Dallas Newspaper's Carl Freund.

Look into the rogue's gallery of mobsters and burglars FBI + CIA + NSC 5412 + OP-40 free agents involved within the assassination of JFK (see pages 156 and 157 of the Robert J. Groden book, *THE KILLING OF A PRESIDENT*). You can see a highly volatile group of insidiously dangerous and ultimately deadly direct enemies of John F. Kennedy and his administration's policies, especially with regard to the Cold War with the Soviet Union and Cuba, as well as the curbing policy Kennedy intended in dealing with Southeast Asia to stop the U.S. troops from continuing deployment in Vietnam. It was a reelection year, which accounted for some lobbying in multiple camps, and as the Kennedy process oscillated, especially traveling through a conservative stronghold state like Texas; it's clear to everyone today that the Vietnam War would not have progressed as costly or deeply as the LBJ campaign eventually did.

Sam Giancana influenced the crucial vote during the 1960 presidential election helping place the son of his former bootlegger partner (Joe Kennedy) in the oval office. He felt betrayed when the Kennedy brothers later went after Mafia business interests in the United States. Santos Trafficante and Carlos Marcello, who were under heavy heat from the McClelland committee, Robert Kennedy-led senate investigations as well as John Roselli and Jimmy Hoffa. Both John Roselli and Sam Giancana leaked out the information that "Kennedy was going to be hit." John Roselli was taped by the FBI clearly saying it aloud, and yet Sam Giancana was in his own way more tactful when he scoffed to a journalist during the McClelland committee probe and said aloud, "*go tell it to your big boss*" repeatedly as if Kennedy's future was the one in jeopardy. As far as his own future, he felt confident to assert that clearly he had nothing to worry about since he knew that the president's watchdog could be avoided by cutting off the head, and it wasn't long after he said it that JFK was hit and the probe's watchdog was put in check. Moving away from the mob side of it (which will have to take a back seat for a moment), we look at the whole picture, including the truer more plot-worthy *architects of fear.* The master planners and the Allen Dulles-led CIA side of it: Robert Maheu, and William "King" Harvey, David Atlee Phillips, and, Richard Helms, and Desmond Fitzgerald, assisting the action end on the playing field which in base scale required mainly two separate shooting teams in principle, with a team of back up marksmen:

Team #1: Texas School Book Depository B Team (2 FBI, 2 Cubans, 1 mobster.) FBI agents in 1963 Bernard Barker, Eugenio Martinez, and two Cuban hit men Pedro Diaz Lanz, Herminio Diaz Garcia and also a fifth man in the background; suspect Eugene Hale Brading. (A.K.A Gene Braden).

Team #2: Grassy Knoll Mechanics, A Team; All 4 CIA, led by Robert Maheu. (Jack Ruby/my p.o.v. under supervision of Robert Maheu.)[11] Howard Hunt, Frank Fiorini (aka Sturgis), Maurice Bishop (aka Frenchy), were the 3

---

11   Inside Z R RIFLE, wherein the Cuban State Department investigation led to uncovering the members of ALPHA 66--BRAVO CLUB including Anthony Veciana and Orlando Bosch, in concert with Nixon's man E. Howard Hunt, and Bernard Barker, Eugenio Martinez, and James McCord, along with Frank Sturgis, Pedro Diaz Lanz, Herminio Diaz Garcia, David Morales, and also C-Cube leader Ed Lansdale. Jack Ruby, via telephone records is a member of this team. However my 30 years research leads me to believe strongly that this A Team was led by Robert Maheu and Edward Lansdale. Therefore implicating the wider web involvement of E. Howard Hunt, Robert Maheu, Howard Hughes and further Richard Nixon; to the CIA's William "King" Harvey... it went all the way to the highest level inside the Central Intelligence Agency's top leadership. (The Hughes--Nixon--Dulles--Barker--Hunt--McCord--Martinez--Lansdale--Sturgis, David Morales, Cord Meyer; and also Richard Helms, William "King" Harvey connection to the CIA hit teams... deployed on 11/22/1963 in Dallas, Texas)

tramps or hobos arrested in Dealey Plaza and whom I firmly believe fired the shots towards the president's limousine, striking JFK from the front: The first bullet just shy of the necktie, and the second bullet hit in the back, the third went into the temple, imploding and exiting the occipital area; the fatal shot that finally killed the 35th president John F. Kennedy, November 22nd, 1963.

Jack Ruby monitored The Knoll: plus *two specialist's*, additional shooters. (Robert Maheu, in the freight yard calling the radio signals to E. Howard Hunt's A-TEAM. Robert Maheu was Howard Hughes agent who would oversee the teams, that included Frank Sturgis, and David Sanchez Morales and the others under the command with Rolando Masferrer: The grassy knoll shooting mechanics with Bravo Club militia, and Alpha 66.)

And toward the FBI side of it which was aiding on scene support in the background areas and greatly helped... with the "cover up" of the president's killers, FBI director J. Edgar Hoover, Guy Bannister, Hugh Ward, and FBI men like James Hosty, and Gordon Shanklin. The Ponchartrain 11, CIA gun running connection of Clay Shaw, David Ferry, Gerry Hemmings, and Tony Veciana, and Orlando Bosch. Bernard Barker, and Eugenio Martinez would assist the FBI coordinating evidence gathering bullets on the scenes clean — up details. It was quite a gathering of the extreme right wing, some very risk-taking men.

And then through the fabric of government conspiracy wrapped up in the peripheral corners and out on the edges of the scope of the efforts of all these powerful factions were the Mafia men recruited vicariously in the effort to corral the actions of higher sources, CIA mostly (creating the plan from the beginning), aided by some key FBI agents *to kill the president* and then to go onward to execute the necessary classic and drastic subterfuge, to funnel all responsibility for the act of this conspiracy... to pin all the actions of several men... to "<u>one man,</u>" named Lee Harvey Oswald. Lee Harvey Oswald was a 24-year-old ex-Marine and intelligence operative for Naval Intelligence and the CIA. Discouraged with his job position as a lower level operative with not much to do, he also worked as an FBI informant, since he was displeased with his treatment by the CIA and Naval Intelligence.

There is more later regarding two additional shooters, insurance hit men. They are revealed afterwards in Closing Statements. Also the positions of the other two men: John Roselli, and Tony Veciana (the umbrella man), are detailed later on in this file.

Oswald's discouragement was clear when he wrote his superiors a note on November 8th, 1963 *two weeks before the Kennedy assassination*. The odd hand-written unenlightened note indicated he was not a man on any kind of mission.

The note was to E. Howard Hunt of the CIA:

Dear Mr. Hunt,

November 8th, 1963

I would like information concerning my position. I am only asking for information.

I am suggesting that we discuss the matter fully before any steps are taken by me or anyone else.

Thank you,

Lee Harvey Oswald

Asking his CIA bosses for clarification of his position was not the mark of a man who knows: this is the voice of a man who doesn't know. Afterwards this information went to David Atlee Phillips as well, and both Hunt and Phillips and Desmond Fitzgerald had to keep things going forward.

Not fully satisfied by the response that had come back from the top from E. Howard Hunt, and a week before the assassination, Lee Harvey Oswald met with David Ferry to talk about his task (not fully knowing the plans that day), and he expressed doubts about his role that was clearly undefined (to him). Whatever the extent of the fully laid plans, he was definitely or clearly uncertain about it. Deeply concerned after he met with Richard Case Nagell.

David Ferry, after his meeting with a shaky Oswald, went to talk it over with Guy Bannister. Guy Bannister and Hugh Ward reported to Carlos Marcello about their problems with Lee Harvey Oswald. Thinking he was about to back out of his assignment (which was still unclear to him), Guy Bannister of the FBI put pressure on Oswald by threatening to have his whole family and his Russian wife, Marina Oswald, deported, possibly sending both her and the children back to Russia. Oswald didn't know it was the work of Guy Bannister, but he suspected it was FBI who made the threats.

A very distraught Oswald bristled at that thought of losing, or being separated from, his family so he contacted James Hosty. Not knowing his role he felt he was being used somehow, and his note explained that he also just wanted more specific clarification from his boss, E. Howard Hunt. In turning to his part-time employer (the FBI) and former agency contact, James Hosty, in an attempt to reduce his culpability, Oswald, to the best of his ability, informed Hosty of the FBI, very carefully, that something was going to happen. Oswald went on to explain he had "no objective or knowledge at his level of standing, as to the extent of what ultimately was going to be happening." Oswald left the meeting with the FBI agent Hosty telling him pretty accurately that he was *confused and tentatively asserting that he was being used somehow. The Nagell warning now becomes clear to Lee Oswald.*

Oswald was desperate for Hunt to explain things to him. Four days after the note to Hunt, Lee Oswald still couldn't gain an understanding and it all began unfolding ("Oswald's confusion")… ten days prior to the date of the assassination. Guy Bannister and David Ferry tried to appease Oswald following instructions from CIA Agent David Phillips (alias Maurice Bishop). The strategy that the agent felt would be best was to tell Oswald, "that he wouldn't be needed that day." Then, calmly, he went on to say, "Just go in to work like you would normally that day." (Oswald worked at the Texas School Book Depository.) Oswald was relieved to go back to work, sort of off the field, and Oswald's tensions subsided. CIA Agent David Phillips told Guy Bannister and David Ferry that Oswald was background anyway, and it wouldn't... change anything. The plan was still a solid "go."

"Bishop" was a shadow man of David Phillips, an undercover former operative of the CIA who was an expert marksman, used in covert CIA operations and preparations for the Bay of Pigs or the group known as Operation 40, the set up of guerrilla mercenary rebels in the 60's (Brigade #2506) to topple Fidel Castro's regime in Cuba. Bishop, who shadowed for David Phillips, was a remarkable taskmaster... Maurice Bishop. Maurice Bishop was also in partnership with an equally deadly accomplice, Frank Fiorini or "Sturgis," who was also the ultimate soldier and taskmaster, and expert marksman in the CIA's plans to route and carry out the demise and elimination of Fidel Castro. You can see them all together in photographs, both as prisoners during the failed Bay of Pigs, and also as the vengeance-inspired tramps who were on the field that mission in Dealey Plaza in Dallas.

See photos on pages 69, 152, and 157 of Frank Fiorini (aka Sturgis), with E. Howard Hunt on page 69 in Robert Groden's truly astounding book of photographs, *THE KILLING OF A PRESIDENT*. Viking Penguin; Penguin Books 1993, 1994. ISBN# 0-14-024003-9, The Blue Cover; Gold Lettering.

Then turn to photographs on pages 140, and 141, of Osvaldo Salas's photographic pictures and text in his wonderful work called, *FIDEL'S CUBA* and you can see Maurice Bishop in action on Cuban soil as he was a captured prisoner during the CIA's bungled Bay of Pigs operation. The most crucial aspect to understand with the assassination's plot and its success is how each piece has an underlying subtext, meaning what's behind one man is usually the work of two, when it comes to the CIA's participation in the conspiracy... to take out... John F. Kennedy.

In Robert J. Groden's remarkable work, *THE KILLING OF A PRESIDENT*, you can witness for yourself the photographic evidence and turn to page 69 and then to page 138... Here you see David Atlee Phillips (top) and the backup man or shadow figure, Bishop,...who appears in custody as one of the three tramps who fled from the grassy knoll. To complicate matters, both CIA men used the alias "Bishop." To examine further evidence, turn to the second "Bishop" behind that one shadow man: Frank Fiorini, aka Sturgis, page 152 and page 157. The two men, brothers in arms, united in the mutual project: Kill the president of the United States, John F. Kennedy, and kill the communist leader of Cuba, Fidel Castro. If you look at the scale model of Dealey Plaza, re-created for the film JFK, on pages 211 and 213 of the Robert Groden book *The Killing Of A President*, you can see how closely the cars were parked right up to the stockade fence. Also on page 213 you can see the original foliage of those trees re-created, that would provide ample coverage to operate for the Grassy Knoll Shooters Group: CIA agents E. Howard Hunt, Frank Fiorini, and Maurice Bishop; The CIA's A Team Hit Squad. If you want to see the actual photographic images of Dealey

Plaza on that clear afternoon in Dallas, November 22nd, 1963, turn to pages 50 and 51 of Robert Groden's book. The stockade fence is five feet in height on the freight yard side and from its next level (from the Pergola structure adjacent landscape in the corner on the other side), it extends, rising past six feet along Elm Street where the road starts a gradual descent to the triple railroad underpass en route to Stemmons freeway. It's the bottom two sharp contrast photographs on these pages that show the best coverage of the camouflage of trees and foliage, as the fence rises even higher at the point of the outside corner.

Anyone who stood here behind the fence, between vehicles parked on the dirt lot, who pointed a rifle over the fence back towards the Dal Tex building, would have a worthy stealth principle and dire vantage point from which to fire on the president's limousine.[12] Also, the photographs of these scale models on pages 211 and 213, show just how short the distance of escape (which was less than two minutes), either by car or by stowing away and then boarding a freight car. Turn to pages 56 and 57 of the Groden book. You can see that the people viewing the president's motorcade had now turned their attention towards the grassy knoll. It appears that there were at least a full 120 seconds before the witnesses watched Kennedy's limousine leave, and then ran up the knoll and climbed the Pergola structure, and then scanned the freight yard (judging by the photograph taken the day of the president's killing, page 150). There was a pocket of time of at least two to possibly three minutes.

Afterwards, the crowd of people who responded after the stunning shots eventually ran up to the grassy knoll. Several Dallas motorcycle police officers stopped and jumped off their bikes, hurriedly double timing it towards the slope of the grassy knoll. With the heightened danger of a shooting team in the area of the grassy knoll, when the crowd of onlookers pursued the assassins getting up to the top of the knoll they were met by Secret Service men flashing badges who delayed the crowd's view of the fleeing shooting team. The shooters ran across the freight yard (in under two minutes), and quickly hopped aboard one of the trains, which made an

---

12   On Pages 49, 50, and 51, THE KILLING OF THE PRESIDENT; in Robert Groden's Book; we see the crowd's movements just moments after the assassination. Robert MacNeil the legendary journalist who ran over to the railroad overpass which aligned with the picket fence that's just above the infamous grassy knoll. Robert Groden points out the man known as Jim Hicks, on page 51; he is carrying a radio transmitter device with an antenna. Jim Hicks confessed to being part of C-Cube, which coincides with the future testimony found inside Z R RIFLE. The C-Cube refers to a command and control team or A-Team. (The Bosch, Lansdale, Ferrie, Sturgis, Hunt, Hughes-Nixon connection.) Orlando Bosch, David Ferrie, Eladio Del Valle connects them (Bosch's partner in Cuba); Luis Posada Carriles, and Pedro Diaz Lanz, and Frank Sturgis, and Richard Cain which included Lenny Patrick and David Yaraz; and all these men were connected to Barker--Howard Hunt--Nixon, and Howard Hughes.

unauthorized departure from the yard. By the time newsman Robert MacNeil reached the railroad overpass, which took approximately three full minutes (after the shooting team had thrown the two rifles into the back of the car), which immediately drove off clearing-away and out of the freight yard, with the two weapons safely out of sight, inside the car's trunk. Another weapon was broken down, a man dressed in a railroad work man's gray uniform then put it inside a tool case. (The story itself has never been refuted by anyone).

The additional insurance shooter wore a Dallas policeman's uniform. See the closing statements, "A Grassy Knoll Witness," Ed Hoffman, in the book known as a JFK cold case bible; Jim Marrs' *CROSSFIRE*, pgs. 81 through 85.

In less than two minutes the shooting team cleared the tracks and made it through to the rail yard's empty freight cars, and successfully boarded one of the trains. By the time the people who stormed up the knoll got a clear view of the stockyard, the shooting team had vanished. The Secret Service men who had deterred and delayed the oncoming crowd long enough to allow the shooting team ample time to escape from this area "unimpeded."

Railroad dispatcher Lee Bowers was sitting in the railroad tower that overlooked the yard and the dirt parking lot on November 22nd, 1963. Lee Bowers reported that a flurry of activity near the stockade fence attracted his attention. Although he was unsure of what exactly he had witnessed, he went on to describe it as if he had seen some smoke near the corner of the stockade fence, or whether it was a quick flash, or flashing of lights, or perhaps he heard something, that had pulled his attention there. He later stated: "there was some unusual occurrence, a flash of light or smoke, or something… which caused me to feel like something out of the ordinary… had occurred there."

Lee Bowers also reported seeing a car with out-of-state plates and political bumper stickers driving into the parking lot just before the assassination. This car, it is the belief of this author given the gravity of the CIA's task of The Grassy Knoll Shooters Group, was driven by none other than top level CIA operative Robert Maheu. It was crucial and absolutely paramount that to kill the president, The Grassy Knoll Shooters Group took *no chances* with their field operation. Going forward they wouldn't risk using <u>anyone but their own CIA Agents</u>. This job came down from the CIA, from the top. It was clearly their payback time, getting even with JFK for The Bay of Pigs, and several… upper echelon or the top CIA guys… were all-in on it.

The car, at some time during the day, held the shooting team of E. Howard Hunt, Frank Fiorini, and Maurice Bishop. But when the president's motorcade left the luncheon at the Trade Mart, the shooting team (Hunt, Fiorini, and Bishop) were already on foot (covering the background-moving themselves, and moving witnesses), out of the dirt lot of the railroad yard. Robert Maheu, who was speaking into a radio micro-phone that was connected to background agents with ear pieces and headsets, continuously kept the shooting team advised of the president's location with the motorcade's slow progression—towards-- Dealey Plaza.

The car slowly drove around, circling the lot, and left, then the same car returned to again circle the lot before leaving a second time. The car came back for the third time, and it parked in the corner near the backdrop of the stockade fence. With the car in position, the three men of the shooting team walked over to the corner near the car and took up positions below the trees, between Robert Maheu's car, and the stockade fence. The team had rifles (already placed there), wrapped up and lying on the ground. Using the car and the fence as cover, Hunt and Maheu communicated exactly where the president's motorcade was in relation to the Book Depository, before it was to turn onto Elm Street. Robert Maheu, is formerly with the FBI, but inside this act of "high treason" he is a leading participating co-conspirator with the A TEAM; the CIA assassination squad.

Frank Fiorini and Maurice Bishop unwrapped their rifles before the motorcade turned off of Main Street, on to Houston Street, and keenly took an aim towards the president's limousine... just as it passed... the Texas School Book Depository. At approximately 12:30, President John Kennedy's limousine was shot at and hit with a barrage of bullets and an extreme hail of rapid rifle fire. It was after the flash of light or the smoke of the rifle shots, Bowers watched the same car leave the parking lot, but he also had noticed that when the car left, Maheu drove away alone, without any passengers. The shooting team's rifles, were inside the trunk, or under a blanket on the floor board in the back seat of the car (all of this depending on how quickly the shooting team fled... to board by hopping onto... a soon departing train).

Witness Ed Hoffman, at 200 yards distance, saw a man in a suit, tie and over coat run along the back side of the picket fence, carrying a rifle in his hands. And, as the man reached a metal pipe railing at the west end of the fence, he tossed the rifle over to another man wearing light coveralls and a railroad worker's hat. The man then ducked and knelt down behind a large railroad switch box and disassembled the rifle, placing it inside a brakeman's brown tool bag. The witness, Ed Hoffman, also watched as the worker continued walking north through the rail yard towards the railroad tower containing Lee Bowers. Bowers witnessed the unusual flashes of light, under the trees; also by the fence.[13]

The CIA assassinated and adroitly murdered the 35th president. In Dealey Plaza there were over 900 or, up towards a thousand witnesses, watching.

The gravity of the CIA operation required that the shooting team would separate themselves from their weapons just in case anyone did catch a brief glimpse of what really happened there. Naturally, if somebody tracked down three CIA men, dressed as hobos or bums, that might've been arrested (just as they were later), then the CIA could arrange to have the arrest records disappear for some 27 years. And, of course, for almost 50 years afterwards,

13   Source: Jim Marrs, CROSSFIRE, pages 81, 82, and 83; A Grassy Knoll Witness. The witness confirms the knoll mechanics were a hit team.

nobody would be the wiser. The team's work was superior that day. You may recall and remember how the Dallas Police Department was told to stand down. There were many other records of similar indications of such direct orders: The morning of the president's visit, Dallas County sheriff Bill Decker assembled his Deputies and clearly instructed all of his men to "Take no part whatsoever in the security of the presidential motorcade." It was also fairly clear that either with or without this order, this also meant that the A-TEAM CIA Mechanics / And Secret Service could go anywhere, driving, walking, entering, and exiting, whenever necessary. No police officer would stop the car that... was containing Robert Maheu–and any assassination shooting teams equipment and tactical gear, or weapons—carried inside it.

NO MATTER WHAT ANYONE WITNESSED IN BROAD DAYLIGHT.

In JFK—A Presidency Revealed—The History Channel,

Producer, David Taylor, Host, Frank Sesno; Circa 2003

It was Hugh Sidey and Ted Kennedy who discussed JFK's "back issues" at some depth. In one facet Teddy relates his mother asked Jack one evening, "you look a little pale...whats wrong dear?" JFK described the horrific pain in his back to his mother whom went immediately—upstairs and returned with what Teddy described it ominously—as "a plaster." Reportedly, she gave the device... to help Jack, by saying; "here dear... why don't you just... try this."

In foresight befitting a brother's love: you cannot say on television that your brother wore his mother's corset—back brace—so it became "a plaster." Albeit modified later on to what Hugh Sidey and Ben Bradlee described as a waistline to the chest line (or) a butt—line to the upper nipple—line, custom made torso fitting back brace. Later on, Jack told his mother that it's the best back fixer; that I have ever tried. In putting aside camelot vanity. Anything that distorted an image of JFKs vim, vigor, and vitality for a young president. These stories vary from each re-telling, depending upon whose relaying their messages, or telling the well worn out story over a period of time. The story I was told relayed here will be added to the Doctor Max Jacobson needle point injections... which always increased, whenever JFK traveled on lengthy trips. Finally, to put the coda on such history, sadly now, this bust to butt plaster or custom made "back brace" would prop him—uptight and upright—in that motorcade limosine... like sturdy bricks in a chess board... "rook piece" that would prevent him from ducking for cover. He rode like a statue into Dealey Plaza—sitting upright in SX—70, unable to bend; as the bullets began to fly.

In a series aired on the History Channel which featured coverage on covert operations ran by the CIA *"The CIA Declassified,"* in a segment concerning one of the many CIA plots to eliminate Fidel Castro... Walt Elder as a former director of covert operations recalls: "At one point we furnished the poisoned capsules to members (of not necessarily members of the Mafia), but to people who were associated with the Mafia." Walt Elder goes on to distinguish CIA plans for Fidel Castro by stating further that "and then the idea was to figure out how to get them from this country to Cuba, and then the major obstacle, once in Cuba…how to then introduce them…to their leader Fidel Castro."

For the assassin: the CIA chose *Marita Lorenz,* who at that time was the current girlfriend of Fidel Castro. In the series presentation, Marita Lorenz remembers that time in history, and vividly recounts it by going on later to carefully describe how the CIA had prepared her for the grim mission: "And they gave me several hours of intensive training, and also these capsules to poison him."

"They said that I was the only one who could do it because I was the closest."

Walt Elder follows up the Marita Lorenz account with a sweeping bold statement of confirmation: "We were in touch with anybody and everybody particularly who had the direct access to Fidel Castro. Why did she have access in the first place? Because she was Castro's loved one… this much we understood, and also the fact that she was so attractive that she could also in our objective, resume this… current currency relationship with Fidel Castro."

Marita Lorenz goes on to recount the rest of her story, by saying that: "I went back to Cuba traveling as a tourist with the camera, and I went to the Hotel Colina, and I had my honorary uniform and I changed clothing, and then I went over to the Hilton. I said hello to the people downstairs… at the desk and I went up to the room and I unlocked the door, and then… I waited for him."

When Fidel Castro finally walked into the room he said to me:

"Where have you been? Where were you? Why were you gone so long?"

"I told him that I was homesick, and that I just wanted to go back to New York and see my family, which was really a lie since I had been in the clutches of the CIA at the time all along, and that I was being trained the whole time."

Things settled down after he questioned her about her absence.

"I remember that he was lying on the bed fully clothed with a cigar in his mouth with his eyes closed, and he just came out with it and said these words to me---"

(Fidel Castro asked her straight out)

'So…did you come to kill me?'

"And, I was just stunned…. and I said…yes. Then he just kept still for a moment, still lying on the bed calmly, and with his eyes still shut and without flinching, and he says to me, 'nobody can kill me…'"

(Marita Lorenz concludes the rest of her vivid story with)

"And then he reached over to the edge where the lamp was and his gun belt hung over the bed's headboard, and he pulls out his 45 pistol… and then he handed it over to me, and I stood there; and I could see that it was rusty but I was dumbfounded, I felt that my body had just went numb…"

"And then I stood there in this kind of mid faux-pas ordeal and finally, after I re-gained myself enough to say… No… Fidel. And, I told him that I couldn't do it… And, I said that I'm not going to do it this way or anyway. I---couldn't take a life…" *The CIA Declassified—*Walt Elder.

Marita Lorenz had lived with Fidel Castro in Havana in 1959 when Frank Fiorini (also known as Sturgis or "Bishop") met her and recruited her for work as a socialite spy for the CIA. She was a cultured, seductive, radiant and beautiful woman with the right stuff that would, a la "TOPAZ", surpass any suspicions from Fidel Castro or his camp. Further connections were drawn from the probe of subsequent later testimony and statements gathered in the mid 70s during the House Assassinations Committee Investigation, as strange interconnections of the conspiracy began to surface. It was during the HACI's probe that the development of a story about Marita Lorenz, the former CIA operative, claimed she had traveled by car from Miami to Dallas with Lee Harvey Oswald, <u>Frank Sturgis,</u> and some Cuban exiles; <u>Orlando Bosch</u> and <u>Pedro Diaz Lanz.</u>

When Kennedy sent the FBI to raid and shut down all these mercenary camps Ponchartrain-11, New Orleans and also No Name Key, in the Florida Everglades as William King Harvey is sent to Rome and all of the Operation Mongoose has been moved into… other hands like Desmond Fitzgerald, and Richard Helms. Kennedy scrapped a second invasion and sent a message to the CIA that clearly… it was all over. "Swing the axe elsewhere" had started.

The tensions boiled over in the Cuban exiles, the brigade #2506, Tony Veciana's ALPHA 66, and Orlando Bosch's MIRR; The word went out and the teams were assembled… to carry out their plan: ZR Rifle to murder the 35th president—John F. Kennedy—in Dallas Texas. 11/22/63.

She added that they had taken rifles along with telescopes on the trip. She said Oswald visited a Cuban training camp in the Florida Everglades, and she also reported seeing Oswald at the pre-road trip meeting in the home of Orlando Bosch. The revelations didn't end there. This is Oswald's most severe depth: How or if he was aware of the rifles and scopes. It's not a fact that he knew all of it. The possibility exists Lee Oswald was probing: *To see how or when, and if it was really a palatable duty, that the CIA—could… uniquely manage… to pull it off somehow.*

When questioned further, Marita Lorenz described Operation 40 in textbook terms, as an "assassination squad" that was made up of the anti-Castro Cubans and their American supporters. She qualified the next statement about the group's activities and agenda, which included direct plans and the objective mission, which was to assassinate Fidel Castro, and President Kennedy. All of the members grouped inside Operation 40 solely blamed their commander in chief--John F. Kennedy--for the ultimate failure of all the plans of brigade force #2506: the failed Bay of Pigs operation.

When Lorenz made that story of the Dallas trip public, Frank Sturgis told reporters that as far as he could recollect, he had personally never met the man known as Lee Harvey Oswald. It was also in the mid-70s, shortly after news of the Dallas trip had appeared in the press coverage, Sturgis paid a visit to Lorenz (to threaten her livelihood), and was subsequently arrested and charged with trespassing. The arrest documented Sturgis's stalking her and kept him from any *direct actions* against Marita Lorenz. It's clear that these loose ends were being handled. Silence was commanded by dire consequences. If you defied it, your life was in danger.

———

After the first threats to Oswald's family Guy Bannister told his superiors, or the New Orleans underworld connection, mobster Carlos Marcello, who finally reported to his bosses Santos Trafficante and Meyer Lansky, that Oswald was getting "cold feet" a week before the coming event. This didn't sit well with either Santos Trafficante or Meyer Lansky (the Fox). It's clear that herein we can see that the mob was very uneasy about the event. (Clearly understandably--Richard Nagell had "spooked" Oswald.)

Meyer Lansky worried that the CIA/FBI patsy or fall guy wouldn't wash in the plan's scheme, especially if Oswald went "squirrel" and decided not to show up at work on that day, at the Schoolbook Depository. The mob bosses figured the weakest link was "going astray" and just might foul up the whole convoluted plot. John Roselli was taped by the FBI saying: "JFK is going to be hit." The voice he used was one that indicated to me (this author's p.o.v. hereafter) that this event was certainly not... a cleverly-Mafia-planned hit.

It sounds on tape like Roselli is stunned by the CIA's audacious plans.

(When the word of Lee Harvey Oswald's cold feet finally reached the top, things happened.)

You have to realize here that Oswald's actions at this point indicated that he had not been given full disclosure of the plan that William "King" Harvey, Allen Dulles, Robert Maheu, David Phillips, J. Edgar Hoover, E. Howard Hunt, Frank Sturgis, Maurice Bishop, Cord Meyer, and also David Morales had in place... because if they had done that with Lee Oswald then none of the strangest behavior in the history of an assassin... would have taken place:

I.E. The handwritten note to E. Howard Hunt, just 10 days prior to the event.

I.E. The threats to the FBI, and the Dallas Police, a few days prior to the event.

Without consulting David Phillips and his shadow man, Frank Fiorini aka "Maurice Bishop," the mob (through the FBI) ended up making similar coercion attempts to scare Lee Harvey Oswald. In effect Lee H. Oswald was being threatened twice. After Guy Bannister and Hugh Ward and David Ferry told their mob bosses their own problems with Oswald, again (conspicuously now), a second series of deportation threats, came down on Oswald's family. They came in an even more vicious manner than previously, and the message was deportation of Marina Oswald. To the Soviet-Russian-born wife and her mother (who preferred life in the United States), going back to Russia was like a KGB death threat. Inside, Lee Oswald was fuming and enraged with anger, but he was boxed in. In a move to first protect his wife and family and to further preserve their right... to remain... in the United States, Lee Harvey Oswald told E. Howard Hunt (this authors p.o.v.) that "he would be there."

An irritated, but finally–coerced and stuck in it just deeply enough Lee Oswald decided—he would sink or swim, but he knew he--would have to be very careful with his movements that day. The message went back over to the knoll shooters group that Lee Oswald would be inside the Texas School Book Depository. (After being warned by Richard Case Nagell he still showed up.)

It was just days before the assassination but Oswald's anger could not be contained long enough to leave his markedly evident wrath of anger that has turned out to be a severe leaking vapor trail in his own signature (calling out to the FBI), when he composed a threatening note to Dallas FBI headquarters and the Dallas Police Department. It was addressed to Special Agent James Hosty, Jr., who had both Oswald and Marina under a crucial and tightly scheduled surveillance. The is exactly what that FBI note read:

"Let this be a warning. I will blow up the FBI and the Dallas Police Department... if you don't stop bothering... my wife."

This is the point in the story that it gets weird... and strangely enough it's the point in the story that is most often lost, but we can see through the whole hoax... if we just look closely at the trail left behind–for all of us to see. The trail of breadcrumbs is tainted if we look at the facts. James Jesus Angleton is the CIA Counter Intelligence expert "responsible for doing shades of gray– all of this hoax... the shadowy past, and all of the sheep dipping-- creating Owald's paper trail... and agency inspired CIA movements." All of this work was perpetrating a false flag operation fall guy scenario under the hand of his handlers George de Mohrenschildt, David Atlee Phillips and James Angleton.

Richard Case Nagell told Oswald, "watch out Lee these guys are not your friends... you are being set up by the company." Oswald refused to believe Nagell's story, but his doubts began to show, when he then wrote the letter to E. Howard Hunt, and also a second threatening note to Dallas police. (However, he got the point across if indeed in person, in handwritten notes.)

It was only two hours after Jack Ruby killed Oswald that Dallas FBI head, then Gordon Shanklin, ordered agent Hosty to destroy the note. Hosty followed the bureau's instructions by flushing Oswald's horrendous and potentially very suspicious evidence straight down the toilet. Lee Harvey Oswald, in a tenacious bold move, had in fact hand delivered the note himself to the Dallas FBI headquarters only a few days before the JFK assassination. The assassination was already successful but those who brought about the conspiracy were not safe: The mobsters were leery enough with the Guy Bannister, Hugh Ward, David Ferry and Oswald problems and, along with Oswald, all of them were eliminated. For Guy Bannister, death was by shotgun less than two weeks... after the president was assassinated.

Hugh Ward died in a plane crash in Mexico arranged by the CIA. The plane's crash follows the web pattern of the Oliver Stone 1991 film—*JFK*; which clearly suggested that the CIA sought to tie up any remaining loose ends connected to Guy Bannister's office.

Jack Ruby was ordered to assassinate Lee Harvey Oswald. The Dallas Police Department and the whole world got to watch and witness it as Jack Ruby shot him while in transit at the Dallas police station, thereby forever keeping the whole thing permanently quiet. Over 77 armed cops were somehow oddly unable to protect Lee Harvey Oswald in the Dallas Police Department basement.

Another problem emerges at the behest of the office of JIM GARRISON.

(Fast forward to 3 years later as things got deadly and severely worse.)

The killings began to accelerate as the investigations of Jim Garrison's probe into the case that he had strung together against Clay Shaw began to unnerve members of the New Orleans underworld and its CIA connections up to and through ex-gun runner Clay Shaw. The CIA teams sent several hit men and *boldly planned accidents in motion* throughout the borders of *the plotters* who assisted in the assassination of President John F. Kennedy.

It was David Ferry who was the most important crucial key witness in Jim Garrison's case against former CIA gunrunner Clay Shaw. David Ferry, also a CIA contract agent, who also had worked for the New Orleans Mafia boss Carlos Marcello, was killed by a <u>forced massive overdose</u> of the drug known as Proloid. Shortly afterward his close friend Eladio Del Valle, was first beaten to death then shot in the heart in Miami, and then with the added Cuban quajiros' touch; He was decapitated, slashed in the head by a machete. Eladio Del Valle was a known anti-Castro exile and was also the CIA paymaster of David Ferry, who was killed by Cuban hit men. (The CIA intended to plug leaks at any cost, no matter who died. The message in the messy signature killing was extremely clear to all of the Cuban exiles. "If you do talk...you will guarantee that you will brutally die.")

Everyone is aware now that both Lee Harvey Oswald and Jack Ruby were acquaintances at his Carousel Nightclub. It is also clear Jack Ruby traveled to Cuba to meet with Meyer Lansky, known to Ruby as "Mr. Fox." Right before John Kennedy's trip to Dallas, two men who worked for Jack Ruby threw stripper Rose Cherami (who worked at the Carousel Nightclub), out of a speeding car and abandoned her by the side of the road. She claimed to know of the plan to kill President Kennedy, which was also depicted in the Oliver Stone film, "JFK." In one of her later statements, she also said that both men, Jack Ruby and Lee Oswald, were involved in a homosexual liaison. There are some quieter rumblings with regard to homosexuality between Jack Ruby and Lee Oswald, but it is less quiet when it comes to rumblings of both David Ferry and Clay Shaw throughout the annals of the New Orleans nightlife circles. This context prompted Jim Garrison's off-color politically incorrect and later-on damaging comment regarding the assassination as *a homosexual thrill killing.* As these skeletons in the closet emerged, Rose Cherami is killed for her talking about the word being out in the underworld' or plans to kill JFK, and her body is dumped on the roadside.

Regardless of the extent of the relationship from Jack Ruby to Lee Oswald and the other relationship with Lee Oswald to David Ferry and up to Clay Shaw:

It marks a distinctive trail right to the CIA. All of it shows further evidence suggesting Oswald was ensnared or *being framed a second time*, which suggests moreover the even greater links and lengths of a larger conspiracy.

The vague description given to the police for the manhunt going on for the president's killer as *"unknown white male, 30s and slender build"* left a lot of room for error, probably nobody inside a Dallas police squad car had any idea who they were supposed to detain, since that wide or broad description applied to countless thousands of private Dallas citizens.

Officer Tippit probably saw Jack Ruby before he ever saw Lee Harvey Oswald and he went to meet him at the agreed spot near the intersection past Tenth and Patton Avenue. But, when Tippet stopped the car, he was relaxed to see a familiar face (his friend from the club), then instantly Ruby turned and fired on Tippit. Jack Ruby and his accomplice then, as they fled the scene, commented about the set up and the hit saying; "the poor dumb cop." If Oswald was anywhere nearby or in sight of <u>anyone</u> after hearing the rifle shots four separate times (and perhaps witnessing the murder or the second frame-up attempt), he just fled the scene as quickly as possible, thinking that the CIA/Mob was out and working on their now' aftermath plan's to kill him.

Aquilla Clemons was an eyewitness to the killing of Dallas police officer J. D. Tippit. She reported seeing two men at the scene of the crime. She said the man who fired on Officer Tippit was heavyset with short hair. Two other witnesses, Domingo Benavides and Jack Tatum, were admonished with coercion to change their stories into stating that Tippit's killer did indeed look like Lee Harvey Oswald: The other witness, Helen Markam, said that Tippits' killer was short and stocky with bushy hair. This matches a filmed interview with Clemons where she said, "the killer was kind of a short guy… kind of heavy." More likely than not these details described it was Jack Ruby.

Oswald's weapon was found in his possession during the time of his arrest at the Texas Theatre. Officer Gerald Hill stated when he radioed in to the dispatcher from the murder scene, saying: "The shells at the scene indicate that the suspect is armed with an automatic .38 rather than a pistol." It is clear that the spent ammunition from the .38 automatic is not the same as from a .38 special. When Officer Hill knew this to be true, it's rumored he checked the weapon Oswald was carrying, and it was clear to that police officer that Oswald's gun hadn't been discharged, or fired at Officer Tippit. A gun that mis-fired is not going to smell like it discharged a live bullet. If I was in the position of an on duty officer holding JFK's alleged assassin, I am certain that I would've checked out that weapon too. (It appears Oswald was framed—twice, in one day.)

Tippit was hit four times, standing by his squad car; the final bullet by the heavyset assailant went into his head. There were two empty cartridges at the murder scene from an automatic weapon, which is more evidence suggesting Oswald never fired his weapon.

I am of the belief that the heavyset man at the scene of the Tippit murder was in fact Jack Ruby. Jack Ruby lived near the Oswald rooming house and Jack Ruby also knew Officer J. D. Tippit through the Carousel Nightclub. I believe it was set up by Jack Ruby to have J. D. Tippit nearby to the Oswald rooming house at 1026 North Beckley and that Jack Ruby had Officer Tippit come to the location the next day. My guess is Ruby told the officer to meet him the next afternoon at the location of Tenth and Patton Avenue at 1 PM. Since Ruby knew Tippit from the Carousel Nightclub, it would be possibly conceivable that he could have talked Tippit into meeting him there, the night before. He could have promised Tippit, who patrolled the neighborhood, that it was very important for him to meet at this spot tomorrow. Even if Oswald (who should not have left the Texas School Book Depository alive), was in custody or *perhaps dead by then*; Jack Ruby would use J.D. Tippit to search Oswald's house to collect any background evidence linking Oswald to Jack Ruby or David Ferry, or any loose ends or, peripheral evidence that Oswald left lying around the house that would suggest Oswald was only a very small part of a larger perhaps more puzzling picture.

Jack Ruby's business needs in the past were met on certain key arrests where Jack Ruby supplied Tippit with the goods on certain enemies that the Mafia-connected club owner sought to eliminate. Naturally, the connection is ever so much clearer with the relative ease in which Jack Ruby obtained his entrance into the basement of the Dallas Police Department. But just before a scheduled security "double check and search," Charles Batchelor, who was then the assistant chief of police, called off the second search. By that time, Officer Roy Vaughn had already let Jack Ruby in, and then Officer Napoleon Daniels saw Jack Ruby... come down the ramp... without a halt of any kind or any restrictions or any kind of contain, and detainment by Dallas Police.

The series of four separate taps on the horn was the audible signal provided to Jack Ruby of the moment when Oswald would finally be moving in transit, to "appear." Police Chief Curry was occupied by a lengthy telephone conversation with Mayor Earle Cabell, who kept the chief on the telephone until Jack Ruby had shot and wounded Lee Harvey Oswald. (Later on, the assistant Charles Batchelor was promoted to become the chief of police.)

Oswald was still alive when Ruby shot him, but two men, "unidentified agents" got into the back of the ambulance and gave the then "still among the living" Mr. Oswald an ill-timed, illogical, and illegitimate heart massage. Oswald, who was already in great pain, was now oddly "deliberately being bled to death by 'unidentified agents'." There were 77 armed policemen inside that basement there... assigned just to protect Lee Harvey Oswald.

Knowing that Lee Oswald's wound did not kill him, the two men who jumped in the ambulance with him pumped his body and, with their own hands, slowly—wrung the life—out of him. (On the television screen in tape black and white video it looks like Eugenio Martinez and Bernard Barker, the men assigned, handling the Texas School Book depository hit team. I viewed the tape *in slow motion several frames*, several times, this is what I can make out of what I could see. However, my angle site was such that it is not crystal clear… that it was these same agents… that handled the Book Depository.)

It was not a long ride to Parkland Hospital, but the two men who assisted with this oddly illegitimate deliberate treatment of heart massage, made sure that Oswald would expire after he had lost enough blood to smother—out whatever life he had left in his body. The ride was delayed just long enough for these "unidentified agents" to make sure *Lee Harvey Oswald was finally pronounced dead… shortly after his arrival over…* at Parkland Hospital.

I heard rumors and the story about classified information that Oswald in one gut shot wound… lost more of his own blood… than JFK who was—hit in the back, and the throat, and he had the top portion of his—head blown off. It's clear that Lee Oswald was not dead when he was put in the ambulance, but it would appear that his body was in my p.o.v. was "blood evacuated to an extreme degree." Enough so, that the amount he lost would make you want to question the two men who hopped into the ambulance, on the final ride to Parkland Hospital. And, my review on the BW tape several frames in slow motion… I see that the men who bled out Oswald, were none other than… the two infamous Nixon—henchman… Bernard Barker and Eugenio Martinez, whom were responsible for allowing—Lee Harvey Oswald to escape from—the Texas School Book Depository. (In my p.o.v.)

If this seems impossible. Watch the extras section in the JFK DVD 1991. In it Oral Ruby (Jack Ruby's Brother), has the auction to sell the pistol that was used to kill Lee Harvey Oswald; in it his brother dryly laments, "he just wanted to wing em' to see him suffer a little bit…he didn't try to kill him. You don't kill a guy by shooting him…in the stomach; he didn't think he'd—die ."

JFK—THE EXTRAS--DVD 1991 Warner Brothers--OLIVER STONE

FIFTEEN

Jack Ruby, The Busiest Man In Dealey Plaza

and at the Dallas Police Department, preparing to kill Lee Oswald...

Lee Oswald was not the only man with cold feet who attempted to get out of his job. Jack Ruby (with $20,000 dollars inside the trunk of his car), tried to get out of killing Lee Oswald while he was in attendance of the midnight press conference–

November 22ⁿᵈ, 1963

He was standing beside reporters as Police Chief Curry made a reference to Jack Ruby, referring to him as a member of the Free Cuba Committee, and then Jack Ruby responded in tone by shouting back and across the gallery of journalists the true correct name of the organization as the: "Fair Play For Cuba Committee."

It was after sensing the high stakes and gravity of his notoriously damaging personal fate over the huge assignment that he was enmeshed or entrusted with *by the mob*, and facing up to *the overwhelming consequences.* Jack Ruby came up *with a ploy—*to get out of his role.

After the midnight press conference that Saturday night, Jack Ruby called police headquarters and ominously, in an anonymous fashion, made a threat that was taken by Dallas police officer Billy Grammer. *Jack Ruby warned the officer* that if the police department *tried to move* Lee Harvey Oswald as planned the next morning:

"We will kill him..."

The warning call that was designed to prevent the Oswald-transfer... didn't work out.

(If Oswald was locked down, Ruby could've claimed that he wasn't able to make the hit.) Jack Ruby then could've returned the 20-thousand back to the mob, and possibly, perhaps *it's certainly probable he* could've pled duress of this police station-house on the lockdown, as his cause with the outfit.

Still trying to avoid the confrontation with Oswald, Jack Ruby showed up at the jail an hour past the prisoner's scheduled transfer time. But the authorities rather uniquely... changed their schedule (*and held up the transfer time*), to coincide with Jack Ruby's *moving into his position* in access and presence inside the garage, to make the hit on Lee Harvey Oswald.

Later on in custody Jack Ruby tried to reconcile what the event required in terms of drugs for him to muster the ample quantity of courage needed to get past the gravity of the whole event in his mind. He prevailed and did the job, the mob's deed, for twenty-grand.

JACK RUBY: *"I walked into a trap when I walked down there. I wasn't clean enough... I'd taken-like 30 antibiotic and Dexedrine pills, just to get it together, to get me down there and to take care of business."*

Numerous pictures are credited inside the material from *THE KILLING OF THE PRESIDENT* by Robert Groden. ([Viking Penguin 1993, 1994);]

THREE DIFFERENT GUNS ARE FOUND AT THE TEXAS SCHOOL BOOK DEPOSITORY.

Of the three weapons found at the Texas School Book Depository:

#1. The 6.5 Mannlicher-Carcano (sixth floor), "The infamous and supposedly declared official murder weapon."

#2. British Enfield .303 (found upon the roof).

#3. The 7.65 Mauser (also located or it was found up on the sixth floor).

The president of the United States of America was murdered November 22nd, 1963. It is rather strangely amazing that the leader of the free world died by rifle shot, and yet impossibly nobody knows how or why, that;

"Two out of three of the weapons found inside the building have mysteriously disappeared." As of this writing, both the Enfield .303 and the other 7.65 Mauser rifles have somehow vanished from the evidence. It is vastly apparent that some group...of the officers involved... had a great deal to hide. It dovetails to information compiled in, Jim Marrs' Crossfire; 1989.

Although it is Officer Gerald Hill who found the spent cartridges on the sixth floor, it was later on, however, reflected in records that the search has been attributed to Dallas Deputy Luke Mooney, who, according to the final police report, found the three rifle shells and a 6.5 Mannlicher-Carcano rifle on the sixth floor of the Texas School Book Depository. Dallas Deputy Sheriff Weitzman, who had an extensive knowledge of firearms, signed an affidavit that the gun found up there on the sixth floor was a 7.65 Mauser, a German-made gun. The reports were radically different and comparatively modified with inexorable discrepancy when the officers' stories didn't match.[14]

The discrepancies between the police officers' statements with regard to just what evidence was found, and the disappearance of two other pieces of evidence (the two rifles), have caused a palpable wave of skepticism to arise over the years, including whether the rifle that was found is the same one that was delivered to the Warren Commission as evidence, and is presently housed in the National Archives. If you want to gather a few more doubts, just go back to page 152 in Robert Groden's *THE KILLING OF A PRESIDENT*: There you can see which of the weapons that CIA Agent *Frank Fiorini* (aka Sturgis), actually prefers as his weapon of choice. The picture reflects the image that gives you an idea of what it must have been like for the three men, on the grassy knoll. In this case the three men on the grassy

---

[14]   Robert Groden's *THE KILLING OF A PRESIDENT*

knoll 11/22/1963 are all part of Operation 40 mercenaries, left on the beach during the failed Bay Of Pigs invasion on Cuban soil at Playa Giron.

In all of this, a tug of war was going on all around Lee Harvey Oswald for the possession of his soul. Here was a man being stretched and pulled and coerced and threatened in all directions. From Jack Ruby to David Ferry to bosses Guy Bannister and Hugh Ward to Clay Shaw. One month prior to the actual assassination, in FBI surveillance tapes on John Roselli it's clearly taped in conversations between the Mafia men, that: "Kennedy is going to be hit." His cavalier tone suggests (in this author's p.o.v.) that it not a Mafia hit.

FBI

Hugh Ward, Guy Bannister, James Hosty, Gordon Shanklin, J. Edgar Hoover, Eugenio Martinez, and Bernard Barker; and Lee Harvey Oswald.

CIA

Robert Maheu, David Phillips, E.H. Hunt, Maurice Bishop, Frank Sturgis, Clay Shaw, Rolando Masferrer, William "King" Harvey, and David Morales.

Mob

Jack Ruby, Carlos Marcello, Santos Trafficante, Meyer Lansky, Sam Giancana, Eugene Hale Brading, Lewis McWillie, and Johnny Roselli.

With this group it's a wonder that somehow Lee Harvey Oswald didn't "commit suicide" instead of actually going in to work on that fateful day.

And what makes it worse is he was <u>grossly underpaid</u> and couldn't be at all happy with the amount of money he was going to be making in all of this. Jack Ruby had close to $20,000 in the trunk of his car and on his person. David Ferry had more than that packed away through Carlos Marcello. Guy Bannister had a sizable bankbook and Clay Shaw's accounts were considerable to astronomical over the years as a CIA ex-gun runner of epic proportional measures, through the Louisiana corridor.

If you look at the bank accounts further of Carlos Marcello, Santos Trafficante and go up to Meyer Lansky, you would be amazed to learn they were some of the Mafia's richest business gainers of their era. If you look at Allen Dulles, William King Harvey, Robert Maheu, David Atlee Phillips, and over to Maurice Bishop, Frank Sturgis and E. Howard Hunt, you would find some of the same ilk of folks (who you could also include), like Bernard Barker, and Eugenio Martinez, into the scale of men who made a great deal of money throughout their tenures in the CIA or the FBI annals, both on the books and particularly their extra *off the books* capital gains. Orlando Bosch, Guy Bannister, Clay Shaw, and Pedro Diaz Lanz, Herminio Diaz Garcia profited greatly.

(The Miami Keyes Royalty—CIA business front—funded operations. Eugenio Martinez, alias "Musculito"/ Bernard Barker-- Keyes Royalty.)[15]

---

15   ZR RIFLE: The Plot to Kill Kennedy and Castro, Claudia Furiati; Talman Company USA Page #119 paperback. Ocean Press, 1994.

(Bosch, Shaw, Lanz, and Sturgis, and Bishop being: The Minutemen Militia, with the Brigade #2506, Pluto, Mongoose, and, Project-- Cuba.)

Lee Harvey Oswald was hired to fill orders at the Texas Book Depository at $1.25 an hour. If you gave me $216 in 1963 and told me to point a rifle out of the TSBD at John Kennedy's passing motorcade, I'd tell you for $54 a week that you're asking me to do an almighty major something for an incredulous nothing. I might even do what Lee Harvey Oswald did, which on that day... was nothing... of the sort.

I admittedly profess that I am no rocket scientist, nor do I hold a Ph.D. in anything. But I do possess some philosophical common sense and also a regular amount of just plain good old common sense when it comes to solving problems, even one as insurmountable as this one seems to be at times. After looking at all of it from... an angle of 360 degrees and in hindsight some odd fifty plus years later... I see it this way.

The old jack rabbit trip by David Ferry in some station wagon all night long through a pouring rainstorm just to go duck hunting doesn't fly with me at all. The ice skate and goose hunting expedition was supposedly for rest and relaxation, but it turns out he drove for 350 miles at night, going nonstop through the worst thunderstorm of the year, arriving in Houston at 4:00 AM in the morning on Saturday. Ironically, Jim Garrison was on the right track of uncovering the getaway pilot in the CIA's web.

It is the movement of CIA contact David Ferry after the assassination that tells me that it wasn't him sitting beside Carlos Marcello inside the courtroom that November afternoon. His big "hunting" trip was to pick up the three tramps at two separate airport pickup spots (which the bums couldn't make), in order to be flown to Mexico. It didn't happen. George Bowers halted the train and had the "CIA shooter, spotter, and watcher hit team" on the grassy knoll. This team, along with some help, fired the shots from the front that killed John Fitzgerald Kennedy on November 22nd, 1963.

There are, however, three things that bother me in trying to explain Lee Harvey Oswald and what he did just the night before the president was shot and killed in Dealey Plaza, and there is a prior event which I cannot refute which perplexes me more than I care to acknowledge. Here are three things that bother me and even perhaps suggest Oswald's guilt that I have trouble explaining away, without trepidation or concern. The three things don't change my mind, but they do provide a hot debate for the lone wolf gunman theorists. Even with these three things taken into consideration (and taking them for reality), I still arrive at my overall thesis, which is that several men were involved in the fabric of JFK's assassination. (This is counter-espionage, the trade at which David A. Phillips specialized; counter intelligence espionage work, with help from James J. Angleton.)

THING NUMBER ONE

The night before the assassination, Oswald went to bed first. Marina followed him without speaking to him, although she thought that as she lay quietly next to him, he had not yet fallen asleep and was awake.

In the morning, Oswald arose early and left the house before anyone else woke up, leaving his wedding ring in a cup on the dresser and also $170 in cash inside a wallet left in a drawer by the bed. Oswald left with no words... to his wife either the night before... or in the morning.

He never said a word and yet he removed his wedding ring and left practically (for all we know) all of the cash he had in a wallet inside a drawer next to the bed. He never said goodbye or anything remotely endearing to her as he left for work that day, supposedly to kill the president of the United States. It seems impossible in my mind to be wordless that night and next day, given the gravity of going off for the last time; on such a grim mission.

THING NUMBER TWO

The apparent attempt by Lee Oswald to kill General Edwin A. Walker:

The author refers to the context shooter, spotter, and watcher when focusing on the three tramps, who were arrested boarding the freight train that dispatcher George Bowers halted as it made an unauthorized departure from the yard. In other contexts, the five men tandem is three shooters, one spotter, one watcher. In the addition there were 2 five men teams, plus two extra men to make... the total number of at least 12 gun men, firing... on the motorcade. This being the opinion in the final conclusions of this author.

On April 10th, about one hour after an attempt was made on Major General Edwin A. Walker, an anti-communist activist in 1963, Marina Oswald found a note for Lee Oswald telling her what to do if he (Oswald), were either killed or arrested. Later on that evening, when Lee Oswald returned home, he told Marina Oswald the news: "I shot Walker." In this attempt it was General Walker who got lucky and moved at the very last second, Oswald's bullet very nearly had taken out the general. Marina Oswald's story was withheld since when questioned, she denied her knowledge about the Walker affair. It was only much later, after a few years passed, that she spoke of the incident. I cannot deny this story and although I have not fully researched it, I believe it could possibly be true. It is worthy of noting the character of Oswald, but even if it is true:

He missed the target. It still stands that Lee Oswald had never killed a man before. Graduating from this failed attempt to the grandest assassination coup in history (11/22/1963) is hard for me to swallow.

The best information ever written regarding Lee Harvey Oswald, which this author read after *The Beachcomber* was completed, is found in the complete volumes of *THE ASSASSINATION CHRONICLES*, Edward J. Epstein, Carroll Graf 1992. The scholarly opinion of David Montgomery.

If you turn to page 124 of the Groden book, you can see the photograph with the '57 Chevy in Walker's driveway with the license plate cut out. The car belongs to one of these Cuban exiles, Orlando Bosch or Pedro Diaz Lanz, which could possibly explain that there was a probable CIA mechanic afoot (involving the help of agency CIA-financed Bosch and Lanz, Cuban exiles), to further frame Oswald and entangle him, tying him into the intrigue that surrounded the supposed attempt that Oswald made (acting alone as it were), in an attempt on General Walker's life. More and more, the Walker attempt looks like an initiation process (set up by the CIA), to allow Oswald to gain access to the "field level operatives" by earning his wings. By taking part in this job, he was to then move up through the ranks and become more than just a paper pusher or flyer distributor for Clay Shaw and Guy Bannister and Hugh Ward's offices in New Orleans.

All along, Oswald sought the approval of his superiors to the point where he wanted to align himself or become more acclimated by doing tasks for the (CIA) agency that would bring him to the class of field operatives like David Ferry and Eladio del Valle, who were proven anti-Castro exiles. They were receiving premium pay per diems doing more highly classified duty working under the agency for Guy Bannister, Hugh Ward, and Clay Shaw, in the highly lucrative arms deals and black market gun running through the New Orleans underworld.

Even in peripheral circumstances concerning Oswald's suspected involvement with the General Walker affair, you can clearly see a pattern of the surreptitious side of the background agents' angle (where several men are involved in a duplicity factor). The fabric of conspiracy was being woven upon every thread of Oswald's subsequent moves, <u>to thereby gain entry earning his wings or passage of acceptance on up into the elite network, and this succession path higher into the circle of the CIA-brotherhood of top level Brigade #2506 Operation 40 agents</u> which included operatives like E. Howard Hunt, Frank Sturgis, and Maurice Bishop. All these agents' steps were directed by both David Atlee Phillips, and James Jesus Angleton.

It also extended further inside this elite club with more heavyweight players: Guy Bannister, Hugh Ward, Clay Shaw, and David Ferry, and also Eladio del Valle... along with two other Cuban exiles, Pedro Diaz Lanz and Orlando Bosch. Oswald's activities reflected a grand pattern of a man (on behalf of the CIA hoops put in a row for him to jump through), who would go through all the necessary steps in the evolution of tasks, doing whatever was required to be a part of the anti-Castro Cubans' elite group of this deadly Operation 40–The Hit Squad. The dangle object to Lee Oswald was to do all of the smaller jobs in front of him earning his stripes...so he could join up with the elite operatives found-- inside Rolando Masferrer's-- mercenary group...the same ones, (funded by Allen Dulles with "Dick" Nixon and Howard Hughes and Clay Shaw) who were training on Howard Hughes ranch. A militia men group of 53, Alpha 66, whom were known as the murder incorporated of the Carribean. (Benton, Rourke, Lauchli, and the Mclaneys.)

In the summer of 1963, Oswald goes to New Orleans and begins a local chapter of a pro-Castro communist movement called Fair Play for Cuba Committee. (He was the only member inside the group at that time.)

In August of that year, while passing out FPCC committee literature on Canal Street, Oswald is set up by the CIA with his first public arrest. Oswald and three anti-Castro Cubans, Dr. Carlos Bringuier, Celso Hernandez, and

Miguel Cruz, got into a disturbing-the-peace episode, which got all four men taken into the police station. Oswald asked to see an FBI agent and soon one arrived there to question him. After a brief summit call out to Guy Bannister, Oswald was released shortly afterward by FBI Agent John Quigley, creating a new history for Lee Harvey Oswald.

In late September that year, Marita Lorenz (the former CIA recruit hired by Frank Sturgis to observe Fidel Castro, report on his habits and personal life, and set up an assassination) confirmed she had traveled by car from Miami to Dallas with Lee Harvey Oswald and Cuban exiles, Orlando Bosch and Pedro Diaz Lanz. She indicated that the men had stowed equipment in tow, which included rifles and telescopes for this trip into Dallas. The men, who were part of Operation 40, a guerrilla-mercenary squad formed by the CIA, were also used in the Bay of Pigs invasion. Oswald's every move was to be telegraphed by the CIA, and every move was re-telegraphed again by former agents (observing him every step of the way), until he climbed so deep into the organization he could not see his way out.

THING NUMBER THREE

How do you get in too deep before you realize it, and why did Oswald (who perhaps realized his own fate) go to an out; or if he needed one, what was it that made him choose to go to the one where he knew he would probably be shot?

He got away from the several men who did fire on the president, and he also knew that the Depository secretary Carolyn Arnold had seen him on the second floor. My belief is that he knew that he never fired on the president's limousine at all, and also he felt it was clear that a witness had seen him no-where near the snipers' nest.

And for that matter, just why in the hell did he work for so little, getting paid next to nearly nothing for committing a background act (by showing up at work that day), in the greatest crime of the 20th century? Oswald was at least culpable and involved in the plot since it would be clearly possible he may have known about the upcoming event in Dallas on November 22nd, 1963. But although you can argue he was a complicit part of the cast of characters involved, he was not going to pull the trigger. He didn't have to, he was the background part that was about to be framed. All of the Book Depository employees that had gathered on the sixth floor to see President Kennedy's motorcade pass through Dealey Plaza were asked by Secret Service men flashing government badges to move down to the fifth floor, while boxes were stacked up to conceal the five agents on the floor.

The same scenario on the grassy knoll: 3 shooters, 1 spotter, and 1 watcher. The five-man team framed Lee Oswald by leaving the weapon after firing shots at the president's motorcade. Later, three FBI agents Bernard Barker, Eugenio Martinez, and watcher Eugene Hale Brading went back to their roles as peripheral agents at a crime scene (one agent was also a Mafia figure). They picked up the pieces that would ensure an appointed arrest of the supposedly "solitary lone gunman" which was the cementation of the fact that this particular lone gunman, Lee Harvey Oswald, had acted alone in the assassination of JFK. (The other shooters were Cuban hit men Pedro Diaz Lanz, Herminio Diaz Garcia.)

Oswald hid in the Book Depository from the five man team who went up to the sixth floor and took care of the job. Oswald was not the marksman to hit the target. He was not a specialist target shooter at all. He had never killed a man before. Worse for the conspirators, there is the stark impossibility of nine shots to come from one single bolt action rifle and make the hit in that amount of time, since the shots' cadence was recorded by officer McClain's Dictabelt motorcycle microphone, which was keyed "open" during the president's killing. The shots from the sixth floor made by these 5 men in tandem were in the same scenario-framework as the men on the grassy knoll; three shooters, a spotter, and a watcher. They left the incriminating evidence of the Mannlicher-Carcano. I offer the following common sense for history.

On page #55, Jim Marrs, inside "Crossfire" there is a chapter called The Triple Underpass. In it: Marrs reports that about a dozen men stood along the eastern edge to watch the presidential motorcade approach, and pass beneath them. On page 56, Jim Marrs reported; "Foster said that he ran from the underpass toward the Texas School Book Depository building, where he watched the rear exits until a sergeant came and told him to check out the railroad cars in the nearby switching yard. However, Foster said he went instead to the front of the Depository and told a supervisor where he was — when shots were fired, then he moved — to down the roadway there...down to see if I could find... where any of the shots hit." He was successful. Foster told the commission he "found where one of the shots hit the turf..." Foster said he found where a bullet had struck the earth near a manhole cover on the south side of Elm Street. Foster remained at this location for a time until the evidence was... taken away by an unidentified man. The spot where Foster found a tear in the grass was near where witness Jean Hill was standing, at the time of the assassination. Shortly after the shooting, she was questioned by Secret Service agents, one of whom... asked her if she saw a bullet land anywhere near her feet.

On Page #68, in THE KILLING OF A PRESIDENT — Robert Groden highlighted the picture of these two agents. Here we can see its Eugenio Martinez examining the divot in the turf, where the bullet was found as Bernard Barker (in his trademark glasses and a cigarette with the hat is looking at his partner;) the photograph is iconic — with the Texas School Book Depository — in the background behind them. **The bullet extracted from the turf — was collected and pocketed by — one of these two men, according to the deputy Buddy Walthers. The bullet was confiscated by either Eugenio Martinez or Bernard Barker. And, the crucial key bullet evidence was never logged in, and also, nor was it ever to be seen again.**

Herein we can reveal the lies we have been told contradict the real truth. We know for a fact today, that 3 bullets struck Governor John Conally; (and) that also 3 bullets struck President John F. Kennedy. And, further-more we do know that 1 bullet shot from the direction of the Grassy Knoll went through the front windshield. Also we know that 1 bullet struck at a bystander and it hit James Tague who stood just below the triple underpass. 1 bullet hit the car from behind, got lodged in the top chrome header frame. 1 bullet shot had missed to the left rear of the limousine and hit the pavement. 1 bullet shot had missed, hitting the grass, that was found by officer Foster.

As many as 11 shots were fired at the SS—100--X ...The JFK limousine. It is crystal clear to this author inside the exquisite Jim Marrs "Crossfire" as to why I think it's so appropriately titled. The crime of the century. It truly fits. *It definitely was a rapid crossfire of bullets.*

Keep in mind that Lee Harvey Oswald was a Texas School Book Depository employee, making about $12 a day in salary. A man with no car and such an entry level low-paying job that he couldn't afford a home for his family (he rented a room alone for himself, while his wife and children stayed close by with friends). Why would he take it upon himself, at that rate of pay, to partake in the Herculean task of assassinating the 35th president of the free world, John Kennedy? And at that particular time, as well as today, how would he, while he was still such a grossly underpaid under-funded assailant? Lee Harvey Oswald was hired at a rate of only $1.40 an hour in salary.

Years later, a Book Depository witness identified two of the men on the 6th floor that asked a group of employees assembled to move down to the lower floors as two of the notorious Watergate 7 burglars who worked for the U.S. Government, Bernard Barker and Eugenio Martinez.

Some witnesses on the ground believe there were at least a dozen shots fired upon Kennedy's limousine. Some witnesses said there were more shots; that they heard 14 shots ringing out that day, in Dealey Plaza; 11/22/1963.

I refer to agent Gene Braden as the Mafia figure contracted by the FBI, to aid the Depository 5 men tandem that were working up on the sixth floor.

One was the bespectacled FBI man whom he identified as Bernard Barker, and the other was the lighter-haired agent known as Eugenio Martinez. The witness refused comment afterwards, saying that he feared for his life. Ever since then, 11/22/63, he changed his story into what he felt they wanted him to say, referring or deferring to the agent's version of events that day: "Either you saw Oswald up there on the sixth floor...or you saw nobody."

You can see them together a lot picking up the pieces of debris that are clues to a unique conspiracy. Look at page 62 and page 68 of the Robert Groden book. You can see both men on the scene covering up key pieces of evidence, like a stray bullet or two fired from the grassy knoll. Keep in mind that Dallas police turned evidence over to these men for what was thought to be "safekeeping." If you look at the murder scene of Mary Meyer, you will see the same two men... Bernard Barker, and Eugenio Martinez... at the scene. (In this author's point of view, it looks like they're detoxifying the crime scene scenario at both places.)

During an examination of the curbing near Elm Street, Dallas Deputy Buddy Walthers found a stray bullet. He turned it over to the two inspecting agents, Bernard Barker and Eugenio Martinez, who immediately pocketed the collected evidence. The bullet disappeared and was never seen again.

With these two men on the ground any counter evidence could be extracted that involves the second shooting team. The intimidation factor of both these agents working on the witness up on the sixth floor and also policing the crime scene below on the streets would prevail for their duty of clean-up detail. (And later on, when it came to the sixth floor of the Texas School Book Depository.) Intimidated by the same men, the witnesses went along with the CIA/FBI agent's station house story:

"I saw nobody... up there." (At least until *Live By The Sword* was published.)

When the coast was clear to Lee Harvey Oswald's satisfaction, he came out of his hiding place on the second floor and proceeded to the lunch room table, calmly sitting there by himself, eating lunch with a Coke. Lee Oswald would make sure that Carolyn Arnold (the Texas School Book Depository secretary), saw him in the lunch room just minutes before the president's limousine started making its way down Elm Street. Oswald did not watch the procession of the motorcade, nor was he up there on the sixth floor when the president's motorcade passed the Depository.

It's clear that Lee Harvey Oswald was never supposed to make it out of the Texas School Book Depository building alive. The 5-man tandem who were there were supposed to contain him: Bernard Barker, and Eugenio Martinez, the other two shooters Lanz, and Garcia, who fled along with the "spotter" Gene Brading. The FBI watcher's also fled the building quickly, never finding or seeing their fall guy Oswald. It was twelve minutes before the entire facility of the Texas School Book Depository was finally sealed off for the investigation by the Dallas police. It was a very slow reaction and recovery time, but it also allowed plenty of time for the real assassins... to escape from the building and make their get away... successfully without fail.

If you read the 1998 *"Live by the Sword"* retelling of the assassination, which is in minute detail by Frontline reporter Gus Russo, you get the rare description of someone who witnessed (from his vantage point) Lee Harvey Oswald commit the actual shooting on the sixth floor. Naturally, this is only my viewpoint in my perception of what I read, but I do not know where the vantage point was.

The witness who couldn't identify Oswald after the day of the actual crime, somehow years later gained the courage to remarkably divulge it and finally report to a reporter what he had seen on that day in Dallas. I wouldn't be surprised if this guy had a CIA paymaster just like Jack Ruby and David Ferry turned out to later have. Both were heavily compensated on the back end for delivering the whole story with such roundabout and turnaround form, of latent candid ground-up truths, that somehow later on turned into gross conviction over all these years.

In no way do I condescend towards Gus Russo. I met the man at The Midnight Special bookstore (when it was on 3rd Street in Santa Monica), at a book signing. What I'm providing now to the quorum is simply a different view of that particular history. Mr. Gus Russo is a well respected reporter.

When the Depository was being searched, employees were excused for the day to go home. Most employees were already outside of the building and many went back inside. Oswald was viewed and seen by Officer Baker and Roy Truly on the second floor just minutes after the shooting, but he was not detained. Oswald left the Depository, but not by the closer rear exit. He walked out the front door and boarded a bus to go home. The traffic was heavy and he got off the bus and got into William Whaley's taxicab and headed towards 1026 North Beckley, but bypassed the house and exited the cab at Neely Street and walked back towards the rooming house. Earline Roberts was watching TV news reports of the assassination and she said to Oswald, "Isn't that terrible about what happened, they shot the president?" According to Roberts, Oswald barely replied, responding with a garbled or noncommittal sigh and grumbled tone. Knowing that he was about to die, if and when he was found, Oswald changed his shirt, and he also picked up his revolver and he left the house headed for a prearranged meeting. There were two places Oswald would go to be picked up and taken to the airport for a flight to Mexico. Obviously, his first ride didn't show and after hearing the shots fired at J.D. Tippit, Oswald went to the second pick-up location.

If there is one certainty to being an agent or even a lower level operative (as was the case with Lee Oswald), it is that you must always be under your handler's control. In Oswald's case those men, "the controllers," were Guy Bannister, Hugh Ward, Jack Ruby, and also David Ferry in contact or in direct communications, along with James Hosty and Clay Shaw and from Clay Shaw, the Oswald/Ferry/Ruby/Shaw connection extended to Carlos Marcello, Santos Trafficante and up to Meyer Lansky, "the Fox." With those heavy hitters in the mix, it was the job of Ruby/Ferry/Shaw to keep Lee Harvey Oswald on the hook and also, by any means necessary, calm and collected during the CIA's entire plan, which was going forward.

I believe Oswald had a pick-up arranged with David Ferry (who was a CIA contract pilot who worked with Oswald in the Civil Air Patrol), and I believe that the pick-up spot, was to be in the vicinity of the Tippit killing. Knowing that Oswald trusted David Ferry more than he trusted Jack Ruby, it was vital to Ruby that David Ferry be the pick-up man since that was who Oswald would entrust to fly him out of the country to Mexico. This scenario coincides with the conclusions of the investigation' led by Jim Garrison.

Although some people claim that David Ferry sat beside Carlos Marcello during his trial at the time of the assassination, and that David Ferry was also inside the New Orleans courtroom during the Tippit killing, it is the opinion of this author that this is not true. If there are witnesses who claim to have seen a man resembling David Ferry sitting beside Carlos Marcello until after 3 PM in that courtroom, I submit that the man was not David Ferry, and it could have in fact been someone who resembled him. I further submit that the man that was used was from New Orleans and also part of the social circuit of the French Quarter night life scene (and yes, he was also gay or homosexual, as was David Ferry), made up to impersonate David Ferry's presence inside the courtroom, providing a concrete alibi for his additional involvement in some peripheral background work involving the conspiracy to kill President John Fitzgerald Kennedy.

Some people have stated off the record that the CIA paymaster, Eladio del Valle, was at the site of the Ruby/Tippit/Ferry meeting, although it has yet to be fully proven. However, it is my belief-- David Ferry-- was going to fly Oswald out of the country that day. During the meeting with Oswald and David Ferry, who was with Jack Ruby, my guess is Ruby had Tippit at the same meeting and Ruby murdered Officer Tippit. (Both Oswald and Ferry fled the murder scene). In my opinion, it was someone who was with Jack Ruby and wore a similar colored white jacket to Oswald's. When <u>Ruby</u> opened fire, killing Tippit who got out of his squad car, that was when both David Ferry, and Lee Harvey Oswald, ran off and just fled from the scene.

I also believe that the back-up was at the shoe store just in case the first-out was blown (which it was, severely). Oswald had no choice but went to it anyway, but David Ferry was too scared to make the second connection to airlift Oswald out of the country to Mexico. The whole thing was an elaborate set up, and I believe a CIA look-alike was used to have the outrageously unbalanced customer, pre-appear a week prior and appear to be Lee Harvey Oswald. His "out" <u>blown</u>, since Ferry didn't show at the Hardy Shoe Store, Johnny Calvin Brewer had recognized him and Brewer followed Oswald over to the Texas Theatre. In *ZR RIFLE: The Plot to Kill Kennedy and Castro*, if you look at the the photograph of Oswald's arrest at the Texas Theatre, it appears as though David Atlee Phillips is there.[16] Oswald is arrested just as someone yells at him, "you've killed the president," as several more officers converge on Lee Oswald; he is arrested, and led away in handcuffs by Dallas police. Such is the work of espionage experts like David Atlee Phillips.

Since his second meeting pick-up was blown, Lee Oswald was arrested for the murder of J.D. Tippit, who was killed outside his police squad car by Jack Ruby. (This being the p.o.v. of this particular author upon my review.)

Those few who witnessed it, identified a heavy-set man who committed Officer Tippit's murder. All of this was to further frame Oswald for two rifle killings in one day. Oswald's revolver, recovered at the Texas Theatre in his possession, had never been fired. His hands, and no doubt also on his face, showed no signs of gunpowder (albeit by rifle or revolver), but during the rush to a rapid judgment "that this case was cinched," officers ignored police nitrate and the standard (GPR) gun powder residue testing.

---

16   Z R RIFLE, Claudia Furiati; OCEAN PRESS 1994. The photo caption reads: Lee Harvey Oswald's--Arrest At The Texas Theatre--November 22nd, 1963.

It is very possible that the prearranged meeting for Oswald was at the Hardy Shoe Store on Jefferson. Manager Johnny Calvin Brewer saw Oswald enter the store's doorway (searching for his contact person to bring him in to safety within the intelligence community). However, neither David Ferry or Eladio del Valle, or the FBI, or the CIA, was at the site location for his pick-up. So, Oswald decided to scramble for the nearest out and seeing the Texas Theatre, he snuck in without... paying for... his ticket. The people who were supposed to help him were now just the people who had "used him." Oswald therefore became the lame duck patsy or fall guy for the FBI. He was soon to become a dead mackerel as the one and the only lone suspect in the whole convoluted CIA plot. It was a little sloppy here, but the plan was salvaged.

It is worth repeating with this text since it is truly so very, very hard to believe. The manager of the Hardy Shoe Store, Johnny Calvin Brewer, had recognized the man because of a set-up incident a week earlier when one of Oswald's CIA hired look-alikes was sent into the Hardy Shoe Store to be a very memorable and a difficult customer. The incident branded Oswald, and Johnny Brewer remembered him. It was not at all a coincidence that the facts of a set-up or a markedly "unlikely previous incident" that was just clearly to me, "most unlike his demeanor." (Oswald was a very quiet loner and an unassuming kind of guy.) He would never ever pitch a fit of rage in a shoe store. He was clearly marked for a pick-up by being told (or foretold) to go back to that same location for a second time. This was the back-up plan of the CIA to bring in their man (the fall guy patsy), just in case Oswald got out of the Texas School Book Depository alive. He was due for a meeting and his subsequent arrest would occur at the site of the shoe store, or very close by, as law enforcement quickly was closing in on him, seeking out... their now... doubly and duly framed "Cop Killer" and "Presidential Killer." The handlers took great lengths... to seal the fate of their fall guy... with a mountain of incriminating evidence, linking Lee Harvey Oswald to these two murders.

If you need more information on Lee Harvey Oswald, read Edward J. Epstein's detailed account: *THE ASSASSINATION CHRONICLES*, Carroll Graf, 1992. A teaching colleague, David Montgomery; he endorses this book.

After absorbing all the material exposed after *The Beachcomber* was completed, I still believe what I have detailed in this chapter does not change, and it does not alter... these written briefs and conclusions herein... at all.

There is a remarkable aspect of the story concerning the mistress of Lee Harvey Oswald that I have chosen to not include in this material. In hearing and seeing the emotions and the pain in telling her story, I felt that it was also necessary on my part not to add any more attention to what she went through with Lee Harvey Oswald, during his final days.

The final telephone call they shared, which lasted about an hour and a half, indicated what I suspected all along. Lee made his return trip from Mexico (he was there to deliver a lethal cancer strain they developed here in the United States, funded by the CIA, to be used against Fidel Castro). It was the last trip he made to that country. The drop pick up was unsuccessful. At that point it seems to be clear that Lee Oswald knew that he was being used, and was being set up by the CIA, or the Company.

The fact that his pick up was poorly planned, whereby David Atlee Phillips, David Ferry, and Guy Bannister mishandled their operative (Lee Oswald) this late in the game, foretold of the nature of Lee Oswald's entire CIA-façade; that what they had created for him was a scam. After his return trip from Mexico, Lee Harvey Oswald it was now clear in his mind, he was expendable. The CIA disallowed his visa. He could've taken off on a plane and gone away to anywhere now. The Richard Case Nagell warning started to come into focus and Oswald may have felt the pressure. Nagell, could be right... he could be set up... to take the fall. So: He then wrote those 2 highly irregular notes to E. Howard Hunt+the Dallas Police, to aid in his... alibi? Surely, the notes would also attest moreso to his likely innocence. My own p.o.v. is that... the notes he left behind for us to see...were interlocking keys?

As the CIA blocked Oswald's ability to flee, it's clear the CIA mechanics tied up any loose ends. Lee Oswald couldn't turn squirrel and run, which was what Meyer Lansky worried might've happened. The conversation with his mistress indicates that a lot of what's written inside The Beachcomber or in the preceding pages, is a reasonable assessment, and routine basis for the arguments that could later on be made for a possibly probable explanation.

In another quadrant for the quorum will be the fact: that this same rare cancer strain was probably injected into Jack Ruby's body <u>to silence</u> any of his own possible future eventual testimonial about the whole CIA operation.

Late September 1963, hurricane Flora hit the southeast through Cuba... it was one of the deadliest storms causing over 7,000 deaths, in its path. It could've disrupted the drop pick up, travel + contacts Oswald--needed.
Jim Marrs reported that Oswald told Judith Baker inside Crossfire, 2013; "If I stay (not run) it could mean that it's one less bullet fired at Kennedy."

CROSSFIRE, Page 147, Paperback Basic Books, Perseus Books; N.Y.[2013]

Allen Dulles led the Warren Commission and as acting head of a newly appointed company investigating the "company" he <u>once headed</u>, he guided and routed the results impacting a total disconnection from his old company's involvement in the crime of the century. William King Harvey and Richard Bissell estimably lost the most, although it seems Maurice Bishop's career disappeared from the radar screen too. Robert Maheu and David Atlee Phillips and E. Howard Hunt stayed on top, but Frank Sturgis, Bernard Barker, and Eugenio Martinez were later arrested as members of Richard Nixon's team of the notorious "Watergate Seven." They're shown in pictures in the Groden book, see page 149 how these agents continued to influence politics during the Nixon administration, both men were heavily involved in assembling an assassination team to eliminate Fidel Castro.

It is interesting to note, also on page 149 of the Groden book, that Richard Nixon also served as the <u>CIA's White House-*Action Officer*</u> for the Bay Of Pigs invasion, run by CIA operative E. Howard Hunt. Afterwards in the Nixon tapes (dated June 23, 1972) that hastened *his departure* from the White House, the former president is <u>boxed</u> and quoted as saying:

"...this Hunt that will uncover a lot of things. You open that scab, there's a hell of a lot of things... This involves these Cubans, Hunt and a lot of hanky-panky..."

(Nixon is stating on tape, it is the belief of this author, that this might open the secrets buried within the Kennedy Assassination File.)

"...and it would be very bad to have this fellow Hunt ah, he knows too damned much, if he was involved... If it gets out that this is all involved, the Cuba thing, it would be a fiasco. It would make the CIA look bad, and it's likely to blow the whole Bay of Pigs thing which we know would be very unfortunate–both for the CIA, and for the country."

<u>You can understand why I feel that portions of this tape were erased.</u>

William King Harvey, the CIA's former Operation Mongoose leader and coordinator, whose drinking excesses had gotten progressively worse during his tenure in Sardinia, Italy (he was exiled to Europe a year before Kennedy's killing), was most prophetic when he summed it all up for the CIA like this: "This was bound to happen," blustered Harvey, "it's probably a good thing it did." Then upon discovering his deputy was helping out local officials with special gifts of several commemorative JFK condolences, he sent the deputy packing for the United States by saying; "I haven't got time for this kind of crap." Previously (Jan. 1963) the once impervious "King" William Harvey had confided (at his farewell party, in bitter tones as the whole Operation Mongoose and Task Force W; how it was dissolved under whiskey) to James Angleton, *accusing <u>the Kennedys</u>* of being responsible—for literally all his current misfortunes. Bobby Kennedy had jack-knifed his entire CIA career.

In reference to Chuck Giancana's book, *Double Cross* it confirms that the assassination was planned in the spring of 1963 in New Orleans, and that those responsible were: John Roselli representing the Mafia, General Charles Cabell, the former deputy chief of the CIA; Frank Sturgis, CIA agent, and Orlando Bosch, linked to Carlos Prio, Gerry Hemmings; and also other high officials of the Agency, especially those who headed the Agency's Special Operations. As it happens this was the key area of David Atlee Phillips, and E. Howard Hunt, Desmond Fitzgerald, and William King Harvey.[17]

THE GRASSY KNOLL SHOOTERS MECHANICS GROUP

The planner's trio: Allen Dulles, William King Harvey, and Richard Helms. Robert Maheu, believed to be the freight yard driver, talking via speaker radio microphone.[18] The shooting teams signals to Chief Field

---

17   *ZR RIFLE: The Plot to Kill Kennedy and Castro*, pg 142

18   *ZR Rifle: The Plot to Kill Kennedy* and Castro, pg. 128

Leader E. Howard Hunt. Shooters Diaz/Garcia/Mertz/Soutre/Sturgis/Bishop/ Morales/Hunt/Masferrer/Martinez/Barker/Cord Meyer/Ed Lansdale.

All these men were quietly praised and reassigned duty, and, Hunt then left the CIA, later to go to work for Richard Nixon. Frank Sturgis continued his intelligence career and stayed within politics and was one of the famous Watergate Seven, but Maurice Bishop was the more radical doer, whenever people spoke out or against him and his radical involvement in the Kennedy killing. He took his field operatives mechanics to work whenever he felt "uncovered" and numerous times "put the work in" to scare off and threaten anyone who implicated him directly to President Kennedy's murder. Evidence exists both Sturgis and Bishop protected themselves from leaks. Robert Maheu was a top aid to Howard Hughes in 1959, pursuant to investments in Cuba; and in Florida Keyes Royalty Miami. It is a resilient fact:

He met with Sam Giancana, and John Roselli, to set up the hit on Fidel Castro.[19] (I do not believe this team was led by Jack Ruby. The gravity of this required top CIA agents to pull it off, with many other members of the CIA in support roles.) I believe that it's Robert Maheu and Howard Hughes acting in concert to head the shooting teams Masferrer/Sturgis/Garcia/Morales/ Hemmings/Mertz/Sarti/Diaz with Hunt, Lansdale, Phillips, and Harvey.

THE TEXAS SCHOOL BOOK DEPOSITORY TASK FORCE

Bernard Barker and Eugenio Martinez, who were also involved in the Watergate scandal, accused of bugging the headquarters of the Democratic National Committee in June of 1971, continued with their careers and were promoted for their ground efforts in taking care of the background pieces that were cleaned up to implicate a single suspect, Lee Oswald, as the daring lone gunman and declassify and fully detox themselves from what Nixon called it all on tape: "hanky-panky" on the 6th floor in Dallas of the infamous Texas School Book Depository.

ZR RIFLE page 119:

> Rolando Eugenio Martinez, alias "Musculito," was the faithful operative of the naval bases of the Cuban exiles. After the huge Watergate scandal broke, Rolando Eugenio Martinez declared that he had conducted 300 clandestine missions... to infiltrate Cuba, before during and after both the CIA operations PLUTO and MONGOOSE. He became a millionaire in the 1970s, and was subsequently hired (allegedly in reward for his efforts in Dallas, 11/22/1963, and in Washington 1971) by—their leader:

> Richard Nixon-- as vice president of Keyes Royalty, of Miami, one of the enterprises with state support that featured figures from the Mafia... and the Batista government, in management positions. The senior CIA

---

[19]   ZR RIFLE: The Plot to Kill Kennedy and Castro, Claudia Furiati and CROSSFIRE, Jim Marrs.

official Richard Helms testified before the Watergate Commision that Martinez was a third-rate agent who was only occasionally paid something for his services, but in reality Martinez... was one of the... best paid CIA operatives inside project CUBA. The interconnection to these men arrested during the Watergate scandal which included Rolando Eugenio Martinez, Bernard Barker, Frank Sturgis, and Virgilio Gonzales (wearing surgical gloves and carrying with them instruments for telephone interception, wire-tapping, and burglary) were caught and taken to a Washington jail. The "operation" was directed by Whitehouse adviser and the veteran CIA agent E. Howard Hunt. Another Cuban, named Felix Rodriguez, was also... detained for his participation in Watergate, and Rafael Quintero, was another Cuban name that came up... along with... Manuel Artime, due to their close relations to Howard Hunt (who is the godfather of his children), Frank Sturgis and Rolando Eugenio Martinez. Faced with the path the Watergate investigation was taking at that time, exploiting the links between Howard Hunt, and the Watergate burglars, President Richard Nixon asked his chief of staff, H.R. Haldeman, to alert the top CIA officials (Richard Helms and also Vernon Walters), so that they could then take all the necessary precautions; because all these investigations could reopen the whole CIA picture regarding the Bay of Pigs question.

Rafael Quintero said publicly that if he were to reveal everything he knew about the Bay of Pigs in 1961, and Dallas in 1963, it would create a huge scandal.

Both the knoll shooters mechanics and the Depository task force group remain free to roam about the country. Gene Brading has had his name coming up a lot in the death of RFK. In 1974 Robert Maheu began to break his silence. Howard Hughes fired him, accusing him of being a thief. Robert Maheu stated in court that Howard Hughes did a delicate job for the CIA connected to a plot to kill Castro. In May 1975, when John Roselli was "retired" and living in Miami, he received a summons to appear before the Senate Intelligence Committee regarding these same alleged plots to eliminate Fidel Castro. According to Senator Frank Church, chairman of the committee, it was John Roselli who then supplied the Church commission with "a detailed account." Robert Maheu also testified revealing various aspects of the case. Sam Giancana was also on the list of those cited to appear, but on the night of June 24th, a few days before he was scheduled to testify before the Church senate committee, someone entered his Chicago home (it appeared that it was a man Sam Giancana had known), and shot him in the head with a 22 caliber gun equipped with a silencer. Later the gun that was used showed up on the banks of the Des Plaines River.

LEST WE FORGET–THE MAFIA GROUP

The Teamsters side of it, Sam Giancana to Meyer Lansky and Carlos Marcello and Santos Trafficante, John Roselli and Jack Ruby, Eugene Brading, and Jimmy Hoffa, all had vivid livelihoods which led to some cases of vivid endings. (Sam Giancana was murdered to keep it all quiet forever.)

Men such as these who would influence commerce and business and the politics of the White House were never targets of my research or interests when I started to write a book about Cuba. If you ask me, they were under their own hands with the scrutiny of *Live by the Sword*. To me the CIA led them... at every step all the way through... in the path to off John Kennedy. In my view of this reality, JFK was killed ultimately by his own government.

In examining the results of the whole effect of the Mafia's record in Cuba, I felt that as an economic stabilizing force they were very good for business, solidifying a type of hedonist nirvana and giving Cuba a rambling guilt-edged bonding to history unlike any other the world has ever known. And yes, it's true that I will forever miss that other dance of millions. It was beginning in 1939 under the careful stewardship of Meyer Lansky, who struck the then unprecedented deal through Fulgencio Batista, and I believe that Meyer was right when he told Lucky Luciano, "This is the best thing that ever happened to us." Even in the movies, as it was depicted in *The Godfather II*... "we're bigger than U.S. steel"...

The family of Amelio Batisitti was running his base at the Hotel Sevilla, a second family, that of Santos Trafficante, Jr., was operating the Sans Souci casino nightclub and the casinos in the Capri, Comodoro, Deauville, and Sevilla-Biltmore Hotels. And overseeing them all was Meyer Lansky, who ran the Montmarte Club, and the International Club of the Hotel Nacional up until he built his opus, the Hotel Riviera and Golf Leaf Casino, opening on December 10th, 1958. After 10 years, 1956 to 1966, time ran out on the mob and the CIA and Allen Dulles.

Robert Maheu, Richard Bissell, William King Harvey, and Ed Lansdale Cord Meyer, and Desmond Fitzgerald, had seen it all go wrong for the CIA, "that the CIA policy makers plans would collapse under Kennedy's orders."

Project AMLASH under Cubela failed to get to Castro since granma in Mexico 56.

The list of the CIA's failures to kill Castro became a reason AMLASH, OP-40, and Alpha-66, Hunt, Phillips, Sturgis, Bishop, William King Harvey, Robert Maheu, Ruby, Gen. Charles Cabell, Guy Bannister, Clay Shaw, and Orlando Bosch, Anthony Veciana, Pedro Diaz Lanz, and also Herminio Diaz Garcia, Garry Hemmings, Rolando Masferrer, and also Cord Meyer, David S. Morales, Bernard Barker, and Eugenio Martinez sought to end their misery.

The CIA plans against Castro, and the Mafia's plans, had not gotten the job done.

The common thread that King Harvey tells to James Angleton is blaming all the CIA's failures in Cuban policy directly on the shoulders of the damn Kennedy brothers. The Bobby and Jack—JFK/RFK factors.

In each scenario the CIA found "a common stopping gap" towards the Kennedy brothers' intermeddling in the CIA's efforts and ended up blaming it all on JFK.

The Bay Of Pigs, 1961, the Missile Crisis, 1962, the second Cuba invasion that is scrapped along with the closing "pulling the plug" of all the mercenary camps. Kennedy told them all to go or to swing your axe elsewhere.

With the opening of the Hotel Riviera, December 10th, 1958: Meyer Lansky went all in, and just like that in a span of twenty one days, "he crapped out."

Then came the ending and the eventually inevitable Castro-led collapse three weeks afterwards, it was all over just like that, from 1939 to 1959, some twenty years of the secondhand "dance of millions" concluded when Castro took over Cuba. I'd have been a customer at Meyer's place and indulged in its riches until I crapped out. And I'd have come back home a rebel in my memories if I were alive at the time. Call me a Mafia-friendly writer, since I, and a few others who know of me could have guaranteed my commission. Call a spade a spade. I was born International Club worthy participancy material and Hotel Nacional or Hotel Riviera rough and ready... So, I can't say as I blame them too much, since it was all truly legal in Cuba. They just wanted to get back into their old businesses in Cuba.

BOBBY WOULD BE BACK ONE DAY TO RUN IN 1968

And what about Bobby, who would have to wait his turn at the oval office? Bobby Kennedy underlined a passage in one of the books in his collection which some writers feel illustrates both the drive and free will of their father Joe Kennedy's influence combining with the great cost or "great price" for what the results of the Kennedy's vision truly was at the end of all their vast sweeping great ambitions. It is in the words of the Greek poet Aeschylus and the stark underlined passage, which could perhaps represent the conclusion he came to over the meaning of his brother's death.

"All arrogance will reap a harvest rich in tears." "God calls men to a heavy reckoning for their own over-weening pride."

There is a lesson for Joe Kennedy in this lecture and wisdom for young men (and all of us young people), in this yet undaunted ambitious young country. Bobby Kennedy, towards the end of his life, pondered that great cost with his own words when he mused that: "I have often wondered at times if we did not pay a very great price for being more energetic than wise about a lot of things, and especially Cuba." Truer words to that effect have never been spoken.

THE CONCLUSION IS SIMPLE

The CIA was the leader, the outfit, the unit, and the Government Agency which collaborated with the Mafia by using some of their mechanics in a plot or co-conspiratorial ploy with several levels of factions and some key players (within the ranks of both said organizations but mostly their own in house CIA agents), that brought about the execution and resulting assassination-murder of the 35th president of the United States, John Fitzgerald Kennedy, in Dallas, November 22, 1963. Albeit a rogue faction of the CIA, the complicity of the web being woven was a highly detailed operation that extended through a series of team tandem thread links, all the way to the top of the CIA leadership. Dulles/Helms/Harvey/Lansdale/Fitzgerald/ and Nixon.

THE TRAGEDY VERSUS REALITY

Here was a twenty-four year-old immigrant father of two who was a lower level ex-Marine and intelligence officer who had never killed a man or had expressed any ill will or harbored any verifiable vilification against President Kennedy or his family. In one day, he was to then decide to plot, plan, and execute a diabolical scheme to kill the leader of the free world (all alone, by himself), not being a marksman of great capacity himself but "to do so" and then kill a president and kill a police officer, all in a day's work and then walk back into a shoe store where he had a blow-up only a week prior (in an effort to evade capture) and then leave rapidly and run inside a nearby crowded movie theatre without paying for a ticket and hide out there from a Dallas police department's manhunt. Extraordinary... is quite the understatement.

There is a theme of Agatha Christie's that comes to mind from *Murder on the Orient Express*. It reads, "They all did it," and the CIA and the Mafia and the FBI (standing on the sidelines), watching it take place and doing nothing to stop it. It was someone in the screenwriting trade in William Goldman's fine book *Adventures In The Screen Trade*, who once referred to the political account of *All The President's Men*, regarding the Woodward/ Bernstein book as sort of like a comic opera. I'm not sure if the same phrase would apply here either.

WHY WHAT WE'RE LEFT WITH, IS WHAT WE ARE LEFT WITH...

DAVID AND GOLIATH

Lee Harvey Oswald was no David, and JFK was a real (at that time) Goliath. It took more than one man to slay that JFK-Goliath, in my opinion.

In the 1960s, we were a young country. The CIA had some pretty unique factions and their influence and activities were *far reaching*, and tantamount toward United States security and foreign policy's sentinel force. And at the time a few members were angry. In the 1960s, we were a young country.

The mob has some pretty unique factions and their influences and activity were *far reaching*, tantamount toward commerce and business throughout the United States as a sentinel force. Back then, at the time, a few members were angry.

There might have been one time in history:

The last of the Mohicans struck an unprecedented arrangement to continue to do business in the United States.

Who else could pull off a story like the *lone wolf nut* and the energizer bunny of *a magic bullet* that could liquidate a president?

It will never happen again in history—

It is true that most of the wiser souls admit (as I do) IT NEVER HAPPENED AT ALL. SOME WILL SAY THIS BOOK, *THE BEACHCOMBER*, IS REALLY FICTION, AND THIS ELASTIC THEORY WORKS OUT... BUT THIS VERY OLD AND TIRED STORY JUST REFUSES TO GO AWAY.

A masterful, divine, clandestine intervention and we're left with a divisionary slice of history that will remain always and forever and again, a clever mysterious mystery. God only knows: Central Intelligence Agency S.O.P. when it comes to secrets, "that bullet hit the target" and you must understand that ["we were never here;"] And, we the people must never hear otherwise.

And yet... Don't we as a people have a right to know?

For over fifty years since, the answer has been no, we do not have the right. The writers that pushed the wheel the opposite way. Most of them have been ignored, in some way. Nevertheless, the wheel has to be spun the other way around... at some point. At least in some small way I looked at the best sources I could find that made sense in their arguments and theories. And alas this cannot be the final attempt to mine this subject. I heard one writer who said, " the statute of this event 11/22/1963, never runs out on murder." So in that sense... if we all fail to get to the truth... it will be eternal (sort of).

SIXTEEN

Circle Talker

There are peripheral politics and roundabout discourses pointing towards LBJ. I don't find any great significance in the discourse, circle talking is more at ease here. I'm just going through the motions for the thought of it since others have thought it too, although in the end I'd say it isn't so.

The power source that arranged President Kennedy's murder was on the inside.

> When those rifles crackled over Dealey Plaza in Dallas Texas November 22nd, 1963…[they] made [their] move into the big time. [They] took control of the president, and the presidency. The man they killed was no longer a problem, and they made certain that his successor heard and remembered the sound of those guns. The Colonel [Colonel Fletcher Prouty, liaison between the CIA and the Pentagon] states the reality that more than one gun was used.[20]

PERIPHERAL POLITICS… POINTING TO LBJ

There were significant events that somehow led Lyndon Johnson to not seek the nomination of his party for re-election in 1968. Dictabelt tape recordings he made of his phone calls to Jackie Kennedy expressed his desires to appoint her as Ambassador to Mexico, noting the Kennedy charm and charisma (which he sorely lacked). He stated "she would have them at her feet, if I could get her to work for me in Mexico."

The Kennedy charm also became his arch rival in his victory speech during 1964 election year when he proclaimed the then-widest popular margin in history by any party and yet privately he murmured his own feelings of limited longevity as president, stating that he felt during the victory in 1964 that both the Kennedys, Bobby and Teddy, cast a long shadow over his leadership's longevity since he could feel the shifting tides in the American voting public, leaning towards that strong Kennedy charisma and charm that was standing nearby waiting in the wings. Lyndon said, "This was my day," and yet he felt the Kennedy legacy was still shining more brightly than his own Texan-bred temporary presidential tin star badge.

Lyndon Johnson felt the palpable Kennedy legacy was doing more than just waiting in the wings. He could sense who would be next, and at the widest margin of victory from his own party, he knew he wouldn't be getting elected again in four years.

The edginess of Johnson's feelings regarding what he may have known regarding the CIA's involvement with Kennedy's murder never left his

---

[20]   Page 5 *The Killing of the President*, Robert Groden.

211

thoughts. He felt that the compelling politics of continuing to escalate the war effort on behalf of the military industrial complex were continually being met with a fiercely intense growing unrest within the political backgrounds of the younger generation who protested the Vietnam war effort abroad. Several destabilizing events would occur throughout both politics and history as a growing dissatisfaction with government and the wave of the hippie peace movement conflicted with the LBJ conservative and almost dinosaur-like limitations. He felt his lack of connection with what was truly happening with the pulse of the real America and this younger generation.

They shot and killed John F. Kennedy on November 22, 1963, next in line was to be Malcolm X, March 22nd, 1965. Then April 4th, 1968, Dr. Martin Luther King, Jr. was assassinated at the Lorraine Motel in Memphis, Tennessee. On June 4th, 1968, Senator Robert F. Kennedy was fatally shot in the back of the head, at a Los Angeles hotel, shortly after winning the California primary. From that moment on, *the wind was knocked out of this country* and very distinctively something went out of this country that would never be recovered. America would wake up in the morning, look at herself in the mirror and fail to recognize herself.

August 29th, 1968. Outside the National Democratic Convention in Chicago, more than 100 anti-war demonstrators (including elderly persons, children, and reporters) are punched, beaten, gassed and maced by Mayor Richard Daley's riot police.

Much has been said in recent years regarding Lyndon Johnson's relationship with Jacqueline Kennedy. The White House tapes as chronicled in the Michael Beschloss book tends to share that vivid portrait of a wily politician who was driven and cornered (as smart as he was, he was in a box he couldn't get out of). It is clear as early as February 1965. As he ordered Operation Rolling Thunder, he stated, "Now we're off to bombing these people." "We're over that hurdle," and then he adds prophetically, "I don't think anything is going to be as bad as losing..." (as he trails off with) "... and, I don't see any way of winning."

The nation's youth movement and political activists, "peace protesters" and the "love and peace...make love not war" hippies, started protesting at the nation's capital and on university campuses beginning April 1965. LBJ tells himself that the anti-war rallies are all communist inspired: "The kids are running up and down parading, and most of them are led by communist groups," and he later adds comments on the weakening effect it brings toward government policy with "They make the North Vietnamese and the Chinese believe that we are about ready to pull out."

Moving back into rumbling rumors about LBJ and Jackie Kennedy...

How their relationship appeared in text form is really not for us to say, since such gentlemanly and parental/fatherly and even flirtatiousness from an older married man could be framed (in a truly light dear-hearted endearment type of sense) to mean something like, "Yeah, Jackie, you are very pretty, and if you ever need a shoulder to cry on, LBJ, the good ole southern man, will be that steady shoulder for you to lean on." And further, as far as we know, that's perhaps all that needs to be said about that.

In answering a question regarding any truth to Lyndon Johnson's possible involvement or prior advance knowledge with regard to JFK's assassination: That is for history's sake, perhaps a good question and a valid one as far as both "good" and "valid" questions go. I personally cannot completely beyond the shadow of a doubt prove at this time, either on paper or in a court of law, that Lyndon Johnson is guilty by association or dubious deployment of conspiratorial actions connected to either direct orders or political ambitions through others that make him a co-conspirator to inherit the job of the presidency of the United States.

There are a few things that I can say raise questions of some partial impropriety on Lyndon Johnson's behalf that spell LBJ's unwittingly unique if not somewhat dubious and conspicuous behavior. That which I distinguish as both dubious and/or clandestine-wise conspicuous is what follows here.

Parkland Hospital–Sunday, November 24th, 1963

THE WHITE HOUSE TELEPHONE CALLS

Dr. Charles Crenshaw writes in his book, *CONSPIRACY OF SILENCE*, that he was on duty at Parkland Hospital when Lee Harvey Oswald was brought there, and he assisted with his treatment. "While standing in the trauma room I noticed a large man in a scrub suit with a gun visible in his pocket. I did not doubt that he was some sort of government agent, and I handed him a sterile mask. At one point a nurse tapped me on the shoulder and asked me to take an urgent telephone call. In an adjoining office, I talked with the president, Lyndon Johnson, who told me that we should try to get a confession from Oswald and that a person was present at the hospital for the purpose of taking that confession."

This story has been challenged (and it is unusual that the FBI would want to) on numerous fronts: particularly by J.A.M.A. and others. James Fetzer's *ASSASSINATION SCIENCE* (page 41 and 42) states:

"It did happen and there is ample proof."

"It should be noted that I have never claimed that President Johnson called personally for me. I was simply tapped on the shoulder by a nurse to take the call. But the call did occur."

Dr. Philip E. Williams, a Dallas neurosurgeon, told *The New York Times*: "I vividly remember someone said…the White House is calling and President Johnson wants to know what the status of Oswald is. I heard the statement in the operating room, and it was not Dr. Crenshaw's book, or anyone else who revived my thoughts about this... because I have said this... for years."

Ms. Phyllis Bartlett was the chief telephone operator at Parkland Hospital that day. She definitely remembers taking the call from a man who identified himself as President Johnson, then transferring the call to the operating room.

"It was Ms. Bartlett who disconnected the line while I was talking to Johnson. She was attempting to transfer the president to the public relations office. Ms. Bartlett wrote to The Dallas Morning News on 15 July 1991: 'There very definitely was a phone call from a man with a loud voice, who identified himself as Lyndon Johnson, and he was connected to the operating room telephone during Lee Harvey Oswald's surgery.'"

The presence of federal agents in the operating room is also well documented. Alex Rosen of the FBI was ordered by Director Hoover to get a man to Parkland to get a statement from the accused assassin. Rosen stated that he had contacted Forrest Sorrels of the Dallas Secret Service office. "Sorrel's says an agent is already there." The time is 12:18 in Dallas. *The Dallas Times Herald* of Sunday, 22 December 1963, carried a story that an agent wearing hospital clothing and a face-mask had waited in vain for a confession from Oswald. In response to this, Dallas SAIC Gordon Shanklin sent an AIRTEL to Hoover which stated in part: "SA Charles T. Brown and SA Wallace R. Heitman made arrangements...to be available... in the event Oswald regained consciousness. In order to save time and be immediately available, these agents did don operating clothing and took positions outside the operating room." But the agents did enter the room. Dr. Paul Peters, who was present and attending Oswald, said: "There were Secret Service men intermingled with the operating room personnel...some were dressed in green clothes, same as the surgeons...two or three shouted in his ear, 'Did you do it? Did you do it?'"

In the fine clinical analysis in a book called *ASSASSINATION SCIENCE*, James Fetzer PHD writes very explicitly about 4 out of 5 doctors who all agreed that both the throat wound and the head wound, were entry wounds.

Doctor Charles Crenshaw, MD; defending his own book, *Conspiracy Of Silence*, a factotum recorded by James Fetzer, published by CATFEET PRESS, 1998.(A reference to that book, in his own book, follows in this segment below.)

Pages 38, 39, 40, 41, 42, 43, 44 in paperback. "Assassination Science."

In the 20-20 story which ABC did on my book: The network reported on an examination of the Johnson log for the time period while Oswald was being attended. Quoting historian William Manchester, ABC reported that Johnson had just told Bobby Kennedy, "We've got to get involved, we've got to do something," or words to that effect.

(Gordon Shanklin, the FBI man, is the same man who ordered agent Hosty into flushing Lee Harvey Oswald's suspicious note straight down the toilet. Oswald wrote them a handwritten note to back off, "Let this be a warning...I will blow----up the FBI...and the Dallas Police Department, if you don't stop bothering my wife. ")

This is repetitive but necessary to illustrate the complicity of LBJ:

Lyndon Johnson's actions (his orders that limousine SX-100 was to be shipped to Detroit to be stripped and totally refurbished) altered any discovery of bullet pathways (through marks on the windshield), or blood traces that would lead to essential clues to *the actual number of shots* and directions of the bullets. Also, Johnson further increased his liability by sending his aide Cliff Carter to remove Governor Connally's clothing (from the office of Congressman Henry Gonzales). Connally's clothing was cleaned and pressed by the time it was handed over to the Warren Commission, and hence was useless as evidence to JFK's assassination. This unique act by LBJ is extraordinarily unusual tidiness.

In a book by William Manchester—THE DEATH OF A PRESIDENT. It refers to JFK—as Lancer, and Jackie is known as—Lace; also in this book as the JFK—limousine is referred to as SS 100 X, (page #160;) Harper and Row. There is the reference material ISBN#0-14-0240030-9, THE KILLING OF A PRESIDENT—Robert Groden's photographic guide to the JFK assassination which has the listing name of the Lancer (JFK Limousine) as SX—70 as well. Each area cited herein, both refer to the very same car that John Fitzgerald Kennedy was killed in 11/22/63.

Doctor Evalea Glanges: who was on duty at Parkland saw a clean bullet hole from the front to the back through the windshield of this car. This author saw pictures to reflect that fact. Later on under LBJ's orders the same car was shipped to a Rouge Factory Plant...under the supervision of George Whitaker who supervised the car...which was stripped and totally rebuilt. Multiple men (including secret service agents employed in the president's protection staff,) identified a bullet hole as coming from the front to the rear through the front windshield. George Whitaker had 30 years experience working with glass; the story he told of these events was recorded by Douglas Weldon, who reported the mind blowing story on the impressive BBC documentary *The Men Who Killed Kennedy*. Nigel Turner, HISTORY CHANNEL.

This evidence sustains the fact multiple firing points shot at this vehicle.

LBJ was in a position... to know that the evidence... had to be destroyed.

Hence he gave the orders to: "Have that car washed and dismantled."

Johnson's other action that caused some additional suspicion to his prior knowledge of the JFK killing was his publication of Executive Order 11652, which locked an immense amount of assassination evidence and documents inside the National Archives, away from the American public's view until the year 2039. It was these and other moves by the vice president, which caused so much speculation in later years about a possible role by Lyndon Johnson in the death of JFK. See the final words of the exhaustive 625 pages found in Jim Marrs' *CROSSFIRE*. Likely, in my point of view the finest assassination chronicle we have, along with ZR Rifle; (And) In A Closing Tomb. The Plot That Killed Kennedy. It ends with William Shakespeare "Et tu, Lyndon."

SEVENTEEN

Kennedy Press Conference

1963

At the time of one of President Kennedy's final press conferences, the count of men in-country on the ground in Vietnam was 5,000 soldiers. Kennedy clearly had intended to decrease the deployment and pull the plug as was indicated by NSA Memorandum #55, and NSA Memorandum #263, when he initiated the withdrawal of a thousand soldiers on October 11th, 1963. After JFK was eliminated by the CIA, the military industrial complex was given a carte blanche activity buildup and escalation through LBJ's tenure as commander-in-chief. The war intensified over the next five years into a catastrophic quagmire in 1968. It was as early as July of 1965 that LBJ privately told Secretary of Defense Robert McNamara, "I'm very depressed about it"...and he would finally add, "I don't believe the North Vietnamese are ever going to quit."

At the height of this escalation of war, the next secretary of defense, Melvin Laird, stated that there were 550,000 men in the country on the ground in Vietnam, with over one million two hundred thousand in Asia deployed–Navy and Air Force–in support of this military operation. It was clearly a massive military operation and political campaign, which ended in a catastrophic failure; and it was only made possible because of LBJ's *inheritance* of the White House.

Around 2 PM at Parkland Hospital, a battle emerged between Dr. Earl Rose and Secret Service agents, under Lyndon Johnson's orders that the body of President Kennedy was immediately to be put on Air Force 1 and transported quickly over to Washington. Texas law was broken under Johnson's demands (the law clearly required Dr. Earl Rose, Dallas County Medical Examiner, to perform an autopsy before anything else was to have taken place). Those who recall the ugly exchange were bullied by Secret Service agents who threatened Dr. Earl Rose with, "You'd better get out of the way if you don't want to be run over." The president's body (which was still warm), then was taken over to Air Force 1.

Prior to this ordeal that afternoon in Dallas with Parkland doctors outside Trauma Room 1, and the over-running of Dr. Earl Rose, "defeating his duty" to perform the autopsy required and mandated by Texas law, another over-riding procedure occurred at the entrance to Parkland Hospital with the president's limousine. Under orders from Lyndon Johnson, the Secret Service began to "wash it out" and destroyed valuable evidence from the scene of the crime. If that wasn't enough, then Johnson ordered to have it completely dismantled; the car was removed, stripped, washed out, and then totally rebuilt. I'm not being unsentimental here or even the least bit sensationalistic when I share all of this rather calculated bloodthirsty ripping of standardized rules of law and order in the United States of America, but with all due respect to the raw nerve of the vice president…"JFK's body wasn't even cold yet, it was still warm meat 98.6 degrees," and this man, LBJ, was running a route's worthy gambit of moves on the playing field.

This is repetitive detail that I've listed a second time because it's both vivid and valuable.

Even though Lyndon Johnson was in a hurry to leave Dallas and a casket was taken to Air Force 1, there is a skepticism surrounding whether or not the president's body was offloaded at the orders from Lyndon Johnson. The body was then taken to an undisclosed location for a government-based autopsy, which included photographs and analysis that skewed some of the facts surrounding the criminal aspects of his assassination. One thing all the criminal forensic pathologists agree on beyond a shadow of a doubt, is that the facts concerning Kennedy's assassination were altered drastically to suit the lone assassin theory. And everyone surrounding the situation knew false information was being put out with regard to the president's wounds, but sadly there truly was nothing they could do about it.

Then came the smooth transition of power. Johnson, perhaps feeling his old rabbit's foot and his Texas born and bred pride "born with boots strapped on," and his eyes wide open on Texas soil, decided to delay takeoff just long enough to be sworn in as the new president at 2:38 PM with Jacqueline Kennedy and Mrs. Johnson standing at his side, 2 hours after JFK's murder.

And after being sworn in (Kennedy's widow, friends and staff, both press and Secret Service, were very much subdued with sorrow), most were still in shock over the day's events in Dallas, but as predicted in the bottom right photo, page 71 of the Groden book, Lyndon Johnson turns to look at Texas democratic Representative Albert Thomas, who winks at the smiling LBJ over a smooth transition of power. LBJ was practically going to be kicked off the vice presidential ticket at some time (it was discussed in great detail over the prior sixty days), and perhaps was to be used just long enough to have JFK re-elected. But now he was riveted, bolted, and completely locked in to be the leader of the free world. The world was stunned. LBJ inherited the U.S. presidency.

Speculation about LBJ, the wily and rude roughneck yahoo politician that he was, is only an easy targeting of an easy target for speculation. It's like picking on the most cunning politically bankrolled talented player in the political player's play arena. LBJ—the man with the most skeletons in the closet—in the entire Kennedy Cabinet combined. I wish I could make it that simple, but I cannot since he was already a Kennedy running mate as the vice president (used for his levy weight), and as a powerful connection to many conservatives. I believe LBJ would have been retained for the second term once Kennedy was re-elected. I feel about 95 to 100 percent certain that Kennedy would have been re-elected, and further LBJ could have maintained his position and waited his turn like other incumbent vice presidents in the past have done. It's yet to be proven (or guaranteed likely) if the existing Bobby Baker/Billy Solesties scandal was strong enough that it could have forced him to resign. However, in the event I am wrong, something would have had to have snapped in LBJ's mind to put him on the list of JFK's enemies. For me that would require some very powerful convincing, and people who have looked at Texas big oil lobbyists would be assuming a great risk to think that circumventing or the plan of elimination of Kennedy would allow the war to be continued through LBJ, since it was clear Kennedy intended to end the war effort. In order for this to have possibly occurred, you would have to give a very big reason for me to believe that it was possible. Hindsight says that it is possible. It was only later that the eight count indictment was later released... we could argue that the charges inside it likely would force LBJ to resign and be possibly convicted... at that trial in connection with at least two murders. The most damaging being the murder of Mr. Henry Marshall. In the counts...I saw that a few, (or some charges in it could be pled down) to manslaughter. I felt that Ed Clark could reduce it. Because I felt Ed Clark and LBJ were just that damn slippery. But jail... was imminent.

The best material that covers the LBJ scandal is Part 9.) THE GUILTY MEN—The Men Who Killed Kennedy, Nigel Turner. In this presentation, Ed Tatro, Walt Brown, and Bar McClelland deliver all of the goods on the story.

One thing is certain, once he was sworn in, the LBJ-Bobby Baker issue died. Some of the 8 counts could be pled down, but LBJ was facing jail time.

Kennedy had made too many enemies in his first 1,000 days in office with the CIA, the FBI, and the military industrial complex and anti-Castro Cubans, along with some RFK-McClelland Committee grist, and the major wrestling show put on by the president's brother, Bobby, who was rattling the mob. Basically, there was enough of a bounty on JFK without adding those big Texas oilmen. The LBJ pendulum of guilt has swung forever yay or nay.

(Nixon stated: JFK would drop LBJ in a close race. It obviously had an effect when he leaked that ugly story to the *Dallas Times Herald* papers .)

So, why then does the nagging question of LBJ's involvement persist? It could only be asked because would Texas oilmen have financed such a madcap scheme? So, then you have to ask why? So, then you would have to make up a scenario which involves them being the *financial aid pact,* worthy of a possible conspiracy to eliminate JFK.

America is a business, and Texas oil is a big part of business, and Texas oil can elect a president. So, then the question becomes, can the same business, Texas oil, perhaps do the opposite?

Ever see the Oliver Stone film, *Nixon*? Can you remember the ironically remarkable scene in the movie where director Oliver Stone had Nixon played by the great Sir Anthony Hopkins? You might like Oliver's casting choice for one of the famous four Texas oilmen, who bent knuckles in verbiage towards Nixon. Who was it you ask? None other than Larry Hagman, who had gained considerable fame as a Texas oilman on the popular TV show, *Dallas*.

Now, if you still believe Texas oilmen can try to exert pressure on the president of the United States, take a good look at that scene again. Nixon threatened J.R., in my view, during the scene which Oliver Stone directed years ago. It was the Larry Hagman character playing big Texas oil, who was threatened by Nixon with a tax audit, among other superlatives. This did not sit very well with the big Texas oilmen. So, if you believe that Texas oilmen can both put a president into office and also be responsible for the reverse of that trend, then you would have to be saying that: The Watergate scandal was helped by somebody connected to Texas oil. Think about this for just a moment if you would, just for kicks.

John Erhlichman quite candidly stated that throughout White House policy during the Nixon administration, a "crisis management system" was always employed during a crisis. In the case of Watergate, the crisis management system was not deployed (meaning it was never utilized or that if it was, somebody *neutralized it,* to the point that... it wasn't deployable). That would mean somebody got to somebody somehow to make sure crisis management in the White House was subverted and that... left somebody naked. In the fine unrivaled great book I read by Jesse Ventura, *AMERICAN CONSPIRACIES*; [2010,] the author includes exquisite references to this illicit connection in striking detail. I've read it about a dozen times, the details fascinated me. Chapter #7, Watergate Revisited, pages 77 through 87. In order to appreciate the details in this book add that chapter—in it's compound fractures—to this chapter. It's all quite revelatory indeed.

Texas oil or the X-men would become what "Deep Throat" was. Then this X-man who would be someone who would uncover somebody or just enough dirt that would bring about the tangible reasons for the eventual downfall of then president Richard Nixon. Bear in mind and please believe what I tell you when I tell you that I don't believe in what I'm saying...when I say to you what I'm truly saying... that it really might have happened.

IT DID NOT HAPPEN THAT WAY.

This would mean that in my lifetime it happened twice in the last fifty years. Call me an idiot if you like, but for whatever my weird ridiculous reasons are (for the life of me I don't know just exactly what they all are), it is my opinion that it is not true and that Texas oilmen did not help the cause to "neutralize JFK and Nixon". Maybe I'm naïve or just maybe Texas oilmen only allow me to think what I'm supposed to be thinking. I think they are innocent men (in the JFK cold case), and I want to add, I know they like me thinking what I am thinking.

So, then my bottom line comes into play and I suppose I understand that I'm far too naïve to understand the big bad world. What I know about Texas oilmen wouldn't even stretch across the bottom of a small teacup (the old William Goldman line on directors), so there in a nutshell is my opinion.

What we're left with is the reality versus the tragedy of Watergate and Kennedy's assassination. I failed to link Texas oil to both crimes' inceptions and conceptions, and nobody else will either. There are people who are much smarter than I am trying to figure out that. If I attend any future conferences over in Dallas, Texas, some very large hat wearing Texan would point to me and say, " he's naïve isn't he." And, likely they would be correct in saying so.

Not only am I *mob friendly*... I'm also a *Texas oil friendly writer.*

So, you have to realize for yourself where the truth is. Follow the money. Kennedy would have pulled the plug on Vietnam with 5,000 men in country. He began the first withdrawal of 1,000 men on October 11, 1963. Literally one month and eleven days later he was killed.

He was assassinated only <u>forty-one days afterwards.</u>

Five years later, under LBJ's tenure as the new commander-in-chief, the Vietnam Campaign had escalated to 550,000 men in-country on the ground, and 1,200,000 in Asia in full tactical readiness. Air Force and Navy deployed in support of this massive military operation. Texas oil and Texas oilmen had to have had a big wedge of this huge delicious economic boondoggle of a wartime pie. It's noblesse oblige that all the flying fighter jets and bombers, all that fire power and the firecracker 550,000 men of armed combat war forces, that were in-country, in Vietnam, required an inexhaustible and extraordinary amount of fuel and oil to run such a devastating and fiercely brutal war machine. Enter the X-man: "Texas oil as fuel for fire power." So, it's what you are left with and you have to ask yourself all those uniquely ardent questions.

I came up empty with my own little exploration into the details on Vietnam. I never found the X-men in the equation, so if it was Texas oil which gave it to Nixon or the same Texas oil, which gave it to Kennedy...

I never saw the X-men. In both cases the X-men got away with it.

The future is up to the rest of us.

We have to wait and see for now (open our eyes wider), perhaps look at our own unique history, but look a little harder at that history and we will have to:

<u>WAIT AND SEE.</u> This seems to be the pattern over the last 40 years. As this book remained unpublished for 10 years, it's been 50 years.

Jim Garrison's closing statements made at the trial of Clay Shaw were fairly accurate and prophetic. He stated that "in recent years...forces have developed in our government over which there is no control and these forces have an authoritarian approach to justice."

———

Johnson was very depressed with the situation in Vietnam. His mood swings with his depression caused some of his aides to seek psychiatric advice to better their efforts to deal with his imbalances. Only five days after Johnson signed the Voting Rights Act, on Sunday, August 15, 1965; some

5,000 rioters broke windows, looted stores and burned buildings. Four people were killed and more than a hundred people were injured during the breakout of the Watts Riots. Two things converged with history, and in trying to build a "Great Society" Johnson knew that the country was going to tear itself apart. Not only had he lost control of the pulse of the people, he realized that he could no longer maintain control over himself, in his depression, nor would he ever be able to continue to control and lead this country. It was clear it was over for him. His time and history's time had passed him, very quickly. Johnson read the writing on the wall and wanted to get out of the hot seat and with great haste after witnessing all that he cared to witness going on throughout the political backgrounds of the United States. He then declined the job to run again for re-election during this wave of social unrest in the <u>historically... hot political climate... by bowing out in 1968.</u>

Anyone reading this material could lay blame on the Writer for drawing such a wide view of the Vietnam conundrum in this profound belief of the importance of this connection to Kennedy's death. However the facts are: The war raged on throughout the Nixon administration until the fall of Saigon. The cost of this lost cause, *known as* Vietnam, was 58,000 American soldiers' lives, matched against 3.4 million Vietnamese people who died in those years during the American war machine's campaign from 1965 through 1975. The raw figures were I think also conservatively estimated by Fletcher Prouty's book *JFK: The CIA, Vietnam and the Plot to Assassinate John F. Kennedy. (Also,) R.J. Rummel's, "VIETNAM DEMOCIDE"; April 10th, 2014.*

It proved to be a very costly decade of up into the vicinity of 550 billion dollars. The Bell helicopter deal netted LBJ 30 to 40 million dollars. LBJ's wealth was estimated to have grown by 350 million dollars in profits from the Vietnam war.

It is within the context of these facts, and also the fact that the crime of the century took place in Dallas, Texas, that questions surrounding LBJ's cronies continually persist. It was the closing Shakespearian phrase in one of the finest works about the case from Jim Marrs' *Crossfire:* Et tu, Lyndon.

My thoughts are differently conjoined than these men as I have said before. (Afterwards in the Kellog, Brown, and Root saga KBR became the newly named Halliburton.)

-The Iraq War skyrocketed and ballooned historically astronomically—leaps and bounds to infinity—way over Vietnam's cost of 550 BILLION DOLLARS—in April of 2008. It has grown to 5 TRILLION DOLLARS over in Afghanistan. It has risen, or overgrown, to 8 TRILLION DOLLARS in the Iraq War's cost today. [These 2008 figures at the apex when Bush left.]

-550 Billion—Vietnam's cost of that lost cause, we lost somehow during 1965 through 1975.

-13 TRILLION in the Afghan—Iraq cost of war throughout that duration 2003 through 2013.

When it's the same company that benefits from the president's administration's policies, you can clearly understand the reason why John Fitzgerald Kennedy was assassinated.

In the DVD extended version of *JFK The Director's Cut* 1991 Warner Brothers:

Tip O'Neill recalls his final conversation with JFK (quote), "I'll never forget it, what he said to me was 'after the elections over…we're going to get the boys out of there… get them out of Vietnam by Christmas 1965.' O'Neill went on to lament, "that there would not have been… that terrible loss of life over there that followed… had he [JFK] lived."

The extras section on the DVD *JFK The Director's Cut* validates Fletcher Prouty's general analysis.

HAROLD WEISBERG AND CYRIL WECHT WHO MODERATE THE VIDEO PRESENTATION OF:

"THE SINGLE BULLET THEORY" – Reasonable Doubt

During the press conference at the time of the announcement of President Kennedy's death, Parkland Hospital doctor Malcolm Perry, in his response to questions, stated specifically that, "the wound in the front of the president's neck was a wound of entrance." And each time he spoke, his superior, Dr. Kemp Clark, also nodded and verbally confirmed what he said to be completely true and correct. Dr. Perry: "It appeared to be coming at him."

Both Harold Weisberg and Dr. Cyril Wecht stated unequivocally, "that the president of the United States got an autopsy that would not have been acceptable for a Bowery bum and the doctors who performed the autopsy were administrative personnel not fully qualified to perform the type of complete forensic and thorough medical autopsy that was required in a murder case involving the president and leader of the Free World."

On the other hand, critically speaking, "Lee Harvey Oswald got an autopsy that would have been acceptable of a president," and further, Harold Weisberg stated, "There are not any questions about Oswald's autopsy, but there are nothing but questions about the president's autopsy." Mr. Weisberg stated this fact with an amazing urgency as a matter of disturbing public record.

"Reasonable Doubt"

C B S FILMS, Inc.

Baltimore, Maryland

Chip Selby; 1988.

EIGHTEEN

In Paraphrasing Mr. Weisberg

In any investigation of this kind concerning a homicide, one of the most important records is the death certificate. What the certificate of death says, which was clearly signed by the president's physician, George Gregory Burkley, R.A.D.M. with no ifs, ands, or buts, was:

<u>"the president was shot at the level of the third thoracic vertebra."</u>

The key bullet location coincides with Robert J. Groden's photographs of the president's clothes. Photographs taken of Kennedy's jacket and shirt confirmed the fact that the bullet had entered six inches lower than what the Warren Commission had claimed in its 888-page report. (There was a cover up.)

Harold Weisberg confirmed that you can't possibly make a mistake like that without "lying," and the Warren Commission's findings "<u>lied</u>" about the position of the president's wounds. With regard to the position of the back wound, "there is no way that they could have made a mistake like that."

It was a deliberate miscalculation by the Warren Commission, moving the bullet location up several inches to coincide with the conclusion of Oswald doing the shooting from the sixth floor window. The sketches made during the night of the autopsy showed the bullet hole almost six inches below the top of the shoulder and yet the bullet emerged from Kennedy's Adam's apple.

The autopsy was written by Doctor James J. Humes who worked late at night in its recreation room and unhurriedly wrote his draft record of the autopsy. However, once he witnessed that Lee Harvey Oswald was assassinated (viewing it on television news), shot and killed by Jack Ruby, he understood the fact that there was never going to be a trial for Lee Harvey Oswald. James J. Humes subsequently destroyed his original draft and rewrote the autopsy. Why he did this when the patient is already dead defies logic to me?

The autopsy revisions began as soon as Jack Ruby shot and killed Lee Harvey Oswald, November 24th, 1963. Report #A53-272. Doctor James J. Humes reported that he had then (destroyed his original documents and) officially transmitted all other papers related to this report on to higher authority. In no uncertain terms, this meant that the government (or in this particular instance more accurately the Agency–the CIA) was that specific so-called uniquely qualified "higher authority."

The pristine specimen, or the bullet exhibit #399 is the biggest chicanery ever perpetuated by any government agency in history, in effect pulling the wool over our eyes. It was supposed to have struck a rib, and also struck a wrist (or a radius), which is a major bone and, to somehow miraculously not be deformed, and to have remained in near-perfect pristine condition. This same bullet that struck both Kennedy and Connally left many fragments inside that were visible through the X-rays taken of their bodies. This clearly proved that Exhibit #399 could not have been the actual bullet that struck both men simply because its weight was "too near capacity" and it lost only 1 to 1 ½ percent of its weight. The bullet that was found weighed 158 point six grains. Its entire weight is no more than 161 grains, and with 25 to 40 grains spread between Kennedy's and Connally's bodies as shown on the X-rays clearly this proves Exhibit #399 (aka the Magic Bullet), was nothing more than a chicanery of falsely acquired material, or clearly faked evidence.

Simply stated for all the citizens of this great United States to forever understand:

Cyril Wecht elaborates and states A RESILIENT AND TRUE FACT.

"Bullet Number #399 could never do in the history of gunfire what this bullet is said to have done." (Also add to that) ... "It is impossible to make this conclusion based on the forensic evidence which is clearly apparent to all the experts who have examined this case and looked at all the facts surrounding the death and assassination of JFK."

Director Oliver Stone stated that his personal film, *JFK–The Story That Won't Go Away* was his aversion to the Warren Commission's 888-page report, and their fact-gathering modifications, concerning the death of JFK. It is the view of this author, beyond a shadow of a doubt, that both Oliver Stone and Robert J. Groden are absolutely correct in their overall conclusions concerning the facts surrounding the death of JFK which points to the CIA and ex-CIA factions. In this case there was another shooting team on the grassy knoll. Overwhelming evidence in this cold case confirms both men are right.

The film *JFK* exists as the counter myth to the Warren Commission's report. Both Robert J. Groden and Oliver Stone, along with Jim Marrs, who basically put the major blanketed collection of all the facts in mosaic text, deserve a position in history for standing apart and alone, under great palpable scrutiny facing both ridicule and adversity: In a quest to prove to the American people that their own United States government, which includes the divisions and sectors of the Central Intelligence Agency, acted in radical and subversive actions to eliminate the 35th president of the United States thereby prompting so many of us U.S. citizens to believe that John Fitzgerald Kennedy was truly killed by his own government. It is a reality as certain as gravity, just like death and taxes are certainties in our living existence in the United States of America.

Adding more to this is the current U. S. led campaign in the Iraq war. Prior to the Iraq War, Dick Cheney's net worth income was listed for the IRS at just a little over a million dollars.

At the end of the 1990s, the Pentagon, under Defense Secretary Cheney, awarded a massive 8.5 million dollar contract to a subsidiary of Halliburton for war-related enterprises. In 1995, Cheney assumed the position of

Chairman and CEO of Halliburton. We understand that Dick Cheney did all of his work for our government legally. The contracts awarded Halliburton were extremely lucrative. They continued to grow and prosper under his tenure as the Vice President of the United States of America, during the Bush presidency. At the time this went to press during the Iraq war the below applied. If history repeats itself one has to stop and take notice of history.

At this stage of the Iraq War, Cheney's wealth has increased to 69 times the pre-war figure.[21]

The memorandum of the acting Deputy Attorney General was most prophetic as written by the hand of Nicholas Katzenbach: On November 25th, 1963, (only one day after Oswald was killed, eliminated by the CIA), even though Jack Ruby had pulled the trigger, Oswald was not going to die until the agents hopped onboard the ambulance and massaged the life out of his body on the short trip to the hospital, which took a little bit longer than it was supposed to take.

When there was absolutely no possibility of an Oswald trial to ever come to pass, Nicholas Katzenbach sent out the memorandum that was to firmly establish the so-called "Government's position," regarding the assassination:

THE MEMORANDUM'S AGENDA WAS VERY SUCCINCT

"The government must be satisfied that Oswald was the lone assassin..."

"...that he did not have confederates that are still at large..."

" ...and further, that the evidence was such that he would have been convicted at a trial..."

From the beginning then, the government concerned itself not with the facts but with restoring confidence...

And in doing so...

They eventually did just the opposite.

(It is as simple as A, B, and C for me.)

A.) It was not a sole assassin.

B.) It was not a neurotic person, Lee Harvey Oswald.

C.) It indeed was a full high-level conspiracy.

---

21   WHY WE FIGHT (documentary), Sony Pictures Classics 2005. A testament about the Military Industrial Complex.

NINETEEN

Closing Statements To Tie Up The Loose Ends

Z R Rifle, C-DAY, and, NSC #5412; The Assassination

THE THEORIES WITH SOME LAST WORDS

One final pass for history's sake and a singular summation and final recount of a truly remarkable 50 year-old political mystery. The many circumstances surrounding the official story of the JFK assassination have always been an extremely difficult subject for the average American citizen to fully resolve without questions. It's still immensely debated and such a truly difficult, difficult, difficult, enigmatic puzzle with stunning global consequences. I wish to refer to three separate and very different individuals. One man is a solidly dedicated reporter who worked in Dallas, Texas. Second is a researcher who spent many hot humid days and nights in Havana, Cuba for three grueling months compiling and also later chronicling the secret files of the Cuban State Department. She reveals the astounding list of all the names involved. Third, a Los Angeles author whose solid work examines the possible additional details and evidence that later concluded with: The connection of the Union Corse Syndicate.

DALLAS JOURNALIST JIM MARRS, Carroll Graf 1989

RESEARCHER/AUTHOR CLAUDIA FURIATI, Ocean Press 1994

RESEARCHER/AUTHOR STEPHEN J. RIVELE, France 1988

All of these three individuals help to lead us on the path of the truth which reflects the most accurate and detailed picture of the distinguished efforts of one very powerful and unique government agency:

THE CENTRAL INTELLIGENCE AGENCY

On page 31 of the Robert Groden book, you can see a finely detailed image (Ike Altgens took that famous photograph), and it is estimated to coincide timing-wise with Zapruder frame number #255…Up on the second floor in the broom closet of the Dal Tex Building, you can see (behind the fire escape), that the window shutters are clearly left open. There is evidence that was suppressed by agents, who coerced witnesses to alter or obscure their testimony: that somewhere inside of the Dal Tex Building, yet another shooter operated from this vantage point and fired upon the president's motorcade, using a rifle equipped with a silencer.

The man sitting on the fire escape despite the muzzled velocity of a rifle being fired out of the building (in other photographs taken that same moment), shows that the witness is clearly moving away, or moreover that he is "stunned," and he reacts by being startled by an apparent "shot" that originated from this area.

Photographs and the witnesses on the fire escape indicated to authorities that it was probable or possible that this shooter could be the infamous Union Corse hit man that was later discussed in theories of many assassination books. Witness testimony was discarded by both the FBI and the CIA; the "muzzled rifle fire" witnesses swore they experienced was dismissed as being most likely just a car engine that back fired. It was important to invalidate the testimony that was in conflict (that another shooter other than the man on the 6th floor, or prescribed by this U.S. government known as Lee Harvey Oswald alone), indicating that certainly he was not a lone gunman.

The idea of ZR Rifle was born in September, 1960 when an attempt was planned against Fidel Castro...

...It was directed initially by Allen Dulles, Richard Bissell, and later by Richard Helms. William Harvey was the original organizer of the operation.[22]

It was interwoven within this research, and others who've given it stock subscribe to this theory, that: The breakthrough in the investigation of John Kennedy's murder hinges upon the disclosure of evidence uncovered by the efforts obtained in those investigative interviews of author Stephen J. Rivele (1988). The two men who were recruited from the international crime syndicate were reputed to be: Lucien Sarti and Michael Victor Mertz. The operation was carried out by one from up high as to indicate the position of The Dal Tex Building. The one down low, over on the grassy knoll, was indicated to be wearing a Dallas policeman's uniform. There is other information to indicate that this shooter operated from the gutter vantage point which would explain why there was a pickup truck, with two wheels over the curb—and in the back cargo bay, witnesses watched an unusual sight–Jack Ruby, in full view, was seen unloading a rifle, to be used by that <u>shooter</u>, after a lengthy hike into the tunnel which led to the gutter's inlet opening, by the grassy knoll; as seen in the film *JFK*. This information stands since its release.

Factor some extra insurance marksmen into the equation, and by utilizing two of the world's most extremely accomplished professional assassins:

The CIA couldn't risk any chance that they might miss because there was the sage old adage: "Once you go shooting at the king, make sure you don't miss."

#1.) Lucien Sarti, by the Grassy Knoll (if not at the gutter's location)

---

22   ZR RIFLE: The Plot to Kill Kennedy and Castro, pg.128

#2.) Michael Mertz in the Dallas Texas Bldg., on a 2ⁿᵈ Floor (Claudia Furiati concluded William Harvey hired the assassins under code name QJ WINN).[23]

Murderers Of John F. Kennedy By Steve J. Rivele, was published in France in 1988. According to Rivele's sources, SARTI also wore a police uniform, and fired from behind the picket fence on the grassy knoll. MERTZ fired from a nearby building, either the second floor window of the Dal Tex Bldg. or from possibly inside the Dallas County Records Bldg.[24]

Richard Helms' testimony given to the Senate Intelligence Committee; QJ WINN's boss on the ZR Rifle team was the CIA's William King Harvey. Harvey's specialty was all of the anti-Castro activities in general, TASK FORCE W and Operation Mongoose included at the heart of this source material. QJ WINN appears to have been Michael Victor Mertz.

Attempts against CASTRO involved John Roselli, and also Florida's Santos Trafficante.

In *Crossfire-The Plot That Killed Kennedy* in paperback, read pages 81 through 85 under the heading: A Grassy Knoll Witness. It is my clearest intention that I highly recommend you must read this book, and the astounding account of what Ed Hoffman witnessed November 22ⁿᵈ, 1963.

The information is both compelling and appetizing for a number of reasons.

In providing another convulsion in the convoluted plotting to the umpteenth detail to show just how clever and insidious was the overall calculated measure, and the great lengths that the CIA would aspire to, to insure the absolute success in their truly radically diverse and diabolical world-altering scheme, to disrupt and corrupt the leadership process; to delete the president of the United States of America. One must pause to take a breath and take it all in... exhale in all the tidiness in these exhaustive details that were interwoven neatly into the CIA's massive conspiracy. In stock or trade, these awesome lengths, and it's huge depth.

However, the facts that many people have battled with accepting over the years are growing in stock. Several sources also concurring that these extra gunmen, perhaps aided by Eugene Hale Brading, could've participated in the conspiracy by completing the disclosed pattern of a military style of "triangular ambush" with three positions of shooters taking out a target at a

23   ZR RIFLE: The Plot to Kill Kennedy and Castro, pg. 127, 128, 129, and top paragraph pg. 130; H.A.S.I. states QJ Winn was from the Corse Union. (The Syndicate)

24   Crossfire, pg 208 (It has not been challenged since released 26 years ago, 1989.)

specific "timing scenario" that involves the two men seen together, sitting on the curbing with the umbrella, and the one, who has been later described over the last 50 years as "the umbrella man."

Photographs and witnesses describe these two men as unusual bystanders in Dealey Plaza, with headset communication devices, possibly signaling the three shooting teams by using the umbrella. The first volley of shots were not fatal as several missed the motorcade and JFK, the second barrage came at the signaling of both opening and closing of this particular umbrella. This motion was pre-planned, just in case the first shots missed; this was their way of indicating that more shots were needed to make the hit fatally complete.

I believe that one man is none other than John Roselli, minus his trademark dark sunglasses, and the man seen next to him was none other than Tony Veciana who was to signal the three shooting teams if the first volley of bullets failed, and didn't completely take out the target. More rounds were fired after these men had signaled the shooting team, and the final barrage was ragged and necessary. The FBI had to pick up a lot of bullets and frags because the shots were not fatal until the final tainted bullet fired from the grassy knoll struck Kennedy, imploding his skull and killing him on that fall afternoon of November 22nd, 1963. My own efforts looking into the assassination lead me to conclude moreover what's known in most publications regarding the subject. However, as more evidence evolves, it will certainly become more resolute, and later on transform to becoming more so in mounting accumulated evolving evidence today as the fact.

On Pages 49, 50, and 51, THE KILLING OF THE PRESIDENT; in Robert Groden's Book; we see the crowd's movements just moments after the assassination. Robert MacNeil, the legendary journalist who ran over to the railroad overpass which aligned with the picket fence that's just above the infamous grassy knoll. Robert Groden points out the man known as Jim Hicks, on page 51. He is carrying a radio transmitter device with an antenna. Jim Hicks confessed to being part of C-Cube, which coincides with the future testimony found inside Z R RIFLE. The C-Cube: refers to a command and control team or A-Team. (The Bosch, Lansdale, Ferrie, Sturgis, Hunt, Maheu, Hughes-Nixon connection.) Orlando Bosch, David Ferrie, Eladio Del Valle connects then, (Bosch's partner in Cuba) Luis Posada Carriles, and Pedro Diaz Lanz, and Frank Sturgis, and Richard Cain which included Lenny Patrick and David Yaraz; and all these men were connected to Bernard Barker, Howard Hunt/Richard Nixon, Howard Hughes, and Ed Lansdale.

Inside Z R RIFLE, wherein the Cuban State Department investigation, led to uncovering the member's of ALPHA 66--BRAVO CLUB--including Anthony Veciana, and Orlando Bosch, in concert with Nixon's man... E. Howard Hunt, and Bernard Barker, along with Frank Sturgis, and, Pedro Diaz Lanz, Herminio Diaz Garcia, David Morales, and also C-Cube leader

Ed Lansdale. Jack Ruby, via telephone records is a member of this team. However my 30 years--research leads me to believe strongly--that this A Team was led by Robert Maheu and Edward Lansdale. Therefore implicating the wider web involvement both E. Howard Hunt, Robert Maheu, Howard Hughes and further Richard Nixon; to the CIA's William "King" Harvey... it went all the way to the highest level... inside the Central intelligence Agency's top leadership. (The Hughes--Nixon--Barker--Hunt--Lansdale--Sturgis, "King" Harvey connection to the CIA "mechanics" hit team.)

The following is an excerpt from *ZR RIFLE: The Plot to Kill Kennedy and Castro*. Claudia Furiati:

Kennedy and the Pluto Disaster—

All of this was the backdrop for the invasion expedition, which on April 17th, 1961 landed on the beaches of Playa Giron on The Bay Of Pigs. The 1400 men who landed on that beach were defeated in 72 hours by Cuban resistance. Weeks earlier, Kennedy received a telegram from Colonel Jack Hawkings, the military coordinator of the brigade, who was in Puerto Cabezas, Nicaragua, the spot selected as the launching site for the invasion. Colonel Hawkings informed him that everything had been arranged according to presidential instructions; but this was not the truth. Kennedy was ignorant of key aspects of the operation: The Brigade was meant as little more than a portable detonator, insufficient by itself. The internal support for the invasion on the island had been knocked out, and air attacks by U.S. forces were indispensable. He was also kept in the dark about the biggest secret of Operation Zapata, in place since Pluto: That the CIA operatives were to dispatch the Brigade at any cost, since the military chiefs at the Pentagon had guaranteed military action after the invasion had begun its course. They deduced that, faced with all the pressure of the moment, Kennedy would end up authorizing military support in order to avoid humiliation.

According to President Fidel Castro, approximately a million Cubans were mobilized, counting both regular forces and the militia. When the mobilized Cubans were already destroying the expeditionary contingent, General Charles Cabell, who was a Deputy Director of the CIA, called President Kennedy, and asked permission to provide air cover for the invasion. Aircraft carriers with fighter planes atop of their runways, "with their motors running were positioned near the Zapata Peninsula." But the president (JFK) would not authorize U.S. military action.[25] The means of deployment and provocation hidden up the sleeve of the CIA also failed: The group of 160 men trained in New Orleans under the command of "Nino" Diaz didn't have the nerve to land in Baracoa, and march to Guantanamo Naval Base. They arrived to guard the coast, but when they were informed that government troops were on a nearby highway, they decided to flee.

Almost two years later, when the prisoners of the invasion were freed by the Cuban government, the major proof surfaced that the CIA was operating on its own and against the instructions of the policies of President John Fitzgerald Kennedy.

Jose Perez San Ramon, head of the "mercenary expedition" and other survivors of the invasion testified that CIA advisers from Trax Base in Guatemala had promised them military support. Also, Colonel Frank, a CIA official, had revealed to Cuban commanders of the brigade that "forces inside the administrative branch of the government were trying to cancel the invasion," but if this were to happen they should seize the U.S. advisers, continue preparations for the attack, and he would give them instructions on the final plan telling them when and how they should proceed to Nicaragua. Ignoring certain conditions of the program and disobeying presidential orders, the CIA had caused a major defeat for Kennedy, who found himself obliged to tell the world that he took full responsibility for the actions. He was furious with the Agency, not for the planning the invasion, but for going beyond their limits. He accused the agency of having gone forward with a plan that was created and approved by the Eisenhower administration, and of having put him "up against the wall" without giving him what he termed as "the proper information."

Kennedy was also furious with Fidel Castro, who, upon exposing the failed U.S. invasion, had publicly embarrassed him. Fidel Castro later reflected, "The Giron [Bay of Pigs] plans presupposed the use of military forces against Cuba....The mercenaries sought to create in our country a kind of Taiwan, installing a type of provisional government. The United States' military forces were already three miles from the coast ready for action. Kennedy, concerned about Latin America, and aware of the military and political error, decided not to give the order of intervention."[26]

A conflict arose: many high officials of the Agency held John Kennedy fully responsible for their defeat. They insisted that there would not have been as many deaths and that the 1,200 men would not have been captured if

---

25   Hunt, E. Howard, Give Us This Day, New York (Arlington House)

26   Tripartite Conference (USA/Soviet Union/Cuba) on the Missile Crisis. Closing speech of President Fidel Castro. Havana. January 1992.

Kennedy had not refused to use the armed forces. The CIA tried to cover up its own responsibility.

Agents quickly flew from Washington to Miami to conceal from family and friends of the members of the expeditionary force, the real number of dead and to urge silence on the issue, alleging reasons of national security and the future liberation of Cuba. A day after the defeat, Kennedy met with the Miami-based Cuban Revolutionary Council. The following day he commented to Richard Nixon, whom he had just summoned to his office, "They're mad... Things just calmed down today and, believe it or not, they're ready to continue and fight again, if we give them the plan and the resources "[27] Nevertheless, the Cuban exiles who did not participate in the invasion took a different view: Miami was both incredulous and agitated. The CIA men *used* and *involved* were inconsolable.

New Perspectives: The Taylor report and the Alliance for Progress

On April 23rd, 1961, Kennedy decided to create an inter-departmental commission to investigate the causes of the failure of the invasion, and to appropriate the new proposals.

The commission would be presided over by General Maxwell Taylor, one of his military advisers. After various interviews with participants in the episode, Taylor finished his report on June 13th, 1961.

The document reviewed the causes of the fiasco in terms of military and paramilitary actions, and its principal political argument changed the traditional focus on the Cuba problem. It proposed that Cuba not be confronted in isolation, but rather in the context of the Cold War. It considered two alternatives: coexist with Cuba and accept it as a reality, or include it in the government program against international communism. Recommendation number six of the report concludes:

> *"We concur in thinking that we cannot live for a long time with Fidel Castro as our neighbor... His presence continues to be an effective exponent of communism, and also anti-Americanism within the community of the hemisphere and constitutes a real threat capable of toppling elected governments in any or in the majority of the weak Latin American republics. There are only two ways of looking at these threats: wait until time and internal discontent finally exterminate them, or take effective measures to force their removal. If it weren't for the time it would take, perhaps a few years more, there are a few small reasons to believe that the first form of action might be effective in Castro's police state. The second has already been made more difficult by*

---

27   Nixon, Richard Memoirs, New York. Grosset and Dunlap. 1978.

*the April fiasco, and now can only be possible through open U.S.
participation, with all the Latin American support that can be
obtained.*

*Neither alternative is attractive, but the first could be opted for
without having to make a decision, although we are personally
inclined to a position of positive action against Fidel Castro, we
recognize the danger of treating the Cuban problem outside of
the context of the situation of the Cold War. It is recommended
that the Cuban situation be reevaluated in the light of all the
presently known factors and that new guidelines be drawn up for
propagandistic, economic, military and political action..."*

General Taylor advised the president to radically reorganize his
government and to reevaluate the emergency military powers within the
framework of the balance of forces between the socialist and capitalist blocs.
It was here during this Cuban Study Group—The Zapata Report—was set up
to detail to JFK what went wrong with the CIA Bay Of Pigs Invasion.
L. Fletcher Prouty stated unequivocally that these findings were very, very
significant to John Fitzgerald Kennedy. RFK—Bobby Kennedy sat in with
the generals and **Walter Beadle Smith**—critically historically—laid into the
CIA directly:

"It's time to take a bucket of slop [meaning shit in his military terms],
and cover up over it." It meant the end of the line for the CIA. **"We have to
put these covert operations under an entirely different roof."**

Everyone in CIA knew from that point on after Allen Dulles, and Richard
Bissell, and William Harvey, and Charles Cabell were all sent packing and
fired—that some drastic changes were in store for the CIA. JFK emerged
from the Bay Of Pigs fiasco with RFK as his strict liaison and then began to
dismantle the CIA—from ever running any covert operations. Memo #55
installed the Joint Chiefs Of Staff in the power position by deflating the CIA
from the operating theatre, on the field, "by pulling their teeth" in the strictest
sense taking the CIA into the ball of JFK's fist... and then scattering it and
splintering it, into the four winds... **"they were through."**

THE FINAL NAILS INTO THE COFFIN SET UP FOR JFK

The Spring Of 1963. They planned it. William Harvey (CIA) along with
Desmond Fitzgerald (CIA), Johnny Roselli and, James Angleton (CIA), also
Cord Meyer, and Richard Nixon—NSC 5412—E. Howard Hunt, and
Bernard Barker... and running the FPCC committee... David Atlee Phillips
with another Nixon man (David Morales) and allegedly, James McCord.
(1961-1963.) Essentially the men running it were connected to the Bay Of
Pigs Cuba team.

Nixon's donors at that time included: Marcello–500K, Hoffa–500K, Trafficante–One Million, Giancana–One Million, Roselli–500K... also the Minutman militia–250K, Guy Bannister and Clay Shaw–500K, Lewis McWilley–250K, Clare Booth Luce and Time-Life–250K, and Keyes Royalty–250K, not to mention Howard Hughes–One Million, as well. We know today Nixon was funded over six million dollars by these donations and that Lewis McWilley, picked up all of Nixon's gambling debts in Cuba. (These above entities bought influence with Nixon... for six million dollars.)

JFK had started a momentum of changes that had a lot of upset people.

Backdrop A.) Pushing aside Governor Wallace at the Alabama University so that Vivian Malone and James Hood (the first black students) could attend.

Backdrop B.) The American University speech following the United Nations speech to challenge the Soviet Union to a peace race as opposed to arms race.

Backdrop C.) The CIA being pushed aside by Memo#55, and Memo#263; while Kennedy shut down the militias, operating in Louisiana and in Florida.

JFK and RFK enrolled the first 2 black students at Alabama University. Once governor George Wallace denied entry to Nicholas Katzenbach as both students waited in the car. After a few hours, waiting inside the dormitory the national guard arrived. The students, with the presence of 100 national guard troops, and led by General Graham convinced the beholder of the crimson tide... as Governor George Wallace was pushed aside... like an antiquated albatross or white trash garbage of an older fossil-like dinosaur's carcas.

Starting at A.) Change came into the homes of every single American:

"I hope that every American will stop and examine his conscience about this and other related incidents." Kennedy told the nation on television after George Wallace was subverted, as two African American students enrolled, "This nation was founded by men of many nations and backgrounds. It was founded on the principle that all men are created equal. The rights of every man are diminished... when the rights of one man... are threatened."

"We are confronted with primarily a moral issue... it's as old as the scriptures and it is as clear... as the American Constitution. The heart of the question is whether all Americans are to be afforded equal rights and equal opportunities. Whether we are going to treat our fellow Americans... as we want to be treated. If an American because his skin is dark... cannot enjoy the full and free life which all of us want... then who among us, would be content to have the color of his skin changed and stand in-place. Who among us would be content... with the... councils of patience, and delay?"

"One hundred years of delay have passed since President Lincoln freed the slaves... and yet their heirs and grandsons are not fully free. They are not yet free from the bonds of injustice. They are not yet freed from social and economic oppression. And this nation for all its hopes, and all its boasts will not be fully free...until all–its–citizens–are–free. "

"We face therefore a moral crisis as a country and a people. It cannot be met by repressive police action. It cannot be left to increased demonstrations in the streets. It cannot be quieted by token moves or talk. It is the time to act in the congress, in your state, and local legislative body. And above all... in our daily lives... this is what we are talking about. And this is what concerns this country and what it stands for. In meeting it... today I ask for the support of all... of our citizens." John F. Kennedy, June 11th, 1963.

Kennedy evoked what he called primarily, "we face a moral crisis...as a country and as a people...in America." This call to question the moral fiber of every citizen was binding to that context... that the country has to ask itself; "Who among us would stand in his place?" Change was on the U.S. horizon.

In the spring 1963 the CIA continued its assassination plots with Johnny Roselli even though Kennedy's own official emissary, James Donovan, was in Cuba at that time, negotiating the release of 27 prisoners, including three CIA agents. James Donovan--The same Brooklyn Lawyer, and the hostage negotiator who was immortalized in the filmed adaptation called "BRIDGE OF SPIES" directed By Steven Spielberg 2015.The CIA would brazenly try to assassinate Castro, while running the risk to endanger their own agents– inside Fidel Castro's jails. Although McCone was out of the loop on covert actions, Richard Helms and William "King" Harvey were at the heart of all the anti Castro plotting. This of course included the clandestine inner secretive–workings of NSC 5412 and Richard Milhouse Nixon... related in this...and all other sets of any previous chapters.

Ironically, it was the dismissal of the three legends in CIA career men, that sparked the urgency among those loyal to whom JFK had fired—Allen Dulles, and Richard Bissell, and William King Harvey. We know that Gen. Charles Cabell who was also fired... went back to the pentagon. This divide critically charged the atmosphere of the men who carried on with their missions. The attitude had changed into the most urgent battleground caveat of: "If JFK can dismiss Allen Dulles, and Richard Bissell, and, William King Harvey... then all of us are in jeopardy... all of us could go or be fired next."

"King" Harvey in particular met with such men and the urgency compounded missions and put the fire under the feet of every covert operation–stamping every step with "do or die," and "life or death," and "we're all going to get creamed, or canned, or, dumped in the river if we don't get immediate results now." All this synergy is well documented 50 years after the fact.

———

Richard Mahoney reported that after "King" Harvey, and Johnny Roselli cemented their plans, Roselli then set up shop at the upscale hotel in Key Biscayne which is Trafficante territory. This is when John Martino and John Roselli "hooked up" with the former mafia electronics technician from the Havana casinos who was recently released from prison in Cuba. Then, when Roselli received money and assets provided by William "King" Harvey; that included extra manpower. Instantly CIA heavyweight heat came on board... with John Martino, David Morales, and Rolando Masferrer, along with Bradley Ayres, Gordon Campbell, and Ted Shackley, Orlando Bosch... had safe houses and contacts and numerous exiles... who were all eager to fight their way back into Cuba. Frank Sturgis, and Anthony Veciana, and Bernard Barker, and E. Howard Hunt had reliable shooters, CIA agents including Eladio del Valle, Thomas Eli Davis, Tony Nestor Izquierdo, Tony Cuesta, and Chuck Nicoletti, James Files, Eugenio Martinez, Reuben Rocky Carbajal, George Johannides, Raphael Quintero, Manuel R. Quesada, and, Gilberto Rodriquez Hernandez, Herminio Diaz Garcia, and Pedro Diaz Lanz. The added extra insurance shooters–the infamous French assassins—QJ Win 1.) Lucien Sarti, and–QJ Win 2.) Michael Victor Mertz; were directly hired on by the CIA operative mastermind, "fired" by JFK; William "King" Harvey.

As we know today from numerous accounts, Clay Shaw, Guy Bannister, David Ferry, and Jack Ruby, and George De Mohrenschildt, and, David Atlee Phillips were all directly manipulating the steps for Lee Harvey Oswald.

The back up to these agents and shooters listed above was a very advanced team of men including Tracey Barnes, Joseph C. King, Gen. Lyman Kirkpatrick, General Robert Cushman, Gary Droller, Robert Maheu, Edward Lansdale, and Desmond Fitzgerald. Financing from the Whitehouse with NSC 5412 / S—Group 40 / Alpha –66 / Richard Milhouse Nixon—via Howard Hughes, Prescot Bush, (and) George Bush, and, Jack Crichton, and H.L.Hunt, Clint Murchison, and; Mr. D.H. Bird...who ran the civil air patrol.

With the resources and manpower already in place and the Kennedys distracted by Bobby running CIA Operation Mongoose–and all of the active co-plotting of the men who JFK fired secretly behind the back of RFK–now William "King" Harvey, and Richard Helms and Allen Dulles, found no boundary; since Bobby was totally occupied by 300 agents, and over 100 million dollars, spread about various operations to unseat Castro, all going on that now he was fully responsible for and running at that time. This was the umbrella for moving all the guns and assassins in relative secrecy within the CIA's covert operations...which gave it wings to the mafia movements: "The secrecy that the mob could rely on... that later on after JFK was killed... that the CIA would use plausible denial tactics cover-up the JFK assassination."

As we know today from highly distinguished authors like Mr. John Davis, or Lamar Waldron, and Thomas Hartmann; Marcello and Roselli got all these hired guns together—in the hit squads that took out JFK—moving assassins through Canada, and then down to Michigan; and then going into the United States. The information dovetails with Fabian Escalante's Cuban State departments revelations found inside the exquisitely direct text made in Claudia Furiati's "Z R Rifle," Ocean Press, (1994). "Ultimate Sacrifice" by Thomas Hartmann Lamar Waldron, Counterpoint Press; New Rights (2005).

There were three cities planned for the JFK assassination. They were plans made to work in Chicago, Tampa, and Dallas, and furthermore there were three separate fall guys who were being set up to take the blame for the crime; Thomas Arthur Valle, Gilberto Carlo Lopez, and Lee Harvey Oswald. Ideally, the reporting from Lamar Waldron and Thomas Hartmann stipulated, the three separate hit men (if you're registering it "fall guys" or "the patsy") for each mob boss's role... in covering up the dire covert operations. AKA Johnny Roselli, Santos Trafficante, and Carlos Marcello. (Source) *Ultimate Sacrifice;* 2005. Given the gravity of these revelations, even a decade later in 2015 there seems to be a lack of the courts trials or any resolution to the fact.

———

Given the long gestation of all these plans, and making sure the back up plans had back ups, it's likely these gunmen had a back up contingency. So the shooters were Trafficante's enforcer, Herminio Diaz Garcia, also, his heroin smuggling partner, Michael Victor Mertz. Chicago hitman Chuck Nicoletti, and, Pedro Diaz Lanz, who was Roselli's handpicked-specialist shooter. The men found inside the JFK file, " The Beachcomber." 2013. Adding this NSC 5412 information just adds to the complicity of Whitehouse room #5412 and Desmond Fitzgerald who along with (FBI) J. Edgar Hoover helped the plotters in Alpha 66 conspire to murder JFK in Dallas, Texas 11/22/1963.

Remember: Richard Case Nagell warned several layers of government JFK was going to be hit. He told the Los Angeles office of the CIA. This meant he told Herbert Leibacher, and Joseph DaVanon. He told U.S. Senator Richard Russell, in Georgia. He told Desmond Fitzgerald, the information to the chain of CIA command that Alpha 66/ Rolando Masferrer/ Lee Harvey Oswald–was getting the MK-Ultra, that hypno therapy from David Ferry. He wrote the FBI directly to J. Edgar Hoover. He writes to Desmond Fitzgerald, and E. Howard Hunt, and Tracey Barnes at the CIA warning them of the Alpha 66 hit squad was planning a hit on the United States President JFK .

———

Richard Helms and William "King" Harvey hadn't given up controlling their own toppling-Castro assassination plotting (mostly involving AMLASH and Rolando Cubela), but David Morales and Desmond Fitzgerald, were actively running the C-Day plans for a coup to overthrow Castro in early December. Members were Tony Varona, Harry Williams, and Manuel Artime.

Tony Varona was bribed with $200,00.00 coming from Sam Giancana paid through Johnny Rosselli, as related historically by Richard Cain. As Varona then reportedly told Rolando Masferrer, certain obstacles were about to be removed (meaning JFK was going to be taken out) so he could emerge with Varona and Harry Williams, and Manuel Artime, in being the part of the new CUBA–once the Juan Almeida / Manolo Ray / C-Day coup was successful.

AM WORLD was separate code name from the C-Day / Am Trunk / Amot Operations. All of this was out of the CIA Miami Station with David Morales, Rolando Masferrer, and E. Howard Hunt, and Cord Meyer, and also Bernard Barker, and also Desmond Fitzgerald. Ted Shackley, and Gordon Campbell (under the CIA supervision of Richard Helms / King Harvey / Desmond Fitzgerald;) and Whitehouse NSC 5412 leaders like Lyman Kirkpatrick, General Robert Cushman and Richard Milhouse Nixon–the highest ranking officer in charge—as we now know today. These details are well documented in "Ultimate Sacrifice" (2005).

Investigations by congress documented the lavish support the CIA gave to Manuel Artime, Harry Williams and Tony Varona. It included "four bases, two in Costa Rica, and two more... in Nicaragua, with two large ships, eight small vessels, plus two speed boats, three planes, and more than 200 tons of weapons and armaments, along with $250,000.00 in electronics equipment."

Miami CIA Officer George Johannides DRE, and David Atlee Phillips, and E. Howard Hunt... were careful to praise in their memoirs the leaders inside DRE. Hunt stressed... Phillips ran DRE but that Johannides was taking over while Phillips focused on several operations at the end of July, 1963.

Johannides had to have the full support and the backing, at the highest levels of CIA operations. We know this today... that this meant approval from Richard Helms. Johannides was part of the SAS faction, that cleared from Desmond Fitzgerald, which meant... Robert Cushman, and also NSC 5412 / S—Group 40 / Alpha—66 / and, future president; Richard Milhouse Nixon. Helms and Fitzgerald were deeply involved in the C-Day / AmWorld plot. Johannides was donating $25,000.00 dollars a month for the CIA which came from the top... that meant that it came from Nixon, Cushman, and Desmond Fitzgerald, Allen Dulles, and Richard Helms (CIA); so this also included the CIA station chief Ted Shackley handling propaganda efforts of DRE. We also know that Johannides and his team of agents were also very effective at their trade. David Atlee Phillips was the lead counter intelligence expert that's highlighted heavily inside Z R Rifle—the top CIA propaganda specialist.

In the pages from *Ultimate Sacrifice* Lamar Waldron and Thomas Hartmann wrote it thusly, talking about the expertise of Mr. David Atlee Phillips; "As one might expect for someone who had written so much effective propaganda for the Central Intelligence Agency. David A. Phiillips was an accomplished Writer, with several books to his credit." In his final project which was an unpublished auto-biographical novel–found after his death–David Atlee Phillip's... handwritten character... had said this:

"I was one of two case officers, who handled Oswald... we gave him missions of killing Castro in Cuba... but instead—JFK was killed with precisely the same plan that we had devised, and used-- against Castro."

Thus the CIA, (David Atlee Phillips asserts forwardly that this revelation administered blame and there is a connection in responsibility–but he leaves room for some doubts, with a caveat;) that we, inside the [CIA] did not fully anticipate... the president's assassination, but, that, the [CIA] was ultimately responsible for it. "I share that guilt." Page #532;) *Ultimate Sacrifice* (2005).

At the height of all these significantly-taxing and perilous CIA operations–as discussed at length by (CIA expert) Dino A. Brugioni; in the early Beachcomber text... RFK was embroiled in the major case prosecuting the most successful crime boss in the history of the American mafia. Just after his 38th birthday, November 20th, 1963...in less than 48 hours...the verdict in the Marcello case would be coming out; the day that JFK was assassinated. (The historic trial was at the apex in November 22nd, 1963.) Along with the intense conclusion of the Marcello trial that was wrapping up then: in the final days leading up to the assassination of JFK there were several CIA operations that were all swirling away simultaneously. In concert operationally were the following and of course there were several others also:

Z R RIFLE	NSC 5412 / S—Group 40—Alpha 66 / CIA
Am Lash (Cubela)	OPERATION MONGOOSE
AM—TRUNK	William "King" Harvey
C—Day Coup	PLUTO
AM—WORLD	RESCATE
Operation TILT	J M WAVE
Q J—WINN	A M O T
Michael Mertz	E. Howard Hunt
Lucien Sarti	Desmond Fitzgerald
Chuck Nicoletti	Bernard Barker
David Morales	Rolando Masferrer

With so many operations in play–especially AMTRUNK which involved several Cuban officials who were about to stage a major coup in December, Castro's intelligence service had an inkling something was brewing. The CIA generated a memo of intelligence on November 6th, 1963... that didn't come out until much later stating: "Fears by Fidel Castro relative to an internal revolt." Someone in the MIRR leaked information to a CIA contact; that Castro feared the possibility of commando insurrections which might take place on a large scale inside Cuba. Along with all that was swirling in the wind four uniquely odd things would transpire in rapid succession in the final countdown towards 11/22/63.

But before we get to that...

Along with all that was swirling in the wind four uniquely odd things would transpire in rapid succession in the final countdown towards 11/22/1963. But before we get to that... we must remind everybody of what JFK started... by unraveling the C.I.A.'s power.

It was very clear to the Agency: in The Bay Of Pigs & Cuba JFK cost the C.I.A. their billion dollar empire. Now, with moves JFK planned in Vietnam... he was about to cost the CIA to 220 to 550 billion... losing Vietnam.

John Kennedy struck a deal with Krushchev that called for the removal of missiles in return for Kennedy's pledge not to support or be active in any part of a new invasion of Cuba. The Soviets backed down and for a moment in time, however briefly, Kennedy's popularity increased significantly—but at the cost of immeasurably "turning off" the policy leaders at the C.I.A. and in the Pentagon. Here it was crystal clear to C.I.A. and the Pentagon: losing Cuba it's not okay but we will have to deal with the consequences of The Bay of Pigs--CIA invasion gone awry. But to lose Vietnam, "it's no way in hell we can ever afford to lose that military contractor's bonanza, or all of those vastly lucrative future Kellogg Brown and Root precipitous cash cow, for war contracts. (They couldn't lose that potential 220 billion in contracts... according to L. Fletcher Prouty, which *arose later*... up to 550 Billion.)

By the end of April 1961, a revised counter-insurgency program had been submitted to president Kennedy without the Lansdale material. Kennedy lost no time in implementing many of its recommendations. The first troop movement, the development of a four-hundred man Special Forces Group to go into South Vietnam was made to accelerate the training of the South Vietnamese. This subtle move was directed by president Kennedy under the terms of National Security Memorandum (NSAM #52), issued on May 11th, 1961. And, strategically six weeks later came the most important paper ever released by the Kennedy-Whitehouse: NSAM #55, that removed the CIA from their active participation... no longer on the playing field on -- **June 28th, 1961.**

Thereby Kennedy with NSAM #55 had made the joint chiefs of staff—the military forces of the United States—responsible for the cold war just as they would be responsible for a real declared state of war among nations, and the CIA would not be involved. No longer ubiquitous and/or able to do clandestine operations beyond a certain size... meaning they were reduced to more of that role that belonged to the Alamo Scouts... or that they were strictly "JAFO" (just another fucking observer). Kennedy had neutered the C.I.A. Using a series of memorandums beginning with the NSAM #52, NSAM #53, NSAM #54, and NSAM #55; culminating in the later NSAM

#56-NSAM #57. (The final NSAM #56 and NSAM #57 were targeting NSC #5412, telling them in effect now you will have to answer to our 400 man Special Forces Group; or General Maxwell Taylor, and McGeorge Bundy [and not] Edward Lansdale.)

Now, everyone in the loop could see how fast things began to spiral out of control for the CIA leadership; as in the rapid succession with which John F. Kennedy had dismissed Allen Dulles, and Richard Bissell, and General Charles Cabell. The writing on the wall had gotten progressively worse when Bobby Kennedy fired William "King" Harvey. The shakeout within **NSAM #55** demonstrated Kennedy was moving the CIA outside of the theater. And that if he (JFK) were allowed to continue as this radical President dismantling all their power then they would be forced into "staying forever outside of the theater." The covert operations of C.I.A. "being abolished." (Basically, JFK sought to turn them back into the gathering intelligence firm, and into doing absolutely nothing more than that. Similar to the Alamo Scouts.)

L. Fletcher Prouty wrote extensively about the new Vietnam policy Kennedy had intended to implement in: "JFK, the CIA, Vietnam & the plot to assassinate John Kennedy," (Skyhorse 2009). When you look at the photograph dated October 2nd, 1963: Turn to page 156, view the fourth and fifth pictures in paperback, and you will see the actual meeting between General Maxwell Taylor and J.F.K., with his defense secretary Mr. Robert McNamara. Kennedy—in the special rocking chair and you'll see the leather bound Vietnam study report... underneath the file folders "visible on the coffee table." It is not possible to invalidate U.S. history. It is the full or non corruptible truth to say that along with Fletcher Prouty, and author Jim Marrs, and/or John Newman (and) if you will indulge in either Claudia Furiati or the filmmaker Oliver Stone—we all see the decision was finally coming into fruition for John Fitzgerald Kennedy, and him making that distinctive decision between **May 11th, 1963** and **October 11th, 1963** (in five months after the Vietnam–Gen. Max Taylor study was completed.) It became crystal clear to this author John F. Kennedy had decided to disengage and pull out of Vietnam by December, 1965.

Jim Marrs wrote on pages 306 and 307 in *Crossfire the plot that killed Kennedy* that Kennedy continued to hesitate about sending combat units into Vietnam. At a news conference he said... "introducing American forces...also is a hazardous course and we want to see if we can work out a peaceful solution." According to assistant secretary of state Roger Hilsman, one of John Kennedy's key advisers, and foreign policy planners reported that JFK confided: "The Bay of Pigs has taught me a number of things. One is not to trust the generals nor the CIA, and the second is that if the American people do not want to use American troops to remove a communist regime 90 miles away from our coast over in Cuba, how can I ask them to use our U S troops to remove a communist regime all the way over there in Vietnam some 9000 miles away."

By mid 1963 after receiving conflicting advice and intelligence regarding Vietnam from his advisors, Kennedy began to reassess his commitment there. He was especially concerned about the treatment of Buddhists under the Diem government. Thousands of Buddhists were demonstrating for freedom and on June 11th, the first Buddhist "suicide by fire" occurred. Reflecting Kennedy's concern, the state department notified Saigon: "If Diem does not take prompt and effective steps to re-establish Buddhist confidence in him, we will have to re-examine our entire relationship with his regime." Diem became more unmanageable as the year drew on, staffing his government with relatives in key positions, and refusing to listen to the pleas of the Buddhists. Talk began about possibly replacing Diem (and) with beginning the safe haven plan (and) adding leaders there, who were more agreeable to the American policy. The talks included Kennedy being so disgusted with Diem that he went on and approved the plan of withdrawing one thousand US military advisers from Vietnam – by the end of the 1963 calendar year.

The American government, including Kennedy, left no doubt of its displeasure with Diem, thus paving the way for yet another Vietnamese coup, which occurred on November 1st, 1963, just three weeks, just twenty-one days, before Kennedy arrived in Dallas, Texas. Accompanied by Lucien Conien, South Vietnamese generals seized key installations and they orchestrated an attack on the presidential palace. After hours of fighting Diem and his brother Ngo Dinh Nhu, finally were forced into surrendering. While being transferred back to general's headquarters both the Diem brothers were brutally--slaughtered inside their transport car.

It was time for a decision in Vietnam—to support a major American military expedition as desired by the Pentagon and the CIA leadership at that time —or to simply withdraw and then take the criticism of the anti-communists. The assassination of both the Diem brothers may have strengthened Kennedy's decision to finally disengage from Vietnam, and there is evidence to suggest factually that he would have ultimately curtailed the Vietnam War. Kennedy, forever the mindful and astute politician, was very aware of the approaching 1964 elections. Senator Mike Mansfield told newsmen that once, following a Whitehouse leadership meeting, Kennedy confided to him that he agreed to: "a complete withdrawal from Vietnam;" but he could not implement these plans... until after he was reelected in 1964. The Nuclear Test Ban Treaty had been signed. Kennedy had spoken at the United Nation's to publicly assert himself onto the world stage by stating that "we must challenge the Soviet Union to a peace race, as opposed to an arms race." The CIA felt that they had lost control of all foreign policy. They felt that Kennedy had gone off his rocker and was about to get away with his ploy to forever-radically divert the CIA from any chance in hell of ever running any more covert operations. In their minds JFK went rogue worldwide; and he went ballistic with the CIA and the Military Industrial Complex, over here, in the USA. Quid Pro Quo—the CIA went rogue and ballistic with JFK—by executing executive action ZR RIFLE and starting their commitment of high treason and/or *the conspiracy* by reversing their commander and chief's orders; and by setting in motion several separate layers of covert operations, *that led to the assassination of the 35th President—John F. Kennedy.*

It is the humble opinion of this author... that despite the grandstanding over Buddhists protests... and the later oscillating gestures towards Kennedy's problems or distractions within policy toward the Diem brothers government:

That JFK preferred dealings with the Diem brothers to remain active in negotiation and he sent a safe haven plane that was in place to protect the Diem's until negotiations finalized a deal to keep power or appease the JFK administration. (Obviously this was to be handled by the catholic church to ultimately meet the demands of Buddhists leadership.)

We know today JFK had bonded with the catholic reformer Ngo Dinh Diem to continue furthering his reform policies to dismantle the heroin trade in Vietnam. This bonding included a safe passage out of the country to the safety of the catholic church, and also the steps for a planned eventual reaffirmation to retain power and to grant "safe haven," until things settled down there afterwards (in Vietnam). The safe haven plan was compromised and subverted by CIA operatives who assassinated the Diem brothers. Pictures depicted a random act. But the reason they did not get on the "safe haven plane" sent by JFK seems entirely set up by agents, non random; **and it looked more so to me... like a planned execution in my point of view.**

This author believes that the Lucien Conien, Edward Lansdale, and James Angleton (under the supervision of Desmond Fitzgerald and William King Harvey) were furthering Whitehouse directives from NSC 5412, from Dulles and Nixon; whose orders set up the assassination of the Diem brothers in Vietnam to escalate the conflict there and to escalate the U S troops involvement. The men mentioned above executed the Diems.[28]

---

28   The Diem brothers were driven to the Tan Son Nhut airport in Saigon, and were seen boarding the "safe haven" (Super Constellation) commercial airplane that was waiting for them. Then, for some totally unexplained and unaccountable reason, President Diem and his brother turned back, and both men disembarked the jet airliner while a few unwitting Americans on-scene looked on, completely stunned by their actions. The CIA, Vietnam and the Plot to Assassinate John F. Kennedy, L. Fletcher Prouty (Source, Skyhorse Publishing 2009).

It was staged to look like a bunch of random bandits, or citizens revolting and then assaulting the getaway car in a sneak attack and killing the Diem brothers. I believe it was staged to look that way to outsiders. But I am of the opinion it was carried out by the CIA assassins Michael Victor Mertz and Lucien Sarti, following direct orders from the CIA and NSC 5412 to secure the heroin trade and to deepen the U.S. commitments, and to escalate deeper U.S. troops being sent to Southeast Asia; sent over there to fight a war in Vietnam.

The leaders inside the French connection like Antoine Guerini, Michael Victor Mertz, and also Paul Mondolini, and Jean Jehan were accurately aware that if Diem's alliance with JFK were allowed to continue it would disrupt the French connection's heroin trafficking trade routes in Vietnam.

Odd thing—Number 1.) Kennedy's attack on the U.S. Mafia bosses threatened the stability of Antoine Guerini's Marseille heroin market. Almost all the heroin trade bought by U.S. addicts came from Marseille after it was processed from the opium base, provided by Ngo Dinh Nhu; who was the brother of the South Vietnamese President Ngo Dinh Diem. Hence, the problem that Guerini would face: as he and his syndicate heroin network had a lot to lose if Kennedy was allowed to maintain his war on the mafia bosses. November 1st, 1963–The Diem brothers were assassinated in Vietnam.

Odd thing—Number 2.) JFK's back channel gesture–sending the French journalist Jean Daniel, was delayed–mysteriously–by three weeks awaiting that peaceful resolution brokered by JFK to Fidel Castro. James Jesus Angleton, David Atlee Phillips, and Desmond Fitzgerald (on behalf of "King" Harvey) conspired to delay this meeting the extra three weeks, altering the timing... just long enough for the Roselli / Harvey / David Morales / Cord Meyer hit on JFK to be carried out over in Dallas, Texas, November 22nd, 1963. The odd 3 week delay made no sense at all.

Odd thing—Number 3.) The Marcello trial was at its apex near a verdict. more importantly though, it appears, the C-Day / Eloy Manolo Ray / and Juan Almeida coup planning truly occupied RFK (Bobby Kennedy) keeping all these Operation Mongoose plots moving forward, until after JFK was assassinated in Dallas, Texas—and placing the C-Day coup after it kept both JFK and RFK (solely focused) on the upcoming coup attempt. Herein again... the timing of this also does not... necessarily make sense to me.

Odd thing—Number 4.) James Angleton, Desmond Fitzgerald, and William "King" Harvey circumvented the secret service protection for the president in Dallas for the JFK motorcade. It had to come from the top from a place high in the chain of command–wherein nobody would question the reversal order to stand down. And it had to be done in a way to be certain Bobby Kennedy was completely unaware to stop the stand down order – over the protests of their unit commander--Maximillian Reich.

It is the opinion of this author that these major distractions–the Marcello trial at the apex, the political problems the Diem brothers were having, and the several Cuban operations Mongoose, JM-Wave, AM-LASH, and C-day, and all the others combined, too many plates were spinning. It led to RFK not having enough eyes and ears focused squarely on Dallas to see or to possibly prevent JFK from being assassinated on November 22nd, 1963.

We know Roselli was involved with Trafficante in the Tampa plot to kill JFK same as Richard Cain was involved in the Chicago plot to kill JFK. In both cases, Roselli / John Martino / Richard Cain / David Morales were involved. But in each case, the facts were covered up by CIA led government authorities and the covert operators that kept the plans secret... such as being the work of the disinformation experts James Jesus Angleton and David Atlee Phillips. Under the rouse of the CIA-Mafia plots to kill Castro, the CIA operatives William King Harvey, Cord Meyer, E. Howard Hunt, and David Morales and John Martino, and Santos Trafficante plotting—was targeting towards JFK. We know today Johnny Roselli was in Tampa November 19th, 1963 through November 20th, 1963. There is an unconfirmed report of Johnny Roselli being in Tampa 11/20/1963 before flying to New Orleans the next day. The report comes from a pilot Robert "Tosh" Plumley, who was a known associate of John Martino. Plumley told William Turner (FBI) that earlier in 1963, he had flown Roselli to meetings with Carlos Prio, and also Manuel Artime, in what appears to be part of the CIA-Mafia / Castro—assassination plots. Plumley says that Roselli stayed in Tampa the night of Nov. 20th, before being flown to New Orleans on November 21st. He says the group then went over to Houston, Texas... before later the next morning going to Dallas, on the dawn of November 22nd, 1963. Robert "Tosh" Plumley says the flight was authorized by "Military Intelligence," with the leaders inside " the CIA," in a supporting role. Page #698, *Ultimate Sacrifice* (2005).

All of this information dovetails to the accounting in the taped presentation entitled "FRAME #313." It also confirms with the Wayne January account that claims the military clearance for the CIA plane that was made ready at Red Bird field by Wayne January for the CIA support team that would eventually fly the JFK assassins out of the country. Mathew Smith, *CONSPIRACY—THE PLOT TO STOP THE KENNEDYS*—Pages 140, through; Pages 146.

Of course we understand today that the film *THE FRENCH CONNECTION* (1971 William Freidkin) depicted the heroin trade over in Marseille, France. Detective Sonny Grosso, NYPD Narcotics Bureau, stated that the king pin who ran this empire from the 1950s through the 1960s was the Corsican Jean Jehan. Although Jean Jehan arranged the famous 1962 deal gone wrong of 64 pounds of pure heroin (with a street value of $250,000.00 thousand dollars), he was never arrested for his involvement in international heroin smuggling. This can only be the work of the CIA's agents protecting this drug operation. All of the warrants for the arrest of Jean Jehan were left open and unresolved. And, this is clearly the work of the CIA hands in the heroin-trades cookie jars and its coffers. KING HARVEY / RICHARD HELMS / and, JAMES JESUS Angleton, and, DESMOND FITZGERALD, and RICHARD MILHOUSE NIXON... through Santos Trafficante, and their strong ties to Lewis McWilley, Johnny Roselli to protect this heroin trade, with the assistance of the top cop... J. Edgar Hoover (The FBI). The reason that Jean Jehan was never arrested was that the men he hired on as the assassins—Johnny Roselli's hit team—were against both JFK and the Diem brothers—they were the same hit team that he used in Dallas, Texas. QJ WINN was Michael Victor Mertz and Lucien Sarti, and were paid with 64 pounds in pure heroin that was worth about $250,000.00 thousand dollars during that time in 1963. This why the story emerged that the JFK assassins were paid in heroin. It was a few weeks later after the heat died down that these assassins were flown to Montreal, Canada. Then next to Europe to return back to France... to remain undetected by customs and the police. The heroin trade was a billion dollar business that just had to be protected. So, if the first 64 pounds of heroin was lost during a seizure, in 1962; it was later replaced with another 64 pounds to–QJ WINN–the JFK assassins were paid a quarter million twice. Once to take out the Diem brothers, and a second quarter million to take out JOHN FITZGERALD KENNEDY 11/22/1963. (Heroin later cut and sold worth five million dollars.)

The Tampa threat. The Chicago threat. The Dallas threat. Three significant times... that JFK was being stalked by major plots to kill him in the last 40 days...and the last 40 nights of his young life as president of the United States Of America. Uniquely all of the data herein reads like a tactical spy novel... of guns, drugs, and the toppling of Castro, and the toppling of the leaders of the U.S.A. and CIA. If you partake in ULTIMATE SACRIFICE—by Lamar Waldron and Thomas Hartmann– It's 904 pages. Its the Ultimate Book. Essentially, if one was to compare it to the Warren Report; you could throw the Warren Report into the nearest trash can. By just reading those 900 pages, and thereby learning more about JFK's history than inside that report by our own U.S. Government. However, the CIA and the mafia both travel in the clandestine shadows. "they mirror themselves to a larger degree...so it is no surprise that in this book, as well as so many countless others....attempting to mine the subject....they work hand in glove, like slippery people should –who work well together and are very hard to pin down—and navigate the watershed trail of their movement." Whether you trust it or not is up to you to decide, since it's such a slippery slope. The most important thing, is your own point of view. All of this crackling tactical spy novel unraveling before you– some 50 years after– the fact. Who's right? And, Who's wrong? It's at best the educated guess after all the data is compiled and later on each strand is assembled and absorbed together as a whole. A decision has to be made...with the author's P.O.V. As the data processor: these decisions on the data become the basic window or the p.o.v. of this author, with all the others... with the many prestigious sources... that are cited herein this text.

If anyone would doubt this aspect of the JFK Cold case, one would only have to refer back to the exquisitely researched document *Ultimate Sacrifice*, Page 307, 308; Lamar Waldron, Thomas Hartmann.

As noted earlier, a Warren Commission document–not cited in their final report–said that Jack Ruby was part of the French Connection heroin network in Dallas, something later confirmed... by a recent history... of the Federal Bureau of Narcotics. The Warren Commission document also said that since 1956, that ; "Jack Ruby of Dallas" gave "the okay to operate" for a "large narcotics set up, operating between Mexico, Texas, and the far east." (A.K.A. SOUTH VIETNAM.)

Also, a recent history of the FBN says that "the Church committee notes that in 1962, QJ WINN 'was about to go on trial in Europe... on smuggling charges,' but the CIA, wished to quash charges or they arrange somehow to salvage QJWINN for our purposes. While the CIA kept QJWINN out of jail, if he lost a quantity of drugs... as had Mertz, that he could have... made that same QJWINN subject to manipulation by Mertz, and Trafficante." (My p.o.v. is that the CIA was paying assassins... to take out JFK in heroin.)

Mertz had several easy ways to get out of the United States, after JFK's death, in addition to using his QJWINN's identity. If Mertz had ever been detained in the U.S.–either before or after the JFK's assassination–it would have been easy for him to get out of custody and the U.S. by revealing his true identity. A Legion of Honor winner... with protection from French Intelligence, a hero who had recently saved de Gaulle's life, Mertz could use diplomatic means to leave the U.S. if need be. Or, to avoid involving French Intelligence while he was still in the U.S. Mertz could pretend to be that someone who was required to be immediately deported if they were ever detained or discovered in the U.S. Mertz had two close associates who had not joined the Resistance in World War II and who were the wanted war criminals in France. If Mertz posed as one of them, and was arrested, he would immediately be expelled from the U.S. and deported (once in France, Mertz could use his own clout to get released from jail). According to those reports from two United States INS officials (detailed later), that's exactly what happened in Dallas, TX right after JFK's assassination, which explains the existing CIA report saying Mertz had been "expelled from the United States at... Dallas, 48 hours after the assassination of president Kennedy." "Imagine how Carlos Marcello–still smarting over his own acrimonious deportation ordeal at the hands of Bobby Kennedy—must have felt after

JFK's assassination, when one of his own hit men was deported to safety by the United states government." We noted earlier that Mertz had been part of an intelligence operation in France that involved his pretending to be pro-OAS, passing out pro-OAS leaflets, then being jailed. The same thing happened to Oswald, in August 1963–only involving pro-Castro leaflets—in a well documented incident detailed in the following chapters. However, it's not widely known that Oswald was also reportedly seen passing out pro-Castro leaflets in Montreal, where Mertz had a base and also where he was a frequent visitor. (This information cements the CIA in this conspiracy.)

Either Oswald was in Montreal or someone impersonating him was, according to a report sent to the US Secret Service, a week after JFK's assassination... from the Senior customs Representative, US Treasury Department Bureau of Customs, Montreal; Canada. The report says that "several persons have contacted this office recently and advised that Lee Oswald, suspected of assassinating the late President Kennedy, was seen distributing pamphlets entitled 'fair play for Cuba,' on St. Jacques and McGill streets, Montreal, Canada during the summer of 1963." Mr. Jean Paul Tremblay, investigator, Customs and Exise, Montreal, stated on November 27th, 1963 that he received one of the above mentioned pamphlets from a man on St. Jacques Street, Montreal, believed to be in August 1963; and, he is positive that this person was Oswald. Mr. Tremblay also stated that... he believes that he could identify the three persons... that accompanied Oswald, and the reason for paying special attention to these persons was because he was working on cases involving Cuba, at that time.

The passage indicates the Montreal incident was the dry run for Lee Oswald's exploits in New Orleans, that included the multiple conspirators with Hunt, Sturgis, Lanz, Garcia, Morales, Masferrer, Phillips, Bosch, Sarti, Mertz, Bannister, Barker, Ferrie, & Shaw.[29] (My p.o.v. is that the C.I.A. was dealing heroin and paying assassins to take out John Fitzgerald Kennedy.)

---

29   Ultimate Sacrifice, Lamar Waldron, Thomas Hartmann 2005. Rights issued, Counterpoint Press, Joe Goodale.

TWENTY

ZR Rifle, The Plot To Kill Kennedy And Castro

It was learned that <u>William King Harvey</u> traveled to Marseilles, France, recruiting the agent code-named QJ Win.[30] House Committee Investigations find he was one of the men from the Corse Union. As Operation Mongoose attempts on Castro failed, and the Cuban missile crisis concluded; Helms was protected, but in January 1963, William King Harvey was fired.

Of the planned attempts against Fidel Castro, we now know that in November 1961, it was <u>William Harvey</u> who personally renewed the contacts with Mafia bosses Sam Giancana, and John Roselli for the capsule case. As head of <u>Task Force W and of Operation Mongoose</u>, he sent agents on special missions to Cuba with the objective of developing an armed uprising; efforts which, as we can see, all fell through. More disastrous was the sequence of events during the Missile Crisis. And, someone had to pay for the failure of Operation Mongoose, so that the Agency and also its high officials (such as the assistant director, Richard Helms) would be protected. That someone was William King Harvey, who seemed to everyone to be an inconvenient and incompetent drunkard. This being the case, he was fired from the center of anti-Cuban operations in January, 1963. And what happened to ZR Rifle? It was taken over by no less than <u>David Atlee Phillips</u>, who at the same time was moving toward the extreme right.

Phillips was extremely adept at social communication. He was a great counterintelligence strategist, an expert in psychological warfare. His background, before the JFK assassination, included several covert actions in Chile (1952), in Guatemala (1954), and in Havana, Cuba (1958, 1959 and 1960); coordinating the area of counterintelligence in the CIA's Cuban plan (1960, 1961, 1962); and also being the CIA station chief in Mexico (1963). Analyzing the evidence of Antonio Veciana about his famous case official, Maurice Bishop, the Cuban State Security Department, delivers the solid conclusion that this was the code name of David Atlee Phillips. In Havana it was David Phillips who recruited Veciana, introducing himself as "Bishop." Proof that David Phillips was residing in that city is contained in information about U.S. citizens residing in Cuba in 1960, which appeared in a guide published by TEXACO and distributed in Havana.

"David Atlee Phillips, Nationality: United States, position in the U.S. embassy in Cuba 1959. Public Relations Consultant; proprietor of David A. Phillips Associates: 106 Humboldt Street apt. #502."

From this point, all of Veciana's comings and goings would be marked by the presence of Phillips, his supervisor in all his anti-Castro activities. In

---

[30]   ZR RIFLE: The Plot to Kill Kennedy and Castro, Claudia Furiati, pgs. 128, 129, and 130

1961, he guided him in the Operation Liborio attempt on Fidel Castro. In 1962, by suggesting to him the creation of Alpha 66, Phillips unleashed a series of terrorist groups. Phillips directed the beginning of the Alpha 66 attacks. These intensified during the Missile Crisis, trying to provoke a political confrontation with President John Kennedy. Phillips told Veciana the terrorist activities were aimed at forcing Kennedy to take a position against Cuba. In 1963, with the Miami camps being dismantled by the police authorities and some of the best commandos relocated to Central America, it was necessary to reunify them. The man chosen for this job was David Atlee Phillips, because of his long association with all of these groups.

Lastly, at this time, where could the necessary capacities for ZR Rifle be found, such as the resources of big business, the Mafia, the anti-Castro groups, or the best marksmen?

In the terrorist groups.

The fact that this was David Atlee Phillips' new job can be confirmed through the testimony of Anthony Veciana: he saw in "Bishop's folder" a memorandum bearing the initials "to H. H." that confirmed commando plans, and contacts and activities. (H. H. could have been either Howard Hunt or Howard Hughes, Robert Maheu's boss in Las Vegas, and head of commercial activities of the CIA.) In September 1963, Veciana again witnessed an encounter between David Atlee Phillips and Lee Harvey Oswald, in Dallas. Lee Oswald was on his way to Mexico and David Phillips was already the CIA's man in that country. After the episode, Veciana recalled that David Phillips ("Bishop") asked him to go to Mexico, and look up his cousin's husband Guillermo Ruiz (the G-2 agent), who at that time was stationed there.

David Phillips proposed that Veciana offer Ruiz a large sum of money to dessert and testify to Lee Harvey Oswald's visit to the Cuban embassy and his pro-Castro affiliation. (Get Ruiz to desert Alpha-66 to further incriminate Lee Harvey Oswald as the fall guy and; as a lone falsified sole JFK assassin.)

The House Assassinations Committee heard two testimonies that shed a ray of light on the participants in the Kennedy assassination. The first was that of Jose Aleman, already related here, which implicated Santos Trafficante in the crime and suggested that three Cubans served as marksmen. The other was that of Marita Lorenz, a beautiful spy recruited by Frank Sturgis in mid-1959, when she maintained relations with people close to Fidel Castro. Lorenz mentioned an encounter she witnessed in Miami in September 1963, at the home of Orlando Bosch, where Pedro Luis Diaz Lanz and Lee Harvey Oswald—whom she had seen earlier in an Operation 40 house—were present. The conversation revolved around a trip to Dallas, Texas.

She said that on November 15th she was part of a group that drove to that city in two cars, and included Orlando Bosch, Frank Sturgis, Pedro Diaz Lanz, Lee Harvey Oswald, and Gerry Hemmings, and the Novo Sampol brothers (Guillermo and Ignacio, from the Movimiento Nacionalista

Cubano–Cuban Nationalist Movement). They stayed at a hotel, in rooms that contained various rifles and shotguns, and that also Jack Ruby paid them a visit there.

Marita Lorenz said that she returned to Miami on November 19th, or November 20th. She also said that she had been coerced by Frank Sturgis not to testify before the (H.A.C.) committee, which ended up judging her statements inconsistent anyway. Nevertheless, the Cuban State Security Department considered the evidence of Marita Lorenz to be important. Following the reasoning of the Cuban State Security Department, we conclude that the Kennedy case involves apparently juxtaposed three separate groupings working simultaneously:

THE COUNTERINTELLIGENCE—Frank Sturgis and Orlando Bosch were two of the principle agents of Operation 40, the "parallel" counterintelligence structure before, during and after the Bay of Pigs invasion. David Atlee Phillips represented the CIA in these operations. Frank Sturgis: Brigade #2506, on Cuban soil; imprisoned by Castro. See photograph Osvaldo Salas, FIDEL'S CUBA Frank Sturgis/Maurice Bishop, pg.140, 141.

THE COMMANDOS—Frank Sturgis was one of the initiators of the International Anti-Communist Brigades, along with Pedro Diaz Lanz, who was in charge of training the elite troops in exile. David Atlee Phillips was the mentor of these terrorist groups. Frank Sturgis and his partner Gerry Hemmings opened the training camp at Lake Ponchartrain, in New Orleans, in the same era as the creation of ALPHA 66. Orlando Bosch was the head of M.I.R.R., one of the most important terrorist groups trained at Lake Ponchartrain. See page #152,) Fiorini; A.K.A. Frank Sturgis inside Cuba. "The Killing Of The President." Viking Penquin — Robert Groden 1993.

THE Mafia—The arms at Lake Ponchartrain were supplied with the cooperation of the Mafia. The Louisiana corridor was controlled in Dallas by Jack Ruby, and in Miami it was controlled by Santos Trafficante. Frank Sturgis had been involved in the contra band arms trade since before the 1959 Cuban Revolution. Santos Trafficante was the bridge between the Mafia and the Cuban Exiles.[31]

The month of August, 1963, was the time and New Orleans, the place. All of the Florida training camps had been liquidated by government order. Ponchartrain, spared by the police authorities, became the center of the illegal counterrevolutionary operations.

Frank Sturgis, Orlando Bosch, Guy Bannister, David Ferrie, Clay Shaw, and Lee Harvey Oswald all participated directly in these. Later, New Orleans became the center for the parallel operation of the CIA. It was in the beginning of August that, due to growing pressure from Kennedy, the FBI was obliged to reveal the secret of Ponchartrain. (The exiled mercenaries

---

[31]   ZR Rifle, Furiati; pg. 130, 131, 132, 133.

who were already inconsolable after the Bay of Pigs, now were determined to strike back on their own.)

(In *JFK* the movie, Oliver Stone's interconnection here is that this event reflects the final straw.) The ultra right understood that the John F. Kennedy government would in no way accept this parallel operation. The CIA had the ideal man in their hands: Lee Harvey Oswald. At this moment, Lee Harvey Oswald was chosen to be accused of the Kennedy assassination, an instrument of the triple plan. On August 9th, while distributing pro Castro literature printed in Guy Bannister's office, he was confronted on the streets of New Orleans by Carlos Bringuer, the leader of the DRE. It was also in August that, according to Jose Aleman Gutierrez's testimony, Santos Trafficante had the conversation about the Kennedy assassination. In the two months that followed, September and October, we see David Atlee Phillips directing Lee Harvey Oswald's steps in Dallas and Mexico. And David Atlee Phillips was the head of ZR Rifle, the source of parallel operations for political assassinations.

Let's get to the final conclusions. The Cuban State Security Department has concluded that those responsible for Kennedy's assassination are David Phillips, as the promoter ZR Rifle; and Santos Trafficante, as the coordinator of the Mafia participation in the operation. And those who fired the shots were Cubans from the "elite troops" in exile. The day of the assassination they were deployed in groups, together or separate, forming a triangle of fire, and one of these groups was under the direct orders of Jack Ruby. And who was the author of this entire scheme?

Richard Helms, the brain of the CIA. Richard Helms was the ultimate chief of the covert and parallel operations from the beginning of <u>Operation Mongoose</u>.

He was the director of the plans that included the capsules, the special missions, the terrorist commandos, the Mafia, the Guy Banister unit, Ponchartrain elite troops, William King Harvey, Manuel Artime, Rolando Cubela, Desmond Fitzgerald, Lee Harvey Oswald, <u>Santos Trafficante, David Atlee Phillips, and ZR Rifle</u>. He was the conductor of the invisible government and the maestro of plausible denial.

Finally, Helms was the link of the Agency with the "hardliners" and the mentor of the provocations during the Kennedy Administration. But Richard Helms' involvement was not apparent; he was behind four walls, an invisible man. After the assassination, Richard Helms was named director of the CIA. He directed the "Phoenix" program in Vietnam, the systematic assassination of persons suspected of belonging to the Viet Cong. One of those named in the Watergate scandal, he was made ambassador to Iran. Currently, he is a business consultant. He is tall, with fine thinning black hair. He is discreet and evasive, the perfect bureaucrat. He is considered the most astute and the coldest of all the directors of the Agency—so cold that he was nicknamed "Mr. Cool." Richard Helms, David Atlee Phillips, and Santos Trafficante equals counterintelligence, Mafia and commandos equals Operation ZR Rifle. The equation is solved.[32]

Jim Marrs' exhaustive fact-filled journal of history, titled "Crossfire The Plot That Killed Kennedy," is a truly remarkable, inordinately resilient, platform of facts; the accounts of immeasurable history and research about all of the facts concerning the Kennedy case are laid out in intimate detail to absolutely form the valid necessary and valuable insights to both the view of November 22nd, 1963, and also the view of the unique "post process" of the government organizations who later obscured the view on that day of history.

Although my conclusion disagrees with the final analysis found inside of Jim Marrs' *Crossfire* (as I see it the CIA is the one team of fowl and the soul proprietorship authenticating an actual plan to execute Kennedy), Jim Marrs' epitaph summation makes the best analysis of JFK's position in political history by acclimating him as only the second intellectual to lead the United States. I summarize Jim Marrs' collection of thoughts concerning the man John Fitzgerald Kennedy. Because of his family's great wealth, John F. Kennedy was insusceptible (as far as the other past leaders were before or after his presidency) into being corrupted by financial deals, or bribes from business, industry banking, or oil magnates, or anybody for that matter. He was the only president since Franklin Roosevelt who was an intellectual. Kennedy had a rich sense of history and a global outlook. He apparently sought to engage people towards his vogue idealistic vision of making the world more peaceful and, interestingly enough, less corrupt.

In other words he really believed in his presidency (and as the leader of the free members of American society to bring about historic strides for a better quality to American life and new ideals), to move ahead as a forward thinking youthful leader to what is otherwise a young country. In blazing the new trail, he set out early to shake up the status quo of Big Banking, Big Oil, Big Military Industrial complex, with its multi-faceted global-reaching Intelligence Community, and also Big Organized Crime syndicate figures that had gained deep inroads into American life since the days of Prohibition. There were—and most certainly remain—numerous ties among all of these powerful factions.

It is now well documented that the mob and the CIA worked hand in glove on many types of operations, including the ugly radical business of assassination. The various U. S. Military intelligence services are closely inter-woven, and in some cases, such as the National Security Agency (NSA), are superior to both the FBI and the CIA. Therefore, when Kennedy and his brother, Attorney General Robert Kennedy, began to wage war on organized crime, it quickly became a matter of self defense to the mob and the banks and industries it controlled. Equally unnerved and previously untainted until Kennedy took oath of office, officials of both the FBI and the

---

[32]   THE PLOT TO KILL KENNEDY AND CASTRO: ZR Rifle. Claudia Furiati, Ocean Press, 1994, Talman Co. USA pages 131, 132, 133, 134, 135, and 136.

CIA likewise were fearful of the Kennedys who had come to realize just how dangerously out of control both of these agencies had become.

The anti-Castro Cubans (along with the CIA-led brigades training for invasion around the world), felt betrayed by President Kennedy because of his last minute orders towards halting the U.S. Military assistance to the Bay of Pigs invaders. And all of these men were quite willing to support and also participate with a top CIA go ahead of carrying out the assassination. Kennedy had angered a long list of very powerful men in the military industrial complex.

If you examine all the documentation surrounding all of the facts concerning the assassination of President Kennedy and particularly the links to members of the Central Intelligence Agency, and conversely some of its key members that John Kennedy dumped after the disastrous Bay of Pigs debacle; it becomes distinctively crystal clear to this author that the plan to eliminate John Kennedy was hatched from the upper echelons of the CIA. In effect its earliest beginnings start with the details of ZR Rifle and the two men that Kennedy inexorably and inevitably inestimably dismissed: its formidable leader, the great white case officer—Allen Dulles, and the covert operative mastermind—William King Harvey—discussed the plan with Robert Maheu, and Richard Bissell. They later planned with David Atlee Phillips, and E. Howard Hunt allegedly with General Charles Cabell, Mayor Earle Cabell, and also Guy Bannister. Plan designs were discussed as early as September 1960, and evolved throughout spring of 1963. It began here from the top... with these men of action inside... the Central Intelligence Agency.

The anti-Castro Cubans and members of the CIA were ready to act, feeling betrayed by Kennedy when he refused air cover for the invasion of CIA-led Brigade #2506...which landed at the Bay of Pigs on April 17th, 1961. The plan was to involve some of the men taken prisoner by Fidel Castro, including CIA mercenary agents Frank Sturgis, and Maurice Bishop. Others under the stewardship of General Edward Lansdale gathered the team including: E. Howard Hunt, General Maxwell Taylor, Bernard Barker, and Eugenio Martinez, Jack Ruby, David Ferry, Guy Bannister, Hugh Ward. Also involved were Orlando Bosch, Tony Veciana, Elladio del Valle, along with Herminio Diaz Garcia, Pedro Diaz Lanz, and Santo Trafficante. The further CIA connections extended into the Louisiana corridor, with John Roselli and Clay Shaw, Tony Verona, Carlos Marcello, which then extended to Meyer Lansky, and Sam Giancana. It was Clay Shaw who supplied nearly all the CIA mercenaries weapons in Latin America, and who did business with the top Mafia chieftains at that time, and also was the central-supplier of all the arms to the various Brigade divisions that were operated by the CIA.

With a deeply rooted invincible connection into the Central Intelligence Agency, Clay Shaw could deal arms freely "without any interference from either the law enforcement, or the state police, or the FBI" throughout the circles of the infamous Louisiana corridor. It was well known that Clay Shaw was to deal arms freely and unhindered since he was "completely untouchable" behind the infinitely powerful clandestine (black ops) muscle of the CIA.

When the Mafia surveillance tapes were passed on to J. Edgar Hoover of the FBI, it was another ironic twist of fate for JFK since the FBI director was a direct enemy of the president. In a clear choice he made for political survival: Hoover took sides with the CIA's plans to eliminate his political enemy first who shortly after his (JFK's) reelection, was going to force the FBI director into an early retirement. It was through the process of work done on behalf of the FBI director's office, and by this level of Hoover's hands-on involvement (especially with the cover up aspects of the JFK killing), and afterwards "the plans of forcibly applying government pressure upon witnesses, by either forcibly using tactics of conversion and or coercion of several key witnesses in the background of Dealey Plaza...whereby the FBI was acting on behalf of the CIA's interests (as well as protecting their own interests to the cover up), in a pattern of fully declassifying... or bringing about the complete detoxification of any fallout of any future probes into the investigation into JFK's ultimate murder."

Kennedy had signed the Nuclear Test Ban Treaty with the Soviet Union, and some of the top Military brass let it be known how they were irrevocably incensed in late 1963 when Kennedy let it be known that he planned to withdraw all the U.S. Military personnel from Vietnam by the end of the year 1965. With this momentous decision, the military turned against him, the military's leadership would not be sorry if something were to happen to Kennedy. This fact is undoubtably what gave grounds for what led the military down the inevitable path to a compliance with the CIA's planned "executive action." The stage was set. General Charles Cabell, the CIA deputy director fired by Kennedy after the Bay of Pigs, was now back at the Pentagon, and his brother, Earle Cabell, was the mayor of Dallas. It was widely known and rumored (back in 1963, as well as in 2003), that Vice President Lyndon Johnson—who was long associated with dirty politics, gamblers, and defense officials—was to be possibly "dropped" from the democratic ticket in 1964. What was even worse was that the platform support of Lyndon Johnson's powerful conservative base of several Texas oilmen (that were staunch friends and literally owned his political career and candidacy), along with the Military Industrial Complex, were very, very distraught with an economic fear of what was about to come to pass if the:

"Kennedy's were talking about doing away with the highly profitable oil depletion allowance." This led to the opening of the keys to the president's security operation in the trip through Dealey Plaza, whereupon General Charles Cabell's brother, who was at that time the mayor of Dallas, Earle Cabell, who with the cooperation of affected oil interests, and other business leaders, especially in the international banking market whom were all equally shocked with another eventual John F. Kennedy reality: When he ordered the treasury department to print its own money, rather than distributing the traditional Federal Reserve notes that carry with them very profitable interest charges. Therefore if you add these two radical changes for the Texas oilmen, and the international banking community, coupled with Kennedy and his brother Attorney General Robert Kennedy, who was waging a newly frenetic, and fanatic, radically dangerous war against organized crime in America:

Jim Marrs:

"It was clear if the CIA wanted to eradicate Kennedy policies the Mafia would do as they were asked to protect their own widely held interests along with the business leaders, banks, and industries they controlled…just like, the Texas oilmen. Soldiers, mobsters, and businessmen were afraid that the changes Kennedy intended for the nation would come at too high a price for themselves."

"Seemingly, it was clear that the gravy train of theirs was about to derail under these policies…and perhaps the apple cart of theirs…was about to be tipped over by this youthful, and zealous forward-thinking president."

The CIA, who were inconsolable after the Bay of Pigs, were counting on a victory when Brigade 2506 landed in Cuba April 17th, 1961. The subsequent Bobby Kennedy take-over of all of the CIA's covert actions against Fidel Castro, pissed off everybody in uniform. Tensions between both of the Kennedys and the Military Industrial Complex snapped the moment that Kennedy stated: He would smash the agency into a thousand pieces, and cast it to the four winds. (In a direct response to Operation Quick Kick, in April of 1962; a year later.)

Kennedy's most momentous decision came to pass in showing the CIA members the price for disobeying his direct orders to cease and disallow all the operations of covert activities preparing for the second invasion against Fidel Castro on Cuban soil: he dispatched the FBI and the local law enforcement agencies into two states to raid and shut down mercenary CIA brigade camps, both Ponchartrain-11, in Lake Ponchartrain, New Orleans, and those camps operating in No Name Key, Florida, and in the Florida Everglades. With this move, John F. Kennedy severed any slim chance for the threads that he still had left holding his tenuous relationship together with the Military Industrial Complex, and some very powerful men… in this inconsolable, fractured, and, boiling-hot and mad… segment of the CIA.

Now they were <u>forced into believing that they shot themselves in the foot</u> with everything that went wrong with Cuba, and the Bay of Pigs, because this time around this president was wary of any covert moves that the CIA intended to make. They began to read the writing on the wall that this battle was for keeps and by shutting down CIA secret bases <u>this president meant business.</u> He had fired Allen Dulles of the CIA. And it was right there that the youthful president made an enemy that the world would regret. The second invasion of Cuba was scrapped by a Kennedy veto and nobody wanted to lose any more ground after the Cuban Missile Crisis.

When William King Harvey was dismissed and sent to exile in Rome, he blamed all of the CIA's failures upon both of the Kennedy brothers. Allen Dulles and William King Harvey sought to restore authority, prestige, and the power it had once known to the CENTRAL INTELLIGENCE AGENCY; returning the Central Intelligence Agency to its original and rightful position in American politics. The ending results of restoring the power and the prestige of the agency's armor for the CIA meant that John Fitzgerald Kennedy had to go. Richard Helms, Desmond Fitzgerald, and Nixon, and Howard Hunt, agreed. November 22nd, 1963 changed our world permanently.

Jim Marrs:

"The changes… like LBJ and Vietnam, or Nixon and Watergate. We never quite looked the same after that time in our history."

Perhaps the most damaging statement that was ever made about the JFK conspiracy was revealed in a statement by CIA agent Gary Underhill. This excerpt from James Fetzer's *Murder In Dealey Plaza* speaks volumes to the afternoon of November 22nd, 1963.

> CIA agent Gary Underhill drives out of Washington D.C. and heads for New York—and the home of Robert Fitzsimmons on Long Island, (Fitzsimmons and his wife are long time friends, whom Underhill believes he can trust). Bob is sleeping when he arrives but Charlene is awake. Underhill tells Charlene that he fears for his life, and he plans on leaving the country. "I've got to get out of this country. This country is too dangerous for me now. I've got to get on a boat. I'm really afraid for my life." As Charlene went on to question him further, Underhill then goes on emphatically explaining that he has information about the Kennedy assassination and that: "Oswald is a patsy. They set him up. It's too much. The bastards have done something so outrageous. They've killed the president, I've been listening too; And hearing things. I couldn't believe they would get away with it… but they did!" Gary Underhill was distraught with emotion as he tried to maintain control of himself, he continued, explaining that—"They've gone mad! They're a bunch of drug runners and gun runners, a real violent group. God, the CIA is under enough pressure already without that bunch in Southeast Asia. I know who they are… and that's the problem. They know that I know and that's why I'm here."

These are in my mind some of the most telling, and also provocative words that were spoken about the set up or the far reaching government hands that were acting on behalf of the Central Intelligence Agency to eliminate the 35th president of the United States, John F. Kennedy. If you want to know how CIA Agent Gary Underhill left this world, turn to page 157 of Robert Groden's "THE KILLING OF THE PRESIDENT;" (top right corner.)

There are, yes, several thousand books written about the Kennedy assassination, far too numerous to mention, and this will not be the last attempt to mine the subject. However, one book of the later years should be offered special mention for its extremely rich text and various points of content with regard to old mysteries about the JFK cold case:

<u>CONSPIRACY: THE PLOT TO STOP THE KENNEDYS</u>, by author <u>Matthew Smith</u>. (Chapter #22 makes for some particularly exotic reading.)

———

One final nail in the coffin to be released publicly in the last few years: The E. Howard Hunt death-bed confession as recorded by his son, St. John Hunt, and video taped by Jesse Ventura (as aired on the True T.V. television program) and accessible on the world wide web. On tape Hunt proclaimed to have participation in the "so-called event in Dallas Texas 11/22/1963." Hunt describes the operation saying that there was major backtracking to cover the tracks of the chain of command—and adds to the list of CIA operatives involved to include Cord Meyer, David Morales, William King Harvey, David Atlee Phillips, and, Frank Sturgis, Antonio Veciana, Lucien Sarti (Corsican assassin and French gunman), Michael Victor Mertz—specialist black ops grassy knoll shooters. He points the finger at LBJ and leaves his boss out? E. Howard Hunt's confession in my p.o.v. "he's covering up for Dick Nixon." (Google search E. Howard Hunt's death bed confession.)

———

THE CIA CUBAN CONNECTION IN FRAME # 313

EDWARD LANSDALE (ZR RIFLE)

WILLIAM KING HARVEY (ZR RIFLE)

JOHNNY ROSELLI (THE HIRED GUNS)

RICHARD HELMS (CIA)	ROLANDO MASFERRER
CORD MEYER (CIA)	JOHN MARTINO
DAVID MORALES (CIA)	GEORGE JOHANNIDES
DAVID ATLEE PHILLIPS (ZR RIFLE)	FALL GUYS

SAM GIANCANA	CHICAGO PLOT	Thomas Arthur Valle
SANTOS TRAFFICANTE	TAMPA PLOT	Gilbert Carlo Lopez
CARLOS MARCELLO	DALLAS	Lee Harvey Oswald
THE MULLEN COMPANY (CIA)		Robert Bennett
THE KEYES ROYALTY (CIA)		Bebe Rebozo

THE SPECIAL ABORT TEAM
CIA BACK-UP TEAM TO COVER FAILURE

ROBERT "TOSH" PLUMLEE (THE MILITARY PILOT)
The Flight: In Operation with *several unidentified intelligence agents;*

IN **FRAME 313** - THE SUPPORTING GROUP - ABOUT A DOZEN MEN.
(8 men on his plane with Robert Tosh Plumley plus others in Dealey Plaza).[33]

SHOOTING TEAMS MEMBERS (A) + (B)

JAMES FILES	PEDRO DIAZ LANZ
MICHAEL VICTOR MERTZ (U. C.)	THOMAS ELI DAVIS
JEAN RENE SOUTRE (U. C.)	HERMINIO DIAZ GARCIA
CHAUNCEY HOLT	TONY NESTOR IZQUIERDO
CHUCK NICOLETTI	FRANK FIORINI STURGIS
ELADIO DEL VALLE	RAPHAEL QUINTERO
RICHARD CAIN	DAVID YARAS
GUILLERMO NOVO SAMPOL	**IGNACIO NOVO SAMPOL**

ORLANDO BOSCH   (ALPHA 66)
LUIS POSADA CARRILES (ALPHA 66)
SAUVEUR PIRONTI (UNION CORSE)
PAUL MONDOLINI   (UNDER BOSS IN THE U.C.)
JEAN JEHAN   (THE TOP BOSS IN THE U.C.)
ANTHONY VECIANA (ALPHA 66) + (NSC 5412)
ROBERT "BARNEY" BAKER (CHICAGO MAFIA)
CLAY SHAW   (CIA) + (FBI) GUY BANNISTER   (FBI)
GERRY HEMMINGS (ALPHA 66)   DAVID FERRIE (CIA PILOT)
MALCOLM "MAC" WALLACE   (LBJ'S TOP GUN)

PRIMARY DISINFORMATION COORDINATOR
JAMES JESUS ANGLETON   (CIA)
Joseph Alsop / Hal Hendrix / Seth Kantor

SECONDARY DISINFORMATION COORDINATOR
DAVID ATLEE PHILLIPS   (CIA)
Henry Luce / Philip Graham / C.D. Jackson

C--CUBE COMMAND AND CONTROL BLACK OPERATIONS
Frank Sturgis, Jack Ruby, Jim Hicks, Lenny Patrick, Tracey Barnes, Robert Maheu,

---

33   Pilot: Robert "Tosh" Plumley, had stated there were "eight men" on board his aircraft, but the information I received on this special big abort team, at least four more men... had joined up with the special team... later on while they were on the ground in Dealey Plaza 11/22/63.

(and) inside the C-CUBE coordination truck; their top leader Edward Lansdale.

THE RICHARD NIXON -- ALL THE PRESIDENT'S MEN
GENERAL ROBERT CUSHMAN (NSC 5412)
ROBERT MAHEU (FBI) + (CIA)
HOWARD HUGHES (HUGHES AIRCRAFT CO# INC.)
DESMOND FITZGERALD (CIA) + (NSC 5412)
E. HOWARD HUNT (CIA) + (NSC 5412)
JAMES MCCORD (CIA) + (NSC 5412)
RAY CLINE (CIA) + (NSC 5412) JORGE MAS CANOSA (CIA) + (F R D)
CARLOS PRIO (CIA) + (F R D)
TONY VARONA (CIA) + (C R C)
MANUEL ARTIME (CIA) + (C R C)
TRACEY BARNES (CIA) + (NSC 5412)
BERNARD BARKER (FBI) + (NSC 5412)
EUGENIO MARTINEZ (FBI) + (NSC5412)
J. EDGAR HOOVER (THE FBI DIRECTOR)
In collusion later...the man who went along in high treason...after the event.
LYNDON BAINES JOHNSON (The Vice President)[34]

It's readily apparent and dramatically transparent—the glass ceiling going upwards, and so high up into the chain of command, leading into the highest sources—deep inside the intelligence community. All the clearance necessary to arrange a free pass to this many shooters involved in the J.F.K. assassination, can only mean that the CIA had to be the lead dog. Only the CIA could make the event/conspiracy materialize/happen as it did happen; in broad daylight, with so many levels of meticulous planning and precision-like execution. The key meeting for me was between William "King" Harvey, and Johnny Roselli. Z R Rifle was organized by William "King" Harvey, it was the keystone plan that simply moved into the United States after its attempts in Cuba against Castro proved not to bear fruit and the plans were then reset to fit... the hit... on J.F.K. James Jesus Angleton and David A. Phillips, led the disinformation apparatus and they both engineered the cover up. In that sense I agree with the findings of Jim Garrison. "the real killers... are the men who were once connected... to the Central Intelligence Agency." In this area Oliver Stone, Jim Garrison, and Robert Groden; are all right.

---

[34] Footnote: Z R RIfle, Claudia Furiati; Ocean Press 1994 Talman (Page 148, Pages 163, up through Page 167). C R C; Cuban Revolutionary Council, F R D; Free Democratic Cuba, U. C.; The French Union Corse. F.B.I. Federal Bureau Of Investigation (USA) C.I.A. Central Intelligence Agency United States U.S.A.

Jim Garrison—THE JFK FILM—On The Mafia

"I don't doubt their involvement...but at a lower level...could the mob change the parade route? Or, eliminate the protection... for the... president? Could the mob send Oswald to Russia, and then get him back, from Russia? Could the mob get the FBI, the CIA, and the Dallas Police to make a mess of the investigation? Could the Mob get the Warren Commission appointed to cover it up? Could the mob influence the national media to go to sleep?"

Anyone. Be you a writer. Be you investigator. Be you laymen. Be you JFK assassination expert. Or even if you're just a regular person who is reviewing all the data that is compiled herein. It is a CIA operation... the typical black operations... and the cover up. The specialty of David Atlee Phillips, and also; James Jesus Angleton. (Jean Renee Soutre—AKA – Lucien Sarti... are one in the same person.)

There was a bullet hole through the windshield in the JFK limousine SS-100- X seen by Doctor Evalea Glanges, at Parkland Hospital. Also seen by three secret service men. It was seen inside of the Ford Factory company by three witnesses, when LBJ later ordered the JFK SS-100 X limousine to be scrapped, stripped... and totally rebuilt. LBJ said "have that car washed dismantled." This was reported by author, and professor Douglas Weldon.

THE MEN WHO KILLED KENNEDY Part 7–The Smoking Guns
Dr. Evalea Glanges, Prof. Douglas Weldon, George Whitaker, Ford Mfg. Co.

A True Story—As Told To Myself And A Witness—May 6th, 2015

The commander of the U.S. Navy carrier that picked up Apollo 7 on 10/22/1968 was also on duty, during the Missile Crisis (1962). The ship's commander said that on November 22nd, 1963, while patrolling waters off Guantanamo Base in Cuba, they received a morse code message from naval communication's headquarters that said President John F. Kennedy had been assassinated. The communication's officer asked the commander, should he read that message to the ship's crew? The message was approved and was read aloud over the P. A. system by that officer to the crew. The message was read at 11:30 a.m. – **one full hour ahead of the actual time J F K was gunned down**—in Dealey Plaza riding in a motorcade through the streets of Dallas, Texas at 12:30 p.m.

The ship's commander and communications officer received a morse code message that John F. Kennedy was killed in Dallas, Texas, one full hour prior to the actual event, or, before the assassination took place? In taking it even one step further. The ship's commander later on reported this complete factual account of the real story to the Warren Commission. The commander told me and also this witness with me that the Warren Commission was not interested in his report. A story... buried for over... 50 years.

It seemed to be clear to us both in using caution by not naming the vessel or any of the ship's crew... since it's stunning that the crime of the century still requires secrecy, and the truth about this complex conspiracy... still haunts us today. That even a commander, in the United States Navy—which employed John F. Kennedy the war hero during WWII in leading his own ships crew of PT—109; those men realized immediately... it was a high treason on the high seas... it was an orchestrated conspiracy... with several layers embedded deep inside the highest levels of Military Intelligence, planning and execution as it was announced to their very own NAVAL COMMAND CENTER, secured frequency... to their own carriers, and the ships... patrolling Cuban waters.

No doubt this book is an amalgamated journey through all of the history surrounding these events. Things came, at random times, which will account for the juxtaposed movement across the time table, where I placed the pieces of the jigsaw puzzle, or the tangible mosaic fabric, by the quilting altogether. Most of these pieces were given in two forms of order... when I got them first and later on the order that I placed them in... second. All of this quilting came from the time period of 1973, when I started up until 2015; at the end of it. The findings represent a patchwork journey, that continues on even as late as May 6th, 2015; as we continuously search for the truth in the JFK cold case.

THE ABORT TEAM

The C I A could say, (that a back up team of their own Agents was on scene in deploy) were on the ground in Dealey Plaza to foil or to subvert or to prevent any attempts of the assassination, or any sniper firing against the JFK motor cade. This was a subordinate's cover mission flown by Robert "Tosh" Plumley. It was clearly a back up, cover operation in case they were caught, or killed, in this Mission Impossible scenario. The mission was a success. Their was no need to expose or deploy this separate subordinate cover group. The C I A plans to kill J F K went off... like clockwork, without a hitch; November 22, 1963.

THE DIEM ASSASSINATION

It was easy to move heroin in a war time environment. The drug trade flourished by leaps and bounds during the Vietnam War. The massive transportation network with Air America of all the manifest support of all the goods, supplies, arms, and equipment, that was going through that war zone from 1965 through 1975 included the drug trade's heroin smuggling. Some of that cache was transported inside the coffins of some 58,000 fallen servicemen... being flown back... to the U.S. in military cargo planes. This proves concretely the CIA was deeply involved in the drug trade.

PART IV

TWENTY-ONE

Little Rojas Ninos Caballos

There was a children's playground park in Campechuela, Cuba, called Little Roja Ninos Caballos Pequenos, because of its miniature horses and many rambunctious children running and riding about and playing along the farm's very large grounds.

The man who owned it was a rich man (by Cuba's standards of wealth) who decided to build up a sixty-acre section of his precious land into a vast children's park. It was known also as a Refugio Para Ninos or, better still, in English, "A Refuge for Children." In Cuba, only certain parks that are approved are allowed to go beyond the land allocation limit.

It was run by Raul Arturo Lopez, a very fit man who was a woodcarver artist. He sculpted wooden shapes of animals made from various trees of many surrounding stalks of timber wood. He carved the wood into all kinds of shapes; horses, owls, birds, frogs... and even at times some more exotic pieces like dolphins, or a big bear, or a tall giraffe. It was a lifetime of creating this stable of sculpture, all by his very own capable hands, a literal handmade personal wilderness tale of artworks.

The children too young yet to ride the horses would play on the sculptured animals or ride in specially made saddles on the live miniature horses. Every child knew of the infamous park created by Raul Arturo Lopez. It's truly a dream park wherein peace of mind can be found.

Raul's lovely wife, Juanita Shelly was her name, was a champion rider herself who had won many a barrel race and many competitions. She was a spirited lady with auburn hair, and well respected and loved for her fabulous cooking by everybody in town. The Lopez's had a daughter named Amber who had beautiful long straight hair that was a shade lighter than her mother's, but they chose the name Amber because it meant something about the wondrous light to be found in her eyes. Amber was full of wonder and full of life.

It was Sunday afternoon and mother and son, Deborah Jean and Joey, Jr., were at the park. Absent: Joe Elliot (Dad) had stayed home because of business. He had to wait for a phone call from his attorney concerning some business that his passed on father (H.B. Goldenberg) was still earning an income from. The transfer of earnings and the current week's sales were scheduled to be reported to him in the Sunday call.

About 1988, Joe Elliot began the company ProFit. It was a modest investment of time and money that evolved into a small chain of sports stores.

It was only four stores up in the Bay Area, but it was a lucrative venture and quite popular with the locals in the neighborhood.

They had shoes, hats, jerseys, sweats, team uniforms and some sports memorabilia. But it was the shoes that were truly the specialty of the place. Back in H.B. Goldenberg's heyday, he wanted to design a specialty shoe department sports store that could meet his high standards and also match the high consumer demands for good service.

One way he did this was from something he realized during his time back in his college days when he was briefly a shoe salesman for a period of two years. He had learned from that experience that the biggest mistake shoe stores made (or could make), was leaving the customer alone while the salesman would disappear (as in other businesses), to go hunt for product in the stockroom. H.B. Goldenberg saw that as wasteful. He designed a system where the shoes came out of a tunnel tube and were called out by a stockman (a person on the floor in management). In this method, the stockman set the table for the salesman since all he or she had to do was sell the shoes, period. The stockman called it and the shoes came zooming out a tube. In this system, the salespeople need never go inside the stockroom.

H.B. Goldenberg was an innovator, much like the infamous creator of Nike, Phil Knight, who began his career in 1971 selling shoes out of his car to various track athletes throughout the humble state of Oregon. His illustrious meteoric rise to the top of the game in the shoe business is a legendary story of market savvy dominance. His products are superior sellers to the competition. Phil Knight was a trailblazer and he ultimately prided himself on being a nonconformist.

As it turns out, ProFit was a huge success. Its motto was, "We court you to the max," and it earned it a very tidy profit.

Joe Elliot had to take that call to get his updates on how the mini-franchise of those four high-output retail stores were doing. Acting now as the CEO in place of his father, Sunday was his only day with the company when his duties were required. A talented staff handled the day-to-day operations of the business, normally about two hours of conference calls with each managerial team in place kept them doing a very good job. The franchise ran smoothly under his stewardship since H.B. Goldenberg had set up such a great team of individual talent to work it. And it worked out very well.

Now back at the park of Little Rojas Ninos Caballos Pequenos, little Joe, Jr. rode the miniature ponies while Deborah went up to the picnic tables on the adjacent hillside, sitting on a wooden bench under the large umbrella tops. She lit up a cigarette to relax in the midday sun and watched her son on the pony ride.

She took a full deep breath of fresh sea-breezed air and closed her eyes and let out an exhale in a sigh of happiness. She thought out loud with, "Hmmm… this truly is a beautiful place and I'm happy with my life." Her eyes closed for a moment again as if she was in praise of the higher power, or prayer of some thankfulness, as she slowly opened them back up to fully appreciate this welcome good blessing that perhaps God had bestowed upon her, as a mother with a healthy child and some harmony. When she had refocused her gaze, she saw the figure of a man in the distance holding her son's hand and walking beside the pony. Bliss bended into fear, the instinct striking right through the relaxing interlude of the moment with a sudden blitz of danger; Joe Jr. was in the company of an unknown stranger.

The figure slowly rounded the curve of the ponies circling. She could see him now. It was Roberto Farshottia, Jr., touching her son in the distance there.

The cigarette dangled and hung on her fingers as she froze like an iceberg, the chill stiletto of fear running through her veins. She sat still, uncertain and not knowing just yet what to do, for a moment she was stunned. The cigarette burned her hand and she let out a vowel's flat steamer note of pain. "Ahh-dammit," she stammered as she threw it to the dirt.

Jumping to her feet she ran the entire distance, some one hundred forty yards down to the pony trail riding circle. She was completely out of breath when she finally reached the edge of the fenced area of the pony ride. She kept pacing through the onlooking crowd of parents and children waiting in line as she searched for Joe Junior but couldn't see him. She panicked and darted forward, out of control, through the crowd, then pleading at the gate with the attendant in the big straw hat shouting, "Where's my son? Where's my Joe, Jr.!"

She started screaming out Joey's name, tugging at the attendant's arm to get past him into the circular area as he held her back with phrases that she must calm down.

Finally, in the melee of her struggling to get past the big guy at the gate, just then Joe, Jr. appeared from behind the hotdog cart, calling back to her. They converged together finally as the crowd parted and applauded their reunification.

She picked him up, tears flowing down her cheeks. This was only the second time she had cried in front of her son. Deborah Jean clutched Joe Junior so tightly that he had to beg her not to squeeze him so hard with, "Mommy, mommy, I can't breathe!"

Deborah Jean: "O.K., Baby, Mommy's here, it's o.k. now." She continued consoling herself and hugging him. Joe Junior: "The man... the man gave me money. He told me I could have a hotdog." (She sets him down.) "Can I buy one, por favor?"

Deborah Jean: "O.k., o.k., we can get one, o.k. But we have to go home now. I have to go meet Daddy."

The heart rate she felt pounding in her soul could not return to a normal resting heart rate. However, she tried to maintain her composure as they ordered from the vendor. She kept her eyes moving all around to find Roberto Farshottia's figure in the faces of the crowd. But like she had seen a ghost, he had completely vanished and disappeared.

She quickly scooted Joe Junior back towards the parking lot, towards the safety of the car, her head bobbing back and forth on the lookout, maintaining her vigil of watch for Roberto Farshottia. When she reached the vehicle and they got inside, she locked all the doors and sped quickly up the dirt road to the roadway in a big rooster-trail cloud of dust. She wiped away the tears in her eyes.

That night, Joe Junior lay awake in bed. It was the first time in his life that he had heard yelling going on in his parents' room.

They were arguing intensely for awhile and Joe Junior was terrified of those noises of anger spilling out through the walls. Finally, as the argument reached a peak, he heard a loud crash. He pulled his covers up over his head and hid himself there in the silence of the aftermath of that big crash.

He heard footsteps on the stairs coming down and then heard the door opening followed by an engine starting up, then tires were squealing in the driveway as the vehicle sped off.

Joe Elliot had raised a chair up in the air and had thrown it across the room. Carefully now, Joe Junior climbed out of bed and took some furtive steps toward his parents' room. He normally made this walk on his way to see his mother in the morning but this time he wasn't sure who would be left behind, if anybody at all.

This kind of tension from husband and wife or a mother and father can only transfer one message to a child of any age.. It's instability of an uneven unbalanced home and it results in a child's fear that they may be in the process of losing either a mom or a dad after the outcome. You place fear in your child that something's wrong and if it persists, it never gets any easier taking the abused side's speeches that it will be all right.

Bravely, Joe Junior entered his parents' room and he saw his mother at the foot of their bed. She sat with her face cupped in her hands. She was crying and she was shaking with her own fears with regard to the outcome of the past day's events. It was hard for Joe Junior to see his mother in pain and he crawled to the end of the bed and put his hands to hers, trying to console her with his presence as he called, "Momma, Momma."

She turned her seating quarters to him guarding her face in shame as he tried to tap her on the back of her shoulders to see what the trouble was. "Please go back to sleep now," she said the muffled words through clasped hands. "Mommy can't talk right now, so go back to bed because it's O.K. now." Then as she spoke the last words, he saw she had a black eye and his father had struck her. Tenderly Joe Junior said, "Momma, I'm afraid." And finally she released her covered face, rushing to embrace him with open arms as she answered with, "Me, too."

In the honest moment the two bonded in their heartfelt embrace as his mother made her consoling promise. "We're going to be O.K." She picked up Joe Junior and they walked into the kitchen. Mom knew what Joe Junior needed was some chocolate milk to lighten up his fears. They had pretty much a routine that when she fixed him up with a cup of that, then he in turn would scrub out the coffee pot and fix her a cup of coffee. This was a favorite ritual, a favor that she did for him and that he did for her. It always brought a smile to Deborah Jean.

He scrubbed the coffee pot with strong hands, the lineage of his grandfather's baby crib-making business. He scrubbed diligently at all of the build-up of stuff on the inside of the old coffee-making pot. He rubbed and scrubbed it until it was spotless clean.

He made her a fresh cup of coffee with the sparkling clean coffee pot while he sipped the second cup of chocolate milk that she made for him. And she told him how much better it tasted, so much better and fresher than anything before because of his handy work. This was Joe Junior's favorite bonding moment that he shared with his mother. The beauty of it was that they needed each other and knew what to do to bring the admiration of respect and love of a mutual smile. The fresh coffee and chocolate milk–sunrise special, it was a very real mother and son connection, if you will.

In the bedroom later on that night, alone, Joe Junior had drawn up a sketch of a safe place like his grandfather Beachcomber had always told him would be the safe place to hide out. He would sleep on it before he decided what to do next. It was the first time his dad had struck his mother and it was unclear to him as to what was the reason.

The arguments didn't give him the whole picture since he couldn't hear it all, so it remained a mystery. Anyway, it was not yet time to abandon the ship.

But what was really puzzling was both times his mother was stalked by Farshottia, Joe Junior was there. It was those two times he witnessed her crying those tears and he could not help himself but to feel it: some partial responsibility in his mother's misery. It was the heart of a child that heals things. But the hurt he witnessed made him yield to the questions he had about these incidents. WAS HE A PART OF HER PAIN?

To a child's eyes… it was a shared shame of damage and breakdown.

The next day Joe Junior went to school as usual. His mother made breakfast and they sat together quietly. When it was time, she handed him his backpack with a hug and a kiss. He stopped as he turned back from the doorway.

Joe Junior kissed his hand and placed it on his mother's healing shiner of an eye. "This is to make Mommy better." She embraced him again and told her son how much she loved him. And he headed off for school.

In the afternoon, Joe Elliot picked his son up from school. Monday was his normal day to pick up Joey, both parents had worked it out. Monday, Tuesday and Wednesday–Dad, and then for Thursday, Friday and Saturday outings; Mom's turn to drive. It was their way of splitting up the duties of parenting and each sharing quality time with Joe Junior.

This evening truly was markedly different since here it was already nightfall and his mother wasn't home yet. There was an unusual silence present at the dinner table tonight. His mother was always home before dark.

In awkward silence, Dad made pork chops with mashed potatoes and gravy. It was ironically her favorite dish of those he could make. Joe Elliot was trying to make up for his domestic violence episode… and things looked bleak. Joe Elliot finished the somber dinner as Joe Junior dutifully looked at his dad with drowning sorrow.

The more time that passed with Debbie gone, the worse it felt for him, and it was plainly expressed on his face. Joe Elliot was a bit sullen because he hadn't quite found the words yet for assurance that everything was going to be all right.

At this point he, too, was uncertain just about anything.

He quietly tucked Joe Junior into bed for the night. He turned out the light and he went to sleep.

Joe Elliot made the same diner the next night. He picked up Joe Junior (not knowing if Deborah would do it) and they went home. At the dinner table the next night, alone again, the both of them sat together amid the silence without Mom sitting at her place at the table. This time, Joe Elliot tried to come up with the words to say to his son but he was interrupted by Joe Junior who beat him to the punch with these words of his own.

JOE JUNIOR: Is Mommy coming back? She never stays out after dark.

JOE ELLIOT: Mommy is coming back. We're going to be O.K.

I want you to know your Mom really loves you.

JOE JUNIOR: I know she loves me.

JOE ELLIOT: She just needed some time alone. I'm sure she'll be letting us know that she's doing O.K. as soon as she can.

Joe Junior leaves the table to get ready for bedtime. He walks with his head down, looking at the floor.

JOE ELLIOT: Joey Junior, I love you, son.

He turned from the doorway to make a flat response.

JOE JUNIOR: Good night, Dad.

FADE OUT

———

All day long, Joe Elliot filled out the forms for a missing persons report. The desk sergeant was named Enrique Cortez, a very tanned and toned man with very large thick-framed glasses. He spoke in a monotone voice, flattened by the infernal toil of his task.. A man can only absorb so much duty before the years wear you down to some mechanical activated drone-like machine; you become the robot's voice that pulls you through your daily routine. A world-weary Enrique had the pipes of an old engine, which just gave him the signature of heavy mileage wear in his vocal character.

It took forever to fill out all of the paperwork and Joe Elliot stood up after finishing the marathon stack as Sgt. Enrique Cortez gruffly braced him with, "Have a seat, Mr. Elliot and Chief Inspector Raul Alcantorropez will be with you." Begrudgingly, Joe Elliot returned to his seat. A half hour more of waiting left Joe Elliot pressed for time and he earnestly tried to get through to the desk sergeant with, "Sergeant Cortez, four hours have gone by. Can you phone Inspector Alcantorropez because I will have to pick my son up from school."

The reply was still cold when he said flatly, "If you'll wait a moment, sir, and please return to your seat again, I'll take care of it, sir."

He picked up the telephone calling the Chief Inspector's office. Joe Elliot looked on, sweat visible on his clenched brows. When Sgt. Cortez hung up the line he said, "Inspector Alcantorropez will see you now."

Joe Elliot went inside the inspector's modest office. It was a hodgepodge of stacks and stacks of paperwork. The chief inspector stood up, still buried behind the mounting piles of paperwork stacks that littered his desktop like a forest.

Raul Alcantorropez: As you can see, we are a very, very busy office when it comes to missing persons.

Joe Elliot: I've waited for over four hours in this sweatbox, chief Inspector Alcantorropez. Can you help me find my wife?

The chief lit up his pipe. He walked over to the single lone glass window and with his back to Joe Elliot, he said,

Raul Alcantorropez: Do you realize how many missing persons reports I get a week, Mr. Elliot? (circling his desk now) This stack is from two weeks ago and this stack is from last week. And over here, this stack is this week's. And this is where I file your wife's report, Mr. Elliot.

Joe Elliot: You mean that's all you're going to do is file it? What about putting out an APB?

Raul Alcantorropez: We do not process all points, Mr. Elliot. Your wife is missing.

Joe Elliot: I want you to put out an APB.

Raul Alcantorropez: Your wife has not been involved in a crime, Mr. Elliot.

Joe Elliot: Please, Chief Inspector Alcantorropez, I need your help on this case, sir.

Raul Alcantorropez: We're doing all we can do.

Joe Elliot: I spent all day here in this sweatbox to find out what it means when you say, we're—doing all—all we can do.

Joe Elliot gets up from his chair to leave the office as Chief Inspector Raul Alcantorropez contends with his dissatisfaction and proceeds.

Raul Alcantorropez: This is Cuba, Mr. Elliot, and things work much differently here than in the United States. We let the people alone to go wherever they want on this very little island, which, as it turns out, in its own way, is a very big little island. Especially for those who choose to make their getaway when they don't want to be found, understood?

Joe Elliot: I understand, Inspector, that I wasted an afternoon, which I could have spent more wisely by looking for her myself. I still have a son to go pick up and I'll just have to find my wife on my own.

He walked out of the police station biting his lip with indignation and in bitterness about the damned hot dragging afternoon that left him fully spent of that day's worth of energy... being forced to sit through such a lengthy ordeal in a foreign country's limited, under-funded, helpless division of a police force that was so lacking in both manpower and capability.

It was another silent drive with Joe Elliot and Joe Junior all the way home after school, neither said a single word towards each other. They glanced at one another intermittently but kept quiet since both had the feeling that things had gone from bad to worse with their facial expressions of despair showing volumes in silent communication.

That night at the dinner table, very little was said as father and son kept their eyes from each other until finally,

JOE JUNIOR: Dad, are you O.K.? Is Mom going to be all right?

JOE ELLIOT: Don't worry, my son, trust in me. I'm going to find your mom myself. We are going to be okay. O.K.?

JOE JUNIOR: Okay we are going to be O.K.

Joe Junior excused himself from the table to go to bed. Joe Elliot dropped his fork and it rattled off his plate. He quickly arose from the table to gather his son's attention by spinning him around to face him.

JOE ELLIOT: Wait a minute, hold up just a second.

(Gripping his son by the shoulders, on one knee)

JOE JUNIOR: I just want to rest now.

JOE ELLIOT: I want you to believe in me, Son, when I tell you I'm going to find your mom, O.K.? I give you my word.

It's a promise, son. A promise, O.K.?

A father trying to do his best in earnest reaching out with the correct resolute energy but his son could only just stare back into his eyes of hope. He hugged his son tightly before he let go and he went off to bed.

TWENTY-TWO

Beachcomber's Grandson's Journey

Drawing a picture of a future paradise

During the night Joe Junior arrived at his own private decision, a day of reckoning for his heart.

His father, Joe Elliot, had tried to reassure him that he would track down his mother. It was going to be difficult, he gathered, since he had seen the fearful tears on his mother's cheeks when the bad man came upon them the first time at the market, and then the second time—the day at Little Rojas Ninos Park.

In his mind his emotions were overpowering him. He remembered how each time was worse for his mother's nerves on those two encounters. So little Joe Junior knew that she was in some kind of deep, deep trouble, and now he feared he would never see his mother again. He felt guilty that he couldn't tell his father about the man who was after Mom.

It was an Oedipal complex in the formative years. He loved his mother deeply and he felt that if he told his dad about the man who was after his mother that he would be punished for telling and that it was his own fault "not telling." And that that was the reason she was gone now.

He was still a boy. He loved his mother. He was in a competition to keep her in his heart. He was too afraid to tell on his mother's business. He was in love with her in his child's mind. In the innocence of his heart, he dared not to sully the swan.

That night he packed some clothes into his pillowcase and he put on a thick layer shirt. He left a hand-sketched picture on his bed and put his trusty pocketknife his grandfather had given him, along with a small photograph of his mother, into his shirt's snap-down pocket with a western cowboy design in the stitching of its sleeves and collar. He would go on the trail himself to find a way to think through the difficulties he was having with his father. He turned towards the window after looking around the walls of his room and then just crawled out over the wooden windowsill to run away.

He would go to a place his older and wiser grandfather, the Beachcomber, had told him of… that would be a safe haven in which to hide.

He couldn't deal with his father maybe finding out that all of this was somehow maybe his fault. But it was also evident he was closer to Mom and without her in the house, things were out of balance inside the home. There was extra tension and Joe Junior, although he adjusted to it over the days she was gone, felt more awkward as time went on.

He knew that he could go off alone like his grandfather had preached he could (to go to a safe place) and things would settle down for him in his mind. He knew that this was what he must do to make things right. To go away with his secrets just like his grandfather Beachcomber had done.

That following morning, Joe Elliot went to his son's room. He saw the freshly drawn pencil sketched portrait of a sandy beach and he noticed a picture had been removed from the small frame on the nightstand next to his bed. The picture was of a young Deborah Jean before she was twenty. It was his son's favorite photo of his mother because he liked the fact that in her youth she was more like a sister to him (in this picture) than really a mom and the bond between them they shared was a very, very strong one of love.

He felt the contours of the bed, which was fully made up and had not been slept in at all. It was at that moment Joe Elliot broke down. He went to his knees immediately and swirled himself up inside the blanket left on the floor. He just laid there, curled into a ball of flesh. He cried there for awhile because the whole thing now was too much for him.

Visions of the boating accident flashed back, along with his father H.B. Goldenberg's shouting voice, telling him to get up off the mat and get going to do something about it. In this vision of his father, H.B. Goldenberg's voice boomed—that he was going to kick his sorry ass if he didn't get up right this second—right now. "Go on, get up," the voice echoed and he snapped out of his collapsed breakdown and became the man of action his father scathingly implored him to become that instant. He snapped himself out of it and got up with a determined H.B. Goldenberg swagger and marched out of the house to his car.

He drove at high speeds, bolting forward down the track like a locomotive train on a mission, to make a deadline at the end of the line. He drove out to the spot of the beach where he was saved so many separate times in his life.

It was like going back to the well of redemption. This stretch of beach was like a fountain of youth. A man could easily spend some nine lives here and like a holy cat somehow survive all the foreshadowing grim reaper's raptures in his soul. But thanks to the Beachcomber Santiago Serna Dominguez who was ever faithful to minding his post, this was truly a lucky spot for living while attempting a premature departure.

The Beachcomber met with Joe Elliot on the sacred sand. The spot by now could be deemed a holy land with the bounty in quantity of how many times a soul was saved in the little patch of paradise here on Earth. The words exchanged between the two men were like a son of god, who pleads with the priest to perform a spiritual miracle. In this case a miracle that might require a holy man to chant verse to a variable legend like a type of demonic exorcism. It was less than a minute before the Beachcomber picked up his knapsack and they walked back to Joe's car and drove straight back to the house as quickly as it was possible to travel in and out of traffic on the road home.

Back at the house, Joe Elliot led the way into the bedroom and Beachcomber picked up the drawing left on the bed by his grandson, Joe Junior, and he began to smile.

BEACHCOMBER: I know from this drawing that he is going to a safe place.

JOE ELLIOT: We go to him then, I mean now if you really know where he is.

Joe Elliot grabbed the sketch from the Beachcomber as both men gripped and pulled at it. Finally, Beachcomber's hands are stronger as he holds it tight, pulling it away from Joe Elliot's grasp with,

BEACHCOMBER: No! We must find Deborah…

Then we go to Joe Junior He will be fine because I taught him well how to survive on that beach. He will be O.K.

JOE ELLIOT: But are you sure he will be O.K.?

BEACHCOMBER: Let's get Deborah back first. C'mon, I know what we can do. I'll call in a favor from an old friend.

JOE ELLIOT: But what if she's already dead?

BEACHCOMBER: No one would ever kill Deborah. She's the spark of this island.

JOE ELLIOT: So where do we go, then?

BEACHCOMBER: We go to see a career soldier.

June Cortez was ready to do whatever Beachcomber asked him. He drove to the supply depot, and he waited at the gatepost until Santiago-Beachcomber drove up to the site with Joe Elliot guiding the wheel, as Beachcomber rode shotgun. They stopped outside the post and Santiago and June Cortez went for a short walk, talking. After their walk, the Beachcomber and June Cortez returned to the area.

June Cortez opened up the trunk of his car. Santiago-Beachcomber removed an army-green duffle bag, fully packed tight with gear.

Beachcomber transferred the duffle bag to Joe Elliot's car and placed it in the trunk as he slammed it shut with June Cortez questioning the size of the arsenal of firepower packed inside the duffle.

JUNE CORTEZ: Are you going to need all that?

BEACHCOMBER: I hope not. It's been a long time since I've used one of them. But you can deliver the scooters, too?

JUNE CORTEZ: It's like riding a bicycle, amigo. The scooters I get after tomorrow and I deliver them myself wherever you need them.

BEACHCOMBER: Can your contact at Papas Beers be trusted not to go to the Don? If he talks, I'll need more than this arsenal of fireworks.

He taps the trunk lid twice with a smile.

JUNE CORTEZ: The guy on the inside has been there for 14 years. He knows how to be not known for what he is.

BEACHCOMBER: You can count on him then to remain silent.

JUNE CORTEZ: Mi familia, Santiago… si It's wise to know the places where everybody takes their drinks in town and where a man can be a man and the girls keep silent—when a man goes out to be a Cuban. (he clutches Beachcomber on both of his shoulder-blades)

He's my brother and he will be there for life; so relax amigo, o.k.? I will have him meet you at the church tomorrow. And he will tell me where you want your scooters.

BEACHCOMBER: Thank you, my friend, for everything.

June Cortez left them, driving east back towards the army base.. Joe Elliot and Beachcomber drove west, back towards the Beachcomber's jungle spot. It was decided between them that it would be best to sleep under the stars and not take a chance staying in a hotel or being caught with weapons on the drive towards the town where the church was located. During the drive the Beachcomber decided to tell Joe Elliot about the first time he went back to Papas Beers about five years ago to find Deborah Jean a long time ago. Joe Elliot listened intently as Santiago Beachcomber related his unique story.

BEACHCOMBER: I came inside the bar and it is after a moment of silence where I think they were stunned by my sight, like seeing a ghost. The people gave me an ovation. It was an incredible feeling, like being a hero to the people of Cuba, for saving so-many American lives… after having been gone away for so long.

The Beachcomber stopped for a moment to fully recognize the importance of that event. It was now that it dawned on him that it was the highest kind of honor that the hardworking common-man (as he once was), and that all of Cuba, from Cuba's working class and the regular people which was the ultimate celebration of pride; in seeing in their eyes that <u>he was their hero</u>. But he knew that tragically he had been less than heroic when it came to the reconciliation with the young daughter he had left behind for several years.

That was his pain (for giving her up), and for which he felt he could not fully live up <u>to that ideal of a real hero</u> or to enjoy the emotion of that moment. He realized mid-story, mid-stream in his retelling of this saga,, just how lucky a man he was... He picked up where he left off …

BEACHCOMBER: After the ovation, before I left the bar that night, a man came up to me. I was just about to walk out the door and I had Deborah Jean behind me. (He stops, lights up a smoke) I notice the guy is still following us and trying to get my attention, see… but, I cannot hear him when he speaks… (blows a long chain of smoke) I extend my hand because I assumed he had seen me on T.V. and wanted to shake hands with me after I had rescued the American football team. He shook my hand tightly and gave me a somber, deadly stare as if he was about to take my life into his very own hands, somehow. He just stared into my soul and I felt it right down to my balls.

It was like I felt it that he looked the life right out of me.

The Beachcomber stopped at that point a second before he began with the rest of the story.

BEACHCOMBER: I finally got him to let go of my hand. But he left something in my palm–a folded piece of paper. So when Deborah and I got back to the beach, I read the note he passed to me.

I'll never forget it in dawn's light. THIS IS WHAT THE NOTE READ: You may be a hero–and you may even be a lucky man, but the girl you're with, my friend, you should know — she's with Roberto Farshottia, Jr., the Owner's son. So, if I were you, I'd get far away from her. You better forget her man. You better turn and run before you could wind up just like me. I was with her, you see, for just one time. That crazy Mafia Don's son–he took out his knife and I lost my tongue.

The Beachcomber was very calm, but he could feel his words reverberating echoes into Joe Elliot's head, for he felt the final piece of the mystery.

BEACHCOMBER: So, there's no mystery now, Joe. Roberto Farshottia's kidnapped her. I'm betting she's still alive because he could never let go.

Upon arrival at the beach, both men exit the car. BEACHCOMBER: It's only a matter of time, 24 hours. The connection will know where they have taken her because I can assure you...

As they put down their bedrolls on the sand, he continued. BEACHCOMBER: When the mob is involved, everybody goes out the same way.

Wrapping himself within the folds of his blanket...

BEACHCOMBER: You get taken to a house. It's just that nobody ever says a word.

Essentially obvious in this testimony was the thin line of a potential minefield of guilt that Santiago was feeling inside for the abandonment of leaving Deborah Jean alone for those ten long years. Joe Elliot kept quiet all along, for he knew any questions he may have had would be better asked at another time.. With the night bird's callings and cricket beats in the background under the stars, they rested for the upcoming task of facing tomorrow.

TWENTY-THREE

For Whom The Bell Tolls

The next nightfall, the church rose up into the moonlit sky like the bell tower of the hunchback. It was 75 feet high, an old mission-style icon that housed a large bell and a staircase. It was an Italian's architectural work… It turns out that it was built before the Castro revolution during Cuba's heyday.

The priest of this parish, Juan Paul Rodriguez, was blessed with a very wealthy brother, John Paul Rodriguez, who happened to build churches in France, Italy and Spain. It was a birthday present to his older brother to construct the most elaborately designed church for him. The vestibule was a very highly cut doorway and the pews sunk lower as you reached the pulpit. It was ahead of its time and truly a remarkable landmark of architectural prestige.

John Paul studied architectural design on a cultural exchange program prior to the Castro regime and with his work with the French, the Italians, and in Spain, he became the most sought-after designer in those countries for some time. And once Castro took over in 1960, he never went back to see his older brother, Juan Paul Rodriguez. His parents eventually over time forgave the world-traveling, wayward son when they realized that the wealth he had accumulated abroad could never be achieved in a country like Cuba. He sent his parents pictures of the wonderful churches he was building all over the world and he told them that this was God's work that he was doing. Seeing the masterful buildings of majestic beauty, the parents forgave their son, John Paul, for dropping out of the priesthood and becoming the building chapel designer for Christ. The extra money he made and sent back to his parents turned into vast amounts of money over the years… and this kind of travel-job money, the parents easily adapted to. The two brothers were unique; Juan Paul, the podium priest, and John Paul, the creative pulpit-making-priest.

This church was the ultimate gift from John Paul to Juan Paul, both the financing, and the designing, of this glorious parish for his beloved brother.

———

The same stained glass window his wife once sat next to seven pews up to the left was just where he left it a decade ago. It brought a flashback to him as he went to the exact pew where she sat, and he gently placed his hands forward and touched the wooden seat rows of the pew. He leaned farther down and placed his temple to rest upon his wrists and clasped his hands together as he lost himself in a deep prayer in Spanish, which translated in English, read as follows:

BEACHCOMBER: I have been away, my father, for ten years. I felt betrayed by my faith when my wife was taken away from me. I blamed

Christ because I thought it was a mistake, and I chose to go away for a long time.

And now I must pray that whatever comes in the aftermath… tonight, I know I will soon join her. But I ask of you only this:

You take me as you've taken her but let me unite my Debbie Jean with her son and may they live in peace.

I ask you Father before I come to you–let me return them… back home… together. May God have mercy on my soul. For once I had forgotten my faith in the True Power you do possess.

As he folded himself in the depths of this heartfelt prayer, he heard the door close behind him, and then several footsteps until a man sat in the pew just two rows ahead of Santiago. Beachcomber Santiago sat upright and began to compose himself, as he dignified himself by wiping away his tears with his shirtsleeves.

He didn't pay attention to the man in front of him. He sat quietly and sighed or breathed some air a moment. He took a few more breaths to regain control of his range of those life-affecting, heartfelt emotions he released.

The man was built like a boxer, sort of tortoise-like in the way that his big head looked like it came out of his shoulders instead of the stem of his neck. He was an old fighter who had too many rounds with too many punchers. He had earned Juan Carlo Farshottia's trust, making him truckloads of cash when he'd bet on him in his heyday. But these days he was the humble head bartender at the Club Papas Beers who went by the name of Jo Jo Torrez. He had grown tired and sold out when the deal of a partnership that Juan Carlo Farshottia promised to him in the last seven years never materialized. Here he was at church making back what he'd lost <u>selling out</u> the boss who had betrayed him with a business deal of a promised partnership at Papas Beers. His deep whispering-baritone voice carried with some echo in the emptiness of the church.

JO JO TORREZ: You must go to Cienfuegos and take the road north to Palmira where the abandoned Esso factory and the old pumping station is. Your daughter is being held by Roberto Farshottia and two other men.

He plans to take her to Venezuela in seven days.

They are planning to make a hit on one of the banks in Biamo Oriente.

BEACHCOMBER: So, Roberto Farshottia intends to branch out on his own, without his father's blessing.

JO JO TORREZ: It turns out that Juan Carlo doesn't trust his son.

He thinks he's too hot to handle. Would you go into business with a firecracker like that?

Anyway, this job will net him enough money to start his own cartel in Caracas, Venezuela.

Santiago, watch your back with this kid.

BEACHCOMBER: Hey, amigo, you watch yours. I only have one true mission in life... to help out my daughter... that's all. You look after yourself, thank you.

Santiago/Beachcomber and Joe Elliot drove to Cienfuegos and traveled the road north to Palmira where they set up camp some 300 yards away from the abandoned Esso factory. They were far enough away not to arouse the men stationed at the pumping station facility.

Using the explosives and equipment, Beachcomber directed Joe Elliot on the demolition work setup. It took two and a half days of preparation before Santiago felt ready. He had to calm the nerves of his partner who kept arching with oscillation in intensity and adrenaline as the days lingered on, closer to the deadline.

The Beachcomber went over their plan by drawing it with a stick in the dirt several times. He explained very carefully that the element of surprise would put the advantage in their favor. But if the rigging of explosives at two critical points missed, it would be a heavy gun battle and rather than face that battle, he told him to launch every grenade in his bag until they could take on the fight and it was down to manageable numbers. This all meant that those few extra days were necessary... and they gave the old Beachcomber some confidence in the rescue plan. He knew that the rigging of explosives was the key to his plan's success since he really didn't know about how well his partner Joe Elliot could handle himself in an all out gun battle. The sooner they gained control of Roberto Farshottia, Jr., the sooner their struggle would be over with what was ultimately going to be the hardest part of their plan.

The day would have to be coming soon... they slept during the day and kept their vigil watch at night. It was day number four in the wait so to himself he felt it... and in keeping it to himself... he allowed his son-in-law to get some needed rest.

He figured tonight had to be the night that Farshottia's band would finally take down the bank.

TWENTY-FOUR

The Bank Robbery Went As Planned

It was a team of a half dozen men with Roberto Farshottia masterminding the carefully plotted heist. They were able to cripple and disable a power grid on the block by detonating a charge on the corner nearby where the bank was fed power. The transformer was hit with double stacked packs of C-4 which, when it exploded, caused a surge in the grid which shut down automatically.

The entire street corner and surrounding three blocks of the power grid went pitch black. Using a pickup truck and two cars, the men sped toward the bank entrance, which had a series of about eight steps to get to the first floor level. The men pulled down their night vision goggles and drove up to the bank's doorway in rapid, fast succession as the pickup truck bounced up the steps and crashed through the thick-glassed double doors. The four men in the two cars leaped out with automatic weapons and barnstormed toward the bank's doorway.

Each man pulled a backpack out of the pickup tailgate carrying extra ammo and explosives and funneled-in, in cover-two formations, working their way towards the vault. The men wore miner's helmets with handheld flashlights and extra lights on their dome helmets and in pitch darkness they could very well see everything with night vision, but the combination multiplying both of them together confused the armed guards who had no idea what numbers of a team force they might be facing. The bank's lone two guards on duty just quickly put their hands up to surrender to the heavily armed assault team, which overwhelmed them. In fear for their lives, they immediately complied with the instructions, quickly lying face down with hands up and outstretched in front.

A thick and very heavy blanket was extracted out of one of the backpacks and covered them up as duct tape was used on each guard individually to tie their hands behind their backs.

A timer was set for a ten second delay as the six men ducked behind the block wall of the bank tellers' windows, crouching very low. Some eight seconds afterwards, the vault's door was blown open along with a huge hole they put inside the roof of the structure. The building reverberated for a few seconds as the mining helmets were thrown off their domes and the men raided the vault, filling three separate huge duffle bags with a cache of cash worth over 8 million dollars.

They were out of the bank in under five minutes. They ran past the pickup truck dropping off some explosives set to a timer that was left inside the bed of the truck. A police siren's howl was whirring in the distance approaching quickly but the six-man hit squad had already sped off into the darkness with two men in the lead car and four men in the trailing car. Two sacks of the duffle bags were in the car with Roberto Farshottia and the trailing vehicle had one duffle bag stuffed in the trunk of their vehicle. The getaway route was unobstructed at this late hour, and the police were too far away off yet (as it appeared), to either take up the chase, or pick up a trail.

The men in both lead car and trailing car began to celebrate their fortune of overall luck that they were sure they had going for them at this juncture.

The pickup device exploded back at the bank, just as the police contingent converged upon the scene.

It launched the truck twenty feet high up into the air. It blew off the entire front face of the bank building. It's a wonder, with the hole in the roof at the vault and with the face of the building obliterated, the thing was still left standing on its own foundation. It was totally blown apart.

The flames by now were blazing way up into the blackness of the sky as fireballs splashed down and flashed like a hailstorm everywhere in the street.

In the police contingent, six patrol cars responded to the scene of the robbery. Three units stopped at the bank while the wild fires continued blazing away. Suddenly, fire truck sirens were heard in the background from far away, approaching the scene. The other three cars, with squealing tires and sirens, chased the two getaway cars.

The officers began crowd control as townspeople gathered and flooded out onto the streets. Two officers went inside the bank to check if any survivors were left alive inside the structure. Fire rescue arrived and began fighting to contain the blaze from reaching further to ignite any of the other existing buildings. Soon hoses were pumped with H2O and pressure and the scene looked like an outdoor block party bonfire with water jets from a dozen different fire hoses trying to douse the uncontrollable flames of the mammoth spectacular blaze... as some multitude of hundreds of stunned Cuban citizens looked upon the extraordinary event.

The three cars of the police contingent gained a fix on the two suspect vehicles as their continued chase reached speeds of up to 90 mph on the roads leading towards Cienfuegos and the Esso factory.

The cars navigated an escape route that took them along a dirt road, which led up to the pumping station and the oil fields.

The chase was kicking up rooster tails of dust some 35 feet in the air. The trailing vehicles did all they could do to cope with their own visibility factors by turning on their wiper blades to wave off the pounding earthen dirt.

Coming towards the incline of Pico San Juan, which was a high mountain pass, the two escape vehicles powered up the hill, reaching a bend in the roadway where they stopped.

A man exited the car there and took out a belt-sheathed machete and struck a rope. The rope, tied off to a tanker trailer, released the tanker, which began descending, rolling backwards down the hill towards the oncoming three police vehicles.

In darkness the tanker trailer overturned and wedged itself across the roadway blocking the only passageway towards Pico San Juan's peak. There was no other way a regular type vehicle could make it up that mountain pass.

Removing a flare gun from his pack, Roberto Farshottia took aim for the overturned tanker's rear quarters' decking and fired off a flare shot. The tanker's rear end release port was leaking fuel since the valve cap had been unscrewed before the rope was machete cut.

The flare shot blazed down the mountainside and hit the quarter panel of the tanker trailer, which exploded in an incendiary fireball blazing flashpoint as the mushroom cloud lit up the mountainside of Pico San Juan.

Roberto Farshottia's crew raised up their fists in celebration of their perfect strike, after shooting off a few rounds into the fireballs of the night sky, casting taunting aspersions at the fate of their crippled foes.

Those three police vehicles were completely stymied by the impossible gauntlet of the fire and obliterated frame and molten metal barrier of the overturned tanker trailer.

Farshottia's crew began laughing at their own luck and the misfortunes of the police pursuit contingent. They returned to their cars and continued on up Pico San Juan towards the Esso oil plant factory rendezvous site. The police could only radio back to their headquarters that they were disabled at Pico San Juan. There was nothing they could do to continue the pursuit of the robbery suspect vehicles without some four-wheel drive SUVs or Jeeps to traverse the steep terrain on the slopes' incline. It would take almost an hour before backup vehicles could pick up the pursuit.

It looked like they got away with it.

From Beachcomber Santiago and Joe Elliot's vantage point –

In the distance the sounds of high-speed cars are heard before their headlights were seen bouncing off the trees traversing the uneven roadway to Palmira, the cars rapidly approaching the pumping station. The men holding Deborah Jean emerge from the second floor upper deck and with night vision binoculars begin to celebrate prematurely before the arrival of the successful bank heist team.

Beachcomber and Joe Elliot quickly uncovered the branches of camouflage and shrubbery, which unveiled the motorcycles. They positioned themselves at the top of the hill. Beachcomber tells Joe Elliot, who was about to hit the kick starter: "No, not yet... let them get closer."

As the Farshottia tandem came rushing and rumbling up the dirt road, until they were about eighty yards away from the ambush point, he silently ticked a countdown as his lips moved in his mental clicks for timing factors. "O.K., Joe, we go now," Beachcomber growled.

In the cover of darkness without lights on motorcycles, like Ninjas they rumble up from the darkness towards the lead car with the four men out front. Joe Elliot uses his baseball skills to pitch a grenade through the side window, which exploded inside the car, killing all four men inside, as the vehicle flipped and rolled over several times in a flaming crash.

The cycle team of Beachcomber and Joe Elliot made a figure eight formation and turned back towards the remaining oncoming Farshottia vehicle, which was behind, trailing its way up to the abandoned oil factory.

Since enough space and darkness was between them, at first the Farshottia team thought that the car ahead had an accident on its own. In the darkness, nobody could see the motorcycles that overtook them.

The Farshottia trailing vehicles heard the motorcycles while Beachcomber Santiago and Joe Elliot surrounded them going pincher-style on either side of the car. Using an Uzi, Beachcomber shot at the driver's side of the car and Roberto Farshottia raised up his torso out of the passenger's side returning fire. In a hail of automatic weapon fire, the driver was hit and the Farshottia vehicle ran along the shoulder of the dirt road.

Roberto Farshottia took over the driver's seat by kicking the body out of the car and careening back on the roadway, speeding into the perimeter of the Esso refinery. He made it to the compound and a wild gun battle erupted. The Beachcomber/Joe Elliot motorcycle team was shooting it out with a group of Farshottia's guards.

As the bullets continued flying overhead with his guards out front, Farshottia retreated to the upper gantry of the building to get to Deborah Jean. From inside, he grabs her by the arm and retreats to the stairwell to climb up to the upper overhead plank catwalk of the connecting tower tanks.

During the blaze of bullets, Juan Carlo Farshottia, Sr.'s men appear out of the darkness and they surround the compound preparing to converge on the unsuspecting participants in the rattling bullets of the gunfight going on at the Esso factory.

Roberto Farshottia steps forward along the overhead planks of the gantry some forty-five feet overhead just as the lights are turned on at the station by Juan Carlo Farshottia, Sr.'s men, who have now overtaken the entire field of battle by outnumbering the four remaining combatants. Surrounded, they surrender with their hands up.

Then Roberto falls through a rusted-out girder grid and plummets forty feet into a storage shack of tin rolled roofing material. He shatters his hip and collarbone and three ribs before his body rolls off the edge of the roof and he thuds down on top of the empty barrels of oil drums.

The wild gun battle is over.

Roberto Farshottia lay motionless across the tops of the emptied 150-gallon drums of oil containers. He would live because he was too stubborn a fighter just to die. However, as the helicopter hovered overhead, a distraught father onboard was being radio signaled to a landing coordinate.

Roberto Farshottia was lucky he was unconscious, since his father was about to discover the indignity of the conspiracy to steal from the bank connected to the cartel that he was an integral part of. It was close to $8 million that the bank was holding (on its way to distribution and laundering) before the strategic moment the heist went down.

These other dons whose stake was stolen would surely annihilate the perpetrators in clockwork-style typical mob payback, elimination… meeting with a swiftly dealt… immediate merciless and mercenary vengeance.

As the chopper landed and Juan Carlo and the armed bodyguards approached, guns tautly pointed waist level on every surrounding man's vision of a 360-degree readiness circling the leader.

Osrah/Debbie Jean descended the metal caged ladder and rushed into the embrace of the arms of the ballplayer Joe Elliot. Beachcomber Santiago stood nearby as the helicopter blades began to spin down to the slow steady sickle slices of a worthy gardener. Beachcomber looked at the blackened earth's dirt wedged between his bare toes, which were oily with the dirt mulch of liquefied petroleum, and watched the reunion. He made a prayer since he was sure that soon he would be buried right there and become part of the earth's crust, right here at this oil field, an inkwell of slick and slippery sludge, at this black hole of abandon.

In his mind he visited his own eminent foreboding demise for every man knows his own life's luck limits when he reaches that point. It was his time of Cabo Blanco.

All he could do was rejoice in the celebration and smile as he looked upon his daughter Debbie Jean and Joe Elliot's passionate lovingly heartfelt reunion. They would be gone soon, but alas, it was… to be forgiven… and to be in love, and in your wife's loving arms. He thought about the beauty of that in the moment there and he mumbled unto to himself in his mind's recognition of registering it.

If there was a good way to die, to go right now to heaven, this would truly be it.

Suddenly, a thundering storm of hoofs drummed across the tar pit as a large contingent of riders on horseback galloped onto the grounds of the old abandoned Esso refinery. There are eight men with eight horses plus two burros. They are Juan Carlos' backup plan to circumvent any police barricades. The group halted and remained mounted as their leader Edarto signaled to Juan Carlo Farshottia by waving his semi automatic Uzi over his head, signaling to him twice, that reception was clear and ready.

The bodyguards eased up their tensions once the group was waved off by Farshottia, who had been smart enough to not tell all of his team the full details of his plans. None of them knew of Edarto coming with horses and this team of extra manpower.

Now his bodyguards in the cover circle put their weapons to their shoulders, pointing upwards, as they marched with him in a unison of cadence, stepping closer until he could see for certain that it was who it was.

And it was. With his own eyes he could see that it was his own son Roberto's body that was sprawled across the barrel tops of several oil drums.

Juan Carlo signaled the two men on his right. Each grabbed his arms and legs and laid him out for display on the ground. One bodyguard quickly removed his black leather jacket and propped up his head to rest upon it. Juan Carlo knelt down to look at his son. All the bodyguards backed off into the background. Every one of the men knew it would be a completely stunning, devastatingly raw blow to his soul.

Silently, the men in the gallery who watched this unfolding before their very own eyes, wondered too; what would he do now about his own son? He knelt there for a long moment. Two minutes later a few men jumped when he snapped:

"Edarto," he yelled across the oilfield. Edarto dismounted and hurried up to be at his right side shoulder, as he leaned down to listen.

JUAN CARLO: Edarto, take my son to the hacienda and put him in his room. I will have a doctor sent to see him there. Do not leave his side until I get there. Take the horses and go, go now, and tell no one <u>nothing</u> of this... comprende, <u>nothing</u>. Go now and take Columbo with you. Columbo, put the money on the burros. You stay with the money and I'll see you at the hacienda tomorrow. (He moves in closer to him.) Keep the men quiet about this. Stay off the roads tonight. We'll tidy up this mess.

EDARTO: Si, patrone. Mañana la casa...

(he yells commands)

Hombres, to la casa hacienda, vamanos.

The two men pick up the don's fallen son. They load some six huge army green duffle bags, three on each mule, and on horseback the men gallop into the blackness towards the hacienda some two hours' ride away. Edarto followed his bosses orders. He knew the ride might kill the injured man. No whirly-bird ride for the kid who nearly succeeded in ripping off his own father's business associates.

Like the infamous horsemen during the times of Genghis Khan, whose times of pillage and rape of villages in the late 13th century gave them the legendary name the "yahoos," they vanished into the darkness of night. They carried a broken yahoo to the hacienda where another heartbroken man (his father) would later come to be with him in the morning after at the hacienda.

A crackling sound of thunder lights up the sky as a steady downpour of rain begins to fall.

JUAN CARLO: Take the girl and the ballplayer to the helicopter.

BODYGUARD: What do we do with this guy here? What about the beach bum hero, Patrone?

JUAN CARLO: The beach bum... hero? Kill him.

The bodyguards grab the shoeless Beachcomber/Santiago and drag him off to a four-foot retainer wall as they prepare to execute him in a reckless roadside hit squad fashion. Back to the wall, he commands one of the executioners to...

BEACHCOMBER: Tell your boss I'd like to have a word.

The bodyguard slugs him in the stomach, he falls to one knee and then several boots are kicking him as he collapses, writhing in pain on the ground. He yells out to Juan Carlo Farshottia who is boarding the chopper.

Overcoming the grasp of the guards, Osrah/Debbie Jean leaps out and rushes to her father's side and on her knees she clings to him begging for his life. She cries out to the several bodyguards.

DEBORAH JEAN: Please don't kill my father! Please don't take my Father—away from me—again.

She sobs at his side as Joe Elliot strains with the grips of his captors aboard the helicopter.

JOE ELLIOT: Please don't kill my wife.

(pleading mercy)

Please don't kill my family, Juan Carlo... please!

Infinitely sudden though it was, his emotions were already switched on and the gangland style hit that was on his mind collapsed into this fleeting plea for mercy, which metamorphosed into a matter of eclipsed anger for Juan Carlo Farshottia. It hit him like an act of some almighty intervention. He began to think clearly for a second and like the miracle of the moment it was, he stopped the execution of Beachcomber Santiago.

JUAN CARLO: Put the drifter into the chopper.

We don't want to leave too many loose ends.

Pick up those bodies in the street and put them in those cars.

Then torch this place... everything burns.

The Beachcomber/Santiago and Osrah/Debbie Jean are hoisted up onto the deck of the chopper, which rises into the air and flies over the compound as the horses gallop away across the Cuban landscape into the darkness.

Very carefully and with a subtle, slow continuous motion, she then removed her scarf and secretly passed it to Beachcomber/Santiago.

The bodyguards demolition wired the plant on a T-box detonator... that would... ignite and blow up—the entire fuel facility. The abandoned Esso factory exploded into a mushroom cloud of black smoke.

The oil gas inferno billowed for miles and miles above the horizon. It was fire in the sky with scattered yahoos on horseback and the escaping yahoos in the helicopter flying through the night sky. No exorcism, at least not on this night's work. Such hazardous ceremonial services would be on another night yet to come.

TWENTY-FIVE

Broken Wings And The Last Roll Of The Dice

The doctor was a broad shouldered stocky-built guy in the old Spencer Tracy tradition. He was an avid soccer player, skilled horseman and expert archer. All of this true spirit of being a sportsman kept him very fit.

He had a goatee but kept it cropped short since he liked the ladies so much. He had the Elvis sideburns and was a devilish kind of handsome who loved to eat pussy.

And being a good doctor, with his well-connected ways, he had woven himself into all versions of the upper strata in Cuba. Such mingling and involvements with those upper social circles put him in touch with the good rich and the bad rich.

The doctor wisely never chose either side. He just treated the injured parties. And privately, of course, that included many clandestine house calls like the one that he was working on now at the behest of the hacienda's distinguished owner, Juan Carlos Farshottia.

Columbia Reyes Quinones was the Don Juan with a stethoscope in Cuba: In dutiful service of both "the good rich," and "the bad rich," including lawyers, Mafia businessmen, and regular businessmen. Naturally, the wives of those infamous men never talked, but Dr. Feelgood was making a lot of those men's wives feel good. You might think that trouble would come of these affairs, but the men who had made their money had little time or interest in their own wives. They had their mistresses for their passions.

They were just glad that visits to the offices of Dr. Quinones made them well. In more ways than anyone ever knew, Columbo Quinones took care of the cream of the crop in Cuba.

Tonight's call was not uncommon. Like the others he had to answer late at night or in the wee hours of the morning, Juan Carlo Farshottia needed his services and Columbo Quinones would oblige and indulge the early call since he knew he would get triple the money that he would get from any other upper middle class Cuban client.

All he needed was the name of the client and he would drive his tan Mercedes up to the hacienda. He was one of the few who owned and drove the highest status-symbol car to be found in Cuba. It was imported by Farshottia's own company for him from Germany some seven years ago, and still in very fine condition. The two men were interconnected on a rewarding basis. The car was just a gift that was given to him.

He was paid for his time at a highly favorable unregulated rate; much, much higher than he would be paid for such services to anyone else. Such was the going rate for his silence as well.

The gates parted at the hacienda and his arrival was radioed by guards to the house. He parked and was greeted by two men at the door. They escorted the doctor to the room where his patient was shaking from the long, wet two-hour ride in the rain. They closed the doors as the doctor went inside at 4:30 in the morning.

His first order was to warm the patient up and he demanded they run a hot bath and bring as many white towels as they could find into the room. The men pulled him from the bathwater and put him on the bed where he was towel wrapped like a mummy. Then Dr. Quinones told them to leave as he cut away the towels where the blood was thickest on the right hip, and he gave him an injection of several powerful drugs for his pain. He then proceeded with his treatment of the complex fractured damaged patient. The ride had nearly killed him. He was near death's door.

By 1:30 the next afternoon, the doctor was done with his work. The time it took to wrap, set and brace the broken hip, without x-rays, was what had taken him the longest.. He set the bones in the best way he could, fit in by feeling them into place. He reset the collar bone, hipbone, left arm and the left ankle. He couldn't take him to the hospital so he had to use his strength to pull and get him back to form. He knew that his patient was young enough that he would heal eventually. The hip, though, would not return back to full function, but that was because the damage was too severe. As it was, he put him back together as well as could be done given the circumstances of the situation. When he emerged from the room, word was sent down to Juan Carlo Farshottia that Doctor Quinones would be ready to discuss his son Roberto's prognosis. He would have to tell him frankly the time it would take to heal the extensive injuries that his son incurred at the factory.

In his experience, he learned it was best to be completely honest with his findings and to explain the prohibitive nature that would befall Roberto Farshottia, Jr., even though he would live through the dangerous fall from the gantry plank.

After descending the wrought iron staircase, Dr. Quinones sat at the table. Juan Carlo quickly ushered in his servants to see about his needs at opposite ends of a very long 24-foot dining table made of a red colored varnished mahogany wood.

Juan Carlo was dining on a snapper fish and he poured himself a large glass of wine. He drank half the glass before he spoke.

JUAN CARLO: I'm having red snapper today.

(he lights up a cigar)

I have the urge for it since I've caught something really big...

(he sips more wine)

Now I have to take the hit with the bad news.

DR. QUINONES: Before I hit you with that, may I have a glass of wine and a cigar, if you don't mind?

JUAN CARLO: One of the best things about being a Cuban is home-grown beauty and the refinement of the tobacco farm.

DR. QUINONES: Indeed it is, Juan Carlo.

The smoke begins to fill the room with clouds.

JUAN CARLO: This is private stock from my best supplier in the country.

DR. QUINONES: Always the best of the best. This is first class treatment.

JUAN CARLO: Speaking of first class treatment... how is the boy?

He blows a drag across the table with a hearty look.

DR. QUINONES: The kid's got spunk, Juan Carlo. But I'm afraid I must tell you this news.

He stops and drinks a long, deep swig of wine, followed by an even deeper drag of the cigar.

DR. QUINONES: He will have a permanent limp. He shattered the hip. When I can get an x-ray to the hacienda, I may be able to tell more. The height of the fall. The landing on metal barrels. The body can only sustain such a force... he's lucky to be alive, Juan Carlo.

He will be crippled for life and your son will have to use crutches and maybe later on only a cane. It will take a year before he can get around on his own and he will have to use a chair for the time of his recovery. I'll have to hire a live-in nurse, Juan Carlo, to take care of him and do the therapy. It will take more money.

JUAN CARLO: You will have more money, Señor Quinones. One year before he can get around on his own, without a wheelchair?

DR. QUINONES: With the aid of a cane perhaps as well, when he does get back on his own power.

JUAN CARLO: Dr. Quinones, will you excuse me?

He rises to his feet and puts out his cigar. He walks up towards the doctor and stops at the midway portion of the 24-foot table. He rests his hand on the back of the chair.

DR. QUINONES: I'm sorry to report this, Juan Carlos. It's not the way a son of yours should live.

JUAN CARLO: Well, this may surprise you, doctor.

It may surprise you a lot but I'm glad he's a cripple. And now, for the first time in his life he will be under control. He will not be able to overtake the business.

As the doctor rises to his feet...

DR. QUINONES: Under control, you say?

JUAN CARLO: He has been the thorn in my side with that nasty temper of his and this last episode would have made us arch rivals in business.

Had he succeeded with the bank job, my cartel connection would have ordered his execution. (he waves his arms)

This way, he lives but he is marked for life.

DR. QUINONES: It's not easy in this business.

JUAN CARLO: With my son's immobilization, believe me, it will be easier for me to conduct business.

Without this percolator of a distraction always blowing off the handle all of the time. He was a disaster waiting to happen.

He walks away fanning his gestures outward, turning around and then stopping.

JUAN CARLO: Now he's a <u>manageable disaster</u>. Me, I should be glad he is in the way that he is, understand?

The doctor sips the wine glass empty and it is slapped down with a hard rap of conclusion on the long wooden table. The two men leave the dining area together as they walk over to the living room. (slapped)

JUAN CARLO: Come with me, I'll give you your cash for all your trouble, doctor.

A large leather black attaché case is on the coffee table. He removes $10,000 from the case and he loads it into his black doctor's bag. He parts and leaves the hacienda with, "Goodnight, Mr. Farshottia."

Pouring yet another drink in his private study at his large mahogany wood desk, approximately thirty minutes, maybe less, had passed by. It was in the beads of sweat that all time was forgotten when the dour businessman's mind was totally infested with his own gutty wheels turning inside his head like a merry-go-round of horror minus the merriment. Juan Carlo Farshottia was brewing a brooding monster of a gut-puncturing decision.

He did his best to keep it under control but there was additional fury in his face's texture, blood veins were visible below his skin. He wasn't tired, but his blood and blood pressure was way, way up. Wiping the pints of sweat at an equal volume to the pace of downing the tequila, he poured himself another drink and lit another cigar from the box on his desk. If you counted the tequilas and the wines that whole day, you could wreck the average man, but Juan Carlo Farshottia was a wrecker of a man, and he was to do all the wrecking himself.

He was just keeping his blood warm.

He picked-up the picture of his wife (she was the one who left him), and like it was an electrical lightning-storm that shocked him; he dropped it on the desktop. He swept it into a bottom drawer, kicking it shut with his foot, and he threw back the shot of tequila like a bullet meant for his own head as he grumbled and remarked to himself, soling his suicide shot with a throwaway lament line

JUAN CARLO FARSHOTTIA: You got off easy, bitch…

I'm the one with the tiger by the tail.

This was the man's way to handle the tough blows that had comprised the news and events of the day that had passed. One fucked up kind of day and night that it really was.

His son was crippled for life, and his own son had just raw outrageously stuck it to him and righteously betrayed him. He could cover it up by returning the money and saying he burned the perpetrators whose bones were going to be found in the trunks of those cars at the abandoned oil factory.

They were of unknown origin—definitely not a random group of Cubans, but either Columbians or a Venezuelan gang. He was still deciding—what he would do.

The meeting was already set for tomorrow night at his club. He had to use this scenario to later play out where it would most work to his advantage.

So he had to decide whom to pin it on that would most benefit and behoove his own motives… in future business with his cartel liaisons, etc.

There was enough abundant restlessness in the drug trade to go around. The DEA put a lid on Miami in the 1980s, so most had sought to run passages of trafficking up and spreading out throughout South America. From there in the jungles and then upwards through the lengthy borders of Mexico.

Most of the bullets were fired in the final leg, into Mexico's softly patrolled and guarded borders with the United States.

Finally, after one more drink down the hatch, he called for Edarto to come into the study. Edarto was wired in with his headset piece and he descended the staircase from his post (monitoring Juan Carlo Farshottia's critically wounded son). At the foot of the stairs, he crossed the hall and walked towards the doorway where two thickly built bodyguards stood their respective watch on Number 1.

He was allowed to go in and he stood before Juan Carlo Farshottia's desk with hands at his sides. He had a resolve running through his own mind that this particular meeting was a pecking order of who gets it first… since that's the way it usually had gone in the past.

Edarto was an efficient executioner: He just liked to get it over quickly and be done with it. Because, in his mind, the quicker the decision, the more clear it was in his own mind that the victim(s) had to die with no other option of resolution. To wait too long for a death was no way to have a good business. Nobody waits for death, when it is necessary. They bring it on very quickly in the more successful outfits.

EDARTO: What shall we do with them?

JUAN CARLO: Nothing tonight, O.K.? We wait until morning.

EDARTO: Till the morning?

After a long puff on his cigar, Juan Carlo Farshottia rises and turns to stare out the window. The smoking cloud continues to build up into a real storm of some vicious gut-wrenching toil.

JUAN CARLO FARSHOTTIA: Tonight I have words with Santiago, first...

The girl and the American ballplayer... (he turns back to face him now) put them together for tonight. Have Santiago brought in to my study.

EDARTO: Si, Patrone.

He goes, turning for the door, just as

JUAN CARLO FARSHOTTIA: Have the cars for transport, Edarto, to the ranch o.k., ready in the morning.

EDARTO: Si, Patrone. Tomorrow morning then.

The ranch was between Yara, and Bartoloma Maso. It was an area 10 miles to the north of the Gran Parque Nacional—known as Santo Domingo— which was a key rebel camp during Fidel Castro's guerrilla campaign in the late 1950s. It's connected by foothills of a river valley where the road winds sinuously like a snake to the Rio Yara, with perilous trails into forested woods better suited to singing birds, or buzzing insects, and little bohios... clinging to precipitous slopes more befitting for the sturdy hooves of the guided mule and a good hunting dog. If anything was ever to be buried—up here, it's never to be found. Edarto knew where a lot of skeletons were buried over in those hills...

With his hands tied up in cuffs behind his back, Beachcomber-Santiago is brought in. Edarto stands back some five feet behind his left shoulder and is quiet. The two bodyguards close the double doors to the office. A silence ensued for 30 seconds before he spoke. .

FARSHOTTIA: Well Santiago Serna Dominguez, what am I to do with you?

BEACHCOMBER: You could just let me go.

He begins to laugh a bit as Edarto slowly starts to laugh also.

FARSHOTTIA: No, Santiago, I don't think so.

(shaking his head)

BEACHCOMBER: You could let me and my family go and nobody would know otherwise. Nobody needs to know anything.

FARSHOTTIA: Yes, nobody needs to know.

But yet, everybody knows you. You have a beautiful daughter and, it turns out, her name was "Osrah" to us. But then we learn she's not Osrah but her real name is Deborah Jean.

Yes, my son had a thing for her. But she went away and left the club for good it seems, or so it was. Then she met up with an American castaway, the ballplayer-Joe… is his name… Joe Elliot.

(he waits, puffs his cigar)

Then it gets very interesting. Yes… indeed, because my altogether bright young son decides to kidnap her from her husband. And if that wasn't enough, he robs a bank connected to my business of some $8 million.

Somehow I don't think letting you go is the most logical answer.

BEACHCOMBER: There is no reason to kill my family. You can take me for your son but please let my family go on without me.

FARSHOTTIA: You crippled my son for life, and you're asking me to have mercy. You will have to be taken away.

BEACHCOMBER: Juan Carlo… Mr. Farshottia, I ask you for a moment of your time to listen to what I must tell you.

He begins rising as Edarto puts a heavy hand onto his shoulder. The force of his strength buckles his legs.

EDARTO: Easy, compadre…sit down.

BEACHCOMBER: At least let me have a last cigarette.

His back turned, his knees on the floor and with his torso and scrunched face pushed into the cushioned seat.

JUAN CARLO FARSHOTTIA: Edarto, put the cuffs in front. Let's give the condemned man his final request.

He rises and is uncuffed from behind as the cuffs are reshackled with his limbs in front of him. Edarto lights him up a cigarette and then puts it near his face. Leaning in, he retrieves the cigarette, taking a series of long drags.

BEACHCOMBER: C'mon, I'm an old man… a beach bum drifter. I can do you no harm. Can we talk, man to man in private? I ask you man to man… please?

Just then at that moment Juan Carlo Farshottia decides that he is right.

FARSHOTTIA: Edarto, wait outside and give us some time.

Edarto gets out of the room. Farshottia then walks behind him as he bolts the double doors shut and completes the circling of his prey as he continues 360 degrees to the desk. There is a gun tucked into his belt just below his belly.

FARSHOTTIA: Man to man… so it is that the condemned man always gets his last wish.

BEACHCOMBER: Well, if I'm going to die by the firing squad in the morning… how 'bout letting me have one of these?

Juan Carlo Farshottia obliges his request by opening the box. As Beachcomber retrieves a cigar, he hands him the clippers as he sits on his desk, then clips his own, lights up another cigar as he pours himself and his guest another drink.

BEACHCOMBER: Well, if I gotta go out... this way I go in style.

He raises his whiskey glass towards the Don with "salud." He puts the glass down on the desk and puffs the cigar a bit. Then the Don looks down at his feet, seeing his bare toes on the wooden flooring.

JUAN CARLO FARSHOTTIA: No shoes...? Tell me how did you do it?

How did you survive out there all those years alone?

BEACHCOMBER: Became a nature lover, I guess. I woke up to the dolphins, sand crabs, and seagulls flying at morning tide.

I learned to sleep to the night birds callings and the cricket beats and the giant sea turtle scratching the sandy beach.

(puffs the cigar)

I became one of them. My heartbeat became a friend of theirs and they accepted me, a man, as one of their own. I had become a creature of nature-

I was just there every sunrise and every sunset.

FARSHOTTIA: Didn't you miss the...?

BEACHCOMBER: What's to miss? Right there at that beach I had everything I needed.

FARSHOTTIA: But what about—your family?

BEACHCOMBER: It's interesting that you would ask me that. It is what I have waited a very long, long time to talk to you about.

FARSHOTTIA: And why do you tell me this, Santiago?

BEACHCOMBER: Because you are the only man who I can possibly believe will understand why I've done what I have done. And you are the only man I can ask to do what I possibly believe you could do.

FARSHOTTIA: I'm growing tired of doing things. After tonight... tomorrow's coming soon...

(he points his cigar like a gun)

I feel closer to a grave than I have ever felt. My son's a cripple. My empire could possibly maybe turn out to be crippled.

(taps the ashtray like a snare drum)

For the first time in my whole life—I don't know what the outcome is going to be.

(a deep puff of smoke)

After tomorrow's meet.

BEACHCOMBER: Mister Juan Carlo, my friend, I swear to you... that's why I went away for so long.

(matches back at him in a deeper puff)

I didn't know what the outcome was going to be tomorrow.

FARSHOTTIA: What outcome is this?

BEACHCOMBER: Each day I woke up to the sunrise, each day I wondered if I should kill — myself?

Juan Carlo Farshottia leans in pulled toward his mysterious lament.

FARSHOTTIA

Why did you want to kill yourself? What was it that caused you to go sand combing the beach?

After a long silence, Santiago/Beachcomber said to Juan Carlo Farshottia, very quietly

BEACHCOMBER: It was that son of yours.

The Don starts to laugh at this revelation.

JUAN CARLO FARSHOTTIA: No… no, you must be mistaken.

BEACHCOMBER: No… no, I'm not mistaken.

(a godlike voice spoken through him)

It was your son, Juan Carlo.

Clenching his fists together over his desk…

JUAN CARLO FARSHOTTIA: How do you mean?

BEACHCOMBER: Ten years ago there was a party. All of Cuba was celebrating.

Late that night, your teenage son who had been drinking got behind the wheel of a car. The stolen car they took on a joyride crashed head-on into my wife's car… the accident on that very night was the one… the one that killed my wife.

(beat)

Your son was only fourteen years old. In your capacity with rank you had the police cover up your son's involvement. My wife, all the world that she meant to me, was gone. You had the report changed and your son, who got away with murder, didn't have to spend one night in jail.

Beachcomber stands up and turns to look outside the window, his back to Juan Carlo.

BEACHCOMBER: That's power…

(beat)

Hmmm, Mr. Farshottia…power.

He turns back to face the man with visible tears streaming down both cheeks.

BEACHCOMBER: I don't have to tell you, Juan Carlo, what my wife meant to me, do I? No, because for ten years I gave up my life. So now… and then, you took care of it.

(beat)

You fix things. Not much has changed for you. A decade goes by and just like you're going to take care of this… His latest thing… he rips off the bank… the Columbians… it starts all over again.

Beachcomber takes a deep drag and blows a trainload of smoke from deep within his lungs.

BEACHCOMBER (continues): Amigo… death is not such a bad thing. Maybe I should get down on my knees and thank you for putting me out of my misery.

Beachcomber stopped himself in this moment of frankness. Surely he can only be saying these words knowing for certain that they truly were to be his last words.

BEACHCOMBER : Juan Carlo… Señor Farshottia…I am honored to be your guest in this fine hacienda. Your son's tragedy tonight and my wife's tragedy a long time ago–this is the gods who punish us for our past mistakes.

(beat)

We live or we die with the <u>past</u>. We all have one… most of life is… that we just wait for our turn.

(beat)

It's my turn tomorrow then.

JUAN CARLO FARSHOTTIA: I am without words, Santiago… I must do what I must do.

BEACHCOMBER: Then that's it.

(beat)

You give me your best whiskey and a fine Cuban cigar. I will die tomorrow a happy man.

FARSHOTTIA: How is that so?

BEACHCOMBER: I finally go to the place it is to see her and that's o.k. for me now…

I go to the place to be with my wife. I want to rest now before I go.

Beachcomber/Santiago rises to his feet. Juan Carlo Farshottia stands to face him. There is a moment where each man's soul gifts the other to feel something.

BEACHCOMBER: I ask you to let me go to sleep, that way my dreams are of her… the vision of her, Señor Farshottia, will be fresh in my mind mañana… when I finally come to see her.

FARSHOTTIA: As you wish, Santiago…you may rest now. (beat)

It's never bad to dream…it's only bad when we stop dreaming.

He summons for the bodyguards to come inside.

BEACHCOMBER: Thank you for the drink, the good cigar, and the chance you gave to me to clear my mind.

Farshottia raises his hand in a motion of a type of quieting farewell. The weight of his words became so momentous in their unfolding of the truth that they left the Don speechless.

Beachcomber turned away and the two bodyguards escorted him out of his office to his quarters for the night.

He slept very soundly with the love of his life, in the comfort of his dreams.

———

Initially the ride along proved to be dubious. They were taken to the house and dropped off at their front door. They exited the vehicles in stunned and overwhelming uncertainty... They knew they were going to die, but the caravan drove off and there they stood: Beachcomber, Joe Elliot, and Deborah Juana, just looked at each other as they stood on their own driveway. Without any indication that they were all dreaming and feeling their own individual hearts beating and in their own souls still alive and breathing.

(Deborah Juana, in Cuban, and Debbie Jean, American, are one and the same.)

They all embraced each other in a family hug that symbolized their freedom. Beachcomber/Santiago told them it was O.K. to go inside the home. Relief abounded as Deborah Juana embraced her father one last time. "Go inside, it's O.K. now." She finally responds, "O.K., we will wait for you like you said." Deborah Juana took her husband's hand and they went inside the house as Beachcomber/Santiago parted with, "I'll bring Joe Junior back in a few hours and we'll all celebrate."

In an instant, Beachcomber vanished to go and get his grandson. The couple, Joe Elliot and Deborah Juana, went into the bedroom to make passionate love. It was to be a testament of their own celebration of their love for each other, and their second chance to make it really real, at life coming back around for them.

Beachcomber/Santiago was less than two hundred yards away when he heard an explosion. He ran back to the home, which was reduced to a smoldering burning pile of rubble as the flames and plumes of smoke filled the morning sky. He began to cry like a man could never have cried. He was crestfallen and collapsed to his knees.

From beside the house, behind a row of bushes, where no one could see him, he heard an engine starting up and he lifted his face from his hands as he saw over the shrubs the face of Juanito Farshottia through the car's big windshield as he hit the gas and then the blue '57 Chevy squealed, burning rubber as he sped off down the road, quickly fleeing the scene of the tragedy. Visible to Santiago/Beachcomber was this bomber inside that car.

It was Farshottia's brother who finally stepped up on his crippled brother's behalf.

Something snapped in Beachcomber's soul. He arose with a face of tempered indomitable resolve, a man at war.

He pulled his blood-red sash, after wiping away his tears, and walked towards a pay-phone and forcefully dialed up June Cortez. He would call in the last favor of his old army buddy. If a bum turned into a warrior, and that warrior became a mad man, the priest was now turned into the spirit of the exorcist incarnate.

TWENTY-SIX

June Cortez

A GOOD SOLDIER GRANTS A WISH

He called June Cortez to meet him, and they met within the hour. He told him what happened and said, "I need to call in one last favor my friend, and that's where it ends. After this, I won't need anything, understand?"

June Cortez responded, "I will get the stuff for you," following up with, "Just tell me what you need."

"Here's the list... I need it by tonight."

June Cortez read the list. "It will be here by tonight at this spot we're standing on before dark." He folded up the list and put it into his shirt pocket. "You have my word on it."

Later that night Beachcomber returned and there was the truck he requested... just as June Cortez promised him.

Beachcomber knew how to build an equalizer for times that he was outnumbered. It was an old guerrilla trick to make a device with scatter damage and pain potential for anyone within forty feet of the blast. It was the gallon grenade, a painful equalizer.

It was a lethal device: Two separate gallon plastic milk cartons with the large handles, pierced by a foot long length of 2x4 wood with 2 grenades wired and attached onto the wood, with an oblong extended pull pin. Tack ties, the kind of 4-spike woven wires that made up the pricks of barbed wire, but longer by about ½ inch. (The 2x4's threaded into plastic milk jugs handle holes and tied up.)

Each jug now filled with gasoline. Whenever the grenades blew, the deadly tacks "scattered and stuck to everything in sight within forty feet of the explosion." If it hit only a portion of a man's body, it tended to make them prone or walk like a zombie in pain. It would put you in the hospital for five days if the blast's scatter fire tacks got on you. If you couldn't walk away fast enough, the ensuing blaze from the fuel would burn you alive. It was one helluvah way to go for someone within range.

Beachcomber was armed with five of these gallon grenades and carried two Uzi machine guns strapped on his back. He had a quajiros machete and two .45 magnums and also an extra 22 caliber pistol strapped to his leg as a just-in-case back-up weapon. There was another weapon in the package. As if all this firepower weren't enough, June Cortez supplied him with a flamethrower, which had a fully fueled cell tank ready for use if he deemed it necessary.

The first thing in vengeance in terms of rules is to isolate the odds and "covet thy secrecy." Second rule is to commit the act of revenge "with boldness and also swiftness," and never leave a trace of your existence. Such contemplation characterizes the best assassins in the Ninja Shoulin, priests of the Chinese culture not unlike Qui Che Chang in Kung Fu. In this case, a priest about to perform an exorcism in the Cuban world, a castaway about to cut away a few of society's rotten souls or some of the undesirable's god mistakenly left behind. It was all forthcoming, a tsunami of revenge, almost as if it was an exorcism of some measure.

Beachcomber got to the club but he held his peace until his prey separated from the pack. Sure enough, there was the car he used out in back of the club. And Santiago/Beachcomber positioned himself in the jeep that June Cortez lent him with four sets of gallon grenades in the back seat plus he had an assortment of other tools of surprise for a sneak attack.

Beachcomber/Santiago had several rolling papers and some of the best tobacco and he smoked voraciously for the three and a half hour duration of the surveillance period. He could see the blue Chevy in the parking lot and he knew that Juanito Farshottia was inside bragging his murderous deeds to those inside. And he thought to himself as he chewed on some sweet Espanola Roja pineapple that he had cut with his machete to pass the time.

Here he was armed to the teeth with weaponry and rations as he munched quietly on pineapple and then rolled himself some fine tobacco. There was his machete resting on the floorboards of the jeep vehicle with the extra gallon grenades (some ten of them loaded into the back seat), and he sat calmly like the submerged crocodile of the Zapata swamps, awaiting the hoofs of his prey to saunter up to the edges of their favorite watering hole.

Papas Beers was only moderately filled that night with patrons of the old club. A typical mid-week Wednesday summer night crowd, as the Beachcomber thought out loud about the passions of his country's Cuban people for a second.

It must have been fate that morning when Beachcomber/Santiago had decided to walk Deborah Juana and Joe Elliot inside the house, after their strange release by Juan Carlo Farshottia's squad of juniors. It truly was just an unbelievable break. But it must have been karma, or some cosmic intervention by the spirits, not just the coincidental type of fate. He still lived on the beach, as one of God's earthly Santeria orisha legends, or as one of his gifted souls, as a human-being, and also as a go between as of one of nature's creatures... In the essence of his true spirit, and in that godlike quality of spiritual armor, he had walked—out the back door—to follow the beach's shoreline to where he knew would be the exact spot to find Joe Junior.

In that back door exit, Juanito Farshottia missed seeing him leave the house and mistakenly believed that he killed them all with that blast.

It was in that sense he never left town or laid-low for awhile, and his return to the club that night seemed perhaps quite logical since no one would suspect him anyway. He was always the watcher when it came to this kind of stuff so he just tried to blend right back in. And in his mind after exacting the deed of blood brotherly revenge now it was done. There was a wise old fat queer chef from a famous restaurant (whom he knew), who used to say many years ago that:

"Once it is done, it is history." He kind of felt relieved of any possibility of retaliatory redemption. It was a gay man's quote but it made sense and it was a simple line that somehow meant, "you could live with it."

Sure enough, he emerged that night with a jinetera on his arm and a couple good bottles of rum making his way to the convertible blue '57 Chevy, headed out for a rendezvous into the night under the stars. Driving somewhere, to some Cubans, is almost as much pleasure as anything. Luxury is found in the freedoms of the old classic American automobile.

TWENTY-SEVEN

Cabo Blanco And Traveling

THE ROAD OF ENDING DOOM

The jinetera rested her head on his lap, giving him a blow-job on the way. They leisurely drove up the coast, heading north to the old smuggling port of Manzanillo. This harbor became a main fishing center and the principal shipping terminal for sugar brought in by trucks or rail from all the little mill towns further south, like Niguero and Le Demajaqua, Media Luna, or Campechuela.

This was a town steeped in rebellion early on as an infamous smugglers' port, and then into the wars of independence. Cuba's first communist cell was organized and started up here in Manzanillo in the 1920s. The only communist mayor, Paquito Rosales, was elected in the 1940s. It was the same timeframe of Jesus Menendez, the famed incorruptible leader of the sugar workers' union, who was assassinated at the Manzanillo railway station platform, after collecting all the workers' grievances in the area.

Juanito Farshottia drove the convertible into the picturesque Parque Cespedes.

Here they got out and walked around the Moorish-influenced buildings and danced for awhile in the glorieta, a very brightly colored and romantically lit up bandstand at center square. It was after a half hour or so that they drove to the railway station.

Beachcomber/Santiago smiled as he watched the ballet of the young lovers, for it reminded him of the old days when he and his beloved wife made the same moves to the same type of music, when he was a young suitor in love.

Here is where Juanito Farshottia let his only passion show. He had a love for trains all his life. He got up on the platform and he danced around with the long legged raven-haired jinetera. Using a blanket that he laid out neatly on the deck area, they went right into a passionate frenzy of lovemaking under the stars while Beachcomber/Santiago quietly watched.

Whether you would know it or not, Beachcomber/Santiago, the old man, was a lifelong romantic. He was fully enjoying the young couple in the throes of passion and he would wait for the man to finish making love. For a Cuban, this would be the best way to check out.

Beachcomber/Santiago, like a cat, quietly climbed up a ladder positioning himself atop the railway gantry spider loader. It was a large spider fork for extraction of the sugar cane to be loaded into freight containers. With a qualified crane operator, this machine could both load and unload about 150 freight cars in a single day.

From atop this crane, Beachcomber/Santiago hit a console contact switch to "on" position, then he pressed a starter button and the crane came to life. He hit the spotlights towards the deck of the railway station. Both Juanito Farshottia and the jinetera were naked, wrapped inside the blanket, and heavily entwined into each other.

This kind of candid camera moment mortified both participants, the jinetera scrambled to her feet fighting off Juanito to get out from under him. She found her feet and she ran off screaming in hysterics all the way down the station ramp. If ever there was a hideously frightening sight, it was the shockingly loud running wildly buck naked jinetera woman, screaming her head off. Never scare the shit out of a Cuban black woman. As if this consequence wasn't dire enough, Juanito Farshottia was in a state of macho and pissed-off disbelief. He stood up naked, staring at the spotlight, at his adversary up on top of the crane, his wet erection still upwards, pointed north to the heavens that had just been interrupted.

With a guiltless Cuban bravado of sworn mortal pride, he issued the damnedest verbiage, "Heh, what's the matter with you?" Then he spouted off into more indignant defiance, "You puta bin dey hoh. Do you know who you're fucking with? Do you know who I am?"

Looking upward in disbelief, Juanito Farshottia defiantly stood erect. He couldn't see upwards fifty feet through the stream of white light's beaming glare of that spotlight, but Beachcomber/Santiago's voice echoed back down upon him as he shouted out with condescending fatherly flair, "Yeah, I know who you are. You're the sick son of a bitch, the sick son of Juan Carlo Farshottia."

A silence ensued: he was stunned by this marquee naming of definitive infamy by Beachcomber/Santiago. He began to stumble for his bag to get to his pants and try and hide from the light's beam.

"Yeah, that's right, you're also a murdering son of a bitch and you're going to die tonight."

He managed to step, hopping up and down on his legs, into the pants legs of his trousers and he fumbled with the contents of the bag and from within the darkness… He raised the gun from behind his back and fired, spending six shells at the gantry loader trying to hit Beachcomber/Santiago's spotlights.

Beachcomber fired back as a wild gun battle erupted, sending sparks of bullets flying and scraping off ricochets and echoes of metal to metal clangs of bullets bouncing off girder beams everywhere.

The train station and gantry platform became a shooting gallery as shots and bullets spraying were echoing off everything in the station platform's structure as both men shielded themselves with cover.

Farshottia ran with his bag and he hid behind a thick steel column post. He pulled an extra pistol out of the bag and reloaded. He had several loads inside packed with extra ammunition, his heartbeat racing and temples blustering with sweat. He prepped both guns to fire everything into the cockpit of the spider crane loader.

Then with both guns pointed upward, he fired continuously and ran for his life as he squeezed both triggers at the same time and ran further down the platform towards the area of the parked car.

Beachcomber shot back firing from overhead and he drove the gantry loader towards the car's location. The metal wheels sounded like trains revving wheels on the steel track. The loader moved quickly and kept him in position with each duck and run for cover Juanito could make. He had the advantage and he had the equalizer.

He pulled the long pins of the gallon grenade and sent it flying towards Juanito Farshottia. The grenade exploded, igniting the station house. Juanito dived behind a long wooden bench, shielding his body from the explosion. The bench was riddled with tacks.

He got up to run again but the gantry loader was still moving rapidly overhead, shadowing his run.

And Beachcomber was gaining advantage over the fleet-footed Juanito Farshottia. He launched the second gallon grenade as Juanito ran for the final leg of the platform's ending edge, which spilled out into a parking lot.

Two gallon jugs with tacks and gasoline wired by wood through the handles with one long pin to hold the key—pin piercing the two grenades… He pulled the long pin and launched it. He struck the target area. It was a direct hit.

Juanito Farshottia was barbecued and prone as his body was puffered and porked with tacks. Over seventy percent of his body was punctured, pierced, and bloodied, in a mangle of carnage.

He could barely walk anymore but he managed to crawl onto his feet like a living zombie who wished he were dead since his whole entire body was in shock with such overwhelming pain. The flames surrounding him were knee high and his shoes were burning as he pushed himself through the fiery flames.

Santiago/Beachcomber descended the gantry loader ladder and he headed his pointed pistol toward Juanito Farshottia's back as his feet dragged across the tarmac towards the car. Santiago/Beachcomber had a machete in his left hand hanging off his wrist, low to the ground, as he followed the slow belly crawling movement of Juanito Farshottia.

He approached this death-walking body welted <u>devil of thorns</u> with an executioner's silence and reverence for the duly condemned man. His death would be a swift one.

It is said there are only two types of emotion: "love" and "fear," and everything else is simply just based on that. If you can characterize life and break it down into its simplest terms then perhaps there it is for us all to see.

Beachcomber/Santiago believed in this philosophy because now it was that a man's impending death—was based on the inherent loss of the ones he loved.

Juanito Farshottia makes it to the'57 Chevy convertible and opens the car door. He turns to Beachcomber/Santiago, attempting to fire his guns but the chambers multiply echoes of click click clickety-click are spent and empty of any bullets in either weapon's revolving cylinders.

He begins to yell as loudly as he can. He is branded in the agony of his wounds, but the more cathartic metamorphosis is he can sense the resolute visitation of fear since he can feel the coming calling voice of the grim reaper. He yelled out again.

He dropped both his pistols and they clickety-clacked on the railway station tarmac. Now, he was exasperated of energy, completely sprawled across the door of the car, almost like the '57 Chevy was a cross of Christ. "Mercy," he begged of him, "I want mercy."

Beachcomber/Santiago eyes his prey and tells him with pirate's blood vengeance and night time chills… of the air channeled and funneling through… the fog of his breath shaping each word.

"I kill you for killing my family: my daughter, and her husband."

Santiago/Beachcomber raised the machete high into the air. The moonlight shined off the serrated edges of its long sickle-like blade. He brought it down with the executioner's guillotine, lopping off Juanito's head, which flipped off the front seat's top edge and went clunking and bouncing into the backseat of the convertible blue Chevy like a bowling ball. It finally thudded onto the floorboards.

Beachcomber/Santiago took his severed mount and stuck the blood-dripping neck on the mast of the Chevy's antenna like a head of cabbage speared by a giant fork. Then he shoved the body of the severed carcass off the door and into the front seat. He shut the door and started the car and drove to the railroad crossing point.

He aimed the car in the direction of the track. The car's wheels were straddled and locked into the railroad's 5 ½ inch bases of the metal spars' of the tracks.

Like a fully gratified executioner, he took great pleasure as he opened a bottle of rum, took a deep long swigging chug-a-lug gut load as it spilled down the corners of his mouth and glistened on his neck bones. He let out an enormous yell that echoed throughout the station.

He poured the rest of the bottle's contents on the body of Juanito Farshottia and onto the car's interior and took another chug before letting out another louder even more earth-rattling king of the tropical jungle lion's roar. Then he looks at the lifeless head of Juanito, "Oh, what, you want a sip, huh?" He began to feel a numbness buzz of powerful Cuban rum. "Well, you know you should never get drunk and then get behind the wheel, or you might lose your head." He took another swig at the bottle and spit on the lifeless head of Juanito. "You don't get any of this," he slobbers a bit and is slurred in his delivery of his speech. "I'm the one who's been in misery for the last ten years."

A train's whistle blast is heard in the distance, it startles Santiago/ Beachcomber to drop his bottle of rum and begin to hasten around for something in his knapsack. He removes the final gallon grenade off his shoulder strap harness to the back seat of the car. He figured on pulling the pins as he reaches over and stops.

The whistle blown by the train is nearing closer and he says to himself, "No, you don't go that easy." He starts breathing heavily, "You get a proper sendoff."

Removing a long piece of thatch wood from his bag and placing it lengthwise over the dashboard, he pushes the body to the passenger's seat and starts up the engine. He begins to laugh as he pulls the dashboard's thatch wood stick and with the car running and in neutral, he posts the wooden stick to wedge between the car's accelerator and the front seat to a high revving of 4000 rpms.

Exiting the car and with a quick spin turn of adjustment with his large hands, he repositions Juanito's severed head atop the antenna mast to face the oncoming freight train. He removes his hands from the skull and like an artist with a mission to get his sculpture to look just the right way, he takes his palms to push deep into Juanito's cheekbones as if he were Maillol creating a masterpiece. He curiously looked upon it as if something was missing. "Come on," he said, coaxing his skull prize to perform some kind of feat, "Where's your smile?"

He extracted his knapsack from the seat and pulled the body back over to the driver's side of the car as he propped the headless corpse upright with both hands affixed to the steering wheel. He takes the final bottle of rum and turns the radio up, blasting a rhythmic Cuban dance song.

He took a swig from the fresh bottle and looked at the head to check his work. He pulled even harder to force the corners of the mouth to careen into a hideous form of a dead man's wicked smile and finally he said, "There, that's it." He backs up a bit to admire his handiwork. "There's a mighty smile of death," he began to clap and sing along in the chorus of music. Beachcomber/Santiago hopped up and down, singing, clapping, bouncing to the Cuban beat as he drank voraciously from the rum bottle and laughed furiously loud as he danced around.

"You get to face fate with a smile," he scoffs, "You get your Cabo Blanco… you're going to hell… with that smile." As a train's blast of the whistle signaled that the train was closer to the station, he stops himself and lets it go out of his soul. "I've been there my friend, I've been in hell for ten years." He takes a gulp of rum and charges up. "You're one puta vato who deserves it. You're taking the midnight train."

The Chevy's engine revving at 4000 rpms and with the train at less than 300 yards—and getting closer—at full speed, he leaned over the car's door and pulled the lever into drive as the '57 Chevy sped off towards the oncoming train.

And in one stupendous blast of metal to metal carnage, the booming fuel cells' explosion of the gallon grenades horrendous shower of fire and pellets shattering the glass and spit out a wildfire way, way up into the night time sky.

The train rammed the car and split it in two and dragged both its pieces on either side of the locomotive for over 400 yards before it was slowed down another 400 more yards further to total 800 yards before it reached its full stop.

Juanito Farshottia went to hell with a smile via a Cabo Blanco freight train.

Beachcomber continued dancing around and he laughed hysterically between chugs off the rum bottle and mocking the sounds of the train with some childhood callings of "choo choo" casting his aspersions and in his own fists of rage mocking dubiously of indignity.

It was a good death that he would celebrate.

He created a perfect revengeful ending avenging the brutal house bombing of his daughter and son-in-law.

Beachcomber/Santiago drove back to Papas Beers. It was a breezy ride in the open roofed jeep as the tropical night dried the sweat off his body. His thoughts were actually muted by the period that he put on Juanito Farshottia's life when he set him ablaze in that creative Cabo Blanco midnight train wreck.

He did not feel any real level of remorse of any kind. The look in his eyes was that of a Shoulin priest, a silent Ninja executioner.

He had a mindset of "one down" and in his eyes it was clear that more work was yet to be done to finish the job. He could see the ending, but it was not over yet until afterwards... until it was all done. He was relaxed and patient altogether since he knew the outcome.

He also knew where he would come out of his vendetta. When it was all over, that would be it and not until then could he be done with it.

In his mind, he was a sane man who was caught up in an insane world of strange circumstances. Once he felt that his job was done, it would be finally over for him, killing all of the demons who had been haunting him in his soul for ten years would be therapeutic to him, and he believed vengeance of this kind was necessary, since sanity had its dangers; you could temporarily go madly insane in today's world. But he swore he would settle this old business once and for all tonight, and end all the unsettling spirits that kept calling him to swing his machete into action.

———

308

June Cortez was not the type of man to involve himself in another man's private vendetta or executioner's actions. He was a very respectable service man who kept his record clean. He would never get involved with any of that. Fidel Castro would have found out about it, number one, and besides, he had a house and family; wife and three kids. It was much too much to lose, so he kept his nose out of anything that didn't smell right.

There was one trafficker whom Fidel found out about during the campaign of Cuban soldiers sent to Angola. The man was publicly executed. General Ochoa Sanchez was executed for alleged drug dealing and the known war hero's death shocked enough soldiers into keeping their noses clean from that point on.

But yet he would help out and it was his help that brought Beachcomber/Santiago the jeep and the cachet of weapons that he would utilize to exact revenge against Juan Carlo Farshottia.

Because June Cortez cared about his friend, he showed up outside of Papas Beers right around closing time. He was dressed in civilian clothes and wearing a fisherman's bucket cap with a long silk brightly printed shirt designed to blend in with the night life. The car was also a rental, but one which could not be traced back to him.

He was sitting there monitoring the scene when Beachcomber/Santiago's jeep pulled up into the front of the club. He looked at the entrance, which was empty since most of the people were gone by that time. A few people were scattered in the parking lot, making out both inside and outside of their cars.

Cuba has such a housing shortage and so many cousins, nephews and family members end up confined into one-room dwellings that most nights you wouldn't be surprised to see such sexual proclivities going on in a public parking lot outside of a popular night spot. Tonight was no exception. The Wednesday night crowd for hump-day, on this summer night, was actively engaged in humping.

Beachcomber/Santiago drove to the furthest edge of the parking lot and began to strap himself with his armaments. He had pulled two Uzi machine guns out of the backseat when June Cortez appeared in front of his jeep. He raised his hat so he could flash a smile. "Heh, amigo, como esta?"

At first Beachcomber/Santiago was startled but just made out the shape of his friend's face as he went about his unloading of merchandise. "Muy bien."

"Compadre, I came to tell you I wish you wouldn't do it this way."

He loaded the flamethrower on his back after he slid his arms into a Kevlar vest which protected him both front and rear of his abdomen as he gruffly responded, "Heh, amigo, I have to do it this way."

Beachcomber/Santiago continued arming himself and he tied up a quajiros machete around his waist that hung in a special sheath that he had constructed out of wood. It hung just below the belt. He pulled a set of CRAF airmen's goggles over his neck, they rested over his chest.

June Cortez lit up a Havana and asked him if he also wanted to join him in a cigar. Beachcomber/Santiago put his hands on his hips signaling him negative. He was loaded with highly flammable weaponry.

June Cortez sighed, "Suit yourself, then." As he lit up his Havana, he went on with a little bit of scripture offered quietly, "Vengeance is mine sayeth the Lord."

Beachcomber/Santiago stopped for a moment. "This is not vengeance, this is not revenge, amigo." He stopped to take a breath. "Tonight is not about getting even or getting anything that isn't duly necessary... Tonight I am the coming of the Lord. I have become what I beheld for ten years and I can hold back no more. Tonight's the one night where you don't want to know this spirit helper... Tonight's spirit helper is from another world."

He strapped extra clips into his bag as he threw it over his other shoulder before he placed his knapsack across his back and rested, palms down, on both of his Uzi machine guns. He placed a pistol in his front shirt and a second inside a belt holster.

"This is the end of that, my friend," with a deep breath parting with, "After tonight, this is where I come out."

June Cortez looked upon his commando-ready friend who he had known for quite some time. He studied his face for awhile and took a deep drag of the Havana and blew out a massive trainload of exhaled smoke. "O.K., this is where you come out, amigo," a moment there... "But let me tell you what you're facing going into that hellhole."

He stomped on his cigar butt and stood face-to-face with Beachcomber/Santiago.

"I want you to come out of it alive."

He began to draw a few lines in the dirt of the parking lot, using an unwrapped Havana, still inside a metal protective case that he carried with him.

"Here is the equalizer... He has 11 men inside there that I could count since the last hour. He will be counting money alone on his desk like he always does. The typical greedy and seedy untrusting shitty son of a bitch— that he's always been."

Beachcomber/Santiago goes to one knee and he listened intently as June Cortez draws the layout into the dirt, marking the spot where the men will be inside the club.

"That much I know where they'll be but there is one problem, the shooter Edarto is mobile. He's floating and he moves all the time. He's carrying two . 45 autos with eight shots. You better see him first because he doesn't miss a lot when he goes off." He takes a deep breath. "He even carries a stiletto that he's good at throwing, so make sure when you put him down." A lengthy silence as he eyes him with, "You put him all the way down."

Beachcomber/Santiago nodded in readiness.

"There's one more guy, but he's the mucho borracione, the mute. He usually sweeps the pesos off the floor after closing. So that's 12 men all together. You got the fix of the layout?"

"Yeah, I got the fix of the layout."

"Good, then you're ready to go."

"As ready as I can be ready."

"Then there's nothing more to say."

Beachcomber/Santiago shook his head and gave him a look that told him that he had to leave him alone with the deed that he indeed intended to carry out without any more words. So June Cortez broke the silent interlude with, "God be with you, my friend." He breathes outwardly and adds, "See you on the other side." He walked away from his old friend and Beachcomber/ Santiago checked his weapons one last time. Donning the CRAF goggles to cover his eyes, he pulled a gallon grenade up off the backseat of the jeep and he stepped closer towards the nightclub's doorway.

As he reached the front step of the saloon, he lit the flamethrower torch, testing it with a few flares of flameouts. The couples making love on car hoods, and in the back seats, began to sit up and take notice of the Beachcomber's display of fireworks.

There were some 30 couples engaged in sex and about two dozen others that were spooning and necking outside the club, and then he set it off. All of them stopped and got up to watch.

Beachcomber/Santiago the flame-throwing dragon lighted the roof of the club with a blazing blast of streams of fire as he ignited the timbers of the wood-shingled roof of Papas Beers Nightclub.

Now you could see over 100 people watching Papas Beers get torched by this man in the CRAF goggles and a full facial mask. Beachcomber/ Santiago kept his back to the crowd. He simply waited for about thirty seconds and he saw them. Three men immediately burst through the saloon doors firing pistols and running formations across the face of the front of the nightclub, and he took aim as gunfire pelted into his Kevlar vest and flame sprayed left and right as he ignited all three men in flames. Couples that were watching now embraced their loved ones as the girls hid their faces into the shoulders of their dates.

It was a human hotdog barbecue of the three men. You could hear the screaming as they were burned alive. A fourth gunman emerged from the club saloon's doorway and another gun battle erupted as both sides exchanged fire. Beachcomber/Santiago torched him at the entrance. The man was burning, his clothes set ablaze as he stumbled back into the bar. He fired shots up in the air as he fell backward through the doorway, calling out to

Edarto to come out of Juan Carlo Farshottia's offices for help . He quickly
ran up to him at his booth where six other men wrapped him into a blanket to
extinguish the fiery flames.

He told the men to "back away" and they were stunned by the carnage of
burns to over 80 percent of his body. The guy looked like a burnt up sausage
on a cheap breakfast plate of a mom and pop-owned diner.

"Cover the windows, cover the doorway, and spread out," Edarto yelled
his commands louder, "fan out!" He kicked and pushed the men aside as the
men moved about in formations to comply. In moving closer to the burned
victim, Edarto leaned in to hear the final words on his breath, "It's the devil
out there," he whispered. "It's a devil coming for all of us." He died with his
eyes open as if he had just seen such a ghostlike figure of just such an evil
spirit.

Glass windows were broken as he directed his men to fire at the man
with the fire tank on his back. Beachcomber/Santiago raced up to charge the
saloon doorway and threw the gallon grenade inside the club, ducking below
the steps as machine gunfire rattled out into the night sky echoing off the
walls and bouncing off metal cars of the parking lot. Then... then the blast
hit. Everyone in the parking lot hit the deck.

In its explosion, two men were blown out of the windows with their
bodies lit on fire and tacked all over. One more staggered out of the door,
burning alive as he tumbled down the stairway.

Several car engines started up in the parking lot as the chaos escalated
into a traffic jam of people leaving the lot. There were three men left with
Edarto and they tried to retreat behind the bar as Edarto ordered them to stay
put, and fight it out until the end. "Columbo, we meet this fucker in hell...
c'mon, amigo, we can take this vato together, O.K.?" The men agreed but,
with sweat beaming on their brows, did not want any more of this battle and
were ready to run off and bolt out the back exit door. With his Uzi drawn,
Edarto forced them to spread their formation and be ready when he gave the
word to fire. The squeal of a live pig came from the back kitchen area,
unnerving the already nervous men.

Beachcomber/Santiago set the flame of his torch and jogged into the
nightclub. He pulled Uzi fire simultaneously as he pulled flamethrower fire.
And in a hail of bullets spun around the room and fired at anything that
moved. The battle lasted for only a couple of minutes as the four men fired
back and the wild gun battle raged on.

The bullets hit his vest but Beachcomber/Santiago was still firing from
the magazine clip of his second weapon. He spent the clips of both and
ducked down low behind an overturned table to reload.

He got up spraying more cover fire and continued spraying flamethrower
—blazes of 360 degrees with full spirals—again until the gunfire that was
coming at him had subsided and he could hear... or see... no more.

He had killed four more men as he moved closer to the office doorway passing Edarto's body as he walked up to the door where Juan Carlo Farshottia's office was. But behind him he didn't see Edarto, who got up… rising, and then he… fired his .45 auto at Beachcomber/Santiago.

Beachcomber/Santiago spun around at the noise of the empty 45 clicking off of the empty weapon's clip. Edarto dropped the gun and pulled his stiletto knife and raised it above his eye level ready to hurl it across the room.

Beachcomber/Santiago fired three quick successive shots into his chest and his whole body stayed upright as he stepped backward till his back was against the wall, with his stiletto still poised above his head. The bullets' mortal shots had froze him with his body stiffened-up, still erect and in shock.

It was like the solar plexus pull with JFK, back in November 22, 1963, just like the bullets ricochet and penetration that caused his arms to clench himself stiff.

This kill had Edarto stiffened like his stiletto knife.

Beachcomber/Santiago grabbed his hand and pulled his arm down turning the knife inside and pelting him in the center of his neck at a 45-degree down angle below his left ear.

Using Edarto's body as a shield, he shot the doorjamb until the knob was blown off and he pushed Edarto forward, kicking his feet to walk as he entered the offices of Juan Carlo Farshottia.

With Beachcomber/Santiago shielded behind Edarto's stiff body, Juan Carlo Farshottia spent the entire six into his own man. Beachcomber/Santiago shoved him to fall forward onto the man's desktop. Money was laid out across the top of it.

Beachcomber/Santiago pulled off his mask and goggles and Juan Carlo went for his back up pistol inside the big oak wood desk's center drawer. Before he could get it halfway palm-held into his grip, "I wouldn't do that if I were you," Beachcomber directed him. "Now use your left hand and put the piece over here very carefully."

Dutifully, Juan Carlo Farshottia—tosses the weapon onto the back of Edarto's body, which is lying—on top of the money spread out over his desk.

Beachcomber/Santiago picks up the weapon off the backside of the carcass of Edarto. He puts the gun into his waist level belt and pulled the stiletto out of the side of his neck.

"I'll keep these as reminders."

He licked the blood off the stiletto, which unnerved Juan Carlo Farshottia as he massaged his own throat looking over at the puffered lump of flesh of his fallen right hand man with disbelief. But with that death behind him, and facing his own, he returned to his seat to regain some of his composure in all this frenzy of epic mind-bending carnage. Juan Carlo Farshottia managed a gruff comeback.

"It's hard to get good help these days."

He managed a deadly smile as he said those words while Beachcomber/ Santiago just nodded his head with noblesse oblige. He then released a momentary sigh of oxygen and continued on with the subtle words of, "Not that it matters much. I assure you I had no idea it would be you."

He pulled out a Havana from his breast pocket and puts it into the base flames of carpet's fire and sat back down in his chair puffing it heavily.

"One last pleasure for the last time." It was the condemned man's last request as he realized this was to be his last cigar for life. It was in the old indomitable Cuban spirit that he would enjoy it to the fullest. This would be the second best way for a Cuban to check out: "With a rum buzz and a fat Havana a la carte."

Even in this state of uncertainty and facing down sudden death, Juan Carlo Farshottia, ever the hustler, would try to negotiate for his final roll of the dice as he tried to put together a deal.

"I could really use a man like you."

Beachcomber/Santiago spray-lined beads of fire on both sides of Juan Carlo Farshottia's desk. The wall of flames burned steadily and brightly at waist high level due to the exceptional thickness of the office's carpeting.

He bosses at him in a snarl of disgust to "stand up, you son of a bitch." Juan Carlo still refused to rise up immediately when he was told and commanded to. He drew heavily, dragging into his Havana cigar, raising his chin and then he casually poured himself a shot of rum. Slamming the bottle onto his desk, he then firmly gripped the shot glass and held it up to Beachcomber/Santiago. "Well, bottoms up," and he threw back the shot. "You kill all my men and now you burn down my place of business... My insurance company is not going to believe this. I drink to you, you fucking beach bum. You sure have an appetite for destruction."

He sat there in defiance as if he chose to die sitting down. Although the floor of the bar was on fire in sections, it would take awhile for the fire, which was started on the roof, to actually burn its way into the next room of Juan Carlo Farshottia's offices. He was behind a very thick wooden fire door since that's where the safe was located, and the actual office section of the structure was the most structurally strong. It was the strongest place to be inside the entire facility, since he had an office like a vault; or a modern day panic room.

You could feel the heat and the connected outer structure to this old place was disintegrating at a steady pace but Beachcomber/Santiago was poised to remain nonchalant, which seems logical since you couldn't help but feel if he himself died on this night, it didn't matter to him since he had lost so much of his life up to this point in time.

He had become an executioner and roughly a form of a devil's advocate of some kind of ghost from hell. It was as if he had turned into the exorcist.

He wanted to see Juan Carlo Farshottia burn in hell and perhaps he just might go out with him in that journey beneath the level of humanity.

He bottoms up drains the shot and pours another one from the rum bottle. "Dare I ask what brought about this episode?" There is a distinct second of silence, both men's hearts beating aloud, before he goes on to add, "after I set you free yesterday morning, both you and your only daughter, and that American yanqui son in law?"

He drinks and pours himself another one but before the glass hits the desk top, Beachcomber/Santiago ignites the flamethrower and he torch sprays the desk like a flaming roman candle as he yells over the inferno.

"Ask your second son, Juanito, about that."

Juan Carlo jumps off his ass and tumbles his desk chair behind him as he staggers off a few stumbles backward aft. Beachcomber implored at him with "Yeah, stand up and face me like a man."

"You know that sick son of yours killed my daughter and her husband. He firebombed the whole house."

Juan Carlo Farshottia responds back with, "I don't know where he is now. He was due back here over an hour ago."

Beachcomber/Santiago: "Maybe he had a train to catch and he had to get away for awhile."

Juan Carlo Farshottia answers, "If he acted, he acted alone on his own. Hey, come on… I had no control over that one."

The desk was a raging inferno, with the papers, box of cigars and calendar paraphernalia that cluttered the desktop lighted up and smoldering, bringing the flames up past levels of his eyeballs. Beachcomber/Santiago spits a ball of saliva onto the burning embers of the desktop. "You have no control over that?"

Beachcomber/Santiago was holding the flamethrower pointed at Juan Carlo Farshottia's chest and he hesitated there for a number of sweating heartbeats. The room's temperature continued rising higher as the paradox of two men facing each other in the inferno of hell strained on.

He was boxed in by flames on either side, with his back up against the wall. He was swarmed and engulfed by fire like a pig on a barbecue grill, fire on both sides of his desk that were melting through the core of Edarto's torso, and burning up to his waist level off the thick carpet. The desk was smoldering and simmering through the frame, the heat compressing the oxygen to such degrees that Juan Carlo Farshottia's eyes bulged like he was about to implode.

There was a second squealing and kicking noise from a live pig that was kicking at his cage from the lower level kitchen area. The sound of this pig's distress laid even more weight of distress upon both men's souls as they continued their earnest discussion over the chaotic melee of the burning barn, with a live pig's squealing chorus in the background.

BEACHCOMBER/SANTIAGO: Well, let's talk about control. Let's talk about when your own children go out of control. You don't have to worry about Juanito. I sent him out on the midnight train to Cabo Blanco... He lost his head on his way to hell.

JUAN CARLO FARSHOTTIA: Beachcomber, I let you go you puta son of a bitch. You kill me for my son's behavior. What kind of man does that?

BEACHCOMBER/SANTIAGO: I tell you, Juan Carlo. I am, to a man who covers for his son's shit. Your son drove the car that killed my wife ten years ago.

JUAN CARLO FARSHOTTIA: Okay, but you killed my son, and you crippled the other one for life. You destroyed my club and my place of business.

BEACHCOMBER/SANTIAGO: Well, you took too much from me a decade ago when your son's car crashed into my wife's car.

(beat) You killed my wife and took away my life for ten years.

JUAN CARLO FARSHOTTIA: But I let you go, Santiago. Please have mercy and let me go as I did for you.

BEACHCOMBER/SANTIAGO: You took too much, Patrone, my wife, my life for ten years. My daughter and her husband... (beat) All I have left is my grandson. I'm going to be good to my grandson. If you would've been a better father to your children, none of this would ever have happened. You built so much hate in them. And if you weren't such a bad father... you might've given them a chance. But the evils of those two sons are like the fruits of a poisonous tree. It's time for this evil to end and for you to say hello to your Cabo Blanco.

I'm going to kill you for everything evil you've done in your whole life, and for the evils of your two sons.

You're a bad father, that's the worst a man can be. You must die.

Beachcomber/Santiago unloaded his Uzi into Juan Carlo Farshottia. His body was pelted with bullets and he staggered towards his desk, leaning upon the desktop of flames. There was a final squeal of the pig in the kitchen as it broke free of its cage, and the then still erect Juan Carlo Farshottia's mouth opened, mouthing out something incomprehensible, trying to breathe.

Beachcomber/Santiago removed the quajiro's machete and swung at his fat pork pig of a neck and lopped off his head, which bounced across the desktop flames onto the floor, rolling past his boots.

The body stood for a few more seconds before the flames penetrated the wood of the desktop and melted out from under his weight and he collapsed forward, splitting the desk in half. His fat headless body burned in a pile of oak and timber wood materials crackling like a stuffed pig in the barbecue pit.

Beachcomber/Santiago picked up the head and put it in his bag.

He unstrapped himself from the flamethrower, placing it down on the floor of Juan Carlo Farshottia's office, which was completely engulfed in fire. Pulling the CRAF goggles and headgear apparatus down over his head, covering his face to mask his identity, he walked out of the office.

Through the billows of fiery smoke plumes he heard coughing. He followed the sounds and found a limp body over at the left corner booth, underneath the table.

Uzi drawn, he raised his mask off. He picked up the man by the back of his shirt, pulling him to a seated upright position.

It was the guy who had his tongue knifed off by Roberto Farshottia. He could barely mouth any words with any comprehension. But if he slowed it down to a gravelly whispered voice, and if you were listening carefully, you could understand him.

Beachcomber/Santiago looked him in the eye and said, "come on, we're going outside."

He pulled his goggles down and readjusted his headgear, shielding his identity. He helped the mute to his feet and, supporting his shoulders, rescued him as both of these men with scars on their souls walked outside of Papas Beers.

Over a hundred Cubans stood around watching the blazing inferno as Beachcomber/Santiago steadily dragged the limp-limbed mute's body through the clouds of thick smoke, flurries of dust created from his heavy footsteps. He emerged from the plumes and dust of the burning inferno of Papas Beers Nightclub and pulled the mute to safety some 35 yards away from the entrance of the nightclub.

There was a vicious cackle and high-pitched animal sounds echoed overhead, sounding like a cockfight that was reaching a crescendo. In its frenetic attempt to escape burning wooden cages up near the apex of the roof's hips, just at the highest peak point, a reddish colored rooster flew out and furiously flapped his wings for the 24 foot long drop off. The men stalled in a freeze framed pause, Beachcomber/Santiago raised his eyes to watch... as he and the mute were overflown in the Passover of the reckless cock of a bird. He bounced across the lot in a tumbleweed of dust, and into the loose dirt of the parking lot.

As if the crowd's murmurs of spirits calling towards the Santeria depths of the Orishas hadn't created enough drama, a,second bird appeared, a black feathered hen this time. It flapped, cackled and popped like a Mexican jumping bean with her wings burning and smoking from the fire as she flew in a haphazard dangerously careless flight from the roof, like a black snowball—from both heaven or hell... but definitely... on its way to hell. It looked for a momentary-second like a tumbler's gymnastics exercise. It bounced and rolled in a vicious tangled wreck of havoc and disorder, black colored frisky-flaming-feathers bouncing left and right and back and forth in barrel rolls until, after a number of seconds, the burning flaming bird's wings finally burnt out, and then the chicken pecking scene of running around all over insane-like… as if its whole head was just cut off… the circus fracas-highlight act was finally over.

Both birds staggered around to find each other: the charred black hen and its partner from hell, the reddish hotheaded cock of a rooster, as both scorched animals then scampered away from the crowd.

Beachcomber/Santiago pulled one of his sleeves to rip and bandage the mute to stop the bleeding over his left earlobe that was struck when he went over the table from the gallon grenade's blast. As he wrapped the man's forehead with the bandage, he had no time to reach for his weapon in the shocking event–a wild pig broke out from the lower burning embers of the nightclub, squealing, char-blackened from burns, and barreled out from underneath the stairwell of Papas Beers' porch. He just ran over the mute's body, leaping over his limp limbs, springing and squealing off into the mesmerized crowd of Cubans.

It was a stunning sequence of events, and the spirited chaotic strangeness multiplied in the rum-buzzed minds of several Cuban onlookers so that the CRAF goggled man, whomever he was, that came out of Papas Beers, that wayward spirit, would be forever steeped in Orisha legend. He was marked as both Shango and Oggun… with the feared signs of the implications of Santeria worship.

The animal freak show unnerved Beachcomber/Santiago. He dragged the mute some thirty more yards toward a retainer rock wall, which lines the parking lot that begins at the other side of it. The stones are all different sizes and shapes and form a wall that is not unlike the stones found at Cabo Blanco, only they are lower, rising no higher than hips of most Cubans.

The mute begged his savior Beachcomber/Santiago, hidden beneath the mask, to help with his broken leg. "No one will help me… I will die right here." Beachcomber/Santiago examined his leg and pulled the sickle to rip away his pants leg to just above his knee. "Please," he goes on with pleading, "they will leave me to die."

Beachcomber/Santiago looks at the crowd gathered and walks back to the burning bar's porch area and with a mighty stomp of his boot cracks some wooden plank of about three feet, smoking in flames, and brings the smoking wood to the mute.

He sees the wood is covered everywhere with ants swarming over the surface, their wooden world a monolithic form of burning hell… like holding the shitty end of the stick as, perhaps in life, the ants were running all over like crazy on the wooden burning beam, all that would be left from the storied Papas Beers landmark.

He pulls a canteen of water from his shoulder strap across his back and opens the canteen's stringed plug and pours it over the ants on the long beam.

BEACHCOMBER/SANTIAGO: You say they would leave you to die.

The masked man pours more water on the burning wood as the mute replied in barely intelligible whispers, his voice stripped and minus a cut off tongue.

MUTE: Yes, if you don't help me, no one will. You are my only hope.

Beachcomber/Santiago continues to sog the porch plank of burning wood, draining the contents of the canteen's capacity across this smoking beam and he mocks the experiment with the line, "It's been a real steam bath this week, we're all in on it and we're all full of god's evil and evil dudes all night tonight."

He ripped the canteen's strap, cutting it into two straps of about 2 ½ feet each with his sickle. All of them, he repeated it several times as he cinch-tied the splint onto the mute's broken leg… "all of them."

He thought of all the deaths of his people: his wife and family and the revenge he had exacted upon Juan Carlo Farshottia, his two sons, Roberto and Juanito and his surrounding company of men that were still burning, both dead and alive inside the bar once known as Papas Beers.

Beachcomber/Santiago looks at the splint he's secured to the mute's leg as the mute said, "You are the Messiah, you are my savior."

Beachcomber/Santiago looked at the mute and he pulled corners on his mouth in a noncommittal pledge of less dignified deity, and spoke. "Just like the ants, I drift along with which way the direction of the wind or the water's going, just like the water I poured from this canteen." He laid the canteen upon his chest as he offered prophetically like a whispered secret to the souls in the world as he told the mute, "Never forget… the meek shall… inherit the earth."

He got up from the mute and pulled his bag off of his shoulders. He pointed his two Uzis at the gathering crowd and motioned for all of them to move back.

The crowd murmured in fear and quickly marched backwards away from this masked man who directed them. Seeing them backing away, he pulled the severed head of Juan Carlo Farshottia from the bag as the crowd then gasped in fear-filled horror at such a morbid sight. He went to further raise the head up higher as he knelt on one knee and picked up a rock that weighed about 5 pounds. He looked Christ-like with a head in one hand and a stone in the other. He pulled a piece of thatched wood about 4 ½ feet long, and using the rock he drove it into the earth with a mighty thrust. He stood back and looked at the crowd of Cubans and raised the severed head again high into the night sky.

With the burning nightclub in the background, he took the severed head of Juan Carlo Farshottia and mounted it, piercing the neck to the wooden mast as he stuck the skull onto the post.

He took the blood-red sash from his own neck and tied it to the forehead of Juan Carlo Farshottia. Having secured the sash upon the severed head, he spun it around on its post so he could watch the fireworks as flames destroyed the saloon known as Papas Beers. With both Uzi weapons pointed skyward, Beachcomber/Santiago started his walk towards the crowd left remaining as those who stayed this long were too mesmerized by this walking vision of a ghostly spirit of death and hung around... just to watch the sighting of the Santeria of a spirit walker. They parted for him like he was some kind of Moses walking into the Red Sea. He walked into the darkness and vanished like the spirit he was, headed for the coastline.

The police arrived at this aftermath, delayed by the melee of the traffic jam tie-up on the one and only roadway to Papas Beers Nightclub, clogged up, bumper to bumper, with cars trying to get away from the scene.

During the questioning, a brave older woman, who begged for pesos outside the nightclub, pointed to the mute as if he would be able to identify the man in the mask since he was the only one to come out who was still alive.

The mute couldn't say anything, barely able to muster the strength to mumble an unintelligible whisper of the horrors of what he had seen.

No one, not a soul, dared to speak to the police about what they witnessed. Papas Beers burned until morning, turning into an ash pile of embers, soon to become legendary Cuban folklore in its retelling the forever crude memorial story of the nightmarish tale.

TWENTY-EIGHT

A Traveler And Her Birthday

9/9/59 AND DAYS THEREAFTER... 9/9/01

(The second to the last heap of the enduring brain-droppings.)

I was intent on finishing the final pages of Beachcomber to coincide with my German girlfriend's birthday 9/9/59 on September 9th, but when I tried to write the ending pages on that day, the ending just didn't happen for me. She had inspired a large part of my reasoning for writing this short story and setting it in Cuba since she had traveled there and told me stories about the tropical island.

(A photo of Gabriella in a white bikini walking the shores of the Veradero... Gaby left me taking away all of the pictures of us as partners together. She was a good friend. She helped by believing in me. No pictures exist. It was a photograph of her walking the Veradero in Cuba that inspired this book. Surely, I met her on the journey to myself. I found myself long after she left me.)

So 9/9/2001 came and went and the writing didn't, for some reason. There was an earthquake on Sunday afternoon after the Vikings had a stinker of a performance on the field the opening weekend of the football season. I was sitting on a sofa at Ken Crane's as the earth violently shook to the tune of a 4.2 level earthquake, which completely wrecked my whole mood and I was off the scale of my creativity. California has a tendency to rock itself like this every so often it seems.

The next night, September 10th, Monday, I tried to settle in and concentrate after work (but still no luck). I went to sleep a frustrated writer with an ending... still waiting to happen.

Then September 11th, 2001, my alarm clock radio tunes in my wake-up as the radio station (92.3) blasts some remarks about an accident at the World Trade Center. I turn on my TV set to see just exactly what had happened.

At 8:45 AM, American Airlines Flight #11, a Boeing 767, hijacked en route from Boston to Los Angeles with 92 passengers aboard, slammed into the upper floors of the North Tower of the World Trade Center.

At 9:06 AM, United Airlines Flight #175, also a Boeing 767, hijacked en route from Boston to Los Angeles with 65 passengers aboard, banks hard and slices into the South Tower.

Then the liquefied spill of the airplanes' jet fuels fireball continually raised the temperature of the buildings' steel framework to levels equivalent to one third the potency of a nuclear bomb the intensity of the bomb at Hiroshima. The steel melted and gave way to the eventual collapse at 10 AM of the South Tower. Thousands of firefighters, rescue workers and tenants were killed in less than ten seconds.

Horrified, New Yorkers ran for their lives on the ground as those who were brave enough to watch witnessed 110 floors crumpling and imploding, raining debris and crushing thousands as one of the twin towers of Manhattan's second tallest buildings was leveled to ground zero and reduced to a smoking ash pile of rubble. Moments after that, at 10:29 AM, less than half an hour later, weakened by its imploded twin, the North Tower imploded and came crashing down, killing thousands more, both on the ground and trapped inside, as the surrounding radius in a circumference area of West Street to Church Street and Liberty Street to Barclay Street became the holy ground of what was now the dead zone in Manhattan. Both buildings, which stood for over thirty years, were gone in thirty minutes. New Yorkers reviled by the disaster rushed to the scene in the Herculean task of culling the war zone for any potential survivors.

American Airlines Flight #77, a Boeing 757, departing Washington Dulles Airport for Los Angeles with 58 passengers and six crew members aboard, plunges into the west side of the Pentagon at 9:40 AM, slashing through the roof top and face of the structure all the way to Sector C Level.

United Airlines Flight #93, also a Boeing 757, leaving Newark for San Francisco with 38 passengers and 7 crew members aboard, was also hijacked, headed for another strategic target, the White House or Congress, but was retaken by passengers before crashing in a field near Shanksville, Pennsylvania, 80 miles southeast of Pittsburgh.

The death toll went beyond 3,000 people of the United States.

It was a bestial act of treacherous evil of some nineteen zealot terrorists, which had commandeered four separate jet liners. Using a team of four men per plane, they overtook the planes with utility knives and box cutters slicing up flight crews and flight attendants to take over the cockpits of the airplanes.

———

It had been close to a month since the attacks on the World Trade Center and the Pentagon and most of us were regaining the semblance of our bearings as to functioning as normally as possible in the wake of such actions on America's soil. As bombing raids continued against the Taliban targets throughout the borders of Afghanistan, which began on Sunday morning, October 7th (on our time table), when it was reported in the news, and we were headed into a new chapter as the October skies of Afghanistan echoed with the American made bombing sounds and the theatre of war.

October 9th, 2001, I was writing and I drafted the final pages of *THE BEACHCOMBER* that were to coincide with an earlier time in history, Che Guevara's birthday, October 9th, 1928. I hoped to bring this novel short story to completion on this day in history. I felt it was a good place to lay down my pen finally and finish what I had begun over a year ago on September 1st, 2000, at the Sunset Millennium Building.

I had written long enough and I was very close to the ending of my fictional story–*THE BEACHCOMBER*.

I cannot truly comment clearly on the response that the country was feeling, or as to what a war of this kind was doing for the American citizenry, or what jitters and bumps and bruises were occurring on the American psyche. But most of this society was jittery and unsettled, like it was on its fifth cappuccino with its handling of the daily grind of all the war-time news stories. There was no way to comment about how badly we felt since whether one was indirectly or directly affected: we as a country took one.

Whatever that experience gave us, whatever it was to all of us, we will never be the same as we once were, before that one.

Businesses were in trouble with economics and the drama of war and the store I worked at was no different; we were off by fifty percent. Many other businesses were hit harder and off by as much as seventy five to ninety percent, especially the travel industry and related businesses, which virtually bottomed out and dried up. Whether you could call it "Osama Drama" or "Anthrax Anxiety," people were altering their lifestyles and stocking up on supplies of winter goods, getting prepared for the worst. A lot of people were not going to be going out too much. Such was the climate and the mood of this country during the completion of the final pages of *THE BEACHCOMBER*.

October 16th, 2001. Draft Date: In History

In discussing that history you realize your own life and limits.

No one is capable of quantifying a type of a Neptune-massive, and no writer living could encapsulate the truth in paragraph.

A fact for anyone who's tried it, but more so in the operative of what is in its true-meaning. It's truly unfathomable territory.

TWENTY-NINE

The After Life Begins

Beachcomber slept at his jungle spot. He had had quite a night of activities to put him into a deep pattern of wistfully wantonly wall-eyed, fully indulgent, heavy sleep. He heard a lapping of the shoreline at morning's tide and woke up to the birds and the dragonflies, the crabs walking, and the passing dolphin pods' morning feedings. He was a bloodshot-eyed sort of combat pirate since he had seen so much action last night.

Life began as he pulled himself forward to sit up, knees bent, barefoot toes in the sand, arms folded across his loins, looking at the morning's sunlight, which sparkled off the sun-warmed lines of lime green hues of the waters of the Caribbean.

There on the shoreline building a significantly ornate castle hacienda made of golden sand was the Beachcomber's grandson, Joe Junior, very carefully packing and patting methodically with his own hands the walls of a fittingly resilient sand castle. In his own way he cemented the idea that his permanent home was somehow ordained to be found right here at this spot on the beach.

Beachcomber/Santiago sat and watched his grandson, and you could see the love in his eyes. Here was the moment that life had shaped for him and tears began their steady stream out of his sockets as if the dam had been cranked up and the waters were set free to run a powerful run. He cried, flowing freely, an outpouring of so many emotions, as he buried his face between his knees, sobbing in the steady release. Many things God had witnessed would remain unforgiven, but at that very moment his soul was redeemable, feeling what he must've been feeling.

IN A DIFFERENT VISION OF A SIMILAR REALITY

We have reached the final brain-dropping.

Nicholas John Lennartson was aware of moments between parents and children and it was one such moment between the mother... observing the daughter... that described it the best for him. It was a beautiful moment of love one day during the hot humid summertime heat in Serra Mesa, San Diego, at 2965 Epaulette Street.

The three-bedroom, two-bath, house had a large sloped hill in the backyard, the hillside was filled with cactus and ice plant. The grass yard extended some twelve feet and the hillside was bayed by a retaining wall about three feet high, built of rocks of various shapes and sizes.

Nicholas John Lennartson's sister, Kathy, was squatting in front of the wall, aiming the garden hose at the rocks. Kathy was watering the faces of these rocks, cooling them off with the careful and delicate precision of a future league cognitive scientist. With the flowing water hose, she showered each of the faces of these multiple rocks all the way down the retaining wall, while her mother looked on at this careful process in wonder.

Karin Lennartson observed her daughter's irrigation movements for the entire length of the rock wall, peering curiously from behind the patio's screen door. Nearing towards the end of the wall, Karin Lennartson made the query into the mystery of the dubious water-hosing project.

MOM: Kathy, what are you doing?

Kathy spun her head around while the water hose continued to spray the faces of the rocks. She answered quickly, responding in defense of her efforts on the job as if it was a ridiculous question to ask; an idiotic interruption.

KATHY: Mom... I'm watering the rocks!

Here the author refers to his mother's experience with her daughter, Kathy.

Karin Esther Lennartson passed away on October 20th, 2004. With or without such a brief window... one senses her love moment there filled with pride.

Karin Esther Lennartson was a maiden name, she later married the tempest Templar Ivory tower of the Czars—the royals of Russia—who became the sergeant here in America—the legend known as Alexander Alexandrovich Gering. (The mold was broken, he was like no other who came before or since... as detailed in the greatest known and also the unknown... all revered him by so many humane reverent measures.)

Whatever it was that caused a woman to alter her life to be with him: one can only mark such a heart as larger than life itself. Karin was gifted with such a pure heart... which was the only way... such a quandary finds its dysfunction, or it was somehow through the gods it was to be quantified for how else could such a bent soul lock on with a great lady? It's nothing personal against him. We deeply mourned the loss of Karin.

———

Beachcomber/Santiago couldn't spoil such a moment. He sobbed for a period of some five and a half minutes in a way that a man of his pride would allow his soul to weep... few men can actually do that. It was a lifetime and a decade of sorrow and exile from everything. He wept it all away.

After five and a half minutes, he heard the rustling of sand as footsteps of beachcombing were moving towards him and stopped in front of him.

He had buried his face between his legs. He kept his head down but opened his eyes. He saw the little bare feet of his grandson, Joe Junior, spreading his toes in the Campechuela-Beachcomber's golden sand.

He wiped his face and looked up at his grandson, Joe Junior.

He flung his arms around his grandson's shoulders as he arose to his knees and embraced him in the forever embrace.

"Grandpa, Grandpa," he said repeatedly, "come see my castle in the sand, my hacienda-castle in the sand."

Beachcomber/Santiago walked over to view the hacienda-castle in the sand.

Nothing could have shaken Beachcomber/Santiago out of the galvanization of that familia fervor, for he knew it was like the fortnight's dangers of events were the gauntlet that he had run, and surviving that test, and to be let out on the other side brought out an upheaval in his soul of emotional tears, knowing that the trial was finally over. He would be able to return to his life and share his humble existence with his grandson, walking the seashores, beachcombing into anonymity.

But a ranging-homing sound of a jet airliner that was flying at a very low altitude was approaching from south-southwest. The aircraft emerged on the horizon with full flaps down, preparing for foreboding consequences. The noises grew louder as the troubled plane came closer to the surface of the water.

What had occurred previous to Beachcomber/Santiago's sighting was a grinding threshing, a metallic metal particle's sounding explosion from the right wing. The plane shuddered, the flight pattern shifted steep right.

In the cockpit, the alarms were sounding and lights flashing. After a series of switches being tapped, the captain and the co-pilot turned off the autopilot and made their adjustments for the lost engine.

Fuel gauges in the cockpit were showing a severe loss of fuel capacity from the damaged wing and the captain knew they would never make it to Miami. The captain told the co-pilot that he would have to land in Cuba at Manzanillo Airport.

Delta Airlines 737, 800 series, heading from Bogota, Colombia, to Miami, Florida, was going down. The 1,500 mile flight was sixty miles past Kingston when she developed engine problems which forced an attempted landing in Manzanillo, Cuba.

The 165,000-pound plane had 158 passengers onboard, apprehensively waiting for the fate of the doomed airliner to come down wherever it was going to come down.

The noise of the jet now sounded like a symphony of a thousand table saws revving making a hellacious ear-piercing and threateningly overpowering racket upon the horizon. To himself, Beachcomber/Santiago felt that only a furniture maker could equate a similar facsimile of those sounds in massing together such quantity and decibels of measure.

It was a soundly constructed aircraft. 129 feet and 6 inches from nose to tail that cost $40 million U.S. dollars for the Boeing Company to build, and of the some 655 crafts ordered, some 224 of them were delivered by spring of the year 2000. This was an aluminum alloy, dual path, fail safe, two-spar tail plane. It consisted of graphite composite ailerons, elevator, and rudder. It was equipped with aluminum honeycomb spoiler/air-brake panels and trailing edges of slats and flaps. Its fuselage construction and structure was that same quality of "fail-safe" aluminum.

Flying controls: convention and powered. All surfaces actuated by two independent hydraulic systems with manual reversion for ailerons and elevator; elevator servo tabs unlock on manual reversion. Rudder has standby hydraulic actuator and system. Three outboard-powered over-wing spoiler panels on each wing assist lateral control and also act as airbrakes. Variable incidence tail plane has two electric motors and manual standby.

It also has leading-edge Krueger flaps inboard, and four sections of slats outboard of engines; two air-brake/lift dumper panels on each wing inboard and outboard of engines; triple slotted trailing edge flaps inboard and outboard of engines.

All of that and the damned thing was going to fall short of its alternate landing site of Manzanillo Airport.

Beachcomber/Santiago wasn't sure if the low flying plane was just going to pass over him or fall right into the ocean.

With the trajectory uncertain in his mind, he decided to move further away for his own safety's sake as the 80-ton plane neared Campechuela, Cuba's coastline. He moved inland for cover nearer to the trees, with his grandson's hand tightly clasped within his own capable grip, bracing for the impact of the descending Boeing passenger jet.

Flight #1167, with 158 nervous passengers, listened to the pilot's voice as he informed the crew to prepare for an emergency landing.

The lead flight attendant and her two attendants were trying their best to calm the passengers and take care of the injured. The flight attendants were just as terrified as the passengers, but they tried not to show their own personal anxiety; such were the classic marks of the professionals on this skilled flight crew.

The captain summoned the lead attendant to the intercom. She picked it up and heard the captain tell her that the damage was severe, and that she should let the passengers know that they would be attempting an emergency landing in Cuba.

The lead attendant made the announcement and then reviewed the emergency landing procedures to the passengers with the help of her attendants. They had each passenger practice the familiar "brace position." As the attendants moved through the aisles, they also adjusted each passenger to be ready; to bend and hold in the proper position.

Then they approached the passengers in the emergency exit sections to make sure they felt secure enough to accept responsibility to open the doors when the time came.

The captain made contact with the airport in Cuba and requested permission for emergency landing. He explained they were losing fuel and that they had no other alternative but to attempt to land at Manzanillo Airport.

The Manzanillo controller confirmed that he had them on radar but could not grant permission to land without consulting the Cuban government, which would take time.

The captain explained he did not have any more time to wait for an answer. He needed an answer of "yes" now. Before the controller could respond, however, the pilots of the doomed plane realized they miscalculated the remaining fuel. The plane was not going to make it to land.

They gunned the remaining engines and tried to raise the nose of the plane before they hit the water. The captain shouted over the P.A.: "BRACE, WE'RE HITTING THE WATER!!!"

The plane nosed up, tail gliding along the water until the right wing touched and the plane bounced, slapping the water until the left wing hit and it parasailed across the surface.

The splashdown of the aluminum fuselage to the calm waters of the Caribbean sounded like a huge streamlined hotel building skiing along the surface, making a horrendous showering and towering racket as the plane skidded over a thousand yards. It finally stopped skimming across the ocean to settle on top of the water, a kind of floating hover-stop on the water's surface some 200 yards from the shoreline just off the coast of Campechuela, Cuba.

Beachcomber/Santiago's grandson was excited by the crash landing and began jumping up and down and exclaiming to his grandfather, a la Tattoo of Fantasy Island, "The plane... the plane."

Beachcomber/Santiago watched as moments later the aircraft wing and aft hatch doors came open. Spring-loaded yellowish-orange rubber evacuation ramps leapt to unfold with the pressure of aeration as the crew prepared to evacuate the cabin, urging passengers into the water to swim for shore. They were using their seat cushions as flotation devices. The flak jacket life vests that were stored nearest to the pilot's cockpit were rationed among the members of the crew per the safety requirements on all the transoceanic flights.

Beachcomber/Santiago watched as some of the passengers emerged from the cabin doors at the front section of the 737 plane. This was followed by the exit of more passengers out of the wing door as they slid down the ramp into the warm waters of the Caribbean. They clutched their seat cushions as buoys and began jogging their feet in slow motion as they dog paddled toward the shoreline.

Beachcomber/Santiago lost the grip of his grandson's hand as he ran back from the safety of the trees and headed straight for the sand to get a closer view of the survivors of the plane crash.

Beachcomber/Santiago felt the sigh of irony in his own soul as he trekked dutifully towards the shoreline, marching the cadence of determined steps of a former soldier in harm's way of yet another anonymity-breaker of his precious rights of humbled privacy. He knew that... well, he had to disappear for a while. And as his steps moved a heavy heaping of Campechuela's sand, he also knew that he would do what he had to do.

He marched up to his grandson, still gesturing profusely at the downed 737, and its approaching castaway cargo of dog paddling passengers filing into the ocean, all 158 of them, churning and kicking with their heels and those of them that knew how to, were swimming eagerly ashore. They had cheated their own Cabo Blanco, and they wanted desperately to celebrate their luck on dry land, as soon as possible.

Beachcomber/Santiago tells his grandson, "We must go, son, we must move on before the authorities arrive," as Joe Junior asked him, "But what about the people?"

"They will be rescued and they will make it to shore."

"How do you know, Grandpa?"

"Because this is the lucky spot, and we will have to get out of here and clear out of our lucky spot for now." He quietly added with a grin, "That way we can come back to it and it will still be ours to claim." He knelt before his grandson and looked into his eyes. "If we stay and help these people, we might not get our lucky spot back." He went on to add that, "They might take Grandpa away again."

Joe Junior: "I don't want them to take you away."

Beachcomber: "Then we must go away for awhile."

Beachcomber/Santiago stopped for a moment and he asked his grandson to do something for him. Kneeling before his grandson, he began, "Son, will you do this for me?" He pulled the sash of Veronica from his neck and tied it to his grandson's neck, like a proper scoutmaster would. "I want you to wear this for me," he said as he tied it into a secure knot.

"O.K., grandpa, I will," he said, not fully understanding, but his grandfather went on to add, "It belonged to your grandmother." He sheds a tear as he goes on. "She was a very, very good woman." He starts to cry and seizes-up, tightening himself on the next words. "She meant the world to me... but God had other plans."

"He took her away from me so I could learn how to live without her." His sobbing continued with his head down and then he wiped his tears. "And it was hard for me but I learned how to go on." He pats his grandson's shoulders after his tears stopped falling. "So we will say our prayers for the people on the plane." They both bowed their heads in a silent moment of prayer.

"Come on, we need to go away for awhile, just me and you."

Joe Junior stares at the dark figure who has silently walked up behind them.

Joe Junior: "But what about this one?" pointing to the Carbanero Che Ortiz.

Beachcomber/Santiago arose from his knees to walk over to Che.

The Carbanero listened to Beachcomber/Santiago and he began to nod his head in agreement. Joe Junior looked confused by the situation. Then Che Ortiz dumped the huge sack from his back onto the sandy beach. He pulled some mangrove twigs and began rubbing the sticks in a rapid and earnest spin of friction.

Beachcomber/Santiago walked back to collect his grandson by the arm as he said to him, "I want you to meet a friend."

They walked together to the place where Che Ortiz was making a rasping noise with the friction of the thatch mangrove sticks. Just then the charcoal lit up as he blew the smoke, fanning to light the charcoal into a fire. Che stood up at the creation of this fire. "Son, this is Che Ortiz, my friend."

Beachcomber/Santiago's grandson took his hand. "Are you coming with us, too?" Che Ortiz began a broad smile as he threw his empty sack over his shoulder. They watched the fire grow as the smoke filled the air with cloud signals of symbology.

Beachcomber/Santiago reached out his hand to his grandson and then Che Ortiz held the hand of Joe Junior, as the little boy between the two of them began taking beachcombing steps across the sand and out of the picture.

Beachcomber/Santiago said to them both, "They will be rescued." They stopped to look back at the plane as the passengers were nearing the shore. "We need to keep going." He kind of waved his hand, "O.K., let's go, let's move along now." He added quietly, "We all... just need... to keep going."

He felt that he himself had been some kind of heavily weighted vessel, a floating monolith of Daedalus. And he knew it was that he had had a lifetime's worth of Spartan heroes and theatrical wunderkind moments wherein he'd taken the reins of overall fate to the farthest limits of what one man could take.

He took a griping hold, clutching his grandson's formative wing. The three of them, Beachcomber, Che Ortiz, and Joe Junior, strode off into the sunlight's shadows marking the trees, far away from harm's way in a cultural sensible bow to the impending disaster of the needy in the airplane's surviving passengers' plight.

He had a life of his own with his grandson and Che Ortiz, and he had already shouldered a massive Caesar's destiny of a major lifetime of hardship with soldiering and sergeanting his private and public wars with so many a witness. A humble sensitive craftsman with the gift of a good spirit, an enrichment born within his soul—the natural tattoo of pride. It never wore off. Even after the lion's share of such terrible trials that was more than any man should take... natural pride despite a few exorcisms with life's demons... with some much needed time off just to rest in between takes. It was a natural and pure coat called pride, and with it any man could be resurrected; even within this wayward drifter, who was resilient.

It was a life filled with so many forlorn wayward and wanton and already deeply passed upon souls of saddening saddlery: these staggering earthly spirits of whom he had always visited regularly in his own life's earnest and earned peace. It was buried and burrowed in the sacrum just above his mantle, the darndest of things, a lurking wrench with a gay wary eye for his cajones, that damned rusty tuner fork's gauge imbedded within him aside, he would try to continue on in his trek. But with that shackle's gloom shadow cast upon foley, he makes a way somehow continuing forward, as the old survivor, in this tainted strange world of life's wreckage, for all his heart's memories endured, stirring around without their souls... that he had yet to daily mourn. It was a life, but it would be one life that was tempered always and every day, in the state of have-not, the part of this have-not meaning, or being, was that this life was... To have not... without pain.

It was his time to return to his humble existence, sharing it this time with Joe Junior, and Che Ortiz, beachcombing through life together, as a family– and beachcombing into history.

THE MEC IRS

It's what this journey is all about...

MILITARY EGALITARIAN CANNONIZATION
INDUSTRIALIZATION REVITALIZATION STRUCTURE
INFRASTRUCTURE REVITALIZATION STRATEGY

The lies were told to reload, and regenerate, and to build more
weapons of War and to stockpile more arms; and even more
Military equipment...to bolster the size of the whole conglomerate
and to make even more money... to fatten up the coffers of the
MILITARY INDUSTRIAL COMPLEX

THE FOREVER CALAMITY WE HAVE FACED
THE LAST 50 YEARS RUNNING...

THE M.E.C. I.R.S. CULTURE

Copyright—Michael Gering—August 1st, 2015

"THE BEACHCOMBER"
THE SECOND EDITION
November 22nd, 2015

BIBLIOGRAPHY

ZR RIFLE – The plot to kill Kennedy and Castro
CUBA OPENS SECRET FILES
Claudia Furiati
Published by OCEAN PRESS
GPO Box #3279 Melbourne, Victoria 3001, AUSTRALIA
Distributed by Talman Company, New York, New York
Permission granted 12/12/16.
A very special thanks to Serina Tremayne.

Page 17, 18; General content

Page 28, 29; <u>Kennedy and the Pluto Disaster</u> (5 paragraphs) Full contents on each of these pages

Page 30, 31; <u>New Perspectives-The Taylor Report</u> (2 paragraphs), Full contents plus footnote

Page 43; Paragraph two

Page 61; 1992 Tripartite Conference, McNamara (paragraph two)

Page 92; On Cuba and world public opinion (paragraph two)

Page 118; Paragraphs one and two, John Roselli and Robert Maheu

Page 119; Full contents, all footnotes, #60, Eugenio Martinez

Page 120; Top paragraph, full content; Robert Maheu / Howard Hughes

Page 128; <u>Let us consider the formation of ZR RIFLE</u>; full content

Page 129; Top paragraph, full content

Page 130; Top paragraph, QJ WIN, 1961 Wm. Harvey traveled to Marseilles

Page 132-135; Full content of basic findings and conclusions

Page 141, 142, 143; <u>The book Double Cross</u>, David Phillips, Howard Hunt.

EYEBALL TO EYEBALL
The inside story of the Cuban Missile Crisis
Anthony D. Brugioni (aka Dino Brugioni)
Edited y Robert F. McCort
Published 1991 by Random House, Inc. New York, New York 10022
USER CALL NUMBER # P N 5524. K 57 2000
Permission received.

Pages 338-341; Full content

Pages 65, 68-70; Full content

MOON HANDBOOKS CUBA
. Christopher P. Baker
Avalon Travel Publishing, 5855 Beaudry St. Emeryville, CA

CROSSFIRE: The Plot That Killed KENNEDY
Jim Marrs
Published by Carroll Graf Publishers, Inc.
Permission received via Harvard lawyer Dale Neal
Permission requested for Pages 55 and 56

Page 81-86; Ed Hoffman, Grassy Knoll Witness (for reference)

Page 204; Paragraph 3, middle page

Page 205; Paragraph 7, bottom page

Page 207; Bottom 4 paragraphs ZR Rifle

Page 208; Bottom 3 paragraphs, Lucien Sarti

Page 272; Bottom 2 paragraphs, Nixon/Hunt

Page 273; Top 2 paragraphs, Nixon/Hunt theory

Page 301-310, concepts + theory

Page 439; (paragraph 4, 5), Sheriff Boone

Page 580-582; conclusion

Page 589, 590; Concept + theory

THE BAY OF PIGS
Howard Jones
Published by Oxford University Press
Permission received

Page 106; Full Context + the analysis, Invoice Ref.#--10952003

Page 107; Full Context + the analysis, Account No.#--90541669

Page 108; Full Context + the analysis

Page 109; Full Context + the analysis, United Kingdom OX2 6DP

Page 110; Full Context + the analysis, Billing # 100 060 422 6737

Page 111; Full Context + the analysis, Richard.Mason@oup.com

ULTIMATE SACRIFICE
Lamar Waldron and Thomas Hartmann
Published by Counterpoint Press
Permission received. Special thanks to Joe Goodale at Counterpoint LLC/
Soft Skull Press; 2560 Ninth Street, Suite 318, Berkeley CA 94710

Page 307; Full context, plus the analysis

Page 308; Full context, plus the analysis

Page 532; Direct text plus any analysis

Page 698; Direct text plus any analysis

THE CIA AND THE CULT OF INTELLIGENCE
Victor Marchetti and John D. Marks
Published by Alfred Knopf
Permission requested

Suggested reading (not in *The Beachcomber*)

AMERICAN CONSPIRACIES
Jesse Ventura and Dick Russell
Published by Skyhorse

MARY'S MOSAIC
Peter Janney
Published by Skyhorse

HIT LIST
Richard Belzer and David Wayne
Published by Skyhorse

Author of *The Beachcomber* disagrees with some portions of the final theory found inside the exquisite Jim Marrs' *Crossfire*, however, there are areas of approach or facts that I have borrowed that intersect and align or concur too.

In the participation in the crime of the century riddle the above is respectfully included. In all cases and in every area of endeavor, requests and also permission were sought from a publisher. "I lawfully submit forthwith, that this is true."

JESSE VENTURA

Jesse Ventura and his writing partner, Dick Russell, collaborated on the fine book, *THEY KILLED OUR PRESIDENT*. In it they focus on 63 facts pointing out that clearly JFK was assassinated as the result of a conspiracy; a wider plot against him.

In a 2014 YouTube video filmed during a book tour promoting that material, you will see Jesse at the podium, filmed by a visitor's camera. It's easy to pull up on YouTube, just search "Jesse Ventura Speech - They Killed our President - JFK Assassination Book" and look for Jesse in a nice cream colored sport coat. The camera filming him is from the second row, right side.

In the video he is brilliant, and you can see immediately why he's a favorite on all the cable news and talk shows we see on television. At least at this event, I found him in fine form.

One question fired off at him (at 16 minutes) was about the level of Lee Oswald's skills with a rifle, on a range. "Was he a sharpshooter... a marksman?" Ventura is an ex Navy Seal, who at the ripe old age of fifty, while still governor in the great state of Minnesota, went out to qualify at sniper training and still qualified as an expert marksman, and he answered candidly. He put it bluntly, "Lee Harvey Oswald was a radar man, he was not combat infantry, he was definitely not a shooter."

Jesse said it like this "not everyone can be a knuckle dragger. He was not a 'knuckle dragger,' as we referred to them [shooters]." (Jesse Ventura, operating as a NAVY SEAL, most certainly *was* a shooter. And he is very proud to have maintained that skill, over so many years.)

Then it came out in a revelation. It is recorded. Ventura made the following brutal observation (27 minutes): "The Mannlicher-Carcano is a Geneva Convention grade weapon. It cannot discharge a frangible bullet (a bullet that breaks apart)... the rifle cannot fire an exploding bullet." He said, *"it can only fire a full metal jacket bullet."* He cited Harold Weisberg's research: "The X-rays of Jack Kennedy's head showed particles of lead throughout his skull cavity." That means John F. Kennedy was hit with a frangible or exploding bullet. The Mannlicher-Carcano (the weapon that Lee Harvey Oswald allegedly used), *"couldn't have fired it."**

My conclusion is very simple—in text book military ballistics and basic sniper fact finding: there had to be multiple assassins involved, firing upon the presidential motorcade. **JFK was killed as the result of a conspiracy.** It is a fact. It is a palpable, unfortunate, and dangerously brutal... cold, hard... fact.

* NOTE: *In quoting excerpts from the Ventura video, we trusted our interpretation of the tape. We heard it, absorbed it, and have made our best effort to portray it correctly.*

ABOUT THE AUTHOR

Michael Gering was born in Petaluma, California in 1960, into a military family. His early schooling was in California, Texas, Japan, and in Germany. Coming back to the US, he was bit by the acting bug initially, but usually miscast in productions early on as a policeman, or big guys, like in John Steinbeck's "Tularaceto." Also, he played a wild drunk in the William Inge: "Come Back Little Sheba." Seeing that casting not going his way he dropped out of acting in plays, and he made a unique decision by walking away from a film director's offer. He attended Columbia School Of Broadcasting. He turned to scriptwriting in 1984 and over the next 20 years penned numerous screenplays (most of which remain unproduced). He has since apologized to great directing talents such as the remarkably visionary Peter Bogdanovich.

At that crossroad back in 1985--no doubt however I tried to define it, or explain it, later on in 2015, its a big error of mine to be so nonchalant cavalier--casting aside offer's. I was pitching so many deals and spinning too many plates topped with my own specials. One dish of my own creation I discovered later on down the road that's called--the hubris. I was there when so many friends didn't get the breaks I had. I just left them all on a table. A brief case filled with this novel and other past missed screenplay's, went along with that. That and a brief handshake at the "The Last Picture Show," at the recent film showcase at the place where, talent and opportunity gathered; in general, I sought to make it right or to fix what I did wrong. I am getting better... at trusting myself. I'm all the way back, to being creating again after a decade long self imposed hiatus. I chose this project after my hiatus. And, it was many reasons I chose this project or this path--as the longer journey to myself.

As a boy in Fort Hood, Texas, Michael's father, Alex Gering, took him to the Texas Theatre. They toured through Dealey Plaza seeing all the historical sights. During this trip through Dallas, a young kid of 13 became fascinated with the Kennedy cold case. The fascination never ended. 40 years later, Mr. Gering pours over books, essays and documentaries on the John F. Kennedy assassination. Even after four decades there is always a strand of the case that surfaces, and one must take a closer examination of that strand. The one last strand for Michael Gering was the Richard Case Nagell story, plus the work of Howard Jones, *The Bay Of Pigs*. And, nuggets from the marvelously well researched book "Ultimate Sacrifice." Thomas Hartman / Lamar Waldron. Credit goes to H.R. Haldeman for fingering Nixon with his book, *The Ends of Power*. And, thank E. Howard Hunt for covering it all up for 45 years.

A culmination of fact fiction, scriptwriting graphic fiction, *The Beachcomer* is Gering's first novel. The first *Beachcomber* edition was completed November 22nd, 2013. Some material was not available as the book went to press. Understanding all this process, taking so much time to secure material... was not the experience of a first-time author. As more material was authorized, details were added to more completely examine the JFK cold case. Those additions formulated what became the second edition of *The Beachcomber*, released in 2015. He combined three books into one book. It's a fact. George Carlin told him he could do it that way.

Michael Gering has lived in Santa Monica, California, since 1991. He truly enjoys football games, documentaries, movies, and occasionally, actual beachcombing. The author freely admits that the loss of his mother in 2004, took too much wind out of his sails, one would not attempt... to mine a deep subject with a great loss looming... at the outer limits of the completion; be that as it may it was the loss of JFK as well as Karin, that shaped the tone. As in any compelling study that begins after high treason, and is beset with lies and betrayal of a country, and a horrible series of murders; one cannot see penance, or penalty exploring it. "This is the world... as I know it to be."

In visits to both graves it is the hope of this author that as he toured the battlefield he respected the subject matter... it is only the subject's abject participants who were the doers of all these rampantly god awful despicable-horrible-dirty deeds. May they, or them, be the subject of their albeit damned judgment, come judgment day; as we sit here today. May we finally expose what one of its participants, Mr. Richard Milhouse Nixon, succinctly called it on the Whitehouse tapes (according to Jesse Ventura in his ground-breaking exposé *American Conspiracies*):

"It's the biggest hoax that has ever been perpetuated."

It is the Da Vinci Code—on the men who killed –John Fitzgerald Kennedy. In 1973—The Fugitive—had the Quinn Martin epilog scene.

In today's wrap up if Horatio Caine were on set, you could imagine that in a CSI Miami--epilog like--scene; that he would offer his favorite saying:

CSI—Horatio Caine likes to—end our story with "You hang in there..."

THE CRIME OF THE CENTURY
November 22nd, 1963

In the last 50 plus years. It has not ended, well.
How long do we have to hang in there Horatio?

Michael Nicholas Gering
November 22nd, 2015
We shall wait... and we shall see--

IN THE FINAL EPITAPH
As We Take The Sad Last Walk Among The Tombstones...

It represents more than three decades of research. In the final code, the book must end on the odd page number 339. The (3) marks three decades. If we add the next number (39), for 3 + 39; it totals 42. The 42 years I've been at it, since age 13 in 1973, when my father took me through the crime scene. For 42 years I wanted to resolve the mystery of the crime of the century.

I realize at this point after all that has been said, or done, by so many others, we have only scratched the surface, because it is still going to be an ongoing challenge to us all. I am not sure that we will ever find that District Attorney (as brave as Jim Garrison existing in this day and age), who would try this case of high treason in a courtroom. I know that I gave the equation or the enigma the best shot I had in me, in years I tried it too. I realize that were all merely just at the beginning of our understanding of the CIA's role in the assassination. And, it might take another 42 years... before we finally crack this awful cold case to get to the bottom of the mystery... surrounding that terrible day in history, November 22nd, 1963.

However, I leave the braindroppings and the clues I found to the young minds who will break through the depths of the abyss; the future generation that will crack this case wide open, and lay to rest the Da Vinci Code—to those next brave detectives—who'll successfully resolve the JFK cold case.

May they bring the story forward...

that finally ends with the truth in the ultimate resolution...

the complete list of who killed John F. Kennedy.

As Director Oliver Stone mildly put it "it's up to you."

I agree with Roger Stone, "I am a warts-and-all realist. It's not a love letter to anybody." And, much worse than that, we know now, after reading all the material I have gathered—

It truly is just what Richard Nixon claimed it was, in the oval office, on the Whitehouse tapes...

"It's the biggest hoax that's ever been perpetuated."